"You shot through a scale," I said. "How?"

"You must know. Gunpowder. Bullet. Load and pull the trigger. Or do you have some magic way of making a gun fire?"

"Don't treat me like a fool. No bullet can go through scaleglass."

I couldn't see the man's face, yet I was sure he grinned. "How very much I would love to stay and enlighten you, to tell you how wrong you are about everything you think you know, but since your friends will soon be here, I suggest you listen if you don't want this to happen again." The man lowered his pistol, and with the immediate threat removed, some of the tension eased from my limbs. Either that or the iishor was fast draining out of me, leaving my knees weak.

Stepping closer, the hooded man pushed aside the barrel of my rifle. "You must take a message to your masters," he said, thrusting his pistol into its holster. "Tell them they have gone too far this time. Tell them they will get only this one warning. We will no longer be your waste pile, your garden, your mine, your slaves. No longer will you take from us and throw back what you do not want. Your next *ride* will be your last. All of you."

Praise for
THE REBORN EMPIRE SERIES

"With prose that rises above most novels, Devin Madson paints evocative scenes to build an engaging story. Highly entertaining, *We Ride the Storm* is certainly worth your attention and Madson is an exciting new author in fantasy."

—Mark Lawrence, author of *Red Sister*

"Intricate, compelling, and vividly imagined, this is the first in a new quartet that I am hugely excited about. Visceral battles, complex politics, and fascinating worldbuilding bring Devin's words to life." —Anna Stephens, author of *Godblind*

"An utterly arresting debut, *Storm*'s heart is in its complex, fascinating characters, each trapped in ever-tightening snarls of war, politics, and magic. Madson's sharp, engaging prose hauls you through an engrossing story that will leave you wishing you'd set aside enough time to read this all in one sitting. One of the best new voices in fantasy." —Sam Hawke, author of *City of Lies*

"A brutal, nonstop ride through an empire built upon violence and lies, a story as gripping as it is unpredictable. Never shying away from the consequences of the past nor its terrible realities, Madson balances characters you want to love with actions you want to hate while mixing in a delightful amount of magic, political intrigue, and lore. This is not a book you'll be able to put down." —K. A. Doore, author of *The Perfect Assassin*

By Devin Madson

THE SHATTERED KINGDOM

Between Dragons and Their Wrath

THE REBORN EMPIRE

We Ride the Storm
We Lie with Death
We Cry for Blood
We Dream of Gods

THE VENGEANCE TRILOGY

The Blood of Whisperers
The Gods of Vice
The Grave at Storm's End

BETWEEN DRAGONS

DRAGONS

AND THEIR

WRATH

THE SHATTERED KINGDOM: BOOK ONE

DEVIN MADSON

orbitbooks.net

Copyright © 2024 by Devin Madson
Excerpt from *The Scarlet Throne* copyright © 2024 by Amy Leow

Cover design by Lisa Marie Pompilio and Lauren Panepinto
Cover illustration by Mike Heath | Magnus Creative
Cover copyright © 2024 by Hachette Book Group, Inc.
Map by Tim Paul
Author photograph by Leah Ladson

Orbit
Hachette Book Group
1290 Avenue of the Americas
New York, NY 10104
orbitbooks.net

First Edition: August 2024
Simultaneously published in Great Britain by Orbit

Orbit is an imprint of Hachette Book Group.
The Orbit name and logo are registered trademarks of Little, Brown Book Group Limited.

The publisher is not responsible for websites (or their content) that are not owned by the publisher.

The Hachette Speakers Bureau provides a wide range of authors for speaking events. To find out more, go to hachettespeakersbureau.com or email HachetteSpeakers@hbgusa.com.

Orbit books may be purchased in bulk for business, educational, or promotional use. For information, please contact your local bookseller or the Hachette Book Group Special Markets Department at special.markets@hbgusa.com.

Library of Congress Cataloging-in-Publication Data
Names: Madson, Devin, author.
Title: Between dragons and their wrath / Devin Madson.
Description: First edition. | New York, NY : Orbit, 2024. | Series: The shattered kingdom ; book 1
Identifiers: LCCN 2023054200 | ISBN 9780316417983 (trade paperback) | ISBN 9780316418096 (ebook)
Subjects: LCGFT: Fantasy fiction. | Novels.
Classification: LCC PR9619.4.M335 B48 2024 | DDC 823/.92—dc23/eng/20231127
LC record available at https://lccn.loc.gov/2023054200

ISBNs: 9780316417983 (trade paperback), 9780316418096 (ebook)

Printed in the United States of America

LSC-C

Printing 2, 2024

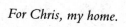

For Chris, my home.

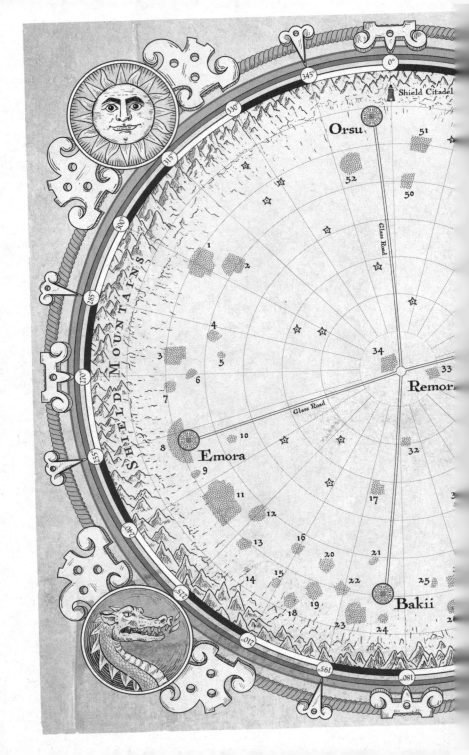

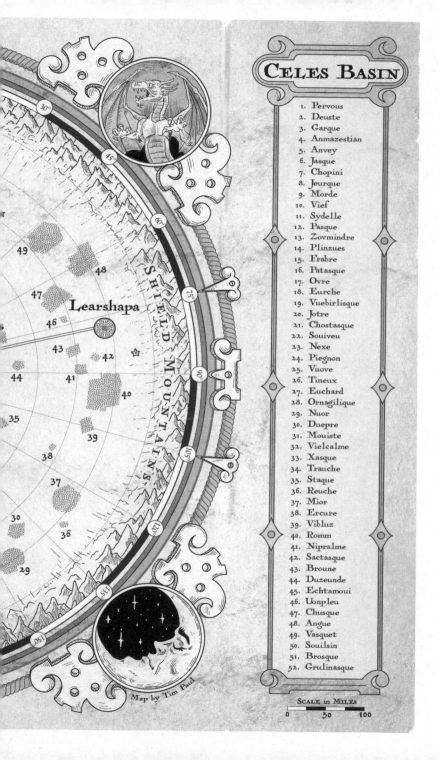

CELES BASIN

SHIELD MOUNTAINS

Learshapa

49
48
47
46
43   42
44   41
40
35
39
38
37   36
30
29

1. Pervous
2. Deuste
3. Garque
4. Anmazestian
5. Anvey
6. Jasque
7. Chopini
8. Jeurque
9. Morde
10. Vief
11. Sydelle
12. Pasque
13. Zovmindre
14. Plinzues
15. Erabre
16. Patasque
17. Ovre
18. Eurche
19. Vuebirlisque
20. Jotre
21. Chostasque
22. Souiveu
23. Nexe
24. Piegnon
25. Vuove
26. Tineux
27. Euchard
28. Ornagilique
29. Nuor
30. Duepre
31. Mouiste
32. Vielcalme
33. Xasque
34. Trauche
35. Staque
36. Reuche
37. Mior
38. Ercure
39. Vibluz
40. Romm
41. Nipralme
42. Sactasque
43. Broune
44. Duzeunde
45. Echtamoui
46. Uonpleu
47. Chusque
48. Angue
49. Vasquet
50. Souilsin
51. Brosque
52. Grulinasque

Map by Tim Paul

SCALE in MILES

0   50   100

Tesha

Afternoon Bulletin

To all criers for announcement throughout Learshapa

Grievous blow for the city as a second critical scale shipment fails to arrive from Therinfrou Mine. Attacks by Lummazzt soldiers to blame.

Emergency council meeting called to discuss rising border tensions with Lummazza, despite initial plans not to meet again until after next week's vote. "We would be stronger together," says Reacher Sormei.

Nine ritual carvings have gone missing from Lord Sactasque's public gallery. It is the second such incident this month. Information is sought regarding this assault on Celessi history.

200:49

The shatter of warm glass hitting stone has a particular tenor, a sound that reaches deep, more feeling than noise. It touches every memory of broken glasswork and shattered dreams, of beauty lost and time torn away. Even when it's Assistant Jul's ugly carafe that looks better as a pile of shards.

"Sweep it up!" Master Hoye called over the roaring furnace. "Life is glass!"

"Life is glass," the boy mumbled back, the lesson still too sharp to fit into the ugly-carafe-shaped hole in his heart. Likely it would be a few more years before he realised what our master's favourite phrase really meant. Not that glasswork was all we lived for, but that life *was* glass. Like life, glass is infinitely malleable when warm and well-tended, yet fragile enough to shatter at a single wrong move. It can be moulded by any hands into any shape, but the more skilled and prepared the hands the better the outcome. Even the addition of scale for strength was akin to the way people gathered wealth and resources about themselves and called it resilience.

I'd been staring out the back window, lost in thought, but as broken glass tinkled into the scrap bucket I shoved the last bite of honey-crusted bread into my mouth. Outside, the slice of Learshapa that had been my lunch-break companion went on unchanged. Overhead, sunlight reflected off whitewashed walls beneath an endless blue sky, yet little light reached the courtyard of faded tiles on the other side of the window. Once it had been a fine atrium, but now it was full of dusty, cobwebbed pots owning lethargic plants more grey than green.

I licked my fingers and wiped the sticky residue down my apron as Master Hoye called, "The gather won't shape itself!"

To Master Hoye, everything was about glass. He likened his desire not to rush out of bed in the morning to glass being stronger when cooled slowly in vermiculite, and the suffering of stress to the drawing of thin canes. Even wrong words spoken at the wrong time earned a hiss from him, like hot glass being dunked in a quenching barrel.

Back at my workbench, I gathered materials for the next job. *Cobalt. A pinch of scale. Sand bed. Two moulds.* Even with the scale shortage, there was a lot to do. The upcoming vote to decide Learshapa's place in the Celes Basin seemed to have energised the city, sending everyone bustling about with renewed purpose and a determination to finish long-neglected projects. That afternoon, my list contained a dozen replacement armour scales, two matching brandy glasses, a trio of scaleglass blades to fit carved handles, and twenty unification badges I would rather have smashed on the floor. *Unification.* I sneered as I laid everything out ready. It was a fine word for conquest.

As I prepared to gather molten glass from the furnace, an arrival sent our bead curtain tinkling. "Good afternoon," a young man said, unclipping his veil and casting his gaze around the large, smoky space.

"Good afternoon." Assistant Borro hurried forward, wiping his hands on his apron as Master Hoye always did. "What can we do for you?"

"I'm hoping to leave a small pile of flyers on your counter in support of the vote." As he spoke, the man handed Borro a paper-wrapped sugar curl from a basket he carried. "Is there perhaps someone more senior I could speak to?"

A glance back found Master Hoye in the middle of shaping a vase and shouting at Assistant Jul, both dripping sweat, and poor Borro rolled his gaze my way.

I strode over, but before I could speak, the young man thrust one of his sugar curls into my hand—a traditional Memento curl of skulls and suns. "A Memento Festival token for next week's Memento Eve vote," he said, all bright cheerfulness. "Might I leave a small pile of flyers here for your customers?"

I glanced down at the flyers, able to make out only two words at the top of the page: *Stronger Together.* "I take it you're supporting the 'conquer us, please, we can't take care of ourselves' vote then," I said, utterly failing at what Master Hoye called civil indifference.

Likely the man had a ready response for most arguments, just not one so blunt. For a long moment he stared at me and I stared back, sugar curl growing sticky in my warm hand.

Behind him, the glass-bead curtain tinkled again, heralding the arrival of two women, arm-in-arm as they let down their veils. "Good afternoon," I said, grateful for the distraction. "Can I help you?"

"We're looking for scaleglass wedding bands," the younger said, a shy glance thrown at her companion. "I know scale is in short supply, but, well, we're asking around anyway."

"Wedding bands?" I scoffed, the disgusted words escaping before I could swallow them. The women froze—a startled tableau of horror.

With a hiss mimicking hot glass hitting water, Master Hoye stepped forward. "That's not Apprentice Tesha's field of expertise," he said, patting my arm with one hand while wiping his damp brow with the other. "Best to speak to me about that. I'm Master Hoye, and you're right, scale is..." His words trailed off as he guided them to the other side of the entry space, away from the ever-present roar of the furnaces. Neither young woman glanced back to see my heated cheeks.

"Oh, so you're that kind of Learshapan, are you?" the man said, finding his voice again. "Traditional. Against all change."

"You say that like change is a neutral term," I snapped back. "Like taking up a new fashion is the same as giving up our ability to decide our own future, because that's what this is. A vote for unification is a vote for assimilation into the Emoran empire."

"And a vote for separation is a vote to stay weak and risk further Lummazzt attacks!"

"Bullshit!"

Master Hoye and the two women broke off their low-voiced conversation, all three turning to stare at us. Cheeks reddening for the second time, I leaned over the counter, bringing my fury face-to-face with the flyer man's. "Lummazza has never attacked us and has no reason to now. But if you give Emora the power to make us in their image there will be no Learshapa. And certainly no Memento Festival." I crushed the softening sugar curl in my fist, snapping its artistry like tiny bones. "The answer is no, you can't leave your flyers here."

"And you think I'm the fear monger," the man scoffed, and in a flurry of skirts, he spun away, pushing through the glass-bead curtain and out into the bright heat before he'd even clipped his veil into place.

"That went well."

I turned to find Master Hoye watching, the two women having departed, leaving our entry empty.

"I'm sorry," I said, anger chilling to regret in a heartbeat. "I ought not to have lost my temper with him. It's not good for business."

"No, but neither is complete Emoran rule, so you're forgiven." There was nothing more to be said, yet he remained watching me.

"What is it?" I said, instantly breathless with worry.

"You need to be more respectful when people come in looking for wedding bands, but I think you know that already, don't you?"

I closed my eyes and gave a solemn nod. "It's just so ridiculous. Especially in a scale shortage."

"Times have been rough." His voice sank to a quiet murmur. "Who am I to judge what people choose to make them happy?"

"Marriage? Family?" I all but spat the words. "You know as well as I do how dangerous those customs are to our communes and care groups."

Master Hoye dropped his hand on my shoulder. "These are

concerns for the meeting house, not my workshop. And yes, I know you haven't been attending meetings, like I know you're a fool who can't find her place in the world, but I'd say it's been long enough, huh?"

I nodded slowly, shame at my outbursts weighing me down. "I'm sorry, Master. I will take more care."

"I know you will."

Again, he patted my shoulder, and would have turned back about his work had not a question burst from my lips. "What did you mean when you said I was 'a fool who can't find her place'?"

"I meant exactly what I said."

"I'm happy here. And in my care group."

"For now, yes. But happy has never been what you're looking for, has it?"

With a wink, he turned away, already calling for Assistant Borro to ready his punty. It was his way of ending conversations that had run out of usefulness, a sure sign that asking what he had meant a second time would earn no better answer.

As I returned to my work, hoping no one else would step through the door, a registered crier passed by in the street shouting the afternoon bulletin. "...scale shipment fails to arrive from Therinfrou Mine. Attacks by Lummazzt soldiers to blame," she called, her voice carrying well in the narrow street. "Emergency council meeting called to discuss rising border tensions with Lummazza, despite initial plans not to meet again until after next week's vote. 'We would be stronger together,' says Reacher Sormei..."

Her voice faded away on the reacher's name, leaving me with the bitter taste of it in my mouth. Reacher Sormei, leader of Emora and the rest of the Celes Basin. At that very moment he was somewhere in Learshapa campaigning for the unification vote so he could rule us too, and people like that idiot with his flyers wanted to help him do it.

A long time ago the Celes Basin had been home only to roaming Apaian tribes, who had done nothing more with the basin's vast scale deposits than carve death mementos into the stone. The discovery that it could be mixed into glass to create a substance stronger than any metal had changed everything. With scaleglass, the Apaians had built permanent settlements, water catchments, and roads that crossed the basin's empty stones, even made an early form of blasting powder that dug the pits of our great cities—Bakii, Orsu, and Learshapa. Perhaps it would have stayed that way had the Emorans not been forced from their own lands into the basin, or perhaps they would have attacked anyway, coveting the scale and all it could do. Either way, as the Lummazzt conquered Emora, Emorans had conquered the basin and built their own city—Emora—from which to govern. The war had been brutal, but so long ago now it hardly seemed real. Only Learshapa had kept any form of democracy when the Emorans finally took over, a concession earned through bloodshed that some were now ready to vote away.

Returning to my abandoned tasks, I couldn't extricate myself from the fear that grew daily. What if the unification vote won? What if my home was about to change forever no matter how tightly I clung? What would become of us then?

I might have relaxed had the day continued like any other, but in the middle of the afternoon it became even less like any other when Sorscha sauntered in, all at ease. His visits to the forge weren't rare enough to herald trouble, but I hadn't seen him for weeks. Not since I'd stopped volunteering at the west quarter meeting house. Not since I'd walked out on Uvao.

"Tesha. Master Hoye," he said, shaking out the dark hair he loosed from his veil. "A fine afternoon to you both."

He leaned on the counter, possessing none of the nervousness I felt at his arrival. As though I'd forgotten how to stand or smile or what to do with my arms. The urge to ask after Uvao was strong.

"Afternoon, yes. Fine, I'm not so sure," Master Hoye said, handing his work to the boys and striding over. "What can we do for you, Sorscha?"

"Always business with you, Master Hoye." Sorscha's smile held a mocking edge, and his single-slit brows hovered low and sleepy. "I'm well, thank you for asking. Though the heat out there is quite something. Almost as bad as the heat in here."

Despite his complaint, he looked cool and at ease, his dark hair ruffled in a careless style and his blackened leather tunic laced tight—as tight as the three brass bands constricting one arm. His glance flicked my way, his mocking smile unmoving, and I could only hope I looked untroubled lest he report my embarrassment to Uvao.

When Master Hoye didn't answer in kind, Sorscha sighed and pulled a folded paper square from his skirt pocket. "Here then," he said, unfolding it with painstaking diligence. "Something to keep you busy for the rest of the afternoon."

"This afternoon? I'm full up."

"Then give this one to Tesha."

"No."

Master Hoye's sharp refusal was entirely expected and yet utterly disappointing—a feeling for which I ought to have been ashamed. The jobs Sorscha sometimes brought in were not only illegal but flouted our customs. Learshapa had always sustained itself by being a collective political community in which decisions were made together, but with that on the verge of change there was much allure in being able to just . . . *do* something about it. Quickly. Quietly. Changing the world.

With a silky hush, Sorscha slid the paper across the counter.

Before Master Hoye snatched it up, I caught the words *identical wine glasses, fast-acting poison,* and *illness.* "And you need it tonight?"

"The client will accept tomorrow morning."

"Then tomorrow morning it is. Come at opening, not before."

"Naturally. Before would mean being up far too early."

Master Hoye grunted and walked away, leaving me facing Sorscha, who remained leaning against the front bench. "Long time, no see, Tesh," he said in his lazy way. "Arguments at the meeting house haven't been as fiery without you. Will you be attending tonight?"

A shrug was all I could manage. Mere weeks ago, I would have been there every night helping out, but accidentally uncovering Uvao's identity had changed everything. No matter how often I might wish, as I lay awake at night, that I'd never found out at all.

"This second scale shipment failing to arrive has everyone on edge," Sorscha went on, thankfully unaware of my thoughts. "Even more on edge than the coming vote and the presence of Reacher Sormei walking the streets shaking everyone's hand, that is."

For people who didn't know him, it was unnerving witnessing Sorscha's shift from charming insouciance to serious political discussion. I'd spent too long in his company to be shocked, but it sent a thrill up my spine every time. "I think we'd all be better off if someone killed Reacher Sormei and let us get on with our lives," he added. "And no, before you ask, that's not the job I just gave Master Hoye. Unfortunately. At least we get to vote, huh? Imagine living in Bakii and having no say over anything at all."

We both grimaced, momentarily in accord as he readied his veil to depart. "Catch you around, Tesh."

"Wait, before you go. Tell me . . . how do you think the vote will go?"

"Are you asking me as me, or asking me as someone whose friend turned out to be an Emoran lord who knows more of what's going on than we do?"

"Both."

A soft laugh brushed his veil as he drew it up, pinning it to his hair. "It's the same answer anyway. I don't know, so I find myself grateful that I'll be at least somewhat protected from the worst of the fallout by said friend turning out to be an Emoran lord. Same place you would be in if you hadn't made such a pointless moral stand when you found out who Uvao was."

"Pointless?"

"You asked," Sorscha said, and with a little wave, he headed for the door, skirt swishing. "Goodbye, Tesh."

He was gone on the words, leaving me stunned and flustered with an increasing urge to run after him and argue. An urge quashed only by Master Hoye dropping half a dozen jobs on my bench.

"No time for daydreaming, Tesha, we're swamped," he said, before retiring to the back of the workshop alone. There, the box he always used for Sorscha's special jobs already sat out. It was flat and rectangular, little bigger than a book, but with wooden panels so finely decorated it would have been worth a fortune even without the secretive contents. Master Hoye had never told me what was inside, but over the years I'd come to believe it was all poisons—poisons over which his hands danced with ease, each vial touched with the gentleness of old friends.

Having chosen vials from the box, he turned to make a fresh gather, and I spun away. Nothing was as sure to incite his ire as curiosity about his box of poisons and the glassware he sometimes put them in for money.

Despite my worries, there was so much work to do that for the rest of the day I lost myself in glass and heat and sweat. For a time, the mysterious box was forgotten, as was the vote, Uvao,

Sorscha, and the political plays of Reacher Sormei, each melting away beneath the singular focus of practising my craft and practising it well.

By the end of the day, I was worn out but satisfied and had started tidying the workshop when a registered crier passed, calling the evening news. As always, we all paused in our work to listen.

"—to the scale shortage, yet another shipment of sand has failed to arrive as scheduled due to ongoing blockades between Orsu and the northern mines. Learshapans advised to ration their glass needs," the crier shouted, slowly passing the open portico. "After this afternoon's emergency council meeting, Lord Councillor Angue is expected to address crowds in the chamber square at sundown, while Reacher Sormei..."

Her voice faded as she moved on, once more taking with her the Reacher's dreaded name and much of the air left in our stifling workshop.

"Sand too," Master Hoye grumbled. "I'll have to go through the orders and see what can be put off."

What more was there to say? With a huff of breath, he waved a hand at the assistants, both elbow-deep in the washing tub and looking miserable. "Go on, run along home, boys. I'll wash up tonight. You too, Tesha. I need to think."

Waved away with a preoccupied scowl, there was nothing to do but swap apron for veil and head out into the street, leaving him to his thoughts.

Although the sun was setting, the air outside still held the day's heat, drying everything it touched. Learshapa could get as hot as our forge, but the city never smelled of burning paper and coal and wax and scale; rather the street held tangs of life, of cooking food and warm earth and sweat, of water and flowers and spilled date brandy. It was all so very *Learshapa* that I breathed deep.

At the end of the street, the public house was already full of noise, all chatter and laughter and the squeak of worn sandals on the glass-tiled floor. A tangle of vines shaded the outdoor plaza, where cooler air gathered around the spill of a central fountain.

It took a few moments to find an empty table near the netting edge, but I soon had a tall glass of brandy laced with benki flowers and my very own sticky cake I utterly deserved. Overhead, the sky was turning pink with the setting sun, which meant Lord Councillor Angue would be speaking soon in the chamber square. I tried not to think about what he might have to say, tried not to think about the vote and its consequences, not to think about war with Lummazza or Reacher Sormei or scale and sand shortages, and ended up thinking about them all. Around me, people chattered and laughed and shared drinks, but not everyone was cheerful. Little knots of argument broke out here and there, each akin to the conversation I'd had with Flyer Man earlier that day. The sense that whatever the vote's outcome, Learshapa was fracturing couldn't but worry at me, and though I drank my brandy and ate my cake, I tasted neither.

Perhaps I ought to go to that evening's meeting after all.

While I weighed my desire for political debate against what I told myself was an aversion to seeing Uvao again, a scuffle broke out near the entrance of the public house. An argument over who was next in line for a table perhaps, fierce enough that someone was shoved against the netting, causing a wave to flow across the sheer roof—a sheer roof beyond which the sun had set. In the upper city, Lord Councillor Angue would already have spoken.

A knot of apprehension tightened in my gut as people at nearby tables rose to stare at the spreading disagreement in the entryway. Whispers hissed around me like a buzz of insects, abruptly cut off as someone cheered. Another screamed. Shouting broke out and patrons turned on one another, fingers jabbing into faces and spit flying, and for a moment all I could do was sit, frozen in place, holding tight to my terror.

At the next table, an old man who'd been drinking with a friend rose to his feet looking as confused as I felt. "What in dragon's breath is going on?" he demanded of no one in particular, but he needn't have.

Rising above the noise came the clear tone of a crier. "Due to the imminent war with Lummazza, the council have used their executive power to accept Reacher Sormei's treaty," she called. "There will be no vote. Learshapa is to unite with the rest of the Celes Basin."

The words rolled over me, along with a tide of shouts and cheers and cries I knew couldn't be real. The Learshapan people had a vote because we'd always had a vote; that was how the city worked. Yet someone threw a punch, others cried, and a group danced on their table while drinks were thrown at them. And amid the noise I found my gaze meeting that of the old man, his horror what made it all too real.

They'd sold us out.

Chest tight, I was up before I had a plan, pushing my way through the chaotic crowd. The crowd pushed back, all manic energy, but I needed to get out, needed answers, so I turned my shoulder and cut my way through, brandy splashing my skirt and fingers catching in my hair.

Outside was little better. Learshapa had erupted, equal parts joy and anguish and hissing with rage wherever the two met, but I had mind only for my destination, and for the question burning my tongue. A question only one person I knew could answer.

I hardly saw the city, hardly felt my own steps, time seeming to freeze and yet speed ahead like it had become untethered from the world, spooling away into nothing. One moment I was pushing through the crowd, the next I was at the back door of the meeting house—the door out which I'd walked when I'd cut

Uvao from my life. Now I dared not think what I would do if he wasn't inside.

The moment I pushed it open, a sweet-scented bundle crashed into me, slowing the world to its natural pace. "Tesh! You came back!"

"Jiiala!" I returned her tight embrace, grateful for the moment of comfort. We were alone in the narrow back room, a tiny air pocket in a world of noise that thrummed through the surrounding walls. "I heard the news. Is...is Uvao here?"

Still holding my arms, she looked up, lips parted upon words she couldn't utter—words lost as the door into the main meeting hall opened and closed upon a short burst of noise, spilling Sorscha free. He'd been bright and full of charm earlier, but this was a Sorscha buckling under unexpected weight.

"It's bad out there," he said, ruffling his hair and dropping onto the bench. "I guess it was always going to be if this happened, but not getting any warning..." He trailed off and blew out a heavy breath. "If you're here to shout at Uvao, Tesh, pick a better time."

"No, I—"

With another short burst of noise, the meeting hall door opened and closed again, wafting the scent of dusky panawood into the room. My chest constricted an instant before Uvao appeared in the corner of my vision—a memory at which I dared not stare. Seemingly as intent on ignoring me, he sighed. "What a fucking nightmare."

"Ought I go back out there?" Sorscha lacked all enthusiasm for his own suggestion.

"Maybe later, if the crowds stick around. I have to go, but I should be back in—"

"Go?" I blurted, forgetting the question that had brought me. "Something is more important than the council surrendering Learshapa?"

Uvao didn't turn, but his dark, tired eyes glanced my way in the barest acknowledgement. "Of course there is," he said. "You don't think my hair stays this nice without constant appointments with a pommadeur, do you?"

Jiiala gave a hearty sniff. "Don't listen to him, Tesh. He's just being silly."

"I would never dare be silly, Jii," Uvao said, grabbing his veil from its hook. "Such a thing is, of course, entirely beneath my exalted position."

Ignoring this jibe my way, I unlatched myself from Jiiala. "And what are you planning to do about all this, given that exalted position of yours?"

He turned then, anger simmering in his bright eyes. "Why, I'm going to wave a magic wand and fix it to my liking because that's what lords do. Strange I didn't think of that when you walked out on me. Now, if you'll excuse me, I really do need to go."

"Where?"

Uvao didn't look up from tying his veil. "To a meeting, if you must know. About *all this* that you want me to fix."

"A meeting of the council?"

Uvao barked a humourless laugh. "Hardly. Now I've let you throw your darts, Tesh, so goodbye."

"No!" I cried, desperation throwing me between him and the door. "No, please. I'm not trying to throw darts. I need to know what we can do. What...what *I* can do. This wasn't supposed to happen, not like this."

Caught there between him and his way out, it was all I could do to hold the fiery heat of his gaze as it raked my features, all anger but for a tiny hint of need that sent my thoughts wheeling back to a better time, when I'd been crushed to the wall by his passion, breathless and ecstatic. That heat boiled all air from the small room, silencing even Sorscha, and though I knew myself a fool for having come, I would have made the same choice given it again. Somehow in this moment he was the only one I trusted to give me answers.

At last, he gave a careless shrug. "Come then, if you must. Behind the old playhouse on Fourth. Twenty minutes. You make your own way."

"That's it?"

"That's it, Tesh, take it or leave it, just get out of my way."

I stepped aside, heart and mind racing with possibilities as he pulled open the door. A nod to Jiiala, a word to Sorscha, and he was gone, leaving me unsure if I still remembered how to breathe.

A clink startled me as Sorscha poured himself a drink. "Better you than me," he said, and raised the glass. "But I guess we all get what we deserve one way or another."

"Shush," Jiiala snapped at him. "Don't be more of a shit than comes naturally, Sorscha. And don't pour a drink without pouring one for me too." Two steps brought her to my side, and she squeezed my arm. "You'd better hurry if you're going, Tesh."

"Yes. Thank you, Jii. I'll..." I gestured to the door. "I guess I'll be going then. Yes."

Sorscha snorted. "Yes, do. Goodbye, Tesh."

Once again out in the warm evening air, the streets through which I hurried were packed with people and a breathless unease. Fear of imminent war sat on the tip of every tongue, and even those grateful for unification decried our lack of choice. The city itself hadn't changed, yet I couldn't shake the feeling I wouldn't recognise it come morning. Somewhere in the upper city, Reacher Sormei would be smiling at the chaos he had wrought—and at the expansion of his empire.

Behind the old playhouse, Uvao had said, and following his instructions I found a run-down, rambling house, built at a time when space hadn't been so tight. It looked empty, dead, but unpinning my veil, I knocked before fear could stop me. The dull sound of knuckles upon stained scaleglass faded quickly, but my thumping heartbeat continued the rhythm while I shifted foot to foot.

The door yanked open, letting free a whiff of stale korsh smoke and date brandy. "What do you want?" came a snap of high-born impatience, and I knew I was in the right place.

"Uvao invited me."

"Ah." The disembodied voice pulled the door open in somewhat reluctant welcome. "Hurry up, don't dawdle."

"I wasn't planning to," I muttered, stepping into the darkness. Inside, the heavy, musky scent had a physical presence, so strong I could taste it. "This place stinks."

"An infelicitous observation," the voice said as it strode deeper into the house.

"Only if it's infelicitous to be honest."

He stopped abruptly. "You know what *infelicitous* means?"

"You're surprised?"

"Only because Uvao's... friends have a tendency to be commoners, even the pretty ones."

"That doesn't mean uneducated" was all I managed before the man strode on, out into an atrium where moonlight sheared through the arches, lighting a garden filled alternately with dead plants and vigorous weeds, tumbling from their beds.

As my guide stepped into the light, I caught my first glimpse of his face—the face of a stranger who nevertheless looked vaguely familiar.

"Don't think you can take note of our identities and use this against us," he said, catching me staring. "It would end very poorly for you."

"That," I said, "would require you to be well-enough known for me to recognise you."

His loud laugh echoed around the atrium, a broad smile manifesting a completely different man. "Well struck, Miss...?"

"No *Miss*, just Tesha."

"Tesha. Like the Tesha who strode the brightstorm's fury in Creshen's Heart? How very fortuitous."

"Like what?"

A smirk teased about his lips. "I thought you said you were educated."

"Educated in important things, not in poetry."

His brows lifted—thin, shaped brows with the half a dozen slits of the upper nobility cut through them. "Are you telling me poetry is not important? To speak your heart in verse is to fly free, at least so Kamadan said, and he's considered quite knowledgeable about such things."

"Emoran men always are," I murmured, earning another grin. It didn't last, however. This Emoran seemed incapable of sustaining the appearance of humanity for more than a few moments at a time before his expression sank back in something I could only call punch-worthy.

"We're through here," he said, gesturing to a door on the far side of the atrium—a door that seemed to open into another house entirely. Lit with pink and gold glass lanterns, the room beyond owned a handful of men in padded chairs, each with a broad back like a petal shaped in twisted cane. Despite a lack of finery, the men were unmistakably Emoran, each layered linen skirt and tight, sleeveless tunic so finely sewn they had no need of the armbands and bracelets they would usually wear to mark their station.

At my arrival, their conversation stammered to a halt, every pair of eyes staring at me from beneath brows slit half a dozen times.

There was no sign of Uvao.

"This is Miss Tesha," my guide said. "One of Uvao's friends. She knows what the word *infelicitous* means, and I don't think she likes us very much."

The man in the chair nearest the door laughed bitterly at that.

"I often don't like us very much either, so she's welcome." He gestured to a chair as he spoke. "Get her a glass, Reve. Once Uvao arrives we can start."

Swallowing the urge to ask what exactly the meeting was about and who they were, I perched on the closest empty chair and tried not to exist. Conversation about the plans they'd dropped to be here murmured around me, cut off upon Uvao's arrival a few minutes later—he able to walk in without the mercurial escort. A perfunctory glance my way and he settled into the remaining chair like one well used to the shape of its cushion.

"I suppose we ought to begin since we're all here," my guide said. Reve, one of them had called him, though that didn't tell me which of our Emoran families he belonged to. "Unfortunately, the news isn't good. Firstly, nothing can be done about the executive order. It's been in the agreement between Learshapa and the ruling council since the beginning; they've just never openly used it because of the chaos it might cause."

"They were right about that," grumbled the man beside me. "We'll be lucky if the whole city isn't on fire come morning."

"Half of that noise is celebration, Jet," Uvao said. "There was always a chance the unification vote would win even without this."

"Then why pull this trick? That's what I don't understand. For weeks people have been talking about nothing but this damn vote, and now—"

"Because Sormei sweetened the pot, and they couldn't risk the city voting to remain independent." As all eyes turned back to Reve, my soul thrummed at being allowed to hear such secrets. "Father has been busy with Reacher Sormei here, so, you know me. I listened, I snuck around, and I found out things I wasn't supposed to know. Like that the council has been meeting frequently in secret, even before today, under pressure from Sormei to do away with the vote and accept the treaty offer."

A few jaded grumbles suggested this was no surprise, though one said, "Meeting in secret? Surely not. That's all right for us, Revennai, but not the council."

Revennai. Lord Revennai Angue? I didn't know many Emoran lords, but as the head of the council, his father Lord Councillor Angue was the most notable around Learshapa.

"You're right so far about the terrible news," said one of the older men present, owning a few greying hairs and a weary expression. "What's the rest?"

Lord Revennai sat back in his chair with a sigh. "That although it's just been announced, I think they agreed to the treaty at least a week ago. Plans for the treaty marriage are already underway. Sormei has put forward his candidate, but I haven't been able to find out who it is yet."

"It's Lord Kiren Sydelle."

Uvao spoke quietly, yet he might as well have shouted for the shock that rippled through the room.

"What?" Lord Revennai snapped. "His brother? Are you sure?"

"Quite sure. Highest possible bid on the table so the council will fight over him."

The man beside me—who I was starting to suspect must be a son of Lord Duzeunde by the symbols on his tunic—dropped his head into his hands. "No wonder they caved and accepted the deal."

I stared at the play of light on the brandy glasses as they threw the conversation back and forth like a ball going over my head. The political customs of our Emoran elite had always been a mystery to me, but as each man sagged with defeat, panic began to worm its way into my gut.

"Right, well, that's it then," said the one I was coming to think of as the Old. "Our hands are tied, because no matter what we suggest, the council will refuse. They've already made their decision. Right up to the point of having a marriage treaty with fucking Lord fucking Kiren fucking Sydelle on the table."

"Fucking is not really his forte," Lord Revennai murmured. "But yes. Something like that."

They lulled into silence, nursing their brandy glasses and glancing sadly at one another, because they had that luxury. Because this decision wouldn't turn their whole world upside down. "Are you telling me there's nothing you can do?" I said. "You're Emoran lords!"

The Old gave a derisive laugh and drank deeply, a few grumbled, and Uvao shot me a warning look. "And you," I added, pointing at Lord Revennai. "Your father is the head of the damn council!"

"We are sons and minor lords, and in Emora that makes you nothing," Lord Revennai said, tone subdued. "Not even trusted by our fathers most of the time. We aren't powerful."

I scoffed, too angry to stay silent. "Not powerful, but certainly protected. You won't have to worry about being conscripted into Reacher Sormei's wars or being forced out of a job when the need to compete with the other cities brings automation to every industry it can. You won't even have to worry about losing your way of life, your culture and communal care networks, because it's *your* way of life that will take over."

"We wouldn't be here if we didn't care about this city," snapped the man beside me. "We started meeting long before this damn vote, when Sormei began squeezing Learshapa with his excise taxes that—"

"*Sormei*," I repeated. "When you're on first-name terms with the tyrant, you'll do just fine."

The man swung his incredulous look toward Uvao. "Why is she here again?"

"Because as annoying as she is, she isn't wrong."

A collective outburst exploded from their puffed chests, but before I could discern individual words from the aggrieved roar, Uvao held up his hands. "Yes, thank you," he said in his best meeting-convenor voice. "But there is actually something we can do, it just isn't . . . nice. Not even safe. If you're in you have to be in all the way; if you can't do that, then you're welcome to leave. No hard feelings."

"Unsafe how?" the Old asked through his glare.

"Potentially reputation ruining. On the other hand, if we can make it work, anyone involved would be a power broker under a new reacher."

"Who?" came Lord Revennai's sharp question.

The Old scoffed. "Lord Romm, obviously, Reve. His father is making another bid for power. In which case, I'm out. No offence to you, Uvao, but you know how it is."

Two others rose from their chairs, followed by two more, each setting down their glasses and mumbling apologies. Uvao nodded to them, his expression blank, all the anger he ought to have been feeling roiling in my gut instead.

When the room settled once more into silence, only three of Uvao's companions remained—Lord Revennai, Definitely Lord Duzeunde's Son, and a man whose name I hadn't yet caught. The nameless one leaned forward, eyes bright. "So, what's the plan?"

"Father dearest wants to pull off an insult bride."

"A what?" the nameless one said.

"Yes, it's perfect." Lord Revennai's lips stretched into a grin with a predatory edge. "It hasn't been done for so long that no one will even think of it, especially since the council practically invited Sormei to take control."

"But what is it?" said Lord Duzeunde's Son.

"The substitution of a commoner in place of a high-born marriage candidate." Lord Revennai's eyes burned bright. "A last-ditch effort to force renegotiation when families were cornered into accepting deals they didn't like. Think of it like a fake relative."

Son of Lord Duzeunde and the Nameless One stared, their disbelief mirrored in the restless churning of my stomach. It sounded risky, a back-alley mugging in political clothes.

"The plan is that my father will deal with the rest of the council to ensure our candidate is most favoured for the match," Uvao said, the four remaining men all leaning forward in their chairs, heads close. "He'll also make the necessary arrangements to pass off our insult bride as a genuine member of the Romm family. My job—our job—is to find an insult bride and train her as fast as possible in everything she'll need to know to pull this off."

A few solemn, thoughtful nods met this, but I'd missed the part that made it all make sense. "But what will it achieve?" I asked. "It sounds like it will just make Reacher Sormei look bad."

"Looking bad is political death in Emora," Lord Revennai said, not looking around. "And even if he weathered it, if Lord Romm has everything in place he could trigger a conclave— that's the election of a new reacher. Likely Lord Romm, especially given how close he came to winning last time."

The Nameless One let out a bitter laugh. "At least he can't send you to the Shield if you fail, Uvao. He'd have no sons left!"

Ignoring this, I looked to Uvao. "And would your father reverse this decision?"

"It's unclear if that's still possible." He shook his head slowly. "But the treaty conditions would be renegotiated, and having a Learshapan reacher would be far better for ensuring the city is neither sucked dry nor used as a shield in a Lummazzt war."

"So we'd just be getting a better dictatorial leader?"

He sighed. "If you've got a better idea, do let us know."

I didn't, because all my ideas relied on the council having no secret executive power to do away with Learshapan democracy.

"Right, well, I'm in," said the young Lord Duzeunde. "I've

got nothing to lose, and if Lord Romm is going to put this on you for his own fucking deniability then we'll make damn sure it works."

Uvao gripped his lips tight and nodded, and it was all I could do not to reach out my own comfort like I'd done when he'd been just Uvao. When he would have taken my sympathy into his arms and held me close, whispering thanks into my hair.

"I'm in too," said the one whose name I didn't know. "So what do we need? I suppose she has to be pretty. And clever enough to learn what she needs to do."

"Has to speak well," Lord Revennai added. "We don't have time to train her out of a slum accent."

They went on talking, but I was no longer listening. I was thinking of a home I would no longer recognise, of a Learshapa lost to war, of Master Hoye's box of poisons and a deep yearning to do something just as powerful that could change the world. Because the woman they were describing was me. Foolish to volunteer for such a scheme, to throw myself into the world of Emoran politics, yet every possibility was an intoxicating whisper. I could do what they needed me to do, but once inside I could do so much more. Once inside, I could bring down Emora.

"Maybe if we—"

"I'll do it," I said, getting to my feet. "I'll be your insult bride."

Four shocked expressions turned my way. I met each with a defiant glare, except for Uvao, who pulled his gaze away to stare at the ceiling. "I could do it," I said into the silence, reassuring myself as much as them. "I am everything you're looking for with the bonus of not having to waste time looking elsewhere."

"She's not wrong," the Nameless One murmured. "Better the bee we have than the dragon we don't."

"That," I said, jabbing a finger at him, "is a very infelicitous remark."

A laugh burst from Lord Revennai, and though he shook his

head, he grinned. "But not infelicitous that you came. I think she'll do very well. Uvao? In fact I think she's perfect."

For a moment that stretched to eternity, Uvao didn't move. Didn't speak. His silence seemed to draw all breath from my body, tightening my chest until, at last, he nodded. "Perfect," he said, the word owning all the tenor of hot glass shattering on stone.

2

Ashadi

Morning Bulletin

To all criers for announcement throughout Orsu and the Shield

Dozens of attacks from The Sands have been thwarted by Shield Riders in the last few weeks. Monster numbers on the rise a cause for concern, the citadel masters say.

Eleven southern scale mines have been attacked by Lummazzt forces in what authorities are calling a concerted effort to weaken Celessi defences ahead of a likely war.

Red dye in short supply throughout the Celes Basin as trade relations with Lummazza plummet.

69:3

Smoke billowed as I lowered my pistol, Manalaii's impressed whistle cutting over the explosive rhythm of the shooting gallery. "Perfect aim," he said, smile appearing through the haze. "And faster than last time. That's quite the pistol."

I lifted an eyebrow. "Don't you mean that I'm quite the shot?"

"Well, yes." His smile took on a lopsided quality. "That too. Of course. Here, I'll reload."

I let him take the gun and wiped both hands on my divided skirts, drying sweat and streaking stray powder onto the dark fabric—an unacceptable habit back home, but thankfully the Shield Citadel was not Emora.

"You should be on your third round by now!" Commander Jasque called over the noise. "Anyone who isn't has to stay back after the session and do timed reloads!"

To my left, Luce grumbled. "Does he want us to just empty the barrel as fast as possible, or actually hit the target?"

Farisque snorted as he handed a pistol to his watcher. "Both, Lucie. Both." He flicked a glance my way, as full of scorn as wariness. "Or get yourself an Apaian watcher like Ashadi's."

"Is that your secret?" Luce said, turning wide eyes toward Manalaii. "I didn't realise the old natives were so good with guns."

If Manalaii heard, he didn't show it, just stood with his back against the wall while with long, deft fingers, he checked my pistol's loading mechanism and filled the chamber with ball and powder. He made quick work of it as always, despite the pistol being a recent acquisition. He had always been the kind of watcher who practised his craft far more than I practised mine.

"No secret, Luce," I said. "Just hit where you aim and you've got it."

"Frabre! Does that look like a killing shot to you?" Commander Jasque shouted farther along the row. "We aren't trying to tickle monsters; we're trying to stop them eating our families. You miss that target again and you've got extra rounds."

While Farisque sniggered, Mana pressed the newly loaded

pistol into my hand. "Lord Ashadi," he said, relinquishing it with a nod and stepping back. With hardly a thought, I raised the pistol, aiming at a target beginning to look more like pumice than paper, and emptied the six-shot repeater in a few glorious seconds.

"Excellent work, Romm!" the commander called, his heavy tread halting behind me amid the tang and bite of smoke. "Romm has emptied seven full pistols already, and every shot a direct hit. If any of you have been wondering why he gets to ride loose, this is why. We're going to keep this up until I have a whole pack of Romms!"

Grumbling met this announcement, and Manalaii took my empty pistol back with a quiet grimace. Raising his pistol beside me, Luce said, "Next time, please miss one. Deliberately, if you have to. You know. For me."

"Just work at it, Lucie!" Farisque laughed, waving away a cloud of smoke as he handed yet another empty pistol to his watcher—a man as dour as Farisque was reckless. "You don't get to be this good by asking other people to be shoddy," he went on. "You can be better than Ashadi if you try, and you don't even need to put up with the creepy death cult stuff."

This time Manalaii couldn't have missed the gesture in his direction had he tried, but while the small painted skull on its leather band around his neck seemed suddenly to glow with the force of our stares, he shrank his attention to the gun in his hands.

Whenever I thought we might finally have moved past jibes at my choice of watcher, someone was determined to prove me wrong.

"You say that like you're better than Ashadi," Luce retorted, turning on Farisque rather than emptying his pistol at the target.

"Impugning my skill, Lucie?"

I turned from the brewing argument to find Mana waiting

with my loaded pistol. I ought to have said something, have apologised for them, but I didn't. "Thank you," I said instead. "Let's load that new seven-shot too, see how she plays."

"Yes, Lord Ashadi."

He hurried away, and as I waited, I realised my error. Luce and Farisque were still arguing, loud enough now to catch the attention of others along the row. "I was talking about Ashadi, since he's the best here," Luce was saying.

"I am quite as good as *Romm*," Farisque scoffed. "He just has fancier toys."

Glances flitted my way at this, and I fought the urge to join in to Farisque's detriment. And failed. "Come now, Farisque," I said in a bored drawl. "You know that's not true. Better than Luce, yes. Better than me, no."

Laughter greeted this—our audience seeming to grow by the moment as riders sought more interesting entertainment than being shouted at by Commander Jasque. Unfortunately, the commander was at the other end of the room, a fact Farisque also noted with a glance and a growing grin. "You're so sure of that?" he said. "How about a little contest then?" He pointed at the new pistol Mana was loading. "Your flashy new pistol against my old reliable. No money on the outcome—neither of us needs it. Let's bet an extra callout instead."

Better to ignore such challenges, but whatever I had hoped upon first arriving, the citadel was just like Emora. Hierarchy. Money. Power. There, one's name was everything, friends were a weakness no one could afford, and mercy tended to backfire.

I sighed and took my new pistol from Mana's hand. "As you wish. I have a few minutes to show you how wrong you are."

"A bet!" Luce cried, loud enough to cut over the remaining noise. "A bet is on! Farisque and Ashadi are shooting for a callout!"

Regret flared, but before I could even consider backing out,

Commander Jasque strode over. "Now this is sport!" he said, rubbing his hands together as riders and watchers alike drew close in a press of chatter, oil, powder, and sweat.

"What were you thinking?" Batien demanded of Farisque with a laugh, his folded arms bulging muscles. "Didn't anyone warn you when you arrived never to challenge Ashadi?"

"I certainly wouldn't dare," Luce agreed, causing a trickle of amused derision.

"Perhaps losing is good for the soul."

"An extra callout? You like hard work and throwing up, huh, Farisque?"

"I'm willing to lay odds on a greater than ten-point difference; any takers?"

I stood heeding none of it, determined to at least appear like a steady rock within the whirlpool while Farisque enjoyed the attention and laughed along, lazy looks beneath his lowered lids sending daggers for my chest.

"Are you sure you want to do this?" Manalaii said, drawing close enough that his words were a breath by my ear. "You could cry off."

"And impugn your honour, my dear?"

"*My* honour?"

I raised a brow at his confusion. "I'm well aware the watchers have a secret betting pool that ranks riders, so don't deny it. Sadly, your secret is not very secret; it's just that nobody cares to stop you."

He mumbled something I didn't catch as Farisque proclaimed his readiness, forcing Mana to step back into the excited buzz.

I had never set out to become some kind of infamous peril people had to be warned against. In my former life, I would have revelled in the thrill of being the best, but here my obsessive shooting practice was born from pain, not joy.

"What good is trauma if you can't profit off it?" I murmured under my breath, adjusting my grip on the new pistol. It was the finest I owned, a newly crafted seven-shot repeating flintlock, something in its precise construction allowing it to fire off seven shots in the same time as other repeaters fired six. Since Farisque carried a slower six-shot, he must have been hoping I wasn't yet used to this new pistol's vagaries, but while today was the first time I'd tested it on the range, his hope reckoned without my insomnia and all the holes in my bedroom walls.

I rotated the loading lever, and with the pistol cocked and ready, let it hang loose at my side.

"Score is by both speed and accuracy," Commander Jasque was saying, his eyes bright with the thrill of precision scoring. "The total of your rings plus the inverse of your time. Four for—"

"With all due respect, Commander, we know how to score," I said. "Can we get on with this so I can get on with my life?"

More sniggers.

"That's one point off for insubordination, Romm," the commander said. "But if you're both ready."

I lifted my arm, levelling the cocked pistol at the distant target. "Farisque?"

"Ready when you are." His grin was a forced rictus, sweat beading on his brow.

"Right then. On three," boomed the commander's voice around us. "One. Two. Three!"

Whatever the realities of being up in the skies, with a stationary target it was possible to unload all seven bullets in mere seconds, cranking the lever between each shot and adjusting sight down the barrel—the whole a smooth, single motion from the first pull of the trigger.

Except when someone ran into the gallery in the middle of the third shot and shouted, "Learshapa has been surrendered!"

I pulled my aim as the words struck me, sending shock rippling through my body. Had I not been well-practised in maintaining focus under pressure I would have lost more than one shot off into the stonework. As it was, the last shots seemed to take forever, each crank of the loading handle and squeeze of the trigger stretching to an age as questions swirled like powder smoke.

I lowered my pistol as the last shot ripped from the barrel. Mana called time, more than a second before Farisque's watcher called his despite my extra shot. Smoke and sharp questions filled the air, both tasting bitter in the aftermath.

"Surrendered?"

"Did Lummazza attack?"

"No, you idiot. He means the people voted to join the rest of the Celes Basin under Reacher Sormei."

"Wasn't the vote next week?"

"Hey, Ashadi, your lands are near Learshapa, aren't they?"

Annoyance bubbled through me. As riders we weren't meant to be members of our families anymore, were meant to be neutral, protecting the basin from outside threat without taking part in its politics. It was true only until something reminded us it wasn't.

I loosened my all-too-tight grip on the pistol. "They are," I said, turning to face the rest of my pack, their interest having shifted from the witnessing of one trauma to another, gazes hungry. "Though I'm hardly the only one here from out east." Not wanting to think about the news, I thrust out my empty pistol without looking, grateful Mana was on hand to take it. "Did I win?" I asked, words forcefully bright.

"It's hardly fair when we were interrupted," Farisque grumbled.

"It's the only way you'll ever get me to pull a shot, so take it or leave it," I said.

This earned some laughter from the tangle of talk as Commander Jasque tallied the score and Farisque went on grumbling, but the world seemed to have faded behind the sheen of smoke. Even Mana's voice sounded distant.

"What?" I snapped.

"Do you want it reloaded?" he said.

"No." I shook my head, thoughts fuzzy. "No, I need some air."

He stepped aside as I strode toward the gallery balcony, only to be brought up short. "Romm by three," Commander Jasque cried. "Everyone except Romm has to shoot two extra rounds. You're allowed to leave only when you get a personal score of at least twenty-five!"

I looked back over my shoulder amid the sudden outcry and complaints of favouritism. "Forget the callout, Farisque. Just don't waste my time again."

Leaving the uproar in my wake, I stepped out onto the balcony, gaining peace and space to think. The integration of Learshapa into the basin had felt inevitable for a long time; it had just taken Sormei Sydelle levels of ambition to make it a reality—a reality that worried at me as I stared out at the barren slopes of the Shield Mountains.

My fingers trembled as I took out a roll of korsh and my striker. The movements were as well-practised as aiming and pulling the trigger, and yet it took me more attempts than I was willing to admit to get the roll alight. Once it was, I shoved the striker back into my pocket, fixed the hang of my pleated skirt, and took a long drag.

The sweet tang of korsh smoke trickled warmth through me, easing my ever-present aches to a slightly more manageable level. Still, I leaned against the stone railing to take some weight off my joints, not at all minding that, for anyone who glanced out, it helped me look broody and inscrutable, staring out at the distant horizon. Others would think twice before trying to talk to me.

"Everything all right, Lord Ashadi?"

Except Mana.

I drew in a breath of korsh and turned, blowing the smoke out as I said, "Are we going to have this conversation again? Ash is fine."

His gaze flittered in the direction of the open door and the collection of riders and watchers still running through practice shots. "It is for you, but not for me. Lord Ashadi. Keeping my job means being respectful."

"Fine, and yes, I'm all right. I'm always all right."

"Always?" His turn to raise his brows in amused question.

"Yes. Always."

It was a ridiculous statement for any rider, yet with impressive faux solemnity, Mana agreed. It was all I could do not to bark a laugh that would have felt like breaking bones.

Suppressing a smile, he came to lean against the railing, just out of reach. Such was the respect expected of watchers, yet I couldn't but wonder if he preferred distance whenever proximity wasn't required of him, so meticulously did he maintain it.

"Are you thinking about what will happen to Learshapa now?" he said, staring at the same nothing at which I stared. "Are you worried for your family?"

"Oh no. Can't say I care very much what happens to them."

Perhaps I shouldn't have said it, but I'd never been good at thinking before speaking, and at least he was well used to that by now. Yet he grimaced, once more glancing at me in that quick, furtive way he had, seeking to gather as much information about my mood and meaning in as little time as possible. "Isn't family important to Emorans? No matter what? Duty, and all that."

"Only for rich ones."

"You say *rich* like it's a dirtier word than *beggar*."

"Because it is."

Mana's brow crinkled. It was adorable and entirely unfair. "Isn't your family rich?"

"Yes. Very."

"One day I will understand the inner workings of your mind."

I blew korsh smoke out on a laugh. "Stars, I hope not."

He grinned and I grinned back, a moment of simple companionship I feared as much as I craved. It lingered longer than usual, long enough to make my chest constrict in the annoying way it had when faced with Mana's decency and care, and this time it was I who looked away.

"Have you ever been to Learshapa?" I asked, breathing in another lungful of korsh.

"No, never. Only Bakii. And before that, our commune, which is halfway to everywhere yet in the middle of nowhere."

"That's a very poetic description," I said, glancing sidelong at him as I breathed out more smoke. That he was one of the few true Apaians left seemed to be all people noticed about Mana, as though the row of dots tattooed in a curved line beneath his left eye obscured everything else. People wondered why he was around, why I hadn't chosen a "normal" watcher, and even questioned his loyalty to the cause. For three years he'd been my watcher, his work no different to that of any other, yet still he stood out as an oddity.

Ashadi's Apaian.

"Poetic?" he said, brows raised. "More likely we just give directions very differently to you. The way to Learshapa from my home is east of the sun four mornings and starfall."

"Now you're just stringing me along."

"Am I?"

His stare was all challenge and I held it, unable to decide and unwilling to fail. As I chewed over an answer, the wind tousled his hair and fluttered his simple skirts—a wind I hadn't noticed until I saw the ways it touched him.

"I think—"

The gong sounded through the citadel like the beginning of a cursed song, ringing into being a world I would rather not join. Even before the third tone rang, signalling my pack, I had the sinking feeling that always came before a ride.

I stubbed the end of my korsh roll on the railing and blew out a last lungful of smoke, catching Mana's worried look.

"I'm fine," I said, or lied, depending on your point of view. "Let's go."

The armoury was already bustling when we arrived, Commander Jasque shouting information at the top of his lungs, not because it was necessary, but because he believed in getting the blood pumping with a good shout.

"—coming in from the northeast, but Frabre and Vibluz will be on circuit duty to check all those tricky dark spots the watchers can't see from the tower," he was saying as I strode toward my armoury chest. Manalaii had darted ahead to unlock it with the key he wore with the skull around his neck.

"—the rest of you will be on offensive," the commander went on, already dressed in his armour at the head of the room. "We're still waiting for a proper estimate on enemy numbers, but if the last few rides are anything to go by, they won't be small."

Being laced into his armour beside me, Luce glanced over. "That's never a good sign, huh?"

"That we're being called out at all is never a good sign," I said, watching Mana unpack my chest plate and long bracers, helmet, and boots.

"Well, yes," Luce agreed. "But if the number is so large that it's hard to count?"

We shared a grimace, but there wasn't time to say more. Mana held up my chest plate, and I slid my arms into it before turning to give him better access to the lacing. He worked quickly, each tightening tug punctuated with brief touches as he slid his fingers beneath the laces—the gentle dance of his hands down my back keeping my attention from the bruises still lingering from the last ride. And the one before that. And the one before that.

With Commander Jasque having finished shouting for now, the armoury was abuzz with low talk as each rider prepared, donning their armour, priming their weapons, and stretching muscles for the ordeal to come.

Ordeal. Perhaps the iishor ought to be renamed to something as honest.

Mana patted my shoulder to show he was finished and had one of my bracers ready before I even turned. Made of thick, hard leather, they were as flame-proof as possible, like the rest of the armour, though I wasn't fool enough to think it would make any difference if I happened to fly into dragon fire.

Manalaii soon had me laced into my bracers too, leaving me to fit my helmet and strap on my holsters while he checked and primed all six pistols, and the two rifles that would hang from Shuala's saddle. As he finished each one, he set them at half-cock and slid them, one after another, into my holsters, slowly weighing me down. It always felt odd to walk into the room dressed in a light divided skirt and sleeveless tunic only to walk out again weighing so much that setting one foot in front of the other became a gruelling task. At least once I was in the air the weight wasn't mine to carry.

Clinking glass heralded the iishor's arrival. With both of my rifles slung over his shoulder, Mana fetched my glass, the murky red liquid within a promise of what was to come. He returned with his usual grimace. He tried to hide it, to look excited or pleased or... whatever he was going for, but he always failed spectacularly. Given the mess he would soon have to deal with, it was no wonder he looked forward to this as little as I did. Yet at the first hint of the iishor's scent, a twisted rush of euphoria flushed through me, its power calling to some deep, dark part of me I refused to acknowledge.

I took the glass from his hand, reluctance warring with need, though I told myself it was duty that won out. I was a rider of the citadel, and this was my sole purpose now. Protecting the cities of the basin from all that came thundering across The Sands.

I lifted the iishor to my lips. A moment of sweetness, then its bitter heat rushed upon my tongue. All around me glasses were smashing, and before the sane part of me could resist, I tipped it all into my mouth and gulped it down, fighting the urge to gag as the last lumpy, tinny fragments slid down my throat.

The glass fell, smashing about my feet—an old tradition. Some riders threw them hard against the walls sending shards flying, but even under the iishor's growing influence, that seemed like all too much effort.

"Lord Ashadi?" Mana stood before me, his words already beginning to quicken, colours shifting. "All well?"

He always asked. I nodded rather than speak, sure my voice would already be slow to him as his was speeding up for me. Just like everything else, from the dance and flicker of lantern flames to the pulse raging within my chest and the movement of riders heading for the door, time sped faster and faster like it had spun loose.

"May the Skies keep you," Mana said, thrusting the pair of rifles into my hands. I took them without thinking, letting my body sink into its practised patterns while my mind unspooled from one reality and sought a foothold in another.

Mana had once asked me what drinking iishor was like. "Like being drunk but nowhere near as fun," I'd said, and it was almost true.

He was gone before I finished my thought, and dragging the weight of my armour and my holsters, my rifles, and my whole self, I started the walk along the passage with my pack. Sometimes the walk dragged like the weight, seeming to take hours, every step a slow, painful thing despite the speeding of the world around me, but other times it was gone in a blink, and there were the lights of the undercroft and the snuffling and scraping and clinking of dragons moving about.

I was there now, everything smelling of old blood and soot and oily wool fresh from pakkas in the high fields. Light glinted and gleamed, and I found myself blinking fast, or perhaps only thought I was because I was still in the awful transition before everything settled. Untethered from any sense of time, I strode the familiar path to Shuala's den, carved into the undercroft along with all the others—each dark arch a dragon's cave.

As I approached, Shuala lifted her head from the shadows and drew a great breath in through her nostrils only to let it out in a disgruntled huff.

Oh. You're back.

She shifted, stretching a foot toward me from the comfort of her woollen bed, claws scratching stone. Behind the claws her glass scales glinted.

You know I get no sleep around here. Someone is always coming and going, and the breeze through the archway is terribly cold.

"You're about as far from the arch as it's possible to get," I said. "And I can feel the warmth of that wool from here."

Oh, that would be right, kicking me out of my bed now too?

"Hardly."

How do you scrawny things even keep warm? She rose as she spoke, stretching out both front legs and lifting her head. *I could always light a nice fire upon your feet.*

"You know what?" I said, stepping back to give her space to emerge. "I think I'll pass. Permission to saddle up?"

You always say that like you're going to do it.

"Yes or no, Shu, we've got incoming."

Then how can I say no?

I pinched the bridge of my nose and blew my frustration out upon a heavy sigh. Around us wings were already beating, and shouts of "Clear!" rang through the undercroft. Shuala just glared at me, her golden eyes seeming to reflect some of my own anger.

At last those golden eyes flicked away. *Fine. Yes. Permission granted. Let's go burn things and see if I can't shake you loose somewhere or scrape you off on a passing mountain.*

"So kind, Shu, you don't know how much I appreciate it."

I gave the signal, and one of the stable hands came running. Growing up on an estate outside Learshapa, stable hands had often been young boys or wiry old men with an affinity for mules, but here they had to be tall, muscular, and indestructible—the kind of men who seemed to be hewn from stone. This one was called Borden. Or... Broden. Or maybe Boroden.

Maybe Boroden heaved Shuala's saddle down from its hook as she slunk reluctantly out of her den, shaking loose the clumps of wool caught to her scales. Her shaking made music like a dozen glass windchimes in a sharp wind, before settling to a gentle tinkle. She eyed Probably Boroden standing patiently beside her.

Why are they always so silent?

"You know the answer to that. Please lie down and let the man do his job."

She gave a little snort. *Why don't they just give these men the drink too?*

"Because it's shit."

At last, she lowered her body onto the stones and let Hopefully Boroden throw the saddle over her wing joint. Working quickly, he adjusted its placement, before scrabbing about on the floor to tighten the thick leather straps, taking care not to cut himself on any of her underscales. Something else a stable hand here needed—very *stable* hands. I grinned to myself, annoyed Mana wasn't around to roll his eyes at that one.

Once it was done, I thanked the man with a nod and stepped back to allow Shuala to fully stretch out, scales clinking. They were glorious things, each about the width of a finger, protruding enough from her skin to make an overlapping pattern of smoky glass, which the iishor turned faintly blue. She wasn't the largest or the strongest or the fastest dragon in the pack, but I'd almost swallowed my tongue the first time I saw her unfold from her den. From a sleepy, shimmering ball she had uncurled into the largest animal I had ever seen, twice my height at the wing joint, standing on four legs each ending with talons of sharpened glass. All the dragons were similar in proportion, with short necks, broad shoulders, and long tails ending in devastating spikes. And then they unfurled their wings.

Job done, Boroden—maybe—dashed out of range while I slid my two rifles into their holsters high on Shuala's back. She made no complaint about the weight or the shifting of the holsters against her scales, but I would check their placement once I was up. I didn't need to be a dragon to know that having something rubbing your scales the wrong way would be uncomfortable.

A touch to each of my pistols and I gripped the saddle, hauling myself up the glinting mountainside that was her back. One leg thrown over, boots hooked into the forward stirrups, reins in hand, and I was all but ready. Luce was ahead of me, making for the archway, so I took a moment to do a final check and be sure neither the saddle nor the holster was making any of her scales stick up.

Are we going or what?

"Excuse me for caring about your well-being. By all means, let's go if you're ready."

If you really cared for my well-being you'd go die somewhere, she said, striding toward the arch as Luce's dragon spread its wings and leapt.

"Someone else would just get assigned to you. Maybe someone not as nice as me."

Is that a threat? It sounds like a threat.

I sighed, though the sound was crushed beneath the thump of

her steps and the scrape of claws on stone. "Not a threat, just an observation."

Like when I observe that your body would look lovely squished flat and not breathing.

As we approached the archway, a sharp wind whipped in, playing music across her scales and making me shiver. Another effect of the iishor was that I was always cold no matter how hot the day—a feeling that was beginning to follow me into my downtime, like my bones were slowly turning to scaleglass.

Reaching the precipice, Shuala unfurled her wings—the only part of her where shimmering glass scales gave way to taut, pale skin, each flap like the cracking of a brightstorm. Half a dozen heavy wing beats and she leapt, launching us both into the deep blue sky. Chill air ripped past my ears, small sounds lost amid the roar of the wind and the crack of wings, even the clink of her scales nothing but memory.

With the iishor humming in my veins, the world came to me in hues of blue and green, only living creatures like the other dragons and riders owning the red and orange of warm-blooded life. They gathered like a flock of red birds just beyond the citadel, and Shuala flew to join them, every fierce flap of her wings pushing us higher. Below, the citadel shrank away while to the south the jagged slopes of the Shield Mountains kept the Celes Basin from view. On this side of the mountains there was just The Sands, stretching as far as the eye could see. And a thickening line of red upon the horizon.

They were coming in fast.

Offence. Ready in one, Shuala said, passing along Commander Jasque's orders with her usual lack of enthusiasm.

"And?"

Flame lines, then you can play.

Standard tactics. Some dragons shared more details with their riders, but I had learned to trust that Shu knew what she was doing. However the dragons communicated with one another, they were capable of flying and burning in formation with no input at all from us.

When the minute was up, Commander Jasque's dragon shot forward and the rest of us followed, Shuala's frenzied flapping sending us into a rapid dive. All I could do was hold tight with both hands and thighs, and grit my teeth as the wind roared past. And on the horizon, the patchwork of blues that made up the world broke upon a mass of bright red monsters. From the open sands they sped toward the foothills, snouts low to the ground and stubby tails wagging. Without the iishor, they were brown, creatures larger than bull pakkas, with leather hides and skinny, misshapen arms that doubled as legs, helping them to balance as they half hopped, half dragged themselves along the uneven terrain at a speed that ought not to have been possible for anything so ungainly.

As we drew close their lines fractured, scattering them off in every direction like a chaotic firework. "Shit," I hissed. That was new, and if we didn't rake them with flame soon some would—

Shuala's back rumbled beneath me, flame readying as we dropped within range. It was like sitting on a boiling pot, every rising bubble vibrating through her scales and into the saddle. As the air grew hotter, I pulled down the tinted glasses hooked onto my riding helmet, muting the white-hot scene as the commander's dragon let out the first gout of flame. It roared free, followed by others, Shuala's head shooting forward as she added her fire to the flames raking through the monsters' splintering ranks. Sparks and hot drops of molten glass flew up from the sand, one landing on my right bracer, but worse than if it had touched skin was the ambient heat. Even high above the fire, it turned the world to a wobbling heat haze, bright and searing upon both flesh and eyes.

Reaching the end of the pack, Shuala wheeled around, banking at such an angle I couldn't but think of her ongoing threats to shake me off. Their first flames had left behind trails of molten glass and scorched earth scattered with dead and dying monsters. The air stank of charred skin and flesh and hair, but half a dozen clusters were still running for the mountains. In formation, the dragons loosed their second gouts, far less powerful but enough to devastate anything that got in their way.

That felt good, Shuala said, pulling out of her dive, heavy wingbeats carrying us back up into the sky. *Hunting time.*

I flipped my glasses back up and surveyed the scattered remains of the horde. Those running off back into The Sands were a problem for another day or another pack, but those sprinting toward the mountains had to be stopped. Far too many had gotten past our initial onslaught, each a bright red blotch of heat upon the otherwise pale bluish landscape. With no time for panic, I drew my first rifle and chose a target.

The first time I'd shot from the back of a dragon I'd cried out at the thrill and the ease, at the speed and strength with which Shuala could carry me through the sky, target to target. Whatever our differences, Shuala responded to the lightest of touches while I cranked the loading lever and fired round after round into the glaring red monsters climbing the foothills toward the citadel and beyond.

The thrill remained no matter how many times we'd done this. I sighted along the barrel and fired at the first target. The warbling squeal of a hit was as satisfying as the click and crunch of the loading lever dropping another ball and powder into the chamber while I sighted the next. They were everywhere, spreading out over the foothills like an army of ungainly fire ants, the air thick with the crack of beating wings and flying shot.

My first rifle clicked empty and I shoved it back into its holster, drawing two pistols in its place.

"Take us lower!" I shouted, and Shuala complied, her recalcitrance saved for the comfort of the undercroft.

Holding her wings still, Shuala soared down. The ground sped by sickeningly fast, each shot I took at a searing red sand monster more instinct than skill, yet screeches rose in our wake. I urged her on, more monsters scattering ahead. A fresh pistol—this my seven-shot—and she dove down close once again, all but able to blow them over with a flap of her wings.

I felled a small clutch of them, yet despite how far we'd flown from the initial group more still stretched ahead.

"How did they get this far? Was this a second group?"

Commander says we're to take them out.

She topped a rise as she spoke, and the few more ahead turned into dozens scattered over the next hill. "Tell him we're going to need backup!" I shouted into the wind.

On our own. Lots of groups got through.

"Shit." I drew another pistol from its holster. "Might need your claws for some of these."

I have a third flame brewing.

"Save it for if we find a pack."

Like that one, she said, topping a second rise to find a dozen clumped together, making for one of the many wider passes.

"Yes, like that one." I flipped my glasses down as her belly began to rumble, and banking back around, she came at them along their longest axis, spewing flame in a roar. The heat made the air waver, and here away from the sand there was no molten glass, only the scorching of rock and dirt and the squeal of monsters as they fell.

I'm out.

"Let's hope I have enough shots then."

She flew on, weaving through the peaks and tracks of the pass hunting individual monsters, scrabbling along on their curved dark claws.

A dropping sensation in my stomach was the first warning the iishor's euphoria was wearing off. Ride by ride it was lasting less time. I needed my dosage increased, an increase I wasn't sure my body could handle. Not a fear I'd shared with Mana. Not a fear I dared dwell on even now.

"Iishor's going, Shu," I said. "Let's finish this up as fast as we can."

Shall I tell the command—

"No."

I could feel her disapproval, but that she'd even asked meant she knew something was wrong. *We should head back.*

"There's still some more ahead. We have to get them first."

If we go much farther, you'll run out before we can get back.

"Can't be helped." I cranked the loading lever, dropping the last ball of the second rifle into the chamber. "Let's finish the job."

I sighted along the barrel as another monster came into view, scrabbling with its misshapen arms up a slope of scree. I fired, hitting it in the back and sending it sliding off balance, Shuala's pace too quick to see if it had died in one shot or would be left bleeding out.

Every time I was sure we'd found the last, the bright red flare of another would appear and we'd press on. Around us the bright blue hue started to drain, revealing the world's rightful colours— colours that spun slowly as nausea built in my gut. I gritted my teeth and pushed it down, drawing my last pistol.

"Almost out, Shu."

Of shots?

"Of everything."

She knew what I meant. Knew she would be making the flight back on her own, a grumble all the answer I got.

The all-too-large group of monsters had finally thinned to a couple making for one of the passes, and I took them out with a hasty shot and reload as Shuala snaked us through the jagged peaks faster than was safe. Heaving a sigh, I was about to turn her back toward the citadel when another appeared a little way on. Waiting until we were in range, I levelled my pistol, hand shaking, arm unsteady. The shot went well wide and I cranked again, cursing my body's weakness, cursing the iishor and its side effects, cursing these damn monsters and their determination to get within our borders.

A second shot went wide too, and a third clipped its foot, barely slowing it down, and that was it. I was out of shots, without resorting to throwing the pistol at it and hoping.

Thankfully, before my hazy brain could decide this was a good idea, Shuala dropped, extending her front claws in a blazing streak of bright, reflective glass, and swept the creature up in her talons. Barely had it squealed than she tore it asunder, dropping the pieces in a fountain of bloody beads that sprayed across her scales.

With no more monsters appearing, there was nothing to do but hope that had been the last and turn back. My light tug upon the reins wasn't needed. Shuala was already banking steeply, beating the air with her great wings and propelling us up, out of the mountain crags and into the sky.

Holding tight, the flight back seemed both far quicker than the flight out and yet interminable. My churning stomach refused to be ignored, and a headache began long before the citadel came into sight.

Silent now, Shuala sped toward one of the undercroft's open archways, taking the entrance much faster than usual. The frantic beat of her wings as she sought to slow filled the space with rushing wind, and her claws scraped the stones as we finally slid to a halt.

My teeth chattered as I pulled my boots from the stirrups and half slid, half fell out of the saddle, one hand on Shuala all that kept me from overbalancing. With the iishor gone, I could no longer hear her, but likely she was saying something snarky about how much trouble I was.

I breathed a delirious laugh and started toward the crowd of onlookers crammed into the doorway.

"Ash!"

Mana. Relief flowed through me. I was going to be all right. "Mana, I—"

I made it only two steps before my legs collapsed, Mana's waiting arms the only reason I didn't hit the floor.

Naili

Morning Bulletin

To all criers for announcement throughout Bakii

In secret, a third merchant ambassador arrived overnight from Lummazza, but the Bastion refuses to confirm his whereabouts amid ongoing protests.

Seigneurs say two ceremonial Apaian bracelets have gone missing from the city estate of Lord Tineux. Reclamation movement suspected. Anyone with information is encouraged to come forward.

After Lummazzt raids on local scale mines, twenty-five more people have been confirmed missing. Jauhai Hatkol, Haassa Loul, Ait Umberkii, Malli Siimo, Een Horn . . .

189:71

Everything has a smell. When I say so, people always claim dozens of counter-examples—glass, air, scale, love, sadness— but they don't understand. To me *everything* has a smell. Even the colour green. Even love. Even sadness. Love smells like clean wool warmed against the body, sadness like waxy tea leaves left out in the sun.

The laundry at Master Occuello's owned the sort of odours everyone could smell, though we didn't always smell the same thing. This morning's batch smelled of dust and bitter herbs and damp goat. Yeloria laughed when I said so, the skin around her eyes crinkling as she stirred, thick wooden paddle in scalded red hands. "And how many damp goats have you stuck your nose on, Nai?" she said.

"None, that's just what it smells like." I had tried explaining, tried to get her, or Chaintho, or Miizhei—anyone—to understand me, only to earn pursed lips and sidelong looks straining with censure. Better to say nothing. To pretend. To smile and take the stirring paddle from Yeloria's shaking hands. "At least that's what I imagine goat smells like. Here, I'll take over. You get the lye."

Time only for a brief smile and she hurried away through the haze, her figure softening around the edges until she was as insubstantial as the other ghosts inhabiting the stifling space. Ghosts that chatted to one another, called for extra hands and shouted warnings as boiling water drained into the black floor grates, sending great billows of steam to swell clouds already obscuring the stone ceiling.

Hugging the lye pot close, Yeloria returned through the mist, sweat sticking strands of hair to her forehead like fine cracks on flushed stone. "I brought the whole pot because there's another load just come."

"Another?" I paused my stirring, only for the current I'd made to almost tear the paddle from my hands.

"Another. He's been busy."

He. The man upstairs. The soiler. We had many names for Master Occuello, the alchemist, as many names as speculations as to what he looked like and how he and his assistants managed to make so much laundry.

I regained momentum with the stirring paddle, pushing sodden cloth beneath the rippling grey water until it almost stirred itself. How much easier to have dropped Master Occuello into the boiler pot instead of his clothes. I'd often imagined tipping him into the scalding water to be poked and swirled and boiled, a pleasant daydream soured only by the knowledge that I was lucky to have work and a roof over my head. Lucky to scrub his stains and soak his clothes, to wring them and crush them and breathe in his chemical concoctions.

"Lucky," I whispered. It was true, and yet the word caught in my throat like it owned barbs.

Lucky.

"Oh, and here." Yeloria tucked a crumpled piece of paper beneath the strap of my shift, straightening and patting my collar as she drew her hand away. "Needs mount up as fast as this laundry!"

She glanced over my shoulder, and though her expression didn't change, I dared not reply in case the matron hovered close in the stifling mists. I couldn't even bring myself to nod, only to keep stirring while the paper scratched against my skin, echoing its existence with every movement. Yeloria would have her own list tucked into her clothing somewhere, because we truly were the lucky ones.

With the large lye jar resting on her hip like a baby, Yeloria tugged off the lid, freeing a puff of pale dust soon smothered by the humid air. "What do you think?" she said, peering into the roiling boiler. "Three scoops? Four?"

What I thought was that the way she held the jar pulled her

tunic tight across her hip, perfectly shaping the curve of her arse in a way that made heat gather between my legs. How many things I would rather be doing to her than recommending scoops of lye.

"Maybe—"

A gust of strong, pungent vanilla had me swallowing my words, my lustful thoughts, even my dreams—crushing them down into my chest where the matron could not hear them. The sharp snap of her shoes followed, a staccato beat in time to which my heart sped.

"Get that lye in, girl." The words were like the crack of old scaleglass and could cut as deep, leaving splinters beneath your skin. "And it needs more heat. No, not you, Billette." The rounded tip of her prodder jabbed me in the back as I turned. "You're on soaker tub two. The load needs moving."

Chaintho's usual tub. It must have been a big load if she needed help, but questions were not to be asked, ever. So without glancing at Yeloria, I dropped the paddle and sped away, hardly having to think about my direction so confidently did my feet guide me. Every worn stone was an old friend that kept me company through thin-soled shoes.

Soaker tub two sat near soaker tub six and boiler five in a decision seemingly designed for confusion, yet Chaintho had worked for Master Occuello long enough that it didn't explain her absence when I arrived. I spun in the mists, setting a hand on the lonely tub's pitted metal rim. From nearby, Miizhei's voice located her as one of the ghosts around boiler five. I hurried over, hoping the matron wasn't watching.

"Miiz," I said, approaching the strengthening smell of acacia shavings, vinegar, and sweet lavender coming from the boiler. "Miiz," I repeated, catching her attention as her edges solidified into life. "Do you know where Chaintho is?"

Sweat gleamed on Miizhei's face and she pursed her lips, a combination seemingly designed to send heat thrilling through me upon memories of joyful nights. Letting Heszia take her paddle, Miizhei wiped both palms down her grey apron and folded her arms—a woman with a story to tell. Her gaze flitted about until, confident that we were safe in our misty hideaway, she said, "Chaintho hasn't left her room this morning. She wasn't at breakfast, and it's not like she has any family here she could be visiting."

"Oh, do you think she's unwell?" I said, knowing the answer would have to be *yes* and *very* for her to be allowed to remain in her room.

Miizhei opted for an irritated shrug. "I can only assume so, and as sorry as I am for her, having to keep an eye on her soaker as well as do my own work has been steadily eating away at my empathy all day. Anyway"—her folded arms tightened—"why do you ask?"

"Matron sent me to change the load," I said hastily, gesturing in what I hoped was the general direction of soaker tub two.

Like a rooster settling ruffled feathers, she uncrossed her arms, and a delicious mixture of relief and satisfaction rushed through me at even so small a sign of jealousy. "Oh good." A lingering glance tore at my clothes and my flesh and my thoughts, before Miizhei turned back to her boiler. "I have enough to be getting on with. If she's run off like Rizzi, I hope they get a replacement faster; that was at least a week of extra work."

I had to agree as I returned to soaker tub two to find its contents could be called green only if one was feeling extremely optimistic. *Muddy* would have been more accurate, or *bog*. Or *smells like sour breath and old, crystallised urine.* The colour and smell could have come either from the clothes or the soaking chemicals, but curiosity wouldn't help me change the load. I reached for the scoop. This one possessed more holes than cane, and I plunged it into the tub knowing I wasn't walking away without hands that stank of bog and piss.

No sooner had I lifted a scoop of dripping clothing than half fell back in with a splash. Drops splattered my face, and I almost lost the rest. Forcing myself to just breathe and ignore the stench, I tipped the half scoop into a large basket beside the tub and went back for more. The big items came out easily enough, swampy water pouring off them like muddy waterfalls, but the small cloths and pouches kept slipping through, reluctant to leave. With each failed scoop, my skin prickled, sure the matron was watching. Swapping a load ought to be a quick job and time wasting attracted her ire, so after yet another failure I dropped the scoop and rolled up my sleeves. Despite the stink, sticking my hands in there wouldn't even make it onto my list of least favourite laundry tasks.

By the time I had finished fishing about in the bog water, the smell had crept its damp touch up my sleeves and spread across my stomach from bending over the tub's edge. The droplets on my face had dried, and it took all my self-control not to scratch them off with my far filthier hands.

"Billette!" The matron's sharp bark almost sent the last cloth tumbling back into its foul bath. "The second load ought to be in already. Hurry up, or it's half rations."

She snapped the threat like a whip, already turning in search of other disappointments. I forced my expression into neutral lines. "Matron?"

Once, she'd docked my food just for speaking, but she must have been in a good mood, for she just turned back, one eyebrow raised. "Speak."

I gestured at my sodden uniform. "Permission to change clothes, Matron. This soaking fluid could damage the other laundry."

The woman stared, her beady, hawkish eyes seeming to look right through me and know that, however true my words, I was itchy and wet and smelled like a sewer and really wished I didn't.

With a little snort, she nodded and jabbed her prodder at the next load. "Get that in first, then you may take your lunch-break early and change in the allotted time."

The already-too-short-to-eat-anything-in time, she meant, but I thanked her, subservient words tripping off my tongue with the ease of long practice.

The new load waited in yet another cane basket, still warm and dry, fresh from upstairs. Every apron and glove and shirt owned different stains; the reason the matron's sorters had lumped these ones together an eternal mystery. The man and his assistants seemed unable to keep anything clean.

I hauled the new load out of its basket in one rumpled, splattered ball and moved it over the tub. And there I held it a moment longer than necessary, two moments even, three. The dry fabric felt blissful against my damp skin, and occasionally I would catch a hint of the elusive scent that sometimes haunted freshly arrived laundry—a smell of star-filled nights, velvet, metallic powder, and broken promises.

At last, I let it drop into the soaking water. One stir to submerge it and my task was done, until the matron ordered me to change the load again with a jab of her prodding stick. I would not have used a prodding stick for anything so dull. Had I been able to jab people into doing my bidding, Miizhei would at last be on her knees between my legs. Floating on such a pleasant dream, I gave her boiler a wide berth as I wound my stinky way stinkily through the laundry to the door, desperate to escape and be stinky elsewhere.

The damp air followed me out into the network of underground passages that made up the servants' quarters. The upper-house servants got the nice rooms nearest the stairs, leaving the rest of us in the narrow, closet-like spaces abutting the drainage channels. The kitchens sat in the centre—the only place even hotter than the laundry, but at least its smells were nice. Today the air was heavy with the scent of overripe mango. That wasn't one of my fanciful scents, however, for trays of sesame slab, each topped with a dollop of mushy mango flesh, filled the servants' table in preparation for lunch. Two upper servants already sat nibbling at them, one having set aside something she was mending, while the other picked strings of mango from his teeth while reading the latest crier's sheet. Neither acknowledged my existence as I grabbed two slabs from the nearest tray and hurried away toward my room.

Situated almost as far from everywhere as was possible, my room was little more than an alcove, enough space beyond the door for a narrow bed, a shelf, and nothing more. Some of the girls kept trinkets on their shelves, or pots of dry herbs to keep the room smelling nice, but I had only my clothes. I'd brought my belongings with me when I'd taken the job, but after two years hadn't yet unpacked them. To unpack would be to admit I was staying, to admit this was my home and my whole future.

Changing from my damp, stinking clothes while shoving sesame slab into my mouth and trying not to slam my elbow against the wall was a greater challenge than I'd hoped. Especially since I had to keep the new uniform clean until the other was washed and dried, because only Miizhei possessed more than two laundry tunics—although the price to borrow one came in heat and flesh and I was always happy to pay. Thoughts of her thighs and the swell of her hips brought heat back to my body as I closed the door behind me, my dirty uniform carefully bundled in my arms. Every part of me yearned for the taste of cheap wine and the slit between Miizhei's legs, Chaintho's fingers dancing over us both.

I glanced along the passage toward Chaintho's door. Communal care wasn't the done thing here as it was in Apaian communes, but it would take only a moment to check on her, to see if she wanted some lunch brought. So decadent a thought as lunch in bed would make her smile too—worth the risk of extra time away from the laundry.

My knock sounded timid though it rattled the thin wood in its frame. "Chaintho?"

No answer. I leaned against the door. "Chaintho, it's Naili. Are you feeling all right? Do you want me to fetch you some lunch?"

Still no answer. Not even a mumble or a groan or a snuffle as she rolled over in her sleep. I set my ear to the door, hoping no one would come by. "Chaintho?"

Nothing. Likely she was sleeping, yet the deep silence gnawed at me. Something could be wrong. She could be really ill and in need of help.

Done thing or not, I pressed down the handle and let the door swing slowly in. As the gap widened, an iridescent glow seeped out, its green-and-gold fingers creeping over my feet and out into the passage. An oil lamp sat burning on a high shelf, but there was no sign of Chaintho. No sign of anyone. Where the bed had been now sat a mass of decomposing wood, moss-covered and crumbling amid a riotous explosion of dying life. Decaying leaves obscured half the floor, vines had grown up one wall to a small crack promising light, while other stems yellowed and drooped, and from everywhere came the wet glimmer of putrescence.

I pressed my sleeve to my nose against the acrid stench. No Chaintho, not even her belongings. Perhaps she had left like Rizzi, but how had so much growth and decay happened so quickly? And where was the bed? And the shelves? Only the lamp remained, burning bright beneath a broken handle.

I tried to blink the scene away like a wild daydream, but it wouldn't leave. One hesitant step over the threshold and my foot sank into the powdery mould colonising the floorboards. A chalky taste filled my mouth. "What is this?" I whispered, suppressing the urge to call out Chaintho's name again.

On one of the rotting shelves, something pale sat caught in the mildew, and without thinking, I grabbed the oil lamp. The broken scaleglass handle bit into my palm and I almost dropped it, possessing enough presence of mind to put it down where I needed it before gripping my bleeding hand. The cut stung, but I gritted my teeth and peered at the illuminated mossy pile. Light gleamed off a sand rose etched onto glass—one of Chaintho's most prized possessions, given to her by her mother. Not something she would leave behind.

I plucked it free of the clinging loam and brushed it off on the part of my apron not doing duty as a bandage. Unlike the rest of the room, the etched rose looked the same as I'd last seen it, its beauty forever preserved upon the smooth glass surface.

"Billette!"

The matron's voice echoed along the passage, sending my heart leaping into my throat. Hastily thrusting the art glass into my apron pocket, I backed from the room, pulling the door closed behind me.

"Billette!"

Her voice preceded her and I hurried toward it, telling myself I hadn't just seen Chaintho's room full of dying plants and mould despite the powdery must lingering on my tongue.

"Billette." The matron halted as I stepped into the main passage. "You're late. You made me leave the laundry."

"I'm sorry, Matron. I—I . . . I accidentally cut myself on some glass while changing and the blood doesn't seem to want to stop."

Her gaze slid down to the hand I had wrapped in my apron, deep red staining its grey fabric. The thick line of her brows creased. "You are wasting time. Get a bandage and be back in the laundry in two minutes or there will be no dinner tonight. As it is, you're now on half rations."

Breathlessly, I gushed out, "Yes, Matron. Thank you, Matron. I'll be as fast as I can." And before she could change her mind, before she could ask what I had been doing, before I could blurt out everything I'd seen, I stepped around her and hurried on along the passage, hardly seeing where I was going. A bandage meant the housekeeper's room, straight on and up the stairs—my feet seemed to know where they were going despite the thoughts swirling sickeningly around my head, each circling back to the same question. Where was Chaintho?

Escaping the underground passages was always a shock. One flight of stairs was all that separated the housekeeper's room from the servants' floor, yet the sudden drying of the air always made my skin tingle. At the top of the stairs, her door sat open, but I knocked anyway. No answer. Chaintho hadn't answered either, and too well could I imagine stepping into still more carious life. But the clean floor I could see from outside was no mirage. The housekeeper's room was as neat and lifeless as ever.

The supply cupboard took up most of the room—a once-grand piece of furniture now chipped and sun-bleached, but however tatty its appearance, it had always struck me as decadent for a housekeeper to have a wooden cabinet. Not just the soft morawood most common around Bakii, but hard lacewood, dark and patterned like they got in the Shield Mountains. That was a world away, just as Mana was a world away and had been for too long, off at the Shield serving his pretty lord because staying had always been harder. Easier to run and keep running as Mama had taught him.

The scent of old lives tumbled free as I opened the cabinet door, but the well-ordered contents were just household necessities. Neatly folded cloths in varying grades, netting patches, sewing needles, thread, paper, quills, boxes of scented linen balls, burning oils, candles, fermented honey paste for bad wounds, and any number of pads and bandages and rags, and of course the three rings full of keys I had always imagined could open every door in the whole city.

Carefully, I peeled my apron away from my palm and peered at the wound. Blood covered the skin, but where there ought to have been a ragged gash, there was nothing. Licking a fingertip, I wiped away some blood, hunting the cut it was surely hiding, yet my palm was entirely intact. But for the tinny taste of my own blood, I could have imagined the whole thing.

"What are you doing, Billette?"

I grabbed the closest bandage and started wrapping it around my hand before I turned, fingers shaking. "Just getting a bandage, Mistress Paiwe."

The housekeeper lifted an eyebrow, accentuating the single slit through it that marked her status. "You seemed to be taking some time about it."

There was nothing unkind in her expression, nothing frightening about her from the soft, almost diaphanous fall of her blouse to the sharp pleats of her divided skirt. She had the sort of gentle authority that made my knees weak and my body hot, yet today it was panic that sped my heart. "I...I...I was admiring—your..." The word was right there, yet instead of coming out, all I could do was flail in the general direction of the neatly stocked cupboard as my cheeks reddened. "It's so organised. And pretty."

Pretty. A stupid word, but I was stuck with it as her brows rose even higher into the soft foam of curls that clustered at her hairline. "You are not being paid to admire my cupboard, Naili."

"Yes, Mistress." I dropped my head, cheeks burning. I wanted to rip the bandage off to be sure—really sure—my wound was gone, to run down to Chaintho's door and be sure—really sure—her room was full of decaying plants, but I could do neither. "Sorry, Mistress."

Mistress Paiwe nodded, the sort of nod that considers the matter closed, before stepping aside that I might escape.

Back in the humid underground passages, I unwound the bandage, hoping to find a cut, no matter how small. There was nothing. To be sure, I rubbed my palm vigorously with the scrunched-up bandage, anticipating the sting of parting skin. Still nothing.

Letting go a shaky breath, I rewrapped my hand, determined to ignore the problem of the vanishing wound until it went away.

Busy hands stop your mind turning, Mama had always said whenever I found her sitting up late tinkering with a new poultice or tincture. Keeping my attention on the laundry worked all afternoon, but when the bell sounded at the end of the day, every worry flooded back. On any other day I might have sought some amusing distraction, but it was my delivery night, so there was time only to change my tunic and grab my half rations on the way to the door.

"You're always in such a hurry, Naili," Alii said, descending the stairs as I made my way out of the kitchen. "Where are you off to?"

My steps stuttered to a halt at the question I couldn't answer, glad it had been asked by only another laundress, not the matron. "Nowhere special," I lied. "I'm seeing a friend."

Alii was the newest laundress yet had the confidence of one who'd been around far longer. She was odd, full of questions and determined to make friends, yet never around when help was needed. I didn't trust her. Yeloria said I was just being Apaian about it, but while I didn't care for the characterisation, she wasn't wrong. I'd grown up in a commune where the elders had only bad things to say about city-dwellers and Emorans, a suspicion I'd carried with me ever since.

"You said that last week too," Alii said, eyes crinkling as though at a joke.

"Because I was also seeing a friend then."

"It's nice of Mistress Paiwe to give you a weekly pass out. Lucky for your friend too."

Lucky. The word seemed to haunt me everywhere I went, its taste as bitter as its smell.

In a hurry to keep moving, I agreed and sped away up the

stairs down which she'd just come. Not as far as the housekeeper's room this time, my destination was a small room right beside it, barely large enough for the desk and chair that filled the space wall-to-wall. Kit sat behind it, scowling as she rifled through a pile of papers—a scowl that eased at sight of me in a way I always enjoyed. "Ah, Nai, there you are. Your pass is...here somewhere? I had it just a moment ago." She shuffled papers, scowl returning. "Oh, here it is." With a flutter and snap of paper, she held it out to me, before pulling a small leather pouch from a drawer. My stomach sank. Its fraying seams and softened sides had been worn out over the last year by each of us delivering it in turn, but I'd forgotten it was my day for that as well.

"Oh, of course." I took the pouch, sharing Kit's grimace as I tucked it into my skirt pocket.

"Be careful," she said. "And I'm sorry, but I can't help out tonight. Mistress Paiwe has me here until all this is done even if it takes until dawn."

"I'm sure we'll manage. At least we'll get done what we can, and that's all we can ever do, right?" We shared another grimace and I turned to go, only to spin back before I'd reached the door. "Oh, before I go, I was wondering...have you heard anything about Chaintho?"

Kit's brows slid low, puckering her forehead. "No? Should I have? Is she all right?"

"I don't know, she wasn't in the laundry today and didn't answer when I knocked on her door."

"That's odd. I'll find out what I can, but you know how it is around here. If it's the workload you're worried about, the mistress did have me put in an order for two of those automated washing machines today. I hope that helps."

"Helps?" I let out a weak laugh but kept my unkind thoughts to myself. Even changing the load in soaker tub two with my bare hands was better than living on the street.

Back down the stairs, pass in hand, I stopped only long enough to pick up the small sack of deliveries someone had left outside the still-room door. A murmur inside meant some of the others were already working—or rather back working, exorcising our guilt at being so very lucky. I would join them when I returned, but first I walked on to the side door, delivery sack clutched in one hand, veil in the other.

From the lower passages, the side door led out to an alley separating Master Occuello's from the linen merchant's establishment next door—an alley all damp corners and the smell of pale melancholy. A man who looked like a clerk sat outside the opposite servant's door, blowing korsh smoke into the narrow space and reminding me of Mana for the second time that day. It had been a while since I'd had a letter—perhaps I ought to ask Miizhei to write a quick one for me, just to be sure he was all right.

Dearest brother, how very busy life must have gotten at the Shield these last months, for you have not written me, I composed in my head as I made for the end of the alley. *Perhaps it is because your beautiful lord has finally eaten you alive.*

If only I dared to be so blunt in writing, but I did not know who read his letters. Very Apaian of me, Yeloria would have said yet again, and again she would have been right.

The street on which Master Occuello's large manor stood was one of the two broad ways that coiled gently down into the city's depths. Walking uphill would have taken me to upper Bakii, to the fine houses of the Emoran nobility and those Celessi rich enough to join them on the rim, while downhill took me everywhere else.

Although the sun was still up, filling the air with heat, the part of the day where it directly struck the streets at this level had passed, leaving me to step into a shaded, stuffy street packed with as many flies as people. Without even a breath of wind, it was like walking through soup, and sweat stuck my tunic to my chest before Occuello's was even out of sight.

At this height, the people filling the streets were mostly well-off merchants and their families, servants and scribes, dressed in Emoran fashions and living the Emoran way. We were all Celessi, all inhabitants of the Celes Basin, but when the Emorans had taken over, they'd remade most of us in their image. Some people said that there were only two kinds of Celessi, Apaian Celessi and Emoran Celessi, that every inhabitant of the basin who wasn't Emoran must be Apaian, and the urge to punch those people was always strong. A long time ago it would have been true, but most people living in Bakii today were as far removed from their Apaian heritage as were the Emorans. They'd stopped seeing culture and belonging as a matter of practice, not bloodline, as though one could be Apaian merely by having an Apaian ancestor. In truth, the majority of the basin was inhabited by Celessi Celessi, people disconnected from both Emoran and Apaian culture and having no claim on either, though they would have spat in my face for saying so.

Slowly, the main street of Bakii spiralled down its gentle slope, fancy façade after fancy façade. As the only street wide enough for carts and double-width mule trains, it was also the most expensive street outside of upper Bakii, where every shopkeeper and artisan sought to have their premises. Yet walk too far down and the buildings on either side became run-down warehouses and dilapidated dwellings, their roofs weathered away, because depth was where the unlucky and unwanted in Bakii went to struggle. To fade. To die. And depth was my destination.

With the direct sunlight gone, lantern lighters were out with their kids, lighting those lampposts that hadn't yet been replaced with automated light orbs. The lantern lighter would stand at the base with his sack, while his kid climbed onto his shoulders and from there up the lamppost—post after post along the road, past the shadowy portals of closed shops and the bright welcome of open tavern doors. Food vendors sat on most corners, filling the night air with spice and the heady mix of sticky sweetbreads and fruit, but such plenty wouldn't last.

On and on down the slope, the air chilled and dampened and smells began clinging to me, some so foul they temporarily ousted the mould that lingered on my tongue. Refuse, stagnant water, wet fabric, and sodden dirt turned to a slurry in the nadirs of Bakii's twisted drains. Though many people still walked the streets, the deeper I went the more furtive the movements became. Quicker. With scurrying steps and glances back over shoulders, no one made eye contact or spoke lest they invite more trouble than they could handle. I put my hand in my pocket, checking I still had my pass—a piece of paper worth more than gold.

I needed it first on the next turn. There, a trio of city guard in their glass-scaled armour were stopping everyone they saw, demanding papers and arresting any who couldn't produce them. Ostensibly it was for our safety, to discourage gang activity and root out Lummazzt sympathisers, but all it did was punish people for being on the streets, whatever their reason. But arguing with them would only get me arrested too, so I pulled out my pass and waited for one of them to wave me on, trying not to look at the heavy truncheons most carried on their hip. Better than guns at least, which only Emoran-born guards were allowed to carry.

Another group of city guard accosted me near the entrance to the deep market. These weren't stopping everyone, but as an Apaian woman with markings tattooed beneath my eye, they always stopped me. "Got a pass there, witch?"

He said the word so easily, but it grated across my nerves, reminding me of the venomous spits of hate as people passed my mother's house, hissing when they caught sight of me sitting on the windowsill amid the jasmine vines. The memories lived in my flesh, visceral, raw, endless, and mine alone. I clamped my lips shut and pulled out my now-crumpled pass.

The guard hardly glanced at it before waving it away. "You going any deeper?"

"No, just to the market."

He grunted, losing interest in me as a shabbily dressed young man came around the corner. "Good," he said, tapping his companion's shoulder and nodding in the direction of a more likely candidate. "Fighting down there. Another Lummazzt gang stormed in snatching people. I'd keep away if I were you."

And leaving those words to shiver through me, he moved on. Lummazzt gangs. Half of the Celes Basin shared a border with Lummazza, and relations had never been good, but in the last year they'd taken a sharp turn for the far worse. Whatever that might mean for the rich people with power to make change, for the poor of the Bakii depths it meant avoiding getting snatched and sold as slaves.

Grateful I had reached my destination, I hurried away from the knot of guards blocking the road and toward the large arch of the deep market. As the name suggested, it was a market deep within the city, a large cavern formed from blasting errors long ago that had been further dug out and hollowed by centuries of use. Lacking all natural light, it was full of smoky old lanterns and crammed-together buildings and stalls, selling everything from food and scavenged goods to clothes thrown away by wealthier citizens. With too low a roof and a stone floor made slippery with damp and refuse, it wasn't my favourite place, but the deep market was where we made our deliveries—a safe place compared to the rest of the depths. I'd heard there was a deeper market, so named with the humour the forgotten wrapped about themselves like a protective shroud, but I'd never dared look. The depths of Bakii were a warren of old tunnels and drains and blasting hollows that weren't safe for anyone.

Opening the sack, I checked the small list—all numbers and symbols that would have made no sense to anyone else. Since most of us couldn't read, Kit and Miizhei had devised a system of markings to signify our regular customers and organised a central drop-off for all new requests—a network of care that meant I had to make only five stops.

Hating the closeness and the smoky lantern light, I pushed my way through the thick crowds, eager to get this job done as quickly as I could. With the list as my guide, I made my way from the trinket stall of old Ardii—signified by a pair of glasses—to Lady Portia's street eats—a semi-circle of lines like the rays of a rising sun—and on to the run-down home of Cutter—a simple slash—leaving little jars and paper pouches and receiving what coin could be spared in return. Shame turned each face away as they apologised for being unable to give more, and I wished I had words that could make them see it was the rich folk who ought to have been ashamed.

Close to being able to escape, I took out the worn little pouch Kit had handed over, and made my way to the emptiest part of the market, where people dared not mill or linger, where people came and went with quick steps and made no eye contact, where a blank red banner hung over a run-down porch. The place belonged to the Hoods, Bakii's oldest and most powerful gang, and my heart hammered as I approached and hammered even harder when I was let inside. There a single room, a single table with a single seated man, a man who watched my every step from the door to the table, where I set down the worn pouch. No words were ever exchanged; he just took the pouch and weighed it thoughtfully in his hand, before tucking it safely away. An empty pouch, equally worn, was handed back, along with a small red ribbon, and there was nothing to do but back gratefully out. The whole took no more than a minute, yet back in the market my heart beat so fast it had surely taken years off my life.

Deliveries done and ribbon in hand, I hurried back up the winding road from the Bakii of the unlucky to the Bakii of the lucky, from the deep markets to Master Occuello's side door, where I hooked the ribbon onto the window bars, replacing last week's faded green strip. Paid up to the Hoods meant safety for our little operation, at least for now, and I stepped back inside the alchemist's manor with a sense of relief I had always hated. But this was, for now, home, and it was safe, and for that I had to be grateful.

The alchemist being what he was, he had little need for the manor's tiny downstairs still-room, so Mistress Paiwe had given permission for us to keep a few plants. A few plants had soon become a lot of plants and a workbench covered in old pots and boards and pestles from the kitchen, along with all the little bottles and stoppers we could salvage. Most were full of ingredients and stood like a messy army clustered in the dark corners. The plants would have done better outside, but the condition on which Mistress Paiwe allowed us to use the room was that no one could know. And that whenever her mother's joints were troubling her, we'd make up a draught.

"All right, Naili?" Yeloria said as I entered, setting the empty delivery sack down by the door.

"Fine," I said. "It's bad out there but no worse than usual."

Yeloria nodded. "Good. Um...if you could help me with one of my tonics I would appreciate it—not now, I'll get through the ones I know first."

"Which one don't you know?" Usually Kit, who took the requests and divided them onto lists, gave us only what she knew we could manage.

Two steps back to her station, and Yeloria returned with her crumpled list. "This one." Her stained fingernail tapped the symbol at the bottom, a coil cut through with two diagonal lines.

"Oh, a full-strength emetic." I grimaced. "I can make that one if you like."

"No, you'd better teach me. It doesn't look like the number of requests is going to decline anytime soon. But I'll finish the one I'm working on first."

While she went back to her bench, I looked at my own crumpled list. I was already behind and needed to get started. First was a cross-hatch beside two round circles—a palliative for an elderly man. That meant fermented honey, olei oil, starlace salts, and some fresh feverfew. And a clean mortar. While the others chatted, I thrust my hand into the feverfew's tangled leaves to pinch off a central stem, before collecting the necessary vials and bottles from the corner.

Back at the bench, I measured the honey and oil into a mixing flask and set to cutting the feverfew.

"Is Yenni not in tonight?" Ambere asked once I sat working with them at the narrow bench.

"No, she has permission to visit her father," Miizhei said, ever the most knowledgeable about such things. "And Kit is working late."

"What is this if not working late?" Yeloria grumbled. "These lists get longer every week, and I still have Chaintho's to do."

I kept cutting the feverfew, slicing the stem and leaf into smaller and smaller pieces until they became more paste than plant. None of the other laundresses had to be here. I had started out using the space to make tonics and poultices for what remained of my mother's old customers, accepting whatever coins or ingredients they could spare in return. One by one the others had found out and started to help. Bit by bit I'd taught them what I knew, and day by day word spread, bringing more and more requests for help from a dying city.

"No one has heard anything?" Yeloria went on, the words quieter and more fearful. "About Chaintho?"

Solemn head-shaking answered, and I fought the urge to spill my fears. We weren't so much friends as a collection of women in the same circumstances, brought together by a desire to help those less fortunate, to exorcise the guilt that plagued us daily. It was a coalition too fragile for troubles. I needed them too much to risk honesty.

"Hopefully she'll be back tomorrow," Heszia said, ever the optimist. "And if she has left, hopefully they hire another girl, since no automated washer can help with this."

Not wanting to think about Kit's washer order, I measured the finely sliced mush of feverfew only to find it wasn't quite enough. Hoping not to draw attention, not to have my opinion sought, I slipped off my stool and back to the plant. It had been a sad and wilty thing, desperate for the sunlight higher up but too weak to reach for it, but when I returned it was to a feverfew that looked lush and green and strong.

I closed my eyes. Opened them. Behind me conversation went on amid chops and scrapes and the tinkle of glass vials, but the plant hadn't changed. One healthy specimen amid a collection made much sadder by comparison.

The feverfew's glossy leaves danced as I ran my hand across them, the whole plant seeming to thrum with life. Beside it, a struggling starlace was all wilted leaves and whippy stalks. I reached out to one broad-lobed leaf, too soft to keep itself fully upright, and like a cat wondering if moving closer would garner more pats, it perked up at my touch. A ridiculous thought, so I touched it again, this time holding the pad of my forefinger to a different leaf—a leaf that lifted, strengthening as though taking in water and turning toward sunlight.

I pulled away like I'd been bitten. An argument had broken out behind me, but I could only stare at the pair of lush, healthy plants and cradle my hand close, every breath coming quick. The room spun. I'd touched these plants hundreds of times and nothing had ever changed, yet no matter how I turned my head, hoping it was a trick of the light, both plants remained innocently green and flourishing.

Numb, I pulled myself up and almost tripped over, all but falling onto Miizhei as I sought my stool. "Hey! Whoa, Naili, are you all right?"

"Yes," I said, though my mind screamed *no*. "I...I think I just need some air. I'm fine, just..." I pulled away, turning toward the door. "I'll step outside a moment. You...you carry on. I'm fine, really."

Leaving murmuring in my wake, I pushed through the stillroom door and out into the passage, where a dim lamp shone through the street door's grating like a beacon. A moment in the cool night air was all I needed. Cool, clean air free from the fumes and steam and powdery mildew that had tainted my mind, filling it with hallucinations.

For the second time that evening, I stepped into the alley. Cold air whipped against my skin now the sun had set and I looked up at the faint stars, drawing a deep breath and letting it go in a rush. The ever-present sounds of Bakii wrapped around me with the comfort of a heavy blanket, all voices and music and buzzing insects. Even the angry shouts of men arguing over a game of Welcome were soothing to the soul and slowly my panic began to ease.

A small limachai seedling sat on the stoop, and determined to prove myself wrong, I picked it up and gripped its stem between thumb and forefinger. Like the feverfew, it pulsed with life—a hum like that of a busy hive in high summer. Swelling, the stem thickened. The stalks lengthened. Leaves unfurled. New stems poked through the dirt, followed by the beginnings of a flower bud. It began slowly, one stem, one leaf, one flower, before stalks surged toward the overhanging roof, fattening and glistening with moisture. Flowers opened in puffs of pollen, and roots broke through the sides of the pot, spilling loam onto the alley stones. Loam that gleamed with damp, sticky putrescence.

"No!"

I dropped the pot as darkness crawled in around the edges of my vision. It smashed on the stones, sending clay shards scattering amid clods of dirt and desperately reaching roots. Stalks sagged and spent flowers dropped, covering the alley in thin red petals like bloody splinters.

"No," I whispered, backing away from the dying plant as fingers of mould crept across the stones. "No." I fought the urge to run and kicked the remains of the plant along the alley, crushing the powdery mould beneath my shoes. No wonder Chaintho had left if she had watched her room turn to dross before her eyes, but I had nowhere to go. Here, I was one of the lucky ones.

And in the back of my mind, a fearful question bloomed. What if Chaintho hadn't left at all?

4

Tesha

Morning Bulletin

To all criers for announcement throughout Learshapa

Calls to freeze the council's executive decision until a vote can be held have been rejected. Unification in the city's best interests, says Lord Councillor Angue.

Ongoing skirmishes with Lummazzt soldiers cause closure of five local scale mines. Reacher Sormei promises advanced forces to deal with the situation as first wounded arrive in Learshapa.

New trade laws put power back in the hands of local merchants by requiring all traders from Lummazza to deal through a central city broker.

343:182

Supplementary Announcement! Explosions from Therinfrou Mine shake Learshapa. Citizens advised not to panic.

Uvao whacked my knee with a thin cane he seemed to have brought with him for no other purpose. "Still bending it," he said. "You look sloppy."

"Knees are supposed to bend!"

"Not while being presented to new people. Do it again."

I let go a long sigh, holding in my frustrations as best I could. We'd been practising this movement and nothing else all day, and my temper was fraying. Uvao, on the other hand, looked as emotional as a rock. I'd been treated to so many of his frowns over the last few days that I'd almost forgotten what he looked like when he smiled, when he laughed, when he brushed hair from my brow and bent his lips to mine.

"Allow me to introduce you to your very dull new husband-to-be," he said, gesturing at empty space with an expression bored enough it could have fallen asleep. "Lady Teshalii, this is Lord Kiren Sydelle."

"A pleasure to meet you, my lord," I said, sliding my foot forward and taking care not to bend my knee as I bobbed in respect. "I—"

The cane whipped my leg. "Sloppy."

"I didn't bend it!"

"Not forward, no, but you twisted."

"How can you even tell? I'm wearing full skirts!"

Uvao rolled his eyes, his disdain palpable. "I can tell because of how it affects the rest of your posture. Straight at the knees keeps everything in line. Try again."

I gestured at the thin cane held loosely in his hand. "Is that necessary? Traditional perhaps, so you can whip your children into perfect little statues."

"Naturally. In fact, my father used an actual whip. He sat in a chair in front of me and shouted orders, lashing out whenever I made a wrong move, like I was a mule."

I narrowed my eyes, but Uvao had practised his blank stare

until he could out-blank an empty canvas. The only way to rattle him was to prod soft spots. "Maybe he only did that because you were the younger son."

His brows creased, a flicker of annoyance there and gone as he folded his arms. "At least your sharp tongue will be right at home in Emora. There may not have been a whip, but my father is a stickler for perfection, so if you're going to pass as a Romm with his blessing you'll have to do a lot better than this. He won't risk going ahead with this plan if you'll give yourself away within two minutes of meeting the Sydelles. Do it again."

It was the most he'd said to me all day, possibly the most he'd said since the day I'd told him we couldn't keep seeing each other, that I could not reconcile it with my conscience to love an Emoran nobleman. Especially not one who had lied for so long about his true identity.

"Allow me to introduce how much I'm getting bored of this," he said, waving the cane vaguely as though at some invisible audience. "Lady Teshalii, this is the Emoran nobleman you're marrying."

I slid my foot forward only to catch a breath on his bitter words and glance up, earning myself another smack with the cane. "Keep your head down until you straighten. If you can't master even that simple step, we'd be better off finding someone else now while we still can."

"You know very well that you goaded me. You aren't making this any easier, Uvao."

"Making this easier for you isn't my job. You think I'm enjoying this? You think I woke up and thought, *Yes, I want to spend my day teaching the woman I loved how to properly genuflect before the lord she's marrying after saying she couldn't keep seeing me because I was a lord*?"

"Uvao—"

"Don't! There is nothing to say. Do it again, on your own this time."

Hands shaking, I stood unsure beneath his fiery glare. Part of me wanted to speak, to reach out, to try to mend what I had broken, but the rest of me just wanted to run. Stubbornness was all that kept me standing in that hall, all that made me once again slide my foot forward, knee perfectly straight as I bobbed my little curtsy of respect. "A pleasure to meet you, my lord," I said, keeping the words slow and fully rounded like someone who has all the time in the world. Every moment I expected him to hit me with the cane again, but this time I managed to rise and lift my head without earning such ire.

"Better," he said. "But it looks stiff and self-conscious. You need to practise until it comes naturally. From now on, whenever you enter a room or talk to anyone, practise. Make it part of your day."

I slid my foot toward him, dropping into the same curtsy. "As you wish, my lord."

Uvao barked a sharp laugh, but when I rose I found no humour in his face. "The Tesha I knew would rather have hit me than say anything so demeaning, but then I'm just the younger son of a Learshapan noble, not the brother of the man who would be king."

"You think I'm doing this because I want an exalted position?"

"I don't care why you're doing this."

"Clearly you do! I want to fight for Learshapa, just like you, so blame the council, or Reacher Sormei, if you have to blame someone."

He shrugged, idly whipping the cane to and fro. "Should I blame him for your decision to hate me for my ancestry too?"

"Uv, I have never hated you." I stepped closer, a wary, tentative step. "I loved you, but—"

"But not enough." He stepped back. "I hope you know Learshapa will never love you back."

Turning sharply, he strode toward the door, the hem of his

skirts dancing about his shins and his bare feet silent on the tiled floor.

"Where are you going?"

"Away from here," he called back without turning.

"And what am I supposed to do?"

"Whatever you want, Tesha. Whatever you want."

Without slowing, he pushed through the heavy curtains covering the arch and was gone, leaving me alone in the empty hall, only my thoughts for company. And the chirp of sunbirds fluttering about in their finely wrought cage. The Romm family seemed to have them everywhere in their palatial manor, filling the house with birdsong that in Uvao's sudden absence took on a sorrowful edge.

Alone, I felt tiny in the large room—a lost sand mouse in a grand song hall. It wasn't as large as an Emoran song hall, but it was big enough to house half a dozen people in comfort yet seemed to own no purpose. Just a hall, Uvao had said, hardly seeming to notice the beautiful mosaic roof or the delicately carved archways leading out to one of many atriums flowing with water. Just a hall. How much more it could have been in the hands of those who needed it.

As I made my way toward the nearby atrium for some air, a deep rumble shook the floor. "More?" I said, as though Uvao had still been present, and gripped the arch pillar. A second explosion. A third. I stood rooted in place, waiting, counting, while above the manor roof, distant smoke billowed into the sky. By the time the ground settled, I'd counted five explosions, all from the direction of Therinfrou Mine.

The first explosions had begun that morning, and I'd been grateful that Lord Romm paid to have crier sheets delivered hot off the press. Lummazza was attacking our mines, though whether they just wanted more scale for themselves or it was a prelude to invasion was impossible to know. All I could do was worry.

With no one to talk to and nothing to do, I walked on into the atrium. By the height of the sun, it was just past noon, but thanks to the trees, the water, and the windcatchers that dotted the manor's roofline, the air was pleasantly cool. Benches sat in shady spots beneath the trees, and a pair of wooden tables stood waiting to be used, but there was no sign of life beyond the little silver fish darting through the water. I couldn't but think how different it was to what faced the miners at Therinfrou, a thought that made my heart ache and my feet need to keep moving. Other archways led to other places, and I walked on, wondering how long it would be until I discovered another human.

Walking in a straight line, I found a second empty hall, a small sitting room of sorts, a library, and a dining room before a distant voice at last promised life. Following it, I found a second, larger atrium standing at what could have been the centre of the manor, a colonnade circling its edge. Two men were crossing it, their profiles just discernible from the shaded arch around which I peered. Both owned the haughty features common to all Emorans, but one was much older than the other and walked half a step behind.

"—better to have them tended where they can be seen," he was saying. "It may help with those still recalcitrant about Learshapa's unification."

"It is already being done," the younger man replied, his voice deep and slow and sure. "You know me; I never leave anything to chance. It was not about the injured mine workers that I came. My spies tell me Lummazza is planning a larger attack, and I want to ensure the city is prepared."

Worry knotted my gut at these words, and I had to fight the urge to follow them and hear more. The older man was surely Lord Romm, to whom I hadn't yet been introduced. Uvao had been keeping me away, and here I was risking being seen, not only by him but by the other stranger too, before I was ready.

"Naturally," Lord Romm said, voice fading as they reached

the other side of the atrium. "We can talk more openly in my office. If you could leave your guards outside, however, I would appreciate retaining my privacy."

No sooner had he mentioned guards than two more men walked into sight, following in their wake. Both wore scaleglass armour on which hundreds of thin scales layered to form a protective coat that shimmered in the sunlight. They tinkled faintly as they moved, a cheerful sound belied by the heavy pistol each carried on their hip.

"Of course," spoke the unnamed stranger as both lords disappeared through a far arch. "So long as you don't intend to murder me, they can wait outside."

Soon the guards disappeared too, leaving me to prise my fingers from the column around which I'd spied, only to jump as a nearby door opened and closed, spilling a scurrying servant into the passage. She checked at sight of me, but hurried on, face a mask. "Excuse me," I said, desperate for an answer. "Who was that with Lord Romm just now?"

The servant barely stopped, bobbing a curtsy to me mid-step. "Lord Reacher Sormei Sydelle, my lady," she said, voice breathless. "Now if you'll excuse me."

"Reacher Sormei," I repeated, thankful the woman had left me to my shock. He'd always just been a distant figure in my life, a name to hate, not one that belonged to a person who walked and talked and breathed. Foolish to be shocked by his corporality, and yet my gaze traced the path he'd walked and found only doubt. Surely he hadn't been old enough, hadn't looked cruel enough. Surely he ought not to have been here at all.

Slowly, I made my way back to the safety of my empty hall with its chirpy sunbirds, worrying all the way over what they had said of attacks. I'd heard so little, yet couldn't but think of the man with his flyers, shouting at me in the workshop about the danger of war. Perhaps he had been right after all.

I returned to the hall to find Lord Revennai waiting, his brow dark. "There you are."

"Yes, here I am. But why are you here?"

"That's no way to speak to a lord in public, *Lady* Teshalii. Try again."

"*Try again.* You sound like Uvao." Halting before him, I slid into the curtsy I'd been practising. "What brings you here this fine afternoon, my lord?"

"Better." Lord Revennai flashed a smile. "And I came to play Lord Kiren in your practice at Uvao's request, but it seems he isn't here."

"He walked out."

His brows flew up, their slits seeming to imitate the rays of a rising sun. "Walked out? But he lives here. What did you do to make him walk out?"

"I reminded him that he is a younger son, defended my choice to stop seeing him, and told him I'd loved him."

To rise farther, Revennai's brows would have had to leave his face. "Loved him? I—oh *no*, don't tell me you're the young woman he was seeing at that meeting house who broke his heart when she found out he was Emoran."

Hearing my actions repeated so bluntly made me sound monstrous, but I would not defend myself for something he would never understand. Instead, I worked my face into a vapid smile and slid once again into a curtsy. "At your service, my lord."

Lord Revennai laughed, somehow also managing to grimace. "My, my, how tangled are the webs we weave. Perhaps I ought to have thought of that possibility when you came to the meeting, but I was rather preoccupied." He ran a hand over his face and looked toward the empty archway. "Well, I guess I had better take over teaching you myself for now. With the city still in uproar and the Lummazzt attacks increasing, there's talk of making sure the treaty is sealed with a marriage as soon as possible."

"Is there any more news? From the mines?"

His brows rose again in mild surprise. "Beyond the fact that those bastards are setting explosives and killing our people? Did you feel the rumbles? The ground was shaking as I arrived."

"I did." My fingers interlaced themselves anxiously. "Do you think it's because of the treaty?"

"What? You think having an Emoran reacher ruling Learshapa has made them hate this city more? When we were already ruled by a council of Emoran lords?"

"Oh, when you put it like that, I guess it makes no sense. I just thought..." I trailed off. What had I thought? That Lummazzt aggression could be entirely blamed on the Emorans alone?

Lord Revennai huffed a bitter little laugh. "You thought it was just us they were after. That might have been true three hundred years ago when we were first forced into these lands, but *Emoran* isn't exactly a fixed category. Half my ancestors were Apaian. No, the Lummazzt are just vicious, pale little bastards who take what they want, and what they want is scale. There's not a lot of it outside the basin, so"—he shrugged, seeming to gesture at everything and yet nothing—"they need the basin."

"Why not just buy it? The scale, I mean. I know they don't like to leave their lands because of their god, but surely they have traders at the border outposts."

"They do buy it. That's what's kept peace for this long. Scale mines just aren't bottomless." Lord Revennai sighed and ran a hand along his smooth hair and down his ponytail. "Anyone who has been paying attention knows this has been coming for a long time; it's just fallen to us to live through it. I am usually the first to speak ill of Sormei, but perhaps this unification came just in time after all. He's responded much quicker to the attacks than the council ever could have. Not to mention that with the treaty as yet incomplete he could, very rightly, claim it isn't his responsibility to deal with, but he hasn't. Still—" He gave himself a shake. "We need a Learshapan reacher to protect this city now he has laid the groundwork, so we'd better get on with your lessons. Let me just channel my best Lord Kiren Sydelle face and we can start."

He had given me so much to think about that I'd almost forgotten I'd seen Lord Kiren's brother mere minutes earlier—a disclosure I kept to myself lest it get me in trouble for wandering. Yet having caught a glimpse of one brother had piqued my curiosity in the other, so tucking the Lummazzt attacks away for later contemplation, I said, "First, tell me what he's like."

"Who? Lord Kiren?"

"Yes, obviously. You lords all know each other, don't you? Spending the season in Emora, regattas at Remorna and all that."

"To an extent that's true, yes. And, well, Lord Kiren is..." He began only for his voice to suspend upon thought, his gaze slipping far away. Into some old memory perhaps, somewhere that made his slit brows drop into that tigerish look he had. "He's a handsome, well-liked, and thoroughly charming man," came the eventual answer, his drawl seeming to mock. "I'm sure even you couldn't dislike him. He's a Sydelle, but he lacks Sormei's... ambition. Second sons, you know."

I didn't, but I found my gaze caught to the slight upturn at the corner of Revennai's lips, wondering what it meant.

"You're staring at me," he said, tigerish look giving way to boyish grin. "Unfortunately, I'm not the man you have the opportunity to marry."

"Seems like that would be quite the step down."

To my surprise, Lord Revennai laughed. "Ah, see, we'll make an Emoran of you yet. Now, to work. I meant to ask whether Uvao has told you about his—*your* family yet? It's important you memorise as much as possible."

"Not yet, no. But his father—Lord Romm, I mean, sounds tyrannical."

"You could call him that, but probably best not to when living in his house. *Ambitious* is a better term, although he did send Lord Ashadi to the Shield, so make of that what you will."

I froze, mind darting back to the older man I'd seen crossing the central atrium. "I'm sorry, are you saying Uvao's older brother is a dragon rider?"

"Yes. If Uvao hasn't told you even that then we're in trouble. We'd better talk history while we practise your movements. Where's your book?"

"Oh." I touched my head as though expecting it to be there. "I must have left it in my room this morning. We could use something else. A cushion perhaps." I pointed to a stack near the sunbirds' cage. "It might stay on better and hurt less."

"That's cheating."

I folded my arms. "It only counts as proper learning if it's uncomfortable?"

"You have a very determined way of twisting my words to fit your opinion of me." He sighed. "Cheating because cushions flop. You could stoop and still keep one on your head. Now, where were you up to?"

"Genuflection," I said. "Uvao would introduce me poorly, I would curtsy, and he would hit me with his cane."

"Unfortunately, I don't have one of those."

"Unfortunately?"

He shrugged. "It sounds fun, but as we have to do without it, let's start at the start. Where will you be standing when they are announced?"

"Beside Uvao, and a step behind Lord Romm because of the difference in our ranks. Which, I would just like to say, is a ridiculous system. What if I wanted to talk to someone lower ranked than I? I would have to turn around but—"

"But you're not allowed to. As always, you've put your keen observation to our social practices and found them wanting. It is, however, handy sometimes to be able to walk into a room and have a visual representation of rank from which to deduce power dynamics."

I tilted my head. "You always have a reply."

"And you always have a complaint. Now, one of the servants will announce them as Lord Reacher Sormei Sydelle, possibly with some additional styles if he chooses to show off, and Lord Kiren Sydelle of Anamoraii."

"Anamoraii?"

"The name of their estate south of Emora. Remember that. And the Romm estate is called Hylanii, southeast of Learshapa. The Romm estate is heavily food production because most of their wealth comes from ore mining and the panawood native to that part of the basin."

"Wood, ore, food. Hylanii."

"Indeed. Now, they've walked in and been announced; what happens next?"

I closed my eyes a moment, running back through all that Uvao had taught me in the last few days. "They have to greet Lord Romm first, then Uvao, because you worship the idea of familial bloodlines and—"

"Tesha." He scowled, the tiger back. "Is it possible for you to go without criticising Emoran culture for even just a few minutes?"

"I'm not sure, is it possible for Emorans to stop crushing and destroying Apaian culture for even just a few minutes?"

Lord Revennai dropped his head into his hands, shaking it slowly. "Now I see why Uvao left." When he looked up, I was surprised to find his scowl had become a wry smile. "You are a handful and a half, Tesha Romm, and will tear your new husband to pieces."

"What's he like? Really."

"You've already asked that and I've already answered."

"Yes, but...well, Uvao said he was dull, and you said he was gentle and charming or whatever you said. I want a real answer. Is he clever? Does he have a mind of his own or does he do what his brother says?"

Like a puppet whose strings had been cut, Lord Revennai collapsed onto the floor with a dramatic sigh and lay staring up at the ceiling. "We're never going to get through this," he said, pressing the heels of his palms to his eyes. "We can't even get through one rehearsal of one meeting without having to stop a dozen times."

I plonked down next to him, nothing ladylike in the way I sprawled full length on the glass tiles. "How about you answer my questions, then I promise we can get through a full rehearsal without interruption."

"I'm not sure you're capable of it," he said, hands still over his face. "Is it some disease perhaps, some degenerative loquaciousness that worsens by the hour?"

"You know it's not." I punched his arm. "Stop being so dramatic and answer my questions so we can move on to all that genuflecting."

"Please don't call it that."

"But that's what it is!"

"Yes, but...just say *curtsying*. Please."

"Why?"

He dropped his arms to the floor at his side and turned a beseeching look my way. "Because I'm telling you that's the way we talk, and before you ask why...it just *is*. Sometimes the answer is...just because I said so."

"Oh, and I have to do what you say?"

"Yes, you have to do what I say! And what Uvao says. That's how we're going to get through this, at least how I thought we were going to get through this. Now I think perhaps we've more chance of surviving a jump off the service walkway above the eastern fall."

I sat a hand on his shoulder rather than punching it. "You are a very dramatic and overwrought young man who shouldn't be jumping anywhere, because it will make a mess of your fine skirts."

"A very dramatic and overwrought young man? I'll have you know I have at least five years on you, likely more, and—" He stopped and scowled. "You're laughing at me."

"Am I?"

"Yes. You are as troublesome and mischievous as a stray cat, and you have the same look, like you've just pushed a valuable vase off the table and yet swear it had nothing at all to do with you."

"One of your cats broke a vase?"

"Several vases. I shall have to rename her Tesha in your honour. Now, please, can we get back to work?"

I shook my head. "Not until you answer my questions about Lord Kiren."

"I don't even remember what you asked."

"I asked if he was boring, or clever or . . . the sort of man who just does what his brother tells him to do."

Seeming to mull over the questions, Lord Revennai folded his arms behind his head and sighed, scanning the ceiling for answers. "He's . . . he doesn't just do whatever Sormei says, but he's also not deliberately obstructive like you. He's the kind of man who thinks about things before deciding, who listens more than he talks, watches, remembers." He gave one of his bitter little laughs. "Trust me, he remembers everything. As to whether he's dull or not, well, that depends on what you like in a person. A lot of people think he's dull because he doesn't draw attention, or talk continuously. Boring in company, perhaps, otherwise not."

"And clever?"

Lord Revennai screwed up his face. "He's not *not* clever, but I wouldn't say he's sharp like Sormei is. Observant and intellectual rather than manipulative and political. I don't know, it's hard to describe people."

"Do you like him?"

His lip twitched, and still staring up at the ceiling, he said, "Everyone likes him."

"Not an answer."

Revennai turned his head, messing up his ponytail on the tiles. "What do you want me to say?"

"The truth."

He looked at me and I looked back, seeking unspoken words in his face. As mercurial and expressive as it usually was, it was intent seriousness that stared back. The sort of expression that made one want to look away, to back down, to apologise for having asked. But I wasn't going to do any of those things.

"The truth is a place not worth exploring," he said at last, looking away. "What I think doesn't matter. What you think of him doesn't even matter, really, since that's not why you're marrying him."

Sitting up on the words, Revennai tightened his ponytail, ran a hand self-consciously across his head to be sure every hair was smoothed into place, and got to his feet. "Now, I've answered your questions. Let's move on."

"To genuflecting."

"To—" He folded his arms. "*Cat.* Come on, get up. You can't genuflect while lying on the floor."

Unsatisfied but knowing that to push further would risk his ire, I held up my hands. "You have to help me up; I'm a poor, gentle lady who cannot do anything for herself."

"You are a cat," he repeated, but took my hands, his warm, tight grip owning more strength than I had expected as he hauled me up with ease. "Now, can we finally start?"

"Yes," I said. "Yes, now we can start."

We practised for the rest of the day. He tested me over and over until I could name everyone in the Romm family and every detail of their estate, and made me curtsy until I could do so with such ease that even Uvao might have been satisfied. He didn't return, and after a dinner spent having my manners shredded and corrected until I was hardly hungry anymore, I gratefully retired to the silence of my room. Uvao had said they were hiring a personal maid for me, but as this woman had not yet arrived, one of the housemaids made sure I was comfortable and ready for bed. She helped with so many things I had been used to doing for myself, and it was all I could do to let her, thank her, and try not to feel ashamed of such demeaning reliance.

Once she had gone, I ought to have slept, but I'd been struggling to do more than fitfully doze in the all-too-comfortable bed since I'd arrived. Everything in the house held a hint of panawood, like Uvao, and everything felt and sounded wrong. Even the air was different in this part of the city, and the sounds of life far more distant. It would be different again in Emora. Life there would be nothing like I could even imagine—certainly nothing like my life in Learshapa with Master Hoye, learning glass.

There'd been no time to do more than leave him a message and hope he understood, but the need to see him face-to-face, to say a proper goodbye, had been eating away at me. Along with the question I needed to ask.

Tonight was as good a time as any.

Moving quickly, I dug a heavy wrap out of one of the clothing chests and shrugged it on. It didn't cover every part of my skin or even all of my bed skirt, but it would do. I wasn't going far, just out into the streets to see my past one last time. Out through the servant's door and into the night, committing the way to memory that I might easily return. From the brightly lit streets of the upper city down into Learshapa proper was a steep walk few Emorans made, but with every stairway and ramp, the streets grew more alive. Though I'd seen it hundreds of times, I halted at the top of the third-tier stairs and took in the view. It never got old, standing on one side of the deep well that was Learshapa proper and looking across the wide gulf to its opposite rim, while in between the rest of the city sloped away, all flickering lights and shifting shadows. In the daytime one could see every narrow alley and reaching tenement, every sharp stair and slowly curving ramp, and every gleaming channel funnelling water into the city centre like veins. Only if one looked up could one see the Emoran rim, all manor houses and private gardens and endless webs of light where none but the wealthiest of non-Emorans dared tread.

Master Hoye's forge sat on the fourth tier, but to reach it meant going through Orial Square—one of the few open plazas in the city proper and tonight home to dozens and dozens of people on stretchers lying amid endless bustle. Netting had been erected to keep the insects away as the healers worked, checking each incoming patient over and sending them off again according to their need. Fearful Learshapans had gathered, asking after loved ones and looking down into the face of every new arrival, while supplies hurried in and whispered stories hurried out. I circled around, not wanting to get in the way of such important work, yet I couldn't but catch the tendrils of talk. About Lummazzt soldiers—"those black-eyed monsters"—about unexpected explosions, about collapsing shafts and shipments of destroyed scale, friends lost and livelihoods destroyed, and it was a heavier heart I carried on toward Master Hoye's dimly lit windows.

"Who in all the damn basin comes calling at this hour?" came Master Hoye's grumble when I knocked. "What do—? Tesha? Tesh, what are you doing here? And dressed in nothing but a wrap? Come, quick."

Hardly taking a breath, he hustled me into the golden warmth of the forge. "I'm sorry, but I had to come," I said as he led me through to the back and pressed me into his favourite chair.

"I didn't get a chance to say goodbye. Or to explain. Or...or anything."

"Your note explained plenty," he said, the words grim. "Left me only wanting to ask if you'd lost your mind. Insult brides. Never heard of those when I worked in Emora, but it sounds exactly like the sort of thing they'd do."

"So you did work in Emora! I thought that might have been where you got the box and where you—"

"Yes, yes." He made a sound between a harrumph and a grumble. "It's not a part of my life I talk about. Nice enough city, mind you, but the work, well, let's say they weren't the finest years of my life. If you'd asked my opinion, I would have told you to stay well away rather than agreeing to some Emoran plot."

The Lummazzt attacks had shaken my resolve to end the unification, but not my resolve to loosen the grip Emorans kept tightening around our throats, and I sat forward, eyes bright. "But, Master Hoye, think a moment," I said. "Agreeing to this plan of theirs gets me right into the heart of Emora, into the reacher's family. From there I can tear them all down."

"Didn't I say you'd lost your mind?"

I sat back with a sigh, throwing up my arms. "All people ever do is talk about changing the world, while every day the Emorans and their money choke more and more life out of the basin, leaving the rest of us living wretched lives. This way we could *do* something. *Really* do something."

Master Hoye's eyes narrowed. *"We?"*

"You could come with me. We could take the box and—"

"No."

"But—"

"No!" He shook his head, turning away to run his hand through thinning hair. "I left that life behind and vowed never to go back. It's bad enough accepting those jobs from Sorscha. I should have thrown the box in the fire long ago." He turned back, resting his hands on the back of his chair and staring down at me. "That city is a viper's nest. People who go there don't come back the same. You think the Emorans here are bad, well!" A snort of humourless laughter and he shook his head again. "No, Tesha. I won't do it and neither should you. They will eat you alive. Here it is safe."

"What if the Lummazzt march on the city?"

"Then it would still be safer than Emora," he said darkly. "We can fight enemies we can see; you can't fight enemies you don't even know are enemies."

He was right, yet it was with a plea for understanding that I looked up at him—this man who had taken me on as an apprentice, had taught me everything I knew, sparing no time or patience, who had counselled me and guided me and been the rock to whom I had tied my confidence in humanity. A sigh trembled past his lips. "You're going anyway."

Statement more than question. He sank back into his chair. "I fear you'll regret your choice, but you've made it, and I can only be proud of your determination to fight, even if I think you'll lose the battle."

"Every battle is lost if we don't fight. Just think, if the Lummazzt really do attack the basin, it's local organising we'll need, not lords sending people out to die from the comfort of their shaded atriums. We need power in the hands of the people."

He huffed a sad laugh. "We lost that fight a very long time ago. But I would love for you to prove me wrong."

It was the best I would get, and I had to be satisfied, even though it meant finding another way to attack Emora from within without his help and his poisons. When it was time to go and he walked me to the door, I hoped he would change his mind, but instead he just said, "Don't let yourself get caught up in their games."

"Games?"

"Emorans," he said darkly. "Most of them have a second, third, and fourth play at all times and a finger in everything they can find, but those who live there all the time, steeped in power and politics, those you cannot trust. They will lure you in and spin you about until it's their song you're dancing to, their fight you're fighting. Don't lose sight of who you really are." He thumped a fist to his chest. "Who you will always be."

Holding in tears, I gave him my word and held him tight for a time, promising that one day I would be back. He took that promise whether he believed it or not, and let me out into the chill street.

The walk back to Romm Manor was long and tiring, uphill all the way as I left the Learshapa I knew and loved behind in a sea of lights and mist and silent worry. Climbing the side fence to avoid any guards, I slipped in through the lower window I had left open and was soon hurrying on quiet steps back to my room. Light pooled beneath the door, and grateful I'd thought to leave a lantern burning, I shouldered my way in ready to collapse upon the bed.

"Tesh!" Arms closed around me, pinning my own arms to my sides as warm breath tickled my neck all panawood and brandy. "Where have you been?" Uvao demanded, stepping back as quickly as he had embraced me, though he still gripped my shoulders as his eyes raked me over. "I have been waiting hours, sure something had happened to you or that you'd run away and—"

"I haven't even been gone hours!" I said, rattled by how like my old Uvao he was in that moment, his blank mask wholly thrown aside.

"It sure felt like hours! Father sent word half an hour ago that he wants to meet you, and I've been racking my brain for some lie that would satisfy him."

I'd been ready to bristle at his suggestion I might run, but at that I froze. "Wants to meet me?"

"Yes! He says it's time he looked you over to see how you're coming along. He needs to make the final decision over whether to put you forward for the treaty marriage tomorrow."

"Oh." I looked down at the wrap poorly covering my bed skirt. My hair was a mess from the wind and the damp night air, and this was the man who would decide if I was good enough. This man who may as well have whipped his children into bowing properly and had definitely sent his oldest son to the Shield Citadel for some unknown crime. I had the sudden urge to be sick.

Uvao squeezed my shoulders. "Tesh? Breathe. Just breathe, and we'll get through the rest together. Here." For the second time that evening, strong hands guided me to a chair, this time at the dressing table. I sat, trying to focus on breathing as commanded while, reflected in the mirror, Uvao started work on my hair. There wasn't time for more than making it look as though I hadn't been out in the wind—a few passes with the brush, his hands smoothing my dark hair with each stroke, and a pair of pins to pull it back from my face.

"That looks terrible," he said, grimacing at his handiwork in the mirror. "But it will have to do."

"It looks fine. Exactly like it would look if I'd been dragged from my bed and had only a few minutes to ready myself."

His grimace became a wry smile. "Right, well then, a few moments to tie a sash around your wrap and we'll be ready."

"Shouldn't I change? These are my bedclothes."

"You look fine. Exactly like you would look if you'd been dragged from your bed with only a few minutes to ready yourself. Given the hour, he's getting what he asked for."

Having grabbed a sash from the nearest chest, Uvao slid it around my waist and made quick work of the knot, and while he did so I couldn't but think of every other time he'd made quick work of my clothing and had to push those thoughts hastily away. If any such memories occurred to him, he didn't show it, dropping the ends of the sash as soon as he was done and heading for the door.

Our walk through the dimly lit manor passed on quick, silent feet, the building as ethereal as I felt hurrying through its large, empty spaces. From the hall where we'd been practising out into the smaller atrium and beyond, I found myself walking the same path from earlier, the destination a memory of a slow, deep voice and a pair of heavily armed guards. We crossed the atrium together, walking through Reacher Sormei's ghost to the archway through which he'd disappeared. Low-burning lights met us, softening a sparse waiting room that lacked any couch, chair, or cushion on which to wait. A closed door stood at the other end, along with a dour man in the plain attire of a clerk. "Ah, Lord Uvao, Lady Teshalii, Lord Romm will see you soon."

"Soon?" Uvao said, halting with a snap of his foot. "He sent for us."

"Yes, and he'll be ready soon," the man said with a forced smile. "Do make yourselves comfortable," he added as though that was even possible in such a space.

With a bow to Uvao and another to me, he walked out, leaving us stranded in the middle of the floor.

"I really hate that man," Uvao whispered once he was gone.

I gripped my lips tight on a sudden urge to laugh, but my little snort drew Uvao's gaze. "It's something about his hair," he added. "It just screams *I'm better than you.*"

"I'm not sure hair can do that," I whispered back. "Though I admit he did seem to enjoy telling us to wait."

"As much as he enjoyed ordering Ashadi's belongings packed up."

The urge to laugh dissipated as though his words were a cold breeze, conjuring a recollection of all I'd heard said of Lord Romm. And though we ought to have just stood still and silent and waited, a question slowly wormed its way from troubled thought to wary tongue. "What did your brother do? To get sent to the Shield, I mean."

His expression darkened, and meeting my gaze with ominous gravity, Uvao said, "He didn't do what he was told."

A little shiver trickled down my spine, and all at once I wished I was somewhere else, anywhere but waiting to meet the man who'd exiled his own son for disobedience.

As he shifted his weight, Uvao's hand brushed mine, only to return, snaking down and gripping my hand in a tight squeeze. "I'm sorry," he said. "About earlier. I...shouldn't have walked out. This has just been...difficult. Harder than I thought it would be, after..."

He made to pull his hand away, but I squeezed back before he could retrieve it. "And I'm sorry, for walking out on you all those weeks ago."

Uvao's laugh was a soft huff of breath as our fingers unlaced, leaving cold air where warm skin had been. "I know why you did it, and I admire your integrity. At least, I do when I imagine it was someone other than me."

What words could follow such an admission? Whatever the urgings of my treacherous heart, I could no more tell him I wished I had not done it than I could turn away now from a plan that meant so much more to me than he could ever guess. Instead, I let long seconds pass in silence, not even a breath of wind disturbing our fragile moment.

"Tesh."

"Yes?" I tried for blithe and carefree and failed. His eyes seemed to burn into the side of my face.

"If this doesn't work out, if...if he doesn't think you're up to the task..."

I'd thought to keep staring ahead, keep looking away, yet his faltering words drew my gaze like a magnet. And having met those dark eyes, I couldn't look away. "Yes?"

"Do you...do you think—"

Lord Romm's office door swung open and I swallowed my held breath, heart racing as I spun back to face the end of the room. Uvao's words had dragged every thought from the moment in which we stood, leaving me to meet his father with hot cheeks and a body all too conscious.

"Uvao," the man said, already turning back into this office. "Do come in. I've been waiting."

I dared not so much as glance Uvao's way as he started toward the door Lord Romm had left open, could only follow, falling in a step behind to mark the difference in our rank.

The office into which we walked could not have been more different to the waiting room had it tried. From sparse to cluttered, lifeless to alive, as though Lord Romm cared only that this one space felt like home. Well-lit, the room contained at least a dozen lanterns, each sending light spilling over the table and the chairs and the many, many shelves—shelves filled with Apaian artifacts. Statuettes and charms and armbands, sandals and veils, small glass blades and bowls. And in pride of place, a skull.

Having strode back behind his desk, Lord Romm nevertheless remained standing, arms folded. "Well?" he said. "Show me what you have for me, boy."

With all the grace he'd tried to drill into me, Uvao stepped forward and bowed. "Father, allow me to introduce Lady Teshalii Romm. Lady Teshalii, this is my father, Lord Ashard Romm of Hylanii."

Trying to recollect every detail of etiquette and not look at the skull that stared down at me, I followed Uvao's lead and slid out my foot, dropping into a curtsy. "My lord, it is a pleasure to meet you at last."

I rose, half expecting Uvao to smack my knee with his stick— the heavy gaze with which Lord Romm surveyed me somehow worse. The man's expression lacked all warmth, but there was something of Uvao about the line of his lips and the way his face settled so easily into a blank mask.

"I see," he said at last. "Attractive enough, I'll grant you that. And I hear her lessons are going well."

On those words, he made his way back out from behind his desk, slow steps bringing him before me. Standing close, his gaze raked my face, my hair, my body, like I was an animal being examined for purchase, and it was all I could do to stand still and pretend I didn't mind, pretend there was anything normal in treating someone so. Without this man's agreement, my own schemes were dead before I'd a chance to begin.

"Hmm," he mused, finally stepping back. "You think she can do it?"

"Yes, Father. She thinks fast and learns fast and in the right clothes will look the part as well as any Emoran."

Lord Romm's cold glance swept over me again, yet hardly seemed to see me at all. "Well then, I shall make the arrangements. The wedding is to take place next songrise, so she'd better be ready. And on your head be it if you're wrong, boy."

Ashadi

Afternoon Bulletin

To all criers for announcement throughout Orsu and the Shield

The Shield Citadel saw two out of the three rider packs called out on the same day yesterday, a first that has many citizens worried.

Raids in Bakii and attacks in Learshapa lead to fears of imminent war with Lummazza.

Understaffed and under pressure—Orsu's port struggles to unload ships and turn on schedule, causing a backlog of vessels as more people escape the growing danger of the Shield.

9:19

There was a point at which, having heaved up what felt like everything I'd ever eaten in my entire life, my body started trying to heave up itself. My conscious, logical mind knew it wasn't possible, but delirious, wracked, and empty me thought it was as inevitable as it would be spectacular.

"Lord Romm?"

"Ash," I croaked in correction. I might not be able to open my eyes enough to see anything clearly or keep any food down, but my hatred of my family name transcended every discomfort.

A pause, then with a sigh and a strained little cough, Mana said, "Lord Ashadi, I'll help you sit; it's time to try water again."

I groaned and tried to snap that I didn't need help and didn't need water, but it all came out as a squealy wheeze. Ignoring both that and my attempt at waving him away, Mana slid his arm beneath me. It ought to have been difficult, I was sure, the lifting of half a person to prop them upon cushions, but the little grunt of effort I expected never came. Manalaii just lifted me as though I were a child, and for a moment I was helpless in his arms, a feeling that spread both shame and joy through my fuzzy thoughts. I always wanted to ask if I was really so light to him, but by the time I regained my voice I'd regained my sanity too—enough at least to bury such questions where they couldn't be heard.

Pillows shifted beneath me, and my next breath was full of lavender smoke as Mana brought the burner closer. As though he had a dozen arms, he pressed a cup to my lips a mere moment later, other fingers gently brushing away the hair stuck to my brow. "Just try a sip."

I grumbled irritably, everything too much effort in my drained and exhausted state. Easier just to die. "Lord Ashadi," Mana said more sharply. "Take a sip or it'll end up poured down you, and you hate that."

I swore at him inside my head, as annoyed that he knew things about me he could exploit as I was exhilarated that he knew things about me he could exploit. An attempt to scowl at him hurt so much that I parted my lips in a pathetic little mewl of pain, only to have water tipped down my throat. I swallowed because the alternative was disgusting, but the pain of it stinging its way down my throat made me wish I'd let it dribble out.

"Qammattz," I wheezed as soon as I was moderately confident talking wouldn't lead to a coughing fit. At least that's what I tried to wheeze; the actual sound that came out wouldn't have been intelligible to anyone who hadn't had to put up with me in this state for three years. Luckily for me, unluckily for him, Mana just repeated the request back to me, and with only a minor pause for disgust or disapproval or some other word beginning with *dis*, he moved away.

Knowing I had some minutes to wait for the coming relief, I leaned my head back against the wall and listened to the small, intimate sounds of Mana working. The tink of spoon on glass, the rustle of oiled paper, a scrape and a tap, followed by a smothered cough as the dust tickled his nose.

A rustle of cloth and the click of Mana's knees heralded his return. "Are you strong enough for this?" he said, keeping his voice low despite the impossibility of anyone overhearing us.

I rolled my head his way, forcing open aching eyes long enough to give him an irritated stare. To which Mana pursed his lips and nodded. "Not strong enough not to," he said, repeating my oft-used phrase. "All right, well, the paper is here in front of you, and I have the cup in my hand. Do you need me to hold the paper?"

A nod was all I could manage beyond silently wondering whether helping a wreck of a lord take illegal drugs had ever featured among Mana's hopes and dreams. Likely not, though it was surely better than all the vomit he had to clean.

The tickle of the paper against my upper lip told me everything was ready before Mana said, "Ready when you are," his fingers remaining around the cup even after pressing it into my hand. "I'll lift, you guide."

Always so thoughtful, so considerate and calm and prepared

for anything. Perhaps one day I would find the ability to thank him without the sincerity singeing my face off.

Or not. Not was easier. Oblivion was even easier and so very close now. Dropping my head, I inhaled deeply, and while the sting and warmth and sweetness ripped through my nose, I poured the cup's contents into my mouth.

Task done, Mana climbed into the bed beside me, the warmth of his body familiar and reassuring. In smaller doses, Qammattz gave one the sense of floating like the bubbles in fizzy water, making it a favourite at social gatherings. A larger dose had the opposite effect, like someone was piling heavy blankets on my face. While it layered on its soft weight, Mana stroked my forehead with gentle fingers and started to hum. Every time, I wondered what the song was but was too weighed down to ask, and every time I forgot before I woke. For three years it had been an elusive tune locked away in faded memories and the sleep-laden seconds between swallowing and sleep, but this time I would remember to ask. This time.

I eyed the thin soup suspiciously, a headache thumping inside my skull. "If that's the same awful bile as last time, I swear I will instantly recover all strength just so I can throw it at you."

Mana's lips twitched as he supressed a smile. "Never would I seek to harm you so, my lord rider. I have been assured it actually has flavour."

"Been assured? You haven't tried some yourself to prevent the risk of poisoning me? You mustn't care for me at all."

For an instant he looked genuinely chastened, before wiggling the spoon still hovering in front of my lips and scowling. "Just eat it."

"What happened to 'my lord rider'?"

"Eat it, *my lord rider,* or I will hold your nose and tip it down your throat. Is that better?"

"Much," I said, and sipped from the edge of the spoon. "I love it when you're mean to me."

Mana's brows creased in confusion as I swallowed the mouthful—not foul, but not what could be called food either. It stung its way down my dry, ravaged throat, but didn't make my stomach lurch. A good sign I might finally keep something down.

It had been a day since the callout, a day that felt like dozens as recovery began with vomiting and bouts of heavy sleep, only to lead to more vomiting, pain in every joint, a hyperaware, restless state, and still more vomiting. The Qammattz had numbed me out on a sea of vague bliss for a time, but left me feeling twice as weak—a steep price for restful sleep when three years of iishor had kept me in a permanent state of recovery.

I sipped more of the soup, my stomach beginning to reawaken at the arrival of fresh food. Soon it would rumble like a thunderstorm as I shifted into the starving phase, when I had to be careful not to shove so much food in my face that I was sick again.

For the next few minutes, we sat in silence as Mana fed me and dabbed my chin with a cloth whenever soup spilled. As always, I felt both grateful and foolish, cared for and beholden, caught in the tangle of confusion his dedication always wrought. Rather than stare rudely at the wall or risk looking him in the eyes, I studied the constellation tattooed on his left cheekbone. I'd never asked what it meant that his people carried tattoos beneath their eyes, and after three years it now seemed too late.

"Would you like me to fetch more?" Manalaii asked as I swallowed the last spoonful.

"No," I said, not having realised I'd finished the whole bowl while staring at his cheek. "I think that might have broken the nausea. I should find something more sustaining before I get ravenous. Else I might eat the spoon. And then your fingers."

As though daring me to try it, he edged his hand closer, all crooked smile and intent, heavy-lidded stare. My heart thudded hard, but before I could even think of snapping my teeth, he pulled his hand away.

"Commander Jasque came by to check on you," he said, rising hastily to set the empty bowl down. "About an hour ago. Maybe two. I told him you were asleep but that you'd been awake for a good stretch."

I'd never asked him to lie, but then I'd never had to ask anything of Mana. He seemed always to just know. "I had better get up and move then," I said. "Load the seven-shot. Let's see how steady my arm is while I wait for my appetite to kick in."

Manalaii's expression carried all the questions he dared not ask, including the censorious *Are you sure this is a good idea?* one he almost never uttered aloud. Even so, I said, "Yes, I'm sure. Load it so I can take my mind off how awful that soup was and how sick I'll feel again after gorging myself."

While Manalaii fetched my pistol, I looked around at the small room. My clothes had been changed at least once, along with the bedsheets, possibly twice or even three times as I sweated them to a sodden mess, but everything else looked as it had before the ride. Each pistol and rifle hung in its place, barrels polished and mechanisms kept clean, while the few things I'd brought with me stood upon the shelf gathering dust amid a jumble of half-read books left open to the page on which I'd lost interest.

The shirt Mana had changed me into wasn't fit to be seen upright in, so with time ticking inevitably toward Commander Jasque returning to check on me, fresh clothes could not wait. Gripping the wrought-iron bedhead, I manoeuvred myself into a better position from which to slide onto my feet, determined to do something for myself. Unfortunately, stealth wasn't my forte and nor was standing, and the sound of clatters and grunts brought Mana hastily back from the small adjoining storage room, powder horn in hand.

"Lord Ashadi, what are you doing?" he said, cruel enough to stand over me looking down from his magnificent height.

"I'm getting up," I said, despite all evidence to the contrary.

"You're lying on the floor."

"Not lying, crouching."

"Having one leg bent underneath you isn't crouching."

"Just stow it and help me up, all right? None of your disapproving old-lady face either, I'm fine. I'm feeling much better already and will dress and head out to the shooting gallery."

Mana stared down at me, his expression inscrutable and no helping hand in sight.

"Mana—"

"Your recoveries have slowed."

"Help me—"

"You're worried about what the masters will say."

I glared up at him. "Didn't your mother ever teach you it was rude to interrupt a man with callous assertions?"

"You mean with the truth."

"Sometimes they are the same thing; now are you going to give me a hand or do I have to shout for help like an unweaned babe?"

"As amusing as that would be, I don't want to lose my job." Mana stuck out his hand upon the words and, gripping mine tightly, hauled me to my feet with as little effort as he showed undertaking every other task. "Your blue skirts, my lord? Or perhaps the sand coloured?"

Not rising to his bait, I made a show of deeply considering his question. "I think the sand today, Manalaii; I'm in a flighty, vast, and unpredictable mood."

"I've always rather thought of The Sands as scratchy and irritating, their vastness extending to every crevice upon the body."

"Charming. Always good to know what you think of me."

His lips twitched, his eyes bright with amusement that edged into something I could almost believe was affection had I let myself see it. Had I let my gaze hold his. Let myself be drawn into the gravity of his presence, the space between us shrinking. Perhaps it had never grown. Perhaps he had never stepped back after helping me to my feet. Perhaps I could just...reach out and touch his chin. His cheek. His lips.

The room spun, only Mana's tight grip on my elbow keeping me from stumbling.

"Are you sure you're all right?" he said, his voice a low, concerned rumble. The words shivered across my skin like I was still cold from the iishor and he was warm, always warm and present and too song-be-damned beautiful. It was getting harder to ignore how intensely my body yearned toward his. How often I thought about touching him. How easy it would be to throw rules to the winds. After all, what could they do? Exile me from my exile?

A manic little laugh brushed past my lips, and caught in the delirious aftermath of the Qammattz, I almost dared. But I could not force myself on him, could not abuse his care and his position. Could not convince myself I was worthy.

"Lord Ashadi, are you sure you're all right? Here—" He started toward the pile of fresh bed linen. "You should get some more rest."

"No! I have to go out there. I have to be seen or they'll ask questions."

"There is no shame in—"

"Yes, there is! I'm their best rider. And if I stop being their best rider then my name won't be enough to stop them watching me all the time, stop them putting up the fucking dose, forcing me through the extra training regimens and writing to my damn father about it all."

In one sharp tirade I'd loosed more honesty than I'd dared in a long time, and Mana just stood and stared like I'd slapped him.

Until pity swept across his features and I turned away. "I need clothes."

"All right. Here, lift your arms."

Like I was a child again, I raised my arms and let him pull my bed shirt up over my head. A clean tunic took its place, followed by skirts fit to be seen in, though my hands trembled and my knees were sure to give way at any moment. An added challenge at the shooting gallery, no more.

"My pistol?" I held out a hand as far as I dared lest he see it shake. "I'll walk over on my own and reload for myself. Let you have some quiet, Lord Ashadi–free time."

His inscrutable look was back—an improvement on the pity. "As you wish, my lord, but call if you need me. I would not wish to be seen failing in my duties."

With loaded pistol and shot bag in hand, I hurried out as fast as my weak knees would carry me, but I barely made it into the hallway before the world started to spin, forcing me to stand a moment with a steadying hand on the stonework.

"Bit wobbly on your feet there, Ashadi?"

I spun and immediately wished I hadn't as pain pierced my temple. The sight of Farisque approaching at ease along the passage only made it worse. "Just a moment of lightheadedness," I said, trying for my usual bored tone. "Often happens when I laze in bed too long on recovery days, enjoying the warmth."

His smile was broad and full of dislike. "As you say." A nod at the pistol in my hand. "How about another challenge to wake you up then, hmm?"

"Such a sacrifice on your part is not required, Farisque. Especially since challenging myself is always far more interesting than beating others easily."

"For a discarded noble like the rest of us, you're an arrogant little shit, Ashadi Romm," Farisque hissed. "What makes you think the desert waters pour from your arse?"

On any other day I would have had a snappy retort for him, some way of extricating myself from the conversation with great satisfaction on my part and great embarrassment on his. Today I hoped pathetically that Mana would open the door and save me, while trying to cow the irritating rider with a glare.

"Thankfully the desert waters do no such thing," I managed eventually. "There is, however, nothing wrong with knowing the value of one's skills."

I made to leave, only to be struck by the words "Why are you here, Ashadi? Whenever I ask anyone about you, all I get are shrugs or whispered tales like you're a grand mystery, and you know what? I think you like it that way. You like being interesting. The only eldest son and heir ever sent to the citadel. You must have done something *terrible*."

He said the word like a man licking his lips after a delicious meal, and upon a spur of revulsion, I turned away—a movement that had never felt so difficult or fraught, as though I stood upon a narrow bridge over boiling glass sands. I managed not to fall to my death nor reach for the wall's support, yet couldn't shake the feeling Farisque was sniggering at my back.

Thankfully, he didn't follow as I strode off along the hallway—*strode* an aspirational word for a desperate attempt to put one foot in front of the other without falling over. Momentum helped, and the weight of the seven-shot pistol balanced me in a way that ought to have made me question how much time I'd spent holding guns in my life, had introspection not been my least favourite activity. I wasn't even sure at this point whether I would be able to pull its trigger when I reached the gallery. If I reached the gallery.

The urge to look back and see if Farisque still watched was almost impossible to suppress, but I made it to the corner where stone passage met more stone passage and felt momentarily safe as I turned out of his sight.

And hit the floor. Knees buckling to meet hard stone, I was thrown forward onto my hands. Panic more than pain filled me as I tried to pull myself back up, sure the whole citadel had just seen me fall.

"Shit, Ashadi," hissed a nearby voice as hands grasped my arms. "Are you all right?"

Luce. I'd never been more thankful for anything. "Just help me up. Quick."

He did so without another word, and having gotten me on my feet, threaded an arm through mine and started walking us, elbows locked, along the passage. "Where were you going?"

I blinked, momentarily unsure where I was, let alone what I'd been doing, the pistol hanging from my hip the only reminder. "Gallery." After a few more steps I dared ask the gnawing question. "Did anyone else see?"

"I don't think so, but it's hard to say. Sometimes I wonder if even the walls in this place have eyes."

I huffed a weak laugh, keeping similar fears to myself.

"Did you hear that Parsek got caught stealing alcohol from the kitchens?" he said. "The masters chose a new watcher for him, and he had to do every callout for a week."

Of course I had heard. Everyone had heard. As the monster attacks had increased, so too had discipline—my name and skill the only reason I'd gotten away with the Qammattz for as long as I had.

"Do you think you can walk on your own now?" he asked as we turned toward the main hall.

"Yes, I'm fine. Really. Just . . . overbalanced."

The sceptical look shot from the corners of his eyes was all the worse for Luce's kind features. "Is it the iishor? Does it . . . does it get worse?"

"It certainly doesn't get better."

"Oh, good. Something to look forward to."

Taking me at my word, he slipped his arm out of mine, and thankfully I didn't fall. His sigh of relief mimicked mine, and we continued companionably on toward the shooting gallery.

"Perhaps I should—"

The gong rang across his words, and my steps shuffled to a halt. One ring meant first pack and plenty of time left for us to recover, but a second tone soon chased the first, cutting that time in half. "Well, shit."

A third tone vibrated through the citadel more horror than sound, hollowing me out as heaving never had. Surely it was too soon. An accident? The third tone had once been sounded by mistake when a new watcher had been left in charge, but no matter how tightly I wanted to hold on to such hope, Luce's grim expression knew the truth.

"Already?" I said, the only word I trusted myself to utter.

"So it would seem," he returned, his carefree shrug forced. "I heard the second pack called out this morning."

No mistake then, yet for seconds that stretched to minutes, neither of us moved, as though perhaps if we stayed caught there in our moment, time would cease to pass and we could put off drinking yet more iishor.

It didn't work. Soon running steps hurried our way as watchers and riders alike sped toward the armoury. Manalaii emerged from the group, his face creased with worry that didn't ease at sight of me. "Lord Ashadi, they've called your pack."

"I heard," I said. "Took you long enough to show up. At this rate we'll be late."

The words were beneath me, but Manalaii took the unworthy rebuke with an expressionless nod and together we joined the others speeding in the direction of iishor and death—*speed* another of those aspirational words I was increasingly clinging to.

We arrived to find the armoury already crowded and Commander Jasque already shouting. "Same place as last ride," he called, his enormous voice failing to fill the growing void inside me. "Seems the bastards are attacking in waves to wear us down."

If that was their goal, they'd already succeeded with me, though I wasn't the only one looking drawn and weary. Worry peered out from every eye and pressed many lips to thin lines— Manalaii's expression doubly concerned as he fetched my armour. It was the work of well-worn habit to slide my arms in and to stand, numb and unmoving, as he laced me into the protective layers of leather hide—chest plate, gauntlets, helmet. Everywhere the click of mechanisms and the hush of dry gunpowder filled the air. At some point Commander Jasque had stopped shouting, his information relayed to everyone who had actually been listening. Everyone except me, standing like a lifeless doll to one side of a room slowly starting to spin.

When Manalaii brought over my glass of iishor he attempted no cheer. We both knew I was far from recovered enough to ride, and drinking iishor on an empty stomach was a terrible idea. I took the glass all the same, and before I could think or even breathe, I poured the thick, warm liquid down my throat. It always burned, but this time it seared along a throat lacerated from endless vomiting, like I had swallowed tiny knives.

The glass smashed at my feet, the sound seeming to come from far away.

"You all right?" Mana said, lowering his face to mine in a way that always exaggerated how much taller he was. "Lord Ashadi?"

With every word his speech sped, colours shifting. I must have managed a nod, for one by one my pistols and rifles began to weigh me down, Manalaii running through his tasks with his usual precision while I was barely keeping myself upright. Despite the spinning room and my churning gut, habit was strong enough that when the time came my feet carried me toward the undercroft without requiring any conscious thought.

Every step was like hauling myself through treacle, but when at last I reached the undercroft, Shuala sat waiting, curled in her wool-lined den and glaring at my approach.

Took you long enough, she said. *The gong sounded eons ago.*

"Permission to mount then, so we can get going."

A low rumble of hot air hissed through her nose. *And why should I give it? I'm still weary from the last flight, and here you are already demanding I take another?*

"Make up your mind, Shu. You can't tell me I'm taking too long but then refuse to fly out."

I can complain as much as I like. Her scales tinkled as she gave herself a small shake—the first step toward stretching out her legs and emerging from her warm cavern. *At least since you barely made it back last time, I can hope this time the iishor will drain even faster and you'll fall to your death.*

"We all have to have our goals," I said with a sigh. "Now, please, permission to mount."

Fine. Let's get this over with, but I want more wool waiting when I get back.

"I'll let the keeper know and she can decide."

With an irritable snuffle, Shuala rose and stalked out of her cave shaking free any clinging pakka wool with musical tinkles. The stable hand whose name definitely started with a *B* and had some *O*s in it stepped forward with my saddle and began the delicate yet tough task of saddling Shuala, surely the least helpful dragon in the citadel's entire history. The man was skilled, quick and sure, yet even he owned the stretched, drawn look of one who'd had far too little sleep.

Around us, dragons were already making for the skies with heavy, thudding runs and cracks of enormous wings. Somewhere Commander Jasque was doing some more shouting.

"We weren't given much in the way of a plan," I said as I mounted Shuala, trying to pretend one foot hadn't slipped and caught a few scales as I climbed. "Let me know what you hear."

Same attack pattern. It seems they've given up on imagination and are trying for brute force.

"Not a lot of time for the commander to come up with new—"

I meant the enemy.

She started forward on the words, urged to motion by my final tug on the straps that held us together. Beyond the undercroft the skies were filling with bright red life as each dragon prepared their flames. Usually, I could bear the initial stages, but today the hot light bit into my eyes, and I snapped my dark goggles down before Shuala even set her claws over the edge of the abyss. No longer in control, there was joy in not having to push myself forward or keep myself moving, able instead to let Shuala take me wherever I needed to go. For now it didn't matter that I felt dizzy or that my stomach was beginning to eat itself with hunger; it was Shuala's strong legs that launched us into the air. To gain height, each fierce flap of her wings had the force of a thunderclap, and wind rushed by as she rose and dove, rose and dove, stretching in readiness. Others were already circling, awaiting Commander Jasque, who was bringing up the rear. While the northern towers always got plenty of warning when a horde was incoming, preparations had felt so slow that it was a relief to find the monsters weren't already upon us.

It's not a small group, Shuala said, passing on information as she received it. *We need to stick close today, not let ourselves be peeled off.*

"No heroics," I said. "I am too tired for those anyway."

Have you told the commander about your resistance?

"No. There will be a better time."

Is that better time never?

I ignored her, grateful that monsters chose that moment to appear on the horizon—a hot red mass thanks to the iishor. With strong legs they propelled their lithe bodies toward us across The Sands, their leathery scales possessing the shine of a hard exoskeleton. Unlike Shuala's glass scales, they weren't impenetrable, but any poorly aimed shot was as likely to deflect as to dig in, and their limbs were as tough as desiccated meat.

Flames first, Shuala said, already banking to join the rest of the pack. *I have only two. Not enough time to replenish three.*

I knew how she felt. But if all went well, we could soon be back in the citadel resting up with perhaps even a whole week until we needed to ride again. Minimal retreats. Maximum carnage.

Without any prompting from me, Shuala took her place in the first flame line and prepared to dive, her belly boiling. A touch assured me I still had my protective glasses down as the dragons let flare their first molten flames, burning and melting the creatures below with their rage. High-pitched squeals followed the crackling fire, before they dissipated into the clink and pop of cooling glass.

First flame spent, Shuala peeled off, banking hard. The ground whipped by, and I held tight, waiting for her to level out again ready for a second run. Instead, she dropped abruptly, sending my stomach into my throat, before she turned again—a sharp bank and twist that would have sent me tumbling to the ground had I not been strapped to the saddle.

"What's going on?" I shouted loud enough to be heard over the wind.

Gunfire. From the ground.

"From the ground?" Not once in the three years I'd been riding had shots ever come from below. The monsters had a variety of tactics, from clumping together and charging to spreading out and charging, none of which had involved shooting back.

She banked again rather than answer, and I leaned out as far as I dared to get a better look. Below, the rocky edge of The Sands met dry scrub in a jagged line like bared teeth, all small caves and carve outs but no sign of movement. The monsters were making for the mountain passes, leaving the sand clear of all but charred corpses as the others readied for their second flames.

"We ought to—"

No, Shuala said. *Commander doesn't like this. Says whoever this is, they need to be taught a lesson or taken out.*

While flames roared behind us, Shuala wheeled about.

"Right, let's get this done fast then." I drew the first of my loaded rifles. "Fly low, and if that doesn't scare them off, they'll get only one warning shot."

A warm harrumph from beneath me was half satisfaction, half annoyance, but I wouldn't kill someone unless I had to—especially not someone who'd had the ill fortune to end up out here. Shuala had no such qualms and started bubbling her second flame as she drew her wings in for a dive.

Hold tight.

I gripped tight with my knees just before she dropped, sending my stomach flying up into my throat. As she dove, wind rushed over her head and right into my face, sending my hair streaming and waking me from my lingering stupor. And for a brief moment I felt fully alive, the iishor balancing out the fatigue and leaving only joy at the raw power beneath me and the perfect mechanism in my hand.

Man. Sand-coloured hood. Rifle. Aiming this—

Shuala broke off with a hiss like an overflowing kettle, her smooth dive broken like she'd hit potholes in the air.

"Shuala?" I held tight and leaned out, only for her to bank sharply, still diving. "Shu?" I cried. "What the fuck is going on?"

The ground rushed toward us, and for a panicked instant I was sure she would slam into it at full pace, crushing us both to paste, but at the last moment she beat her wings hard, slowing us enough that she could land at a run on the shifting sands. A run that lasted four steps before she fell forward, momentum leading to an ungraceful landing. And to my face slamming into the back of Shuala's scaled neck. Glass cut into my skin, spilling blood into my eyes and leaving me stunned in a moment of white-hot vision.

Beneath me Shuala writhed, and with shaking hands, I tugged at the straps of my saddle. "Shu! Shu! What happened?"

Bullet. Hit me.

"What? How?" I got the straps unclipped and all but fell from the saddle to land, winded, upon the sand.

Don't know. Commander says you must protect me while we wait for help. No one can come yet. Man. There.

Using my rifle as a stick, I hauled myself up, ribs aching and eye stinging from the blood. Wiping it away seemed to do nothing beyond clearing my vision for a few seconds before it filled with blood again—blood made gritty as sand swirled around me.

"Where did it hit you?"

Left. Flank.

The side she hadn't buried in the sand. I scrambled around, disoriented but hardly caring. Nothing ought to be able to get through a dragon's glass scales, certainly not a bullet shot from a distance. Still using my rifle as a staff, I circled Shuala's heaving body, tracing my free hand along her scintillating scales.

Ash! The man!

I felt the blood before I saw it, gritty with sand like my own but so much hotter. Bright, dark red due to the lingering iishor, it hissed as it hit the sand, and I pulled my hand from its boiling heat. It dripped from the middle of a scale, where glass had cracked around the entry point.

"It went through the middle of the scale," I said, wiping away the hot blood with a quick swish of my sleeve. "The middle of a fucking scale!"

Ash!

"What?"

The man!

"What man?"

"I believe she means me."

I spun and found myself staring down the barrel of a long

pistol. A leather glove the colour of sand held a finger poised over the trigger, its owner little more than a similarly sandy-wrapped figure behind it. Dark eyes gleamed from the depths of a protective hood, and though the steady hand upon the pistol was all promise, it was anger, not fear, that surged up my throat.

"You shot my dragon," I said. "You shot my fucking dragon. Who the fuck are you and what are you doing out here?"

"I am no one," the man said. "A messenger, if you will."

"That doesn't explain why you shot my dragon!"

"No, but next time my aim won't be so merciful."

"What next time?" I lifted my rifle, not caring it wasn't a close-quarters weapon. "This ends now."

The pistol aimed at my face didn't so much as twitch, the man's hand steady as rock. "I hope you are right; I would rather not have to come back and speak to any of you rock-dwellers again. So put away that weapon and listen to me, or I'll shoot down another rider who will."

"You shot through a scale," I said. "How?"

"You must know. Gunpowder. Bullet. Load and pull the trigger. Or do you have some magic way of making a gun fire?"

"Don't treat me like a fool. No bullet can go through scaleglass."

I couldn't see the man's face, yet I was sure he grinned. "How very much I would love to stay and enlighten you, to tell you how wrong you are about everything you think you know, but since your friends will soon be here, I suggest you listen if you don't want this to happen again." The man lowered his pistol, and with the immediate threat removed, some of the tension eased from my limbs. Either that or the iishor was fast draining out of me, leaving my knees weak.

Stepping closer, the hooded man pushed aside the barrel of my rifle. "You must take a message to your masters," he said, thrusting his pistol into its holster. "Tell them they have gone too far this time. Tell them they will get only this one warning. We will no longer be your waste pile, your garden, your mine, your slaves. No longer will you take from us and throw back what you do not want. Your next *ride* will be your last. All of you."

For a few seconds that seemed to stretch to minutes—hours—days—the man stared at me from the shadow of his hood and I stared back, his easy confidence as much a promise as his steady hand had been. I'd heard his words, yet they made no sense, and questions piled upon my tongue. The first to make its way out was a weak "Who are you?"

"I am no one. Just tell them."

As though we were done, he turned from me, one step taking him to Shuala's side. There, he pulled off one of his gloves and set his hand gently upon her scales, bare skin to glass. "I'm sorry for everything that has been done to you. May you one day find the grace to forgive us, and we the courage to forgive ourselves."

Barely were the words out of his mouth than his head snapped my way, a man catching sight of shifting prey. "And as for you. You had better hope we never meet again."

With that, he turned his back on me and walked away, splayed steps taking him halfway up a low, rocky dune, his scarf swirling. Halting there, he brought two fingers to his lips and whistled, a high, demanding shriek that seemed to shake the ground beneath us. Sand slid down the dune. Small rocks tumbled. And a lithe, dark creature emerged from beneath the man's feet in an eruption of sand. I blinked, clearing the grit from my eyes in time to see the creature leap into motion. Strong legs propelled it at a half run, half bound much faster than I could have given chase, while upon its back, the man sat seemingly at his ease, guiding the creature—more monster than animal—away along the curve of a rocky rise before dropping out of sight.

Beside me Shuala was still breathing, hot rasping breaths that promised she lived, though her voice had long since stopped vibrating in my mind as the iishor fled. It had taken not only her voice but my strength, and my knees gave way, landing me in a sprawl of sand and blood. As I settled next to Shuala's glass scales, the strange man's warning circled through my head, but it was his gentle apology to her that haunted me. How he'd drawn off his glove. Had touched her. Seeking forgiveness for something that made no sense.

Side by side in the sand, Shuala and I lay waiting for the incoming flap of winged rescue, the silence between us no longer just the lack of iishor but the growing realisation that I knew nothing about her at all.

6

Tesha

Afternoon Bulletin

To all criers for announcement throughout Learshapa

*Continued protests outside the upper city council chambers
have led to clashes between unification and separatist groups,
many injured.*

*Three hundred soldiers from Emora have been dispatched to
Learshapan scale mines to repel Lummazzt attacks. Fear of war
on the rise across the city.*

*This morning, Reacher Sormei addresses city officials,
promising minimal interference in local affairs.*

422:2

Finger pressed to the number on the latest crier sheet, I flipped
pages of *The Book of the Song* until I reached the right one,

before counting the words. *Drop*. I scribbled a note. The code from the morning bulletin had been the word *two*, but it would be a few more days before a full location could be decoded. Not that I could do anything about it from the empty halls of Romm Manor, but it was nice to feel connected to my old life in little ways. Little reminders that I was, deep down, still just Tesha.

It had been Sorscha who'd first introduced me to the reclamation movement—a loose collection of people interested in returning Apaian artifacts to their rightful owners. Messages came through the crier sheets, and when there were enough instructions to act, our small group gathered to assign the task and ensure it got done. Mostly it involved picking up parcels from one location and taking them to another, easy work with the bonus of knowing you were annoying Emorans. If only someone would organise to steal Lord Romm's collection next.

I sighed and slipped a slice of orange into my mouth. The only problem with keeping up with the codes was also reading every crier sheet. News was rarely good, but it was getting worse by the day. At least down in the city I'd always felt I could do something about it, that I was a part of it. Here I could only remind myself what I was trying to achieve.

And keep hiding from Lord Revennai.

We were meant to be practising attending a party together, but I'd slipped away with some food for a few moments' peace. In the two days since Lord Romm had given his blessing, he had continued to show no personal interest in my Emoran education, but Uvao and Lord Revennai barely let me rest.

"Oh, Lady Teshalii, there you are!"

I shoved my collection of crier sheets back into my skirt pocket and threw *The Book of the Song* into a nearby bush. My new maid approached, relief colouring her features. I got hastily to my feet, immediately feeling bad for having found a quiet corner of the atrium to hide in.

"I'm sorry, Biiella, do you need something?"

"Oh no, my lady. I'm sorry to disturb you, but Lord Uvao and Lord Revennai are looking for you. And the pommadeur is here to see you, along with the seamstress."

"The pommadeur? But why?" I brushed my hands down my skirt as I stepped onto the tiles, abandoning both my orange slices and the Emoran holy book to the garden bed.

"I couldn't say, my lady. I was merely instructed to find you as quickly as I could. They're waiting for you in the hall."

They were indeed waiting for me in the hall, the pair of them looking as grim as I had ever seen them—so grim my heart both sank and sped as I approached, heedless of my bulging skirt pocket and fingers sticky with orange juice. "What is it?"

Lord Revennai flicked a glance at Uvao's silent profile before clearing his throat. "Have you been keeping abreast of the news the last few days?"

"About the Lummazzt attacks? Have they...?"

"No, not yet. But with the situation with Lummazza getting much more serious, Reacher Sormei wants to put an end to the treaty protests, so..."

Lord Revennai trailed off with a grimace, leaving Uvao to step in as though they'd practised their speech together. "They want to bring the wedding forward," Uvao said, looking past me to the archway. "They think waiting until songrise is too risky."

"And likely Sormei wants to get back to Emora," Lord Revennai added with a grumble. "He's not very patient at the best of times and doesn't like being away. Especially not with a crisis brewing."

I waved this off impatiently, breath caught in my tightening chest. "Bring it forward?" I said, the words more gasp than I'd hoped. "To when?"

"To the end of the week."

For a moment we stood in silence while my stomach churned,

spinning the hall around me. "Three days," I whispered when at last I found my voice. "You mean in three days?"

Lord Revennai's nod held a wry grimace. "Yes, in three days. To which end, Reacher Sormei has asked to meet you."

"When?"

"This afternoon."

No longer able to keep myself standing, I dropped into a crouch, bending my head between my knees. This afternoon. The reacher of Emora wanted to meet me that afternoon, and I had to make him believe I'd been born a lady of house Romm. "I'm not ready," I said, lacing my fingers behind my head and staring at the shifting tiles. "I'm not ready. I'm not. He'll know, he'll see right through me. It's too soon." I shook my head, tears pricking my eyes. "I can't do it. I can't. So stupid to ever think I could."

In a rustle of crisp cloth, Uvao crouched before me. "That's not the Tesha I know," he said, gripping my shoulders tight. "The Tesha I know would say, *Fuck what that arsehole thinks, I'm going to make him wish he was as smart as he thinks he is.*"

"Perhaps best not said directly to Sormei's face," Lord Revennai murmured above us.

"My Tesha," Uvao went on, ignoring him, "would sweep up her shattered pieces and give herself a shake. Because life is glass."

"Life is glass," I whispered back, recalling with a stab of sadness how interested he'd been in learning about my work, how he'd always listened, always been there. Until he hadn't been the man I'd thought he was. "Life is glass."

Perhaps if I shattered someone could sweep me up and throw me away, somewhere I could hide from the world. But Uvao was right. I had agreed to this for a reason and there was no going back, nothing to do but sweep away the pieces of my old life and step fully into the new, nothing to do but grip Emora by the throat and try to change the world. If I did not even try, I would never forgive myself.

I sniffed and wiped my sleeve across my eyes, wishing no one had been present to see my fear win. "Life is glass," I said again, stronger this time, and nodded.

Uvao squeezed my shoulders. "That's my Tesha. Now, when you're ready, the pommadeur is waiting. It's time you looked the part."

I returned to my room to find a trio of maids helping a seamstress about her work, and a pommadeur who had set up by the window for the best light.

"Ah, Lady Teshalii," the pommadeur crooned, sailing over to me the moment I stepped in the doorway. He shot daggers at the seamstress as he passed, but she ignored him, continuing to work about the hem of a skirt hanging on a wire frame. "Do come and sit down, please, we have much to do. Sit, sit." He flourished a hand at the chair, sunlight spilling over its light, soft wood. "We must see to these brows, we must. Be very still and this will soon be done, then we can move on to the far more exciting part of styling your hair for this afternoon."

Razor held almost loosely in his hand, the man worked quickly on my brows, hardly seeming to give the task a thought. Within little more than a minute he was tidying his work with tweezers, and it was all I could do not to hiss at each stray hair he plucked.

"There now, all better," he said, stepping back to examine his handiwork. "Always easier to keep up than to do all over again, though," he added in mock censure.

"I don't think anyone could have called that difficult; you work so quickly."

"Ah, thank you, my lady, that I do. Much practice. Now your hair."

Once the pommadeur had finished, it was the seamstress's turn to flutter about as I put on the four glorious skirts she'd brought with her. I'd always thought it pointless to wear more than one, but the way she had designed the colours and textures to fall together... "It's beautiful," I said, and was surprised to find I meant it.

"Thank you, my lady. If you're satisfied, we'll fit your tunic now."

Fit was the right word, so tightly did it follow my form. Two dozen tiny glass buttons glimmered down the front like raindrops on pale, dusty red. Part ribbon, part fabric, part sheer magic, it was perfectly fitted to my skin and yet comfortable like the finest glove, its neckline dropping low with a broad, embroidered collar.

As the seamstress fastened the final button, a servant arrived, a little out of breath. "Lord Romm wants to leave in ten minutes," he said, and was gone again, leaving the maids to cluster about me. One slid bands onto my left arm, another dusted my face with powder, while a third laid out my shoes. All I could do was stand and wait, heart hammering so quick I was sure to faint if they did not soon give me air.

Instead, another knock sounded upon the door, and stealing the last of my breath, Uvao appeared upon the threshold. His eyes widened as he looked me up and down, staring like I had been replaced with a stranger. Perhaps I had; I'd never felt less myself in all my life.

At his appearance, each maid curtsied and hurried out of the way, leaving me stranded in the middle of the floor, shoes waiting on the tiles before me.

"Uvao," I said, his name but a breath.

"Lady Teshalii," he returned, and cleared his throat. "Allow me to compliment you on your attire; you look exquisite."

So much I wanted to say, so much I wanted to ask, but all I could do was slide my foot out into a curtsy and thank him. The beginning flicker of a smile was crushed by firm lips, and he pointed down. "Shoes. It's time to go."

A maid knelt at my feet, and though it felt wrong to let her help me into my shoes, I wasn't sure I could sit down without ruining all their fine work. Once she had finished, I turned a glance at the mirror and found a stranger staring back. Gone was Apprentice Tesha, replaced with an Emoran woman I didn't know and, despite Uvao's admiring stare, wasn't sure I wanted to.

"Come, cousin." Uvao held out his arm. "We cannot be late."

"No, of course we cannot."

I took his arm, glad of his support and of the closeness of his body but unable to say so. Unable to say the scent of panawood that always hung about him squeezed my heart with every breath. Unable to thank him. Unable to say I was sorry. Unable to tell him how much fear I carried for us both.

In the grand entry hall, Lord Romm stood tapping his foot, all scowl and azure cloth. "You have kept me waiting," he said in welcome, holding out his hands in what I now knew was a formal greeting. Uvao took his father's hands and lifted them to his lips before stepping back, leaving space for me to perform the same formality. We'd practised it over and over, but this was the first time it had been someone other than Uvao and Lord Revennai, and my heartbeat sped sickeningly. Trying to imagine Lord Romm was just Uvao in different clothes, I stepped forward and took his hands—*not too tight, not too loose!*—lifted them to my lips—*don't lick your lips beforehand!*—and gently pecked first his left hand then his right—*just the dry part of your lips, no wetness!*—before releasing them. I stepped back as Uvao had done, and found Lord Romm once again looking me over like something he was trying to value.

"You have polished up well, Lady Teshalii," he said, and with a start I realised it was the first time he'd addressed me directly. "Has my son explained the importance of this meeting to you? As owner of the largest estate in the Learshapan reaches, it was no great difficulty to ensure my candidate got precedence, and as a Romm you join a select group highly sought after in marriage contracts, but as the instigator of this treaty it is Lord Reacher Sormei's prerogative to accept you for his brother only if he so chooses."

"Surely he would need a good reason to refuse," Uvao said, earning a disdainful glance from his father.

"In theory, yes. In practice, he is the reacher and the head of the Sydelle family, so he can do whatever he likes. That makes this meeting critical. You must not only show an easy capability with our ways such that he doesn't question your credentials, but must also show that you would make Lord Kiren a good wife. If you cannot then Uvao will have failed me and I will move on with other plans."

With a nasty little click, his disinterest in my training suddenly made sense. This wasn't everything to him, just one iron in one fire, one way out of many he could gain enough power to challenge for the reachership. If I failed today, he would blame Uvao and move on unscathed. Only if I was accepted would I start to matter.

Awaiting no reply, Lord Romm turned and strode toward the open doors, leaving us to follow. Uvao went first, and I dared not risk so much as a glance his way, dared not let him see how utterly his father's words had chilled me to the bone.

I'd been inside a litter only a handful of times, always after a long night when walking another step had felt too hard and the coin worth it to be carried home. The litters down in the city were old and dusty with questionable smells, but Lord Romm's was like a diaphanous cake, all soft, pale cushions and layers of netting to keep out the flies. A muscular man made shiny with fly-repellent clove oil stood waiting at each of the four poles, while a fifth pulled back the netting to allow Lord Romm to step inside. Uvao followed, leaving me to climb in after them as gracefully as I could in my tight new garments.

No sooner had we all settled cross-legged in the small space than Lord Romm gave the order and we were on the move, swaying out through the manor's courtyard gardens and into the street. The layers of netting turned everything we passed to pale ghosts, every grand house, every shopfront and market, every garden and fountain. I took it all in, yet my curiosity was increasingly tainted with anger as I watched people in fine clothes walk around, talking and laughing without a care in the world. Here there might have been no Lummazzt attacks and no injured miners, no thwarted vote and no fear of unification, the lives of our Emoran elite nothing like the lives of everyday Learshapans. It wasn't new knowledge, yet it twisted uncomfortably in my stomach as I was carried from one manor to another, dressed in fine clothing and playing their game.

As we turned toward the open gates of the Sydelle family manor, I held Master Hoye's warning words close. *Don't let yourself get caught up in their games,* he had said. *Don't lose sight of who you really are. Who you will always be.*

"I won't," I whispered under my breath. "I promise."

Sydelle House was neither the largest nor the tallest manor in upper Learshapa, the original builders having sacrificed size to maintain a large private garden on all sides—a dense nest of flowering trees and vine-tangled arbours within a forbidding outer wall. Once through the gates, we wound along a twisting drive toward the half-hidden house, and Lord Romm broke his silence with a sniff. "This place always makes me want to sneeze," he said, before swinging a look of lazy amusement my way. "I hope you're ready to take on a reacher, my dear."

I murmured a reply—at least I thought I did—but all I could hear was the thundering of my heart.

Once the grand façade loomed over us, the litter carriers halted, lowering us to a mosaic-covered mounting stone, well hidden from the street we'd left behind. Another sniff, and Lord Romm stepped out, followed by Uvao, leaving me to make my legs work. I could do this, I could, I told myself, forcing myself out of the litter to join my companions in the shaded courtyard, but no sooner had I reached Uvao's side than I caught sight of the guards. Just like the men who had followed Reacher Sormei at Romm Manor, these wore thick scaleglass armour like dragonhides, but in addition to their heavy pistols, they also held long-barrelled and very deadly-looking rifles. Two stood on either side of the main entrance, four more visible inside, and a prickling sensation on the back of my neck made me wonder how many hid in the garden around us. I kept myself from turning to look and tried not to stare, tried to focus on the flowers embroidered on the back of Lord Romm's tunic to the exclusion of all deadly weapons.

"Ah, Lord Romm," a servant said, stepping out to greet us with a bored drawl. "Lord Reacher Sydelle is awaiting you within. If you would follow me."

More armed guards awaited us inside. Standing by doors and at the corner of every passage, they formed something of a reflective glass corridor through which we walked, allowing me to see nothing else as we passed. Whatever beauty the house might have owned, all I really saw was gun after gun after gun. Since Emorans were the only ones allowed to carry such weapons, they were rare sightings in Learshapa proper, and I was fast finding I preferred it that way.

At last the servant led us into a small sitting room open to an atrium on one side. The room had a homely feel, full of mismatched cushions and unorganised bookshelves—one of which owned a cat curled up in a bolt of sunlight—the whole nothing like Lord Romm's empty, austere halls.

"Lord Romm, Lord Uvao, and Lady Teshalii to see you, my

lord reacher," the servant said, his lack of grand formality leaving me little time to prepare myself.

From a long couch in the centre of the room, a figure rose, and I found myself staring at Lord Reacher Sormei Sydelle. And he stared right back, ignoring the superior claims of my companions' rank. The day I'd caught sight of him crossing the atrium with Lord Romm, I'd seen enough only to sense he wasn't what I'd expected; now I stood face-to-face with perfection. From his high cheekbones to his elegant, even features, Sormei Sydelle was a work of art shaped in flesh. Finely arched brows; intense, dark eyes; rounded lips; and enough muscle to make his trio of wrought armbands stretch—had we worshipped a god like the Lummazzt, such beauty could have inspired its form.

I knew I was staring and I ought not, yet dragging my gaze away was an effort. As though he could read my thoughts, an amused smile twitched the reacher's lips and he turned to greet Lord Romm with a nod. Waving away the offer of a formal greeting from Lord Romm, Reacher Sormei once again looked my way. "I will, however, accept a kiss from Lady Teshalii, given we have not met before."

He held out his hands, and in a daze I took them, lifting them to my lips one after the other. Firm grip, gentle peck—I tried to focus on what I needed to remember, but the scent of his skin had an intoxicating hint of spice. Yet when I stepped back and dared a glance up, his amused look had died, leaving behind a flicker of something darker—something hard and determined, there and gone, chilling me to the bone.

"There, now that we all know each other properly, we may sit down," he said, gesturing to the two couches across from his. "Ah, and here are the refreshments," he added as two servants entered carrying a large tray between them. "Some brandy, some of those sticky Learshapan cakes you all like so much, and I'm sure we'll all be firm friends."

His smile seemed genuine enough, though it didn't quite reach his eyes. Once the tray sat on the table between us, he picked a syrup cake up between thumb and forefinger and set it on a small glass plate with a filigree edge. There he left it and gestured to one of his guards. Wordlessly, the man left his post by the atrium arch to stride over, and silently taking a small fork from the tray, he cut a tiny wedge into the cake and lifted it to his own mouth.

"I hear your speech this morning was well received," Lord Romm said, ignoring this strange theatre and taking his own cake from the tray. "Much applause."

"Organised speeches given to the converted always go well," Reacher Sormei said while his guard slowly chewed the piece of cake. "It is the rest of Learshapa I must convince, it seems. But then, that's why we're here, isn't it."

I once again found his intent gaze upon me, a hint of something chilly beneath the beauty. "Tell me about yourself, Lady Teshalii. I believe I'm correct in saying we have not yet had the pleasure of your company in Emora for the season. I'm sure I would have remembered your face."

It felt ridiculous for him to compliment anyone else's appearance, but thankfully this was familiar ground. Uvao had made me practise telling my new life story dozens of times in different ways, always beginning with a grateful smile to show I knew it was kind of people to ask.

"There isn't much to tell," I said, while across the table the slowly masticating guard finally swallowed his mouthful. "As a younger son of a younger son, my papa was rather removed from the main family, and we spent most of our time travelling between Hylanii and Learshapa, working in the family interest. Until the marriage of first my cousin Ellbette, then Cousin Etta, made me the highest-ranked Romm woman in the family line." I gave a sweet little shrug I'd practised over and over. "Now here I am, first lady of house Romm. It has always been my dream, and I'm so proud to be able to represent my family."

Having eaten a piece of the reacher's cake and sipped from his brandy glass, the guard at last returned to his post, leaving Reacher Sormei smiling faintly at my well-rehearsed story. "How very dull and unremarkable a dream, Lady Teshalii," he said, pinching off a piece of cake and putting it in his own mouth. "You and every other lesser-ranked woman of a fine family. At least aspire to be the wife of a reacher's brother."

Lord Romm saved me from answering with a harsh laugh around his mouthful. "In that case why not the reacher himself? May as well think big when the reachership is far more precarious than being a family's first lady."

"Is it?"

The quiet question seemed to slice air and throats alike, so deep was the silence that ensued. I suppressed a shiver, gaze caught to the reacher's beautiful face as he went on eating his cake a pinch at a time.

Eventually, Lord Romm huffed a dry laugh. "We both suffered for that, and there it ended."

"And there it ended," Reacher Sormei repeated. "Until now."

Glancing from one to the other, I took a bite of my own cake to hide my confusion. At first it had seemed the reacher had taken Lord Romm's comment about precarity as a threat, but now I wasn't so sure. Every shred of warmth had fled the room, even the cat on the bookshelf jumped down and stalked off as though in search of a more comfortable space. It brushed past Reacher Sormei's couch on its way, earning a scratch behind its ears and a wry smile. "Sick of us already, Mitzy. Very understandable."

"Never been one for cats myself," Lord Romm said, taking a mouthful of brandy and deciding to act as though the previous conversation hadn't happened. "Can't say I even like the damn sunbirds, but they have been in the family for generations, so I'm stuck with them."

"Mmm, you see the beautiful thing about cats is that it's the other way around," the reacher said, watching Mitzy amble out into the atrium, heedless of his heavily armed guards. "They are stuck with you. Nothing humbles quite like a cat's disdain."

Freed from its earlier tension, the conversation slid into banal commonplaces, from discussions of their respective sand ships to the upcoming season in Emora. The reacher asked Uvao if he would be attending this year, which Lord Romm answered for him in the affirmative, leaving Uvao nothing to do but ask about some regatta and inspire a return to the detailed discussion of winds. It seemed a topic of great interest and might have gone on forever, but a light tap on the door heralded the return of the servant with the bored drawl. He strode without a word to the reacher's couch and, heedless of the conversation, bent to whisper in Reacher Sormei's ear, causing the beautiful man's heavily slit brows first to dip, then lift in genuine surprise.

"Truly?" he said, turning to face the servant as he straightened.

"Truly, my lord reacher."

"What peculiar timing. I feel the divine song is playing a jest on us." With that, he fixed his intent stare on Lord Romm. "News you will likely have waiting for you when you return home, Romm, but you may as well hear it from me. It seems Ashadi's dragon got shot down over The Sands yesterday."

A beat of silent horror, before Lord Romm erupted from his chair. "What?"

The crack of emotion in the desperate word was the first sign of humanity I'd seen him display, and I hated him slightly less for it. Reacher Sormei, however, seemed to find it amusing.

"Calm yourself," he said, eyes crinkling with laughter. "He is quite unharmed. Were there any more details, Grim?" he added, glancing up at his servant.

"Only that they are unsure who shot him, but that the bullet went through the middle of one of his dragon's scales."

Again, Reacher Sormei's brows rose in faint surprise—a far

calmer reaction than the information warranted. "Through the middle of a scale?" I said, looking from the stoic servant to the reacher and back. "But that cannot be right. Unless it is made much too thin, scaleglass is strong enough to withstand a bullet even at close range—else you would not attire all your guards in glass from head to toe. There must be some mistake."

As the last words spilled indignantly from my lips, I realised I'd said far more than I ought, and for the third time, Reacher Sormei stared silently at me as though he could see right into my head. "You are, of course, very correct, Lady Teshalii," he said at last. "It is a very curious piece of news, is it not. What explanation can there be, do you think?"

"Oh, I...I am hardly an expert, my lord reacher, I have always just found dragons so fascinating. Natural scaleglass is so rare, after all."

"Then you think someone is lying?"

"No! Of course not, but perhaps mistaken. Maybe a bullet chipped the edge of a scale, or hit a scale that wasn't sitting flat."

His eyelids sank lower, his smile all lazy mockery. "And if they are not mistaken, Lady Teshalii, how do you think it might have been achieved?"

I forced out a laugh in the hope his question was a joke, only for him to go on staring, awaiting my answer. The problem was one of hardness and density and the crystalline formation of glass—all things I was meant to know nothing about. But I'd already proved I did. "Short of inventing something harder than scaleglass, Lord Reacher, I couldn't say. Even close up, a dragon's scales are impenetrable. Was their impossible armour not what made them such formidable foes for our ancestors?"

I was proud of that one, proud of how easily the Emoran point of view had found its way to my tongue.

Reacher Sormei clapped his hands, amusement not leaving his eyes. "She has opinions *and* she knows her history. What a gem you have kept hidden from us all, Lord Romm. But you are right, Lady Teshalii, it is certainly troubling and something I will have to look into. Attacks against the Shield have increased dramatically these last few weeks, which was bad enough without monsters learning to use firearms and inventing something harder than scaleglass. We are, it seems, under attack from every direction."

His words brought on a moment of silence, and I realised Lord Romm hadn't spoken since confirming the news about his son. Reacher Sormei must have noticed too, for his gaze slid in Lord Romm's direction. "Perhaps it is time for us to adjourn to my office for further negotiations. If this contract is to go ahead you and I have a lot of terms to discuss and agree upon."

"The council's treaty—" Lord Romm began.

"The council's treaty is what it is," the reacher interrupted with a sleek smile, more tiger than housecat. "We must, of course, also come to our own terms." He rose on the words, abandoning the uneaten half of his cake. "It was a pleasure to meet you, Lady Teshalii, and to see you again, Lord Uvao, but you must excuse us now. Grim will see you out."

The bored servant hadn't left his master's side since bringing the news from the Shield, but he stepped back at this, gesturing for us to go before him out of the room. For all the formal farewells I'd been made to practise, Reacher Sormei wanted none of them. Without so much as a second glance our way, he strode off like we had ceased existing the moment he didn't need us, leaving Uvao and I nothing to do but walk out as quickly as we dared.

Once back in the litter, I let go a shuddering breath, but kept my mouth shut until we were safely back in the bustling street. "He knows," I said, finally able to give voice to the fear quaking through me. "He knows, I'm sure of it."

"Nonsense, he wouldn't have sought further negotiations if he thought there was anything suspicious going on. Trying to wring every concession and coin he can out of my father in the process. Likely he'll get it too, and we'll have to put up with the resulting fury when father gets home."

His confidence eased some of my fear. Of course it wasn't in Reacher Sormei's interest to go ahead with a marriage treaty that would end poorly for him; I just couldn't quite let go of the worry the man knew a lot more than he ever said aloud.

"What did you think of him?" Uvao asked abruptly as the carriers wound their way through the baking streets.

"Think of—oh, Reacher Sormei?" I brought my attention back from the small room filled with warmth and life and enough ammunition to kill everyone in sight. "He was not what I expected."

Uvao huffed a laugh. "No, I imagine he strikes a lot of people like that and works hard to ensure it stays that way. Expect a monster, get a pretty face, and people are thrown off balance every time."

I kept a grimace to myself, his description exactly how I had felt.

"You did well," Uvao added when I didn't speak. "I thought you might have ruined it with the scaleglass, but it's not such an odd thing for an Emoran noble to know, and you saved it with the comment about our history. He seemed quite taken with you."

His final words turned bitter, and he punctuated them with a laugh that seemed to mock himself more than the reacher. "Thank you," I said, unsure what else to say, every thought a tangle in the wake of having time so suddenly cut from beneath me. If all went to plan, I would be married by the end of the week.

"You play the part well," he went on, sliding his hand onto my knee. "I couldn't keep my eyes off you."

Despite my tangled thoughts, I was suddenly all too aware of his proximity, of the warmth of his skin and the faint scent of panawood that always hung about him. Beyond the layers of pale netting, people were going about their afternoon unaware of how easily he could shift heat about my body with nothing but a few words. A look. A touch. His hand felt heavy on my knee, hot even through the many layers of my fine skirts—skirts I suddenly wished elsewhere despite the risk.

Too great a risk.

I shook my head in an attempt to clear it. "Do you think they'll come to terms?" I said, as much to say something as to voice the lingering fear that Reacher Sormei knew the truth. "Do you think it'll go ahead?"

"Do you want it to?" He stared at me, the darkness in his eyes at odds with the searing sunshine.

"Of course I do. That's what all of this has been about."

"Has it?"

His hand didn't shift from my knee as he leaned closer. "Has it?" I repeated, hoping the words sounded breathless only to me. "Uvao, this is what you've been training me for, and if it falls through now your father will blame you and—"

"Let him. I don't care."

I could not hold his intent gaze and looked away. "Yes, you do. This is your world. Your people. Your life."

"Because I was born to it? Does that mean I can never change? Never want something different? I'd have given it all up for you."

The words whispered past my cheek, hollowing my stomach with a deep sense of loss. How quick I had been to reject him when I'd found out the truth, how focused on my own reaction that I'd not considered other possibilities. Not given him space to make up his own mind.

"I'm sorry," I whispered back, our lips barely a breath apart. "I—"

He pressed his lips to mine, tentative, gentle, unsure for a heartbeat before he leaned close, pressing me into the cushions and devouring me whole. He was all heat and I was all need, and for a moment there was no litter, no carriers, no upper city streets, no

Reacher Sormei and his cold, beautiful eyes, just Uvao's body and mine and a desire for more hands than I possessed. Until with a little bump, our litter stopped moving. Back outside Romm Manor.

With a gasp I pulled away, lips wet, body hot, a mere moment before hurried footsteps approached from inside the house. "Lord Uvao," someone said in agitated tones. "Lord Uvao!"

"What?" he snapped, dragging his gaze from me like it weighed the world.

"My lord," the servant said, lifting the netting for him to alight. "My apologies, but there is a man here with a delivery. Unfortunately, he is refusing to leave...Whatever it is that he has brought he won't leave in any hands but yours and will not be dissuaded."

"What?" Uvao said again, more confused this time as he stepped out, leaving me a moment to catch my breath, to tuck each lustful want away where it couldn't be seen or guessed or even desired.

The servant went on holding the netting open for me, and I would have made him wait, had not a familiar and unexpected voice jolted the last of the heat from my body. "You know me, not one to be put off by arseholes looking down their noses at me."

"Sorscha?" I all but leapt out of the litter, ignoring the servant's disdainful glance as I hurried inside in Uvao's wake. "Sorscha, it is you!"

He stood leaning at ease in the entry hall with a parcel under one arm, heedless of the large number of servants who seemed to have gathered merely to keep an eye on him. Uvao sent them on their way with scowls and snaps—an anger that didn't dissipate as he led the way inside leaving Sorscha and I to follow.

"Why'd you come?" Uvao asked, breaking his silence only once we'd reached the relative safety of a small sitting room. "Given your many and varied lines of work it's not exactly safe for you to be here."

"I know," Sorscha said, dropping onto one of the narrow couches, the parcel on his lap. "Which is why I expect immense gratitude for my sacrifice."

Uvao rolled his eyes. "Naturally." He held out his hand. "Well, what is this special delivery then?"

With a click of his tongue, Sorscha pulled it away from him. "Not for you, Uv, forgive my lies. I didn't think they'd let me wait around with it if I'd told the truth. It's for Tesh."

"For me? But..."

"Now, before you thank me, I want you to know I didn't take this risk for you," he said, sliding the parcel toward me. "I did it for Master Hoye."

At my master's name, my gaze snapped up, meeting Sorscha's across the small table. Across the square, box-shaped parcel he'd set between us. And the answer to my unspoken question was there in Sorscha's eyes.

"That's mean even by your standards, Sorscha," Uvao chided him, unaware of the communication that had passed between us.

For a heartbeat longer, Sorscha held my gaze meaningfully, before turning away with an easy smile. "Isn't it just? Don't worry, Uv, Tesha and I get along better when we're being mean to each other, don't we, Tesh?"

"Wouldn't have it any other way," I managed brightly, forcing myself to look up from the box. "But even though you didn't do it for me, I'll thank you for bringing this all the same. Master Hoye said he was going to gather some of my things and send them along for me to remember home by. I'll go put them somewhere safe and leave you to your boy talk."

I swept up the parcel as I spoke, grinned at their twin outbursts—"Boy talk!"—and hurried away to the safety of my room. There, I locked the door behind me and set the parcel on the bed, where it sat like an innocent gift. Despite my shaking hands, I made quick work of the knotted string and tore off the double layer of paper, exposing a familiar pattern of woodwork. It really was Master Hoye's box—the box that came out only when Sorscha brought in illegal jobs. Now it was sitting on my bed.

The sight of it squeezed my heart tight, and my hands shook all the more as I flicked open the small latch and lifted the lid. Inside sat dozens of tiny bottles, each with an engraved glass stopper that glinted gold in the sunlight. They all had their own little space in which to nestle, protected by a furry woollen lining, and lying atop one side, a letter.

Tesha. You talked and I didn't listen. I'd hoped I'd left all this behind me, that I didn't need to fight for anything in Learshapa, but I was wrong because I was afraid. If we do not fight for everything while we still have it, we'll only have to fight to get it back. I can't come with you. I'm too old, too tired, too scared, but I can give you what you need. Take care with this; the power you wield with it is stronger than you can imagine. The suffering you don't see, you don't mind.

Remember there is always a home here for you if you want it.

Wiping damp eyes on my sleeve, I folded the letter tightly and tucked it down the side of the box. The first bottle I took out was a finely made little thing, its glass perfectly clear though that did nothing to help me identify the contents—some dozen or so pale yellow balls the size of peppercorns, but slightly dusty. It had no label, nor did the second one—a shimmering grey powder that looked as soft as ashes. None of them seemed to be labelled, but none of the bottles were quite the same either—possessing slight variations that might not have been noticeable to those who hadn't studied and worked with glass. There had to be more though, had to be something to identify them, or Master Hoye wouldn't have given it to me, and so I searched. I took out each stoppered vial and bottle and set them in lines on the floor, checked underneath the compartments, the underside of the lid and the sides of the box. It was the base that eventually slid out, able to be unhooked and pulled loose. One side was the box's exterior, but the other was covered in markings and notes and names and doses, and for a time all I could do was stare at it, hardly remembering to breathe.

It was almost dark by the time I packed it all away. Almost dark before the news came to my door on Biiella's hasty steps that Lord Romm and Reacher Sormei had come to an agreement. The wedding was going ahead. In three days, I would be married to Reacher Sormei's brother. In three days, I would leave Learshapa.

But now I was going to Emora with a box of poisons.

7

Naili

Morning Bulletin

To all criers for announcement throughout Bakii

End of separation! The city-state of Learshapa has at last agreed to join the Celessi alliance under Reacher Sormei, unifying the basin for the first time in centuries. A unified basin will allow us to stand against Lummazza's ongoing intrusion into Bakiian territory.

Raids ongoing at local scale mines, as three people have been saved from a Lummazzt slave caravan after being tracked down by concerned family members. Talks with Lummazza's new ambassador stall.

Fierce protests continue today as fourteen more people have been confirmed missing. Elle Taan, Horjyon Bell, Impira Mylii, Ettala Piit, Vel Kiivi...

The smell of burned bread filled the kitchen, yet still the stink of mould lined the inside of my nose. I hadn't slept and had only nibbled at my breakfast, gaze darting always to the door in the hope Chaintho would walk in. She didn't. Miizhei grumbled about the workload, and Alii fretted that Chaintho's illness might be infectious. The urge to tell them what I had seen lasted a mere instant before I tucked so perilous a thought back down where it belonged. What I'd seen—what I'd done—was wrong, and wrong didn't last long in Bakii. Wrong was dangerous, and danger buckled all degrees of loyalty. I'd lived long enough to know that if push came to shove, people shoved.

All too soon the matron swept in amid her cloud of pungent vanilla and clapped her hands, making me jump. "Get moving," she snapped, barely halting in her stride toward the laundry. "Nothing gets washed by wasting time."

First thing in the morning was the only time you could see the entire laundry end to end, from the sorting tables and mending stations through to the largest boilers near the drying yard. Yeloria was on drying duty today, while I had been shunted across the room to work with Miizhei, tending not only her main boiler but also the endlessly foul soaker tub two.

"Nai! Look where you're going!" Miizhei stepped out of my way, scowling over an armload of laundry. "I'd rather get this in the tub than on your head."

I murmured an apology, and she clicked her tongue irritably. The laundry landed in the tub with more splash than usual.

"I hope you're not going to have your head in the clouds all day," Miizhei said as she went back for the rest. "There's already too much work."

I mumbled a second apology and picked up the paddle. I needed to focus, or Miizhei would chew me up and spit me out before ever I incurred the matron's ire.

Thankfully, Miizhei had a steady rhythm to the way she

worked and tended to fill every moment with talk, her knowledge and interests broader than anyone else's I'd ever met. She'd even been taught to read, though how and why she had never said.

"Did you hear about Learshapa?" she said, drawing me into her rhythmic talk.

"No, what happened?"

"They've finally been forced to join the rest of us. A unified Celes Basin, they're calling it, if you can believe that."

Unified was a fanciful word for even just the relationship between Emora and Bakii, let alone the addition of the radical remnants of Learshapa, but it was her choice of words that gave me pause. "Forced? I didn't miss a war, did I?"

"No! At least not a real one. But Reacher Sormei isn't the kind of man who asks nicely. Gets things done whatever it takes, that one." Her eyes sparkled in mocking laughter. "I know you can't read, but that's why the criers shout the news, right?"

"Yes, but getting shouted at by criers means having to step outside, and I would rather not risk it just now."

Miizhei agreed with a disgusted grunt. "It gets worse by the day out there. Those foul monsters are getting away with snatching people from their homes just because the seigneurs don't care. You can be sure the moment some ambitious black-eye takes someone rich then there will be trouble."

"You really think the Lummazzt would go that far? Incursions into Bakii already seem extreme for a people who don't like to leave their homeland."

"We call them monsters for a reason. They'll take the whole basin if we let them, then this will be their homeland too."

"You're even more cynical than—"

"Shh!" Miizhei hissed, and I pinched my lips closed as Alii came floating past, carrying a small armful of laundry. Weaving through the steam, she drew close, slowing her steps and smiling at us as she passed. I possessed no smile to return, while Miizhei had eyes only for the boiler in front of her. For a moment that seemed to stretch into uncomfortable eternity I stood pulled taut between them, until at last Alii's slow progress took her out of sight.

I spun on Miizhei. "You don't trust her either?"

"Not for a second." Miizhei shrugged one bony shoulder and dumped a few scoops of lye into the boiler. "She's been asking too many questions."

"What sort of questions?"

"The sort of questions that are suspicious when you can amble about the laundry without getting screeched at by Matron. What's your reason?"

I had many little reasons, but they'd all come from one big reason, and though I knew Miizhei would roll her eyes, I said, "Because she smells wrong."

As expected, Miizhei rolled her eyes. "Really, Nai?"

"Really." I kept stirring, pushing the clumps of wet laundry beneath the steaming surface. "Like an oily short-haired cat sitting in the sun."

"Now I know you're just being ridiculous." Miizhei returned the lye bucket to its stand. "How much longer do you think this has?"

I looked down into the boiler but saw no water or laundry, no steam or lye or glass, only the face of the man who'd long ago convinced my mother she had to part with her tiny savings or the Hoods would take her children. He'd smelled just the same. Although now that the Hoods' control over the lower city tightened year by year and people kept disappearing, perhaps he'd been right.

Thankfully, in Miizhei's company, the rest of the morning disappeared in steam and chatter, the call for break upon us before my arms had even begun to tire. Sesame slab awaited us once more in the dining hall, the mango plopped atop even darker than the day before. Amid the grumbles, I slipped away into the narrow passages, the need to check Chaintho's room once more overriding any hunger.

With lunch served, no one else was in the far passages, and I made it to my own door without being seen. From there it was only a short distance and many nervous glances to Chaintho's. My heart hammered all the way, leaving me lightheaded as I once again knocked upon the thin wood. "Chaintho?" I said, and closed my eyes, silently pleading for a reply. None came. "Chaintho?" I pressed down on the handle, but this time the door didn't open. The wood bowed as I tried again to no avail. Our rooms didn't have locks, yet a shiny brass keyhole now sat below the handle, its glint a wicked smile. I touched it to be sure it was real, its smooth metal cool.

A glance around proved I was still alone in the passage, and that no other doors had locks. I was running out of time, yet I crouched to peer through the keyhole. Gloom peered back, musty and smothering. The gap at the bottom of the door was little better, but as I rose from hands and knees, something soft tickled my cheek. A small hank of hair had caught on the bottom of the door-frame—dark hair covered in pale dust. No, not dust. Dozens upon dozens of tiny white flowers were growing on the hairs, each dark thread a stem full of life. A faint aroma of sand roses hung in the humid air.

A shiver spread through my skin, my own hairs standing proud. This was wrong. It was all wrong. I stepped back, bumping into the opposite door. It rattled, bowing in its frame, while on the floor, Chaintho's hair shifted in the breeze my movement made.

"No," I whispered, and slid along the wall, not taking my eyes off the hair. "No."

Forcing myself to turn and walk away, my first thought was to tell Miizhei when I got back to the laundry—a thought that slowly died upon the chalky taste of mould creeping onto my tongue and the fear she wouldn't believe me.

By the time I reached the laundry, my panic had dissipated enough that I was convinced I'd imagined the whole. I found Miizhei full of complaints, some about how sesame hulls always got stuck between her teeth, but most about soaker tub two. It sat by the far wall, its soaking water innocently uninviting.

"If Chaintho isn't back tomorrow, I swear I will make her drink that stuff until she really *is* unwell," Miiz huffed, already wiping sweat and steam from her brow as she dunked the paddle back in the boiler.

"You don't think she's actually unwell?" I said, watching her out of the corner of my eye.

"Oh no, I'm sure she has run away." Miizhei jutted out a hip and scowled. "If she was sick we would still have seen her."

"You'd think she would tell someone she was leaving though."

Miizhei stared at me through the roiling steam. "And risk someone snitching to the matron for better treatment? Wise that she didn't."

She was right, and yet doubt scratched at my thoughts. Telling anyone about Chaintho's room or Chaintho's hair, or about the plant I'd grown with a touch was dangerous, yet was silence truly any safer?

The previous day I'd tried not to think about it, tried to keep myself busy, but now I could think of nothing else no matter how hard I worked. We boiled and stirred and scrubbed, we measured out lye and brighthorn, and Miizhei chatted away all the while, not a word making it past my ears. Whenever I tried to drag my mind to something else, it would creep back to that locked door in a passage of unlocked doors. The keys in Mistress Paiwe's cabinet might not have opened every door in the city, but they would open one—one she had locked so no one could see within. Such had Chaintho's silence earned her.

When it came time to swap the soaking load, I stared into the soup that was soaker tub two. It looked the same as it had that morning and the day before, yet its green hue had taken on a sinister tinge. The taste of mould crept back onto my tongue.

Miizhei took up the scoop with a sigh. "You watch the boiler, I'll get this done."

The taste of mould that seemed part of me now.

"No, here." I took the scoop from Miizhei's hands. "I'll do it. May as well have only one of us stinking like bog."

She eyed me a moment, brows drawn close, but she let the scoop go with a shrug. "It's not like I'm going to fight you for it."

Miiz returned to the boiler, her gaze a heavy weight upon my back as I gingerly lowered the scoop into the greenish water of soaker tub two—water that was starting to take on the guise of an evil spectre in my mind. It was childish. As nonsensical as all the strange things I thought I'd seen.

Telling myself for the hundredth time that I had imagined it all, I pulled out the first scoop and let it slop into the waiting basket. Small items once again slid through the holes, escaping back into the water before I could free them. Half a dozen scoops got as much of the load as I was ever going to without using my hands, after which I set the scoop down. At our boiler, Miizhei's ghostly outline stood still as though watching me. The room was full of its usual chatter and clanging, shouts and footsteps and gushing water, yet it all sounded far away, muted by a buzzing in my ears.

I slid my hands into the soaking water, trying not to breathe. The same small cloths and mismatched pairs of gloves wallowed at the bottom of the tub, darting away like frightened fish as I tried to grab them. The trick was to move slowly, not to create a current, but that meant keeping my hands in the tub longer. They were already tingling, like my skin wanted to crawl away, stripping my bones.

One handful. Two. I had to breathe deeply despite the smell

to keep panic from overflowing as I felt around for the last strag-
glers. At last, having gathered them up, I straightened, dropping
two gloves into the basket atop the rest. The breath I released
trembled.

"You all right, Nai?" Miizhei stood watching, arms crossed,
paddle still in hand. She scowled because she always scowled,
but no matter how much genuine care or worry might have lain
beneath it, I nodded.

"I'm fine," I said. "Except for once again being soaked through
with this piss water."

"You had better change. I'll tell the matron we need a new
scoop here, unless she wants us all smelling of piss water."

"I don't have a fresh change after yesterday, and she won't let
me take a second break. It's fine, I'm sure it'll dry off soon."

Miizhei chewed her bottom lip, still glaring at me. At last, she
released her crossed arms and swung the paddle back into its place
against the boiler. "Then don't ask her. Go get a fresh uniform
from my room, and I'll keep her busy by demanding a new scoop."

"But—"

"Just go, Naili. I don't want to work with a bog monster for
the rest of the day. You stink."

I went, cheeks burning. My uniform stuck to me, the shape-
less tunic beneath my apron sucking close to my skin as I hurried out—out of the laundry and into the humid underground
passages, walking a path I knew so well I could have walked it
with my eyes closed. And I wanted to close them, wanted to
cease existing for one blissful moment of peace. But there were
no moments of peace beneath the matron's rule. She could come
after me at any moment.

Miizhei's room wasn't as far to walk as mine, and I was soon
pulling a fresh uniform from her jumbled shelves. Balled-up
clothes sat next to books and trinkets, sketches of people I'd never
met, and long-emptied bottles of huren wine.

Checking only that the door was closed, I dropped my wet apron to the floor and peeled my tunic up over my head. My shift was wet too, and I pulled it off with a shiver, half cold, half supressed disgust, and let it fall, tangled, atop of the rest. I rubbed my bare forearms, chill with the damp. My hairs stood on end and my skin was pimpling, yet my hands sloughed off dust rather than imbuing warmth. The dust left a white powder on my hands and the scent of jasmine in the air, faint but cloying. I hadn't smelled anything like it since moving into the city proper, since I'd last seen my mother's tumbledown cottage held up by love and a tangled nest of jasmine vines.

Jasmine. My stomach lurched in fearful certainty, and I peered at the dust to find it wasn't dust at all. It was hundreds of tiny white flowers. With a strangled cry, I brushed them off on my damp skirt, a shudder rippling through me.

"No, no," I whispered as though in prayer as I looked from arm to arm. Tiny flowers bloomed on my hairs, each short strand home to many. Heart thumping in my throat, I bent to see my legs, and my stomach lurched. They were everywhere. "Just dust," I said, rubbing them all off and knowing my words for a lie. "Just dust; you are not turning into a plant, Naili Billette, because that's ridiculous."

I pulled Miizhei's clean tunic on so fast it almost tore. I needed to move, to do something, anything, so long as it wasn't standing there thinking about Chaintho's hairs caught in the door-frame and that swampy green soaking water. Whatever Master Occuello had been doing upstairs, his experiments had made it downstairs and into that tub. Into Chaintho. Into me. He had changed my body, was twisting my spirit, turning me into something I didn't understand.

I slammed Miizhei's door as I left, breathing so fast I was sure to be sick. No questions were to be asked, that was the matron's rule. No questions. Because we were the lucky ones and we wanted to stay lucky, to keep the roof over our heads and the food in our stomachs. No, I could not risk questions or complaints down here and would get no answers if I did. But silence hadn't helped Chaintho and it wouldn't help me. If only to warn others, I had to speak.

From beyond the still-room door came voices like scratchy whispers. I'd stood there at least a week, surely, a month even, an eternity, courage guttering. I knew what I needed to do, what I ought to do, yet knowing and doing aren't the same, and so my feet remained planted—ha!—upon the ground.

"Where's Naili?" I couldn't tell who voiced the question, but it ought to have acted as a spur to my hesitation, providing the perfect moment in which to step in and proclaim grandly that I was present, that I existed, but how could I claim as much when I wasn't sure myself that I did? Perhaps I was merely a dream. Or perhaps that was just wishful thinking for how much easier that would be.

I needed to open the door. To walk in. To speak the words that had spun over and over in my mind grinding a groove inside my skull. There is something wrong with me. Is there something wrong with you too?

My hand shook as I gripped the handle, and with a burst of force, I thrust the door open and stepped inside. Yenni glanced up, words faltering on her lips. Ambere turned too, breaking off conversation with Miizhei, until one by one all six of the laundresses who'd chosen to help me sat staring. For a moment we might have been frozen, sealed in glass for an eternity, until with a twitch of one shoulder and a haunted look, Miizhei turned away. Heszia gripped her hands tight in her lap. Yenni seemed not even to breathe.

"You know," I said to all of them, fear and relief warring in my chest. "You've seen them too. The flowers." I drew up my long-sleeved tunic, baring my arm with its pale dusting of jasmine blooms, to the still-room's oily light. "All of you?"

Yeloria unfroze first, turning to look at the others, before drawing up her own sleeve with shaking fingers. A puff of pink dust emerged as the cuff dragged up her arm, leaving behind blotchy pink patches on her skin.

"They started on my arms," she said, her voice the barest whisper. "But they've spread. I've been...rubbing them off the back of my neck for days."

Heszia slid from her stool to her feet, a half-step forward ending in a cracked sob. "Mine...mine isn't flowers. I thought...I thought I was losing my mind." She hoisted the hem of her tunic to reveal the side of her belly, where smooth skin gave way to a patch of moss, all brilliant green life growing as though from damp earth. Scratches cut across both flesh and moss, and Heszia averted her gaze. "What is wrong with me?"

Her plea broke the dam, both Ambere and Yenni wrapping their arms around her and rolling up their own sleeves, while Yeloria shuffled toward me, tears streaming. Her embrace was so tight it constricted my lungs for a moment, before she let me go in a cloud of rose scent. Amid the hubbub of relief, Miizhei sat unmoving. I met her gaze over Yeloria's shoulder, my silent question earning a humourless smile and one of her single-shouldered shrugs.

"Of course me too," she said. "But I will not be joining in your weeping. I refuse to be anything but angry."

"You think it's from the laundry?"

"Oh, I know it's from the laundry." Miiz crossed her arms tight. "I've heard no whispers from elsewhere in the house, and you know I hear everything."

With the tears had come tales of how each of them had discovered their affliction, a collective babble that healed what it could not illuminate, but at Miizhei's words the others grew quiet. For a time, no one spoke, and the enormity of our situation crept upon me, casting a long, cold shadow in which I shivered.

"I don't think Chaintho left," I whispered. "I found some of her hairs with desert roses growing on them, and her room... there's a lock now. On the door. So, they must know something is wrong, the matron and Mistress Paiwe at least, and..."

"And they don't care," Yenni finished, her face still flushed.

"Of course they don't care," Miizhei said. "That cannot surprise you. They're already replacing us as fast as they can with machines, and there are thousands of people in this city without work who would happily take our places, danger or no, should we abruptly drop dead."

"Do you think..." Yenni began only to falter. "Do you think Rizzi left or..."

The question remained hanging—a question none of us could answer with anything but the doubt weighing heavy in our guts. How long had this been happening?

"Yen," Ambere said, gripping the woman's arm. "If this...if this killed Rizzi and Chaintho, then...that could happen to any of us at any moment. Are we all going to die?"

I wanted to reassure her, to ease the fear in those wide, youthful eyes, but what could I say that wasn't lies? Speculation was as little comfort as silence.

The knowledge that my body could turn to dross at any moment, possibly without any warning, made every inch of my skin tingle. But standing in the middle of our fearful huddle, Miizhei folded her arms, a gesture comforting for both its familiarity and its refusal to brook nonsense. "Let's not get too ahead of ourselves," she said. "There might have been something else that predisposed Chaintho and Rizzi to such an end. I assume I'm not the only one who is doing more than just growing unwanted flowers on my skin."

As she spoke, she reached out to a nearby seedling. I held my breath, waiting to see her grow the plant as I had grown the limachai in the alleyway, but at a touch little more than the brush of her fingertip, the seedling wilted. Green to black and shrivelled in a blink. No growth, no mould or putrescence, just dead.

"Miiz," I breathed. "That's..."

"Terrifying," Yeloria finished, seeming to step back even though she didn't move. "I...I can't do anything like that."

"Neither can I," Yenni said, glancing around at the rest of us.

A glimpse of something all too like terror flickered across Miizhei's sharp features, the look she threw my way full of a desperation I'd never seen before.

"I can," I said, taking up her plea. "Just...the other way around. Yen, give me the other seedling."

Not glancing at Miizhei, Yenni reached past her for the second seedling on the narrow bench and held it out to me.

The weight of their gazes made my heart beat fast, made doubts creep into the edge of my vision like gathering darkness, but I set my finger to the seedling stem before fear could change my mind. Once again the hum of life spread through me like a vibrating heartbeat outside of my skin, and the seedling started to grow, stem swelling first before it shot upward, unfurling leaves as it went. Gasps sounded around me, and I yanked my hand clear before the plant grew too big.

As I handed the much heavier pot back to Yenni, its plant now large and drooping, the still-room door opened.

"Evening, girls," came Kit's voice followed by the scuff of steps that never seemed to lift far off the floor. "Oh, what is it? What has happened?" I turned to find her paused halfway across the floor, hair spilling from a bun and dark-rimmed eyes more alert than usual. "Is it about Alii?"

"Alii?" Miiz said, the question breaking us from our collective shock. "What about her?"

"Oh, I just passed her in the passage. She seemed annoyed about something, so I thought maybe she'd asked about helping out and been turned down. I was going to ask why since we need as much help as we can get. More requests came in this evening, you'll hate to know."

Her words met silence, and she looked from one of us to the next around the group. "Is...is everything all right?"

No one answered. Kit was one of us, but she also wasn't one of us. As Mistress Paiwe's secretary, she'd never had to stick her hands in a laundry boiler or suffer the matron's prods and demands.

"Something has...gone wrong, Kit," Heszia said, finally breaking the silence.

"What do you mean?"

Heszia didn't answer with words, instead sticking her finger into the base of the plant Miizhei had killed at a touch. Around her implanted finger, the soil seemed to bubble like the surface of a boiler, before pale globes pushed through the dirt, each the head of a mushroom blooming into the oily light.

"What the fuck?" Kit cried, the curse word at odds with her always tousled yet proper appearance. "How did you do that?"

The initial hubbub returned, the need to exorcise our souls of our secrets, to share our pains, stronger than I'd thought possible. Together we were not freaks. Together we were not broken. Sleeves were pulled up and skin bared, dozens of tiny little flowers of all sorts dancing before Kit's eyes as she stared at each of us, peppering the air with half-formed questions. Eventually she managed a full one. "You really think the laundry water did this to you?"

However ridiculous it might have sounded, it was the only explanation, and the alchemist the only possible source.

"What else could it be?" I said. "What else connects us all, and Chaintho?"

"But..." Kit said, more frazzled than ever as she looked, pained, at each of us. "Have you told the matron?"

"No," I said.

"And we won't," Miizhei added.

"But... what about Mistress Pai—"

"No." Miiz's vehement reply was clipped short by the closing of her thin lips, and she looked away, leaving me to describe what I'd seen in Chaintho's room. About the dross and the hair and the locked door. By the end, Kit had paled and her fingers were knotting about each other in agitation.

"So you think they know? And it could happen to any of you at any time?" Kit shook her head. "I don't believe this. I don't want to." Upon a sudden thought, she drew up her own sleeves and began inspecting each arm. "Can you see anything on me?"

While the others looked her over, Miizhei drew close to me. "Life and death we are then, huh?" she said in a low murmur. "Can't say I'm thrilled about being the dark to your light, Nai."

"I'm sorry. Is it just...?"

I couldn't finish the question, trying to recall the last time she'd touched me.

Miiz pressed a wry grimace flat between her thin lips. "Just plants? Seems to be. Once I noticed, I asked others to get the herbs I needed, and tested the death touch thing on the matron. Might have been nice if it had worked."

I gripped her arm and laughed, though it would have been better described as a snort. "Miiz!" I cried, my amusement causing crinkles to appear at the corners of her eyes.

"You disagree?" she said, heedless of the glances thrown our way.

"Not at all! I'm just... just imagining you standing over her, all innocent, like... 'I just found her all shrivelled like that, I swear.'"

That set her off, and for a whole minute neither of us could stop laughing. It felt good to laugh, clutching at one another for support as tears trickled down our cheeks and our stomach muscles ached, more joy in that moment than we'd had in any before the alchemist had cursed us with his experiments.

When at last we caught our breath, we found the others waiting impatiently, stares deadly serious.

"Oh no." Miizhei giggled as we came out of the clouds. "Reality is back."

"We were saying," Yeloria said rather sternly, "that perhaps we ought to go straight to Master Occuello, since it seems unlikely the matron or Mistress Paiwe can do anything about this."

Still clutching Miizhei's arm, I hit the ground with a thud. "Go to Master Occuello? They won't let us into that part of the house."

"No, but one of us could sneak up there when they aren't looking. Late one evening, perhaps, after everyone has gone."

I realised they were staring at us with the intensity of people awaiting a reply to a question that hadn't yet been asked. A question they didn't want to voice.

"You think one of us should go," I said.

Yenni looked at her feet. The others at their hands. "You're the only ones without anyone relying on you."

The final piece of the puzzle fell into place, and I let go of Miizhei's arm, all desire to laugh having fled. They all had family they sent money to, people dependent on them for their survival. Miiz and I had no one who needed us. No one who would suffer if something went wrong.

"That annual dinner for the guild types is on later in the week," Kit said to break the silence. "Master Occuello is sure to attend, and since he doesn't go out much, it's a good time to sneak upstairs and lie in wait for him."

It was both a brilliant idea and a terrible one—perhaps the very reason I felt drawn to it. To its wildness and its possibility, and to the chance of standing face-to-face with the man who had done this to us and demanding answers.

Miizhei said nothing, just scowled as was her way. She wasn't the gentle, protective type, sure to sacrifice herself for the betterment of her friends, whether because such was her nature or because all sentimentality had been crushed by her fall into Bakii's underbelly. Not that it mattered, I realised. I wasn't going to let her go anyway.

"I'll do it," I said.

The clang of the bell always marked day's end. Outside in the real world, the sound would fill Bakii's old, winding streets with people, veils drawn against evening bites, but in the world of Master Occuello's laundry, it said, *It's time.*

While the other laundresses hurried out, I hung back to check I'd taken all my baskets in for sorting and properly stowed the stirring paddles. Miizhei was first out of the room, a glance all I got for good luck as she went about her task—distraction and watching the only two roles that could make my mission easier. Yeloria lingered longest, rubbing the back of her neck and nodding to me, but there was little to say that hadn't been said. We'd commiserated and then we'd planned, refusing silence.

The sounds of dinner came to me as I stepped out of the laundry, all distant clinks and scrapes and the muffled murmur of weary conversation. The urge to join them instead of risking everything was strong, but I'd chosen the harder road of caring and I wouldn't risk our fragile new solidarity by failing my friends now. All I had to do was sneak upstairs, wait for Master Occuello, and get the answers we needed. So simple, yet I'd never been farther than Mistress Paiwe's office, the rest of upstairs a mystery to me—a mystery I had to navigate without being caught if I wanted to remain one of the lucky ones.

Ambere stood at the end of the underground passage, busying

herself with fixing the worn strap on her shoe. She glanced up, and in a passably disinterested tone, said, "Naili." A cough echoed from the end of the secondary passage, followed by another atop the stairs, and Ambere nodded. My heart hammered and my body fizzed like a boiling salt poultice. The way was clear. It was time to go.

With clenched fists, I started up the stairs. Every step brought with it drier air and the buzz of evening insects, but though the air was warm my skin pimpled, standing my hairs on end—hairs fast regrowing the tiny flowers I kept rubbing off.

At the top of the stairs, there was no sign of Yeloria. The housekeeper's room stood on the right, its door ajar, soft light spilling through the narrow gap and across the floor like a line I knew I ought not to cross. A line from beyond which answers beckoned as growing petals tickled my skin. Mistress Paiwe wasn't in, and with the murmur of dinner underway behind me, no one was in the passage to see me step over the line of light like it was a jagged crevasse, one wrong step sure to send me falling upon sharp crags. But there was no crack of stone, no slip as rocks bounced and tumbled; there was just the other side of the housekeeper's door and a passage stretching away before me—endless yet possessing only one destination.

Miizhei stood at a window at the end of the main hallway, folded into the shadows beside the iron bars. She'd said it overlooked the yard from which Master Occuello's sedan chair came and went, and daring no whisper, her nod was all I needed to know the alchemist had not yet returned from his fancy dinner at the Bastion. I walked on, determination gathering with every step. I would not die, nor let any of my friends die, for anyone, let alone for an alchemist who didn't even know who we were. If I was going to die it would be with my name, heavy with guilt, upon his lips.

At the end of a second long passage, murmuring approached.

The muted sound seemed to come from both directions, growing ever louder. Doorways lined the passage and I pushed open the closest, stepping into darkness. It deepened as I closed the door over behind me, not daring to click it shut. Scuffing footsteps approached, and a laugh—harsh and humourless—rattled along the passage. I closed my eyes. Held my breath. My heart stung, thundering within its tight cage.

"That's what new men are for though, right?"

I sucked in a breath. The voice was right outside.

"Except for the pretty ones," came the reply. "Leave the pretty ones."

That laugh again. A set of footsteps scuffed to a halt.

"They're all yours."

The door beside me snapped closed. I jumped, hands leaping to my mouth to push my cry back down, while outside the steps moved on, carrying their conversation with them.

When at last my heartbeat slowed and the steps had disappeared, I slowly turned the handle and eased open the door. At a chink of glass scales I fell back again, sweeping the door closed so fast it almost caught my toes. Unable to shut it all the way, I peered through the narrow gap, each jangle of glass like an unwelcome hand creeping down my spine. On light steps, a man in scaleglass armour drifted by, the light orb on his belt illuminating the length of his holstered pistol. Master Occuello was an important figure in Bakii, but scaleglass armoured guards and heavy pistols? Surely only the city's seigneurs were that important.

Once the guard had gone, I once again risked the passage. No footsteps this time, no voices or clinking armour, just the silence of a lifeless house.

When at last I found the stairs, I hurried toward them only for a clink of glass to break the silence. A clink and a step, and I spun, hunting safety and finding none. The footsteps closed in on a wave of tinkling scales and low whispers, and with nowhere to hide, I ran, speeding the rest of the way as quietly as I could. Quiet but for the thud of my heart, beating out its panic like it wanted me to get caught, to be thrown out or jailed, to no longer be one of the lucky ones. Catching my toe on the bottom step, I bit my tongue as I stumbled forward, instinct all that kept me moving—clambering on all fours—up the stairs. At the first glint of light on glass, I froze. I hadn't reached a hiding place, but movement would give me away, and for all that the sickening swirl in my gut urged me to run, I stayed crouched halfway up the stairs, a mere statue in the deep shadows.

Eyes squeezed shut and breath held, I gripped the stair banister and waited. Footsteps grew louder. Closer. A shout was sure to come at any moment, then hands would grip my clothes and I would be dragged away. Until I wasn't. Until the footsteps started to fade. Until they were gone, taking the menacing chink of their glass scales away into the gloomy house. Only when the silence below matched the silence above did I dare to uncurl myself and keep moving.

The stairs emerged into a room far grander than the one in which they'd begun, though it was just as dark, with deep shadows hanging in every elegantly carved corner like spider nests. A painted arch opened onto a large, open space where a lamp had been left burning low on a cluttered table. Like our small workspace in the still-room downstairs, here were dense gatherings of bottles and vials, little boxes, bowls, tubes, and scales. Books lay scattered about, one with its pages half-covered in an inky crimson scrawl. At another workstation, a small army of herbs and flowers surrounded a black scaleglass cutting board and knife. Scaleglass made for sharp blades, and picking it up took the edge off my dread.

More workrooms followed, and storerooms with shelves that reached floor to ceiling, piled with books and paper, with scaleglass bowls and fire boxes, with baskets of clean gloves and cloths and towels. The plan was to lie in wait for him, but it wasn't until I'd made it halfway around the central rooms that I found the first living space—a small sitting room of sorts with uncomfortable-looking chairs upholstered in crimson cloth.

From the sitting room led a dimly lit passage, and as I began to look about for a good place to wait, a faint hum grew upon the silence. I hesitated, hand to the wall. Was the alchemist back already? Or was that someone else? I had to find out, so I adjusted my grip on the scaleglass blade and followed the sound. It drew me to a door inset with shimmering glass, beyond which a dark figure moved. A cough. The rustle of clothing. The sticky peel of bare feet on glass. Pale golden light seeped beneath the frame as I reached for the door.

The handle turned without a sound, the mechanism so well-oiled and smooth that the door slowly swung open upon its own weight, spilling light onto my feet. On the floor beyond sat a pile of dark cloth with a master's formal hat perched atop it. Master Occuello. I hitched a breath. The pile made it look as though he had vanished, leaving behind only his clothes, but he stood with his back to me, a hand dipped into steaming bath water. With him dressed only in a shift and cincher, I stood unsure whether to enter or retreat and remained rooted to the floor halfway between. Any moment and he would see me. Hear me. Feel a cold breeze through the open door and turn. But first he reached both hands to his head and made short work of a series of twists and pins, letting long, dark hair down in a tumble of flattened curls. Before I could breathe, he unhooked his cincher, and it dropped unceremoniously from about his chest, ending in a tangle of ribbing on the floor.

Before more clothes could fall, I adjusted my grip on the scaleglass blade and forced out words. "Master Occuello, please, I need your help."

He spun, crossing his arms over his chest and scowling from

behind his sweep of dark hair. Irritation deepened at sight of me. "Who are *you*?"

I parted my lips to answer, but my tongue formed no words, became nothing but a useless flap of flesh in the face of all before me. The alchemist watched me through half-lidded eyes, annoyance fading to boredom even in the face of a blade—far more at ease in the presence of sharp scaleglass than I was in the presence of—of *her*. Of her jutting hip and her thin linen shift and her increasingly amused sneer.

"One of my servants, I take it," she said, the dismissive words a slap. "I'm sure my guards would like to know how you got past them."

She stepped toward the door, but I could not let her go, could not be thrown out with no answers. "No." I strengthened my grip on the blade and held it firm, standing my ground.

"No?" Her growl was all threat that turned my anger from a spark to a blaze.

"No," I repeated, determined to hold myself together. "You're not going anywhere until you help me."

8

Ashadi

Evening Bulletin

To all criers for announcement throughout Orsu and the Shield

It is still unknown who shot the dragon brought down north of the Shield earlier this week, though a stray shot is suspected.

Sand prices soar as the basin prepares for war with Lummazza, though locals fear increasing attacks against the Shield more than distant battles.

Many ships left stranded this morning as labour shortages cause chaos at the harbour. Ship crews forced to work on the sands to manage backlog in turnarounds.

181:24

I stood in the centre of the ugly crimson rug and stared at nothing, eyes unfocused. The citadel masters had a way of asking questions that would have made the most attentive mind melt and dribble away.

"And you're saying this man wasn't attired in Apaian or Celessi garb?" Master Freesh said, he a man who liked precision in his words.

"Yes, Master," I said. "Never seen anything like it."

They sat at a long table before me, mere shadows in the corner of my unfocused vision. Master Hershal leaned forward. "Describe him for us."

A more accurate request would have been *Describe him for us—again*. I swallowed my sigh, knowing the quickest way to get through this was to answer and repeat and dance to their tune until they were done. Complaints only made everything take twice as long.

"He wore sand-coloured leathers, a large hood and gloves... and a scarf. As I've said, I am a little hazy on the details because my vision was blurred by blood." Someone had stitched my brow closed when I'd been brought in, though whether it had been Mana or the healer I didn't know. It had been at least a day before I'd known anything at all, so exhausted I had been from the double ride and the shock.

"And you said he took his gloves off," Master Freesh again, his voice the deep grating of a blade across a sewer grate. "Describe his hands."

"Glove," I corrected. "He took only one glove off. But his hand, it was..." I closed my eyes, sliding back into fast-fracturing memories. They were all sand and heat and anger and panic and words that seemed to have no set place, floating untethered from time. "His hand wasn't remarkable. Dark skin. Long fingers. Steady. Used to holding a weapon and pulling the trigger."

Every memory of the man himself seemed to have frozen like a painting in my mind, every detail present and demanding, nibbling at my attention. However, telling the masters that I'd spent every waking hour thinking about him seemed unwise. The smooth skin. The deep, confident voice. And the steadiness with which he'd levelled his pistol at me, untroubled by the possibility of putting a bullet through my eye.

"And his voice?" Master Razard asked, his own voice far more musical than the others. "Did he speak with an accent or as though our language was not his language?"

"No," I said. "His voice would not have been out of place on any street from Learshapa to Bakii."

Silence met my answer, silence but for the distant hum of activity as citadel life went on. There had been no gong since I'd woken, but there were always dozens of other things to do—scouting rides, armour and weapon maintenance, marksmanship practice, recovery, and, of course, needling one another about all the ways we'd failed our families to end up at the Shield in the first place.

"And the man's weapon?" Master Razard asked, finally breaking the silence. "Tell us about that."

"It was a long-barrelled six-shot repeating pistol. I didn't recognise the make, but it looked both well-kept and expensive, of the highest quality. Likely, he shot us down with a rifle, but I didn't see that."

A few more beats of silence and I forced myself to bring the room into focus, to care for even a moment about my duty. The four masters—Freesh, Hershal, Razard, and the far more watchful and silent Master Leossai—sat at intervals along their meeting table, hands folded in some configuration of scarred and wrinkled fingers. All four stared unblinking, like they were trying to scrape information from my mind with the power of their eyes, the result so unnerving that I itched to leave.

Eventually, Razard glanced at his fellow masters. "That's everything we need for now, Lord Ashadi. If we have further questions, we'll send for you."

In any other situation, I would have drawled that I couldn't wait, that I would be thrilled to return and repeat answers to the same questions over and over again, but the masters strongly disapproved of sarcasm. It was hard to believe they'd ever been riders. Perhaps this was what a lifetime of iishor did to a man.

As much as I wanted to immediately escape their stuffy space and their ugly carpet, I stood my ground. "A question, if I may?"

"That will depend on the nature of your question, Romm," Master Hershal said.

"I only wish to know how Shuala is. I asked one of the keepers but was not allowed to see her."

"You know the dragons are secretive about their business. It isn't our place to interfere."

"Yes, Master, I know and I don't wish to interfere, only to know if she is all right."

Again, Master Razard glanced at his fellow masters before replying. "The last we heard she was recovering well. The bullet had been removed and her scale patched, but it will be some weeks before she is strong enough to fly."

Which they didn't need to add meant some weeks before I was called out on a ride, as bonding to a new dragon could take much longer.

I ought to have left then, having already pushed my luck, but I couldn't let go of the questions crowding through my mind. "The bullet," I said. "It went through the middle of a scale. How?"

"You are not here to ask questions, Lord Ashadi, only to answer them. You may go."

"And that man. What did his warning mean?"

"Mere ravings, Romm, now you may—"

"But no one has ever shot at us before. No one even lives—"

"You may go," Master Razard snapped.

Knowing I would get nothing more, I spun on my heel and made my escape, taking my fizzing pile of questions with me out the arched door and down the spiral stairs, the masters' sharp gazes seeming to follow me all the way.

Over the last two days, I'd recovered most of my physical strength and stability, but with it had come a discomfort I couldn't explain. Everything felt wrong. I felt numb and yet sensitive to every touch and sound, calm and yet buzzing with questions, trapped and yet as though a door sat just within reach.

The dinner bell had already rung by the time I reached the main hall, and though I had no interest in talking, at least amid the general noise I would hear something other than the haunting memory of cracking glass and Shuala's hot blood hissing upon the sand. The masters had said she was recovering—something I ought not to doubt. But then I'd never doubted The Sands were empty until a leather-clad sharpshooter levelled a pistol at my face.

The sounds of chatter rose as I approached the doors, hooking into me with the promise of losing myself. The noise grew louder, the occasional laugh thrown in among the clatter of cutlery and incessant talk. A full dining hall had been a rarity of late, so often were packs out or recovering from their iishor. Tonight it was full of riders and watchers, full of food and drink and flickering light, with serving staff winding their way between long tables, sweat sparkling on their brows.

I paused a moment in the archway, getting my bearings and hunting out a free seat, only for every pair of eyes to turn my way one by one. Voices trailed off, some halting mid-sentence to stare, while others showed their interest by turning to whisper to their neighbour. It was like the barrel of that pistol all over again, only the weapon was my brethren and the bullet their curiosity— the way they nipped at gossip and spread their own stories for entertainment.

I ought to have made an ironic bow, have looked behind me or otherwise made their interest appear foolish, but the ability to do anything beyond exist had been left out on the sand with Shuala's blood. Instead, I unstuck myself from the floor and walked on, trying not to collapse beneath the weight of so many stares.

From the narrow watcher's table at the far end of the room, Mana's eyes followed me as they always did, all the way from the door to the free place at my pack's table—a place next to Luce and across from Farisque, the former ever a pleasure, the latter making me wonder if throwing myself off the undercroft wouldn't be a better use of my time.

"Ashadi," Farisque crooned as I took the seat. "How good to see you up and about. Shame about the eyebrow."

"Shame it makes me look more rakish?" I said, glad I could still manage a retort, my protective snark working without input from my brain. "Diminishing my charm will not enhance yours."

Buoyed by the sniggers along the table, I reached unseeing for the dish before me, desperate to keep moving. Bread dipped in oil and baked with cassa berries and cheese—not my favourite, but I put two slices on my plate and shoved a third into my mouth. Around us, chatter slowly resumed, the citadel's inhabitants losing interest when I proved to be uninteresting.

"I heard you were called in to see the masters again," Luce said, jabbing his food with unnecessary ferocity.

"If you're wondering if they had anything new to ask, then no," I said, all nearby riders turning my way. "They just seem keen on getting me to repeat myself, hoping I'll come up with new details."

"And have you?"

"No."

Farisque waved a dismissive hand. "Well, at least you have plenty of time to try now you're not riding out with us."

"Not that we've been called out since," Luce said. "I think this is the longest break between gongs since I got here."

"That's just because you're new," Batien said, a nod making his greying hair dance. "We used to get about a week off between rides when I started almost fifteen years back. Seems the passage of time makes the world worse, not better."

"That's depressing," came a disembodied grumble, accompanied by morose agreement.

"I say things as I see them."

There seemed hardly enough air around the table as they went on to discuss possible reasons why there had been no call-outs. Everything from the shift in the weather to the dwindling of monster numbers to the deterrent scent of dragon blood we'd left behind. The hard truth was that there were no answers. The monsters had always just been there, always been charging the Shield Mountains, and always needing to be turned back. And every attempt to find out where they came from and why had failed. That was the first thing riders learned when they arrived. Even in the last fifty years, six expeditions had flown north and six expeditions had failed to return. The Sands were not just an open desert, impossible to survive in without supplies, but a dangerous place that spawned endless monsters, in which no one lived and out of which no one had ever walked.

"Who do you think he was?" The question had been circling around my head, and it took me a moment to realise I'd asked it aloud, that everyone nearby had stopped eating to stare at me. "The man," I added. "Who shot me down. He had unusual clothes but he sounded like a Celessi, and his pistol was modern and well-made."

"And a figment of your imagination, perhaps," Farisque drawled, breaking the silence. "Brought on by stress and increasing iishor resistance."

"What?" Horror hollowed my gut as I stared at him, the sense I'd fallen into a dream strengthening at the murmurs of agreement that followed.

"It's hardly surprising," Batien said, not meeting my gaze. "Iishor messes us all up sooner or later."

I stared from sympathetic face to sympathetic face and found no belief in any of them. Clamping shaking hands to fists, I said, "And the bullet? I suppose I imagined that into being too?"

"Stray bullets aren't that uncommon when we're all firing."

"None of you were firing! You were all in the second flame line when it happened!"

For the second time the room stuttered into silence and everyone stared at me. I'd half stood, voice raised, heart a staccato beat that pulled toward nausea. Every rider at my table looked away, embarrassed by my scene. Even Luce didn't meet my eye. "You don't believe me," I said, the words a whisper. "None of you believe me."

"No one lives in The Sands, Ashadi," Farisque said, his annoyance that of one explaining the obvious to a difficult child. "No one ever has and no one ever will. Especially not Celessi men with expensive firearms. It's all monsters and death and sand and nothing else."

Murmurs of agreement bubbled around us, and I wanted to be sick. I had been there. Had felt Shuala bucking and diving to avoid the bullets coming from the ground, had heard the orders passed on by Commander Jasque, had seen the man with my own eyes and stared down the barrel of that gun, and yet the disbelief surrounding me called it all into question. Had I imagined it in a fit of iishor fever? Imagined the man and the gun, the warning and the gentle way he'd set his hand on Shuala and begged her forgiveness? The nagging thought that it was possible nipped at my mind, yet a deep, visceral sense of certainty filled my body, and I shook my head.

"I was there. I know what I saw."

"And still needed to be questioned three times to get a solid answer," someone muttered. A someone who might have faced the full roar of my fury had the gong not rung, sucking all air out of the room and replacing it with dread. One ring of the gong meant first pack, and though I would not have been riding out regardless, I felt a familiar relief at the sight of others rising from their table. For a moment all was noise as the riders and watchers of first pack abandoned their meals, filling the space between tables with moving bodies and murmured fears. They were gone almost as abruptly, leaving a diminished dining hall in their wake. Gone too was the chatter and the energy and our collective appetite, and one by one other riders and watchers rose to depart.

Farisque got to his feet first, breaking up our little group as Batien grumbled. "I knew the peace wouldn't last. Only a matter of time."

"Do you think this is just a one-off?" Luce asked, wiping his mouth and letting his napkin fall as the serving staff gathered plates. "Or are we back to daily callouts now?"

"Couldn't say, kid, but a lull isn't comforting in a season that's had more callouts so far than we used to get in a whole year." Batien picked a piece of food from between his teeth and got to his feet. "Better get a good sleep," he added, patting Luce's shoulder. "Could be a long couple of days."

One by one they walked out without so much as a glance in my direction. I had ceased existing the moment I refused to reject my truth for their lies, but the gong had stolen my anger, leaving only fear in its place. Fear at the memory of a very real man's very real warning. *Your next ride will be your last. All of you.*

Despite Batien's good advice, the moment I got back to my room I loaded every one of my pistols and dug out the questionable alcohol I'd smuggled in a few weeks earlier. It tasted like piss that had already been drunk and pissed out again, but it would do for now, its only job to keep me company as I peppered the walls with bullet holes.

When Mana returned from dinner, he busied himself about his usual work without so much as a censorious click of the tongue, leaving me to my destructive coping mechanisms. Normally drink and gunpowder were enough, but as I emptied shot after shot at the same spot on the wall, the need for something stronger crept upon me—a need I kept at bay only until Mana disappeared into the adjoining storage room, at which I set down my pistol.

The chest made a faint, protesting creak as I pushed it open, loosing the scent of panawood shavings my clothes were folded with. A pouch sat atop where I had left it, and I fished it out, only for doubt to set in. Too light. I didn't need to open it to know it was empty, but I did anyway, refusing to believe all the Qammattz was gone without seeing the bare leather. Unsurprisingly, seeing it didn't make the drug's absence any easier to bear.

A step, a rustle—something—made me turn. Manalaii stood in the doorway, shoulder to the frame, solemnly watching. He knew. I knew that he knew and yet neither of us spoke, caught instead to the safety of silence. Until it stretched so thin it could no longer protect either of us.

"Do you happen to know where my other pouch is?" I said, lifting the one in my hand as though without the example he wouldn't know what I was talking about.

"It's in the end chest, but . . . it won't have what you're looking for either." Arms folded, gaze focused upon the floor, I'd never seen him look so defensive. "I'm sorry, Lord Ashadi. I had no choice."

I set a hand to my forehead in an attempt to steady whirling thoughts. "Are you talking about the Qammattz or something else?"

"Orders came this afternoon."

Dropping the pouch, I pressed the heels of my palms into my eyes, everything scrunched like I was a thwarted child back in the nursery. "Damn meddling husks." I could probably find more somewhere, but that would get Mana in trouble with the masters. From there he might lose his job, and I would lose him.

My foot twitched, then started to tap a rapid beat upon the floor.

"I..." Mana fidgeted in the doorway. "If you need...I could—"

"No."

"If you give me an order, I have to obey it. Though I think they're watching me too."

"That only makes it worse. No. No, no, no. Besides, we both have to answer to the masters in the end, I just wish they'd given me the order instead of messing around with all the..." I waved a hand in Mana's direction, seeking the right words. "Games and guilt."

"Aren't games and guilt what you Emoran nobles do for fun?" He said it with a smile, the kind of smile that sought to jest at truth with one hand and stick in a blade with the other. A smile that faded when I didn't laugh. "Apologies, Lord Ashadi. I have been too free with my humour."

"Or too astute in your perception." I pulled myself to my feet, swaying a little but refusing the hand Mana instinctively reached out. "I suppose the masters are worried about what might happen and want to ensure every rider is clean and ready."

Mana's lips parted, the beginnings of a silent objection hastily frowned away.

"What?" I said.

"What what?" he returned, brows raised.

"You were going to say something and thought better of it, and don't pretend you didn't. Games and guilt are my forte, remember? Spit it out."

He sighed, slumping back against the door-frame with a grimace. "It's not every rider. It's...just you. There are whispers that you're not well, and so I was...instructed to—"

"That I'm not well," I repeated, the words coming out more

vicious than I'd intended. "They're really doing everything they can to make it look as though I'm out of my mind. Trying to discredit me. Even keeping me coming back and repeating my story so it looked like I couldn't remember properly, but I remember every detail of that man like he is etched upon my mind. The Sands contain only monsters and death, yet he was there." I met Mana's blank stare and huffed a bitter laugh. "You don't believe me either."

"Oh, I believe you."

I gave him a suspicious look out the corners of my eyes. "Why? No one lives in The Sands. Everyone says so. As did every book my tutors gave me."

"What books did they give you?"

"I don't remember their names, only that they were dull. Even the books on dragons were boring and couldn't agree on a single point. It's like—"

"It's like they were all written by Emorans," Mana said, before pursing his lips in apology. "You may as well try to understand a painting by listening to the man who stole it rather than the man who painted it."

"What do you mean?" I said warily. I might regret the question, but he'd offered me a crack through which I could peer, and I couldn't look away.

He perched on the edge of a storage chest and sighed. "The citadel wasn't built for Emoran dragon riders," he said, voice low. "These halls were carved by ancient Apaian monks—followers of Shiirami back when some of the tribes believed in gods. They came here to worship her sun aspect. That's why the undercroft opens to the sky at angles that make the sun most visible. I believe there were set ceremonies for certain times of the day and year, but I've never met anyone who knows more detail. It was a long time ago even for us."

"I...Are you sure?" I looked around at the old stone walls as though expecting them to defend themselves. "I've never heard anything about that."

"Because all of your books were written by Emorans," he repeated. "Or at least by Celessi brought up to the Emoran way of life and taught Emoran history."

"Yes, but surely there are books written by Apaians too."

"We don't write things down as much as you; we tell stories." Mana shrugged. "And besides, who would print our history and what libraries would keep our books? Our version of history differs from yours as much as our culture does. Did."

Did. A bitter word for a man whose only nod to his culture seemed to be the markings under his eye and the memento skull he wore around his neck.

There ought to have been something smart to say, something wise and considered, but whatever it was fled my mind before a wave of anger that spared no one. What proof was there beyond Manalaii's word? A word far below that of the acclaimed tutors who had given me my education.

"It doesn't matter about the citadel," I snapped as though Mana had spoken again. "Are you telling me there are people who live out in The Sands too?"

Shoulders hunched like a child in trouble, Mana nodded. "I don't know what made relations so poor, but they've always been there. There are stories, of course, of shared histories long ago, but I don't know anything about them except that there used to be trade routes that ran through the pass."

"But why haven't I heard of them? Do they not want us to know they're there?"

Mana shook his head, slow and sad. "I don't know. I never learned much history. You'd have to ask someone who knows the right stories."

"You don't know much, yet it's still more than I do. Are these people in The Sands the reason no expedition comes back? They aren't Lummazzt, are they? He didn't look like a black-eyed monster. His skin was too dark."

"I shouldn't think so, we don't have stories about Lummazzt like you do."

"I wish they were stories," I said with a huffed laugh. "But if these people in The Sands have been killing dragons on expeditions, why apologise to Shuala? He seemed to know more about her than I do, but..."

I trailed off in the face of Mana's blank look, annoyed that while he had some answers, they weren't the full answers I needed. I dropped onto the edge of my bed with a heavy sigh. "No one else believes me. They say a stray shot must have got her, but the others were all in the second flame line when the commander ordered us to take the shooter out."

"Then at least he must know the truth."

"Yes. Yes, he must." I paused, an idea sending my mind wheeling away. "And you know what? I'm going to ask him what happened, see if I can get a straight answer from someone. It's not like I have anything else to do."

Mana grimaced, but whatever he might have thought regarding the folly of such a plan, he kept his doubts to himself. What an Emoran noble could get away with far exceeded that of an Apaian watcher.

Before even I could think better of such an idea, I let my indignation carry me out into the passage. At this hour, the citadel was usually quiet with all attempts at evening cheer and camaraderie having been tucked away where the masters could not see, but tonight even the serving staff I passed spoke in low whispers. It wasn't far to the commander's room, but the back of my neck prickled all the way.

Hardly had my knuckles fallen upon Commander Jasque's door than it was torn open, the commander's watcher glaring at me in welcome. "What do you want?"

"I wish to speak to the commander," I said, choosing to swallow both my disrespect and a reminder that, beyond these walls, I outranked practically everyone, Jasque included.

"He's not here," the snappy little man said. "He's gone to the undercroft, so you'll have to wait until tomorrow."

"Could you let him——?"

The door slammed upon my question, leaving me scowling at the old, stained wood. "Well fuck you too," I muttered and turned away, but my intention of returning to my room was speedily overtaken by the deeper instinct of a Romm, bred into my bones—to get what I had come for. And so I spun back and walked on toward the undercroft. Whatever business Commander Jasque had there between rides could be made to include answering my questions.

As I approached the undercroft, sounds of activity filtered out along the passage. Snuffles and scrapes and clinks of glass scales, rumbles and running steps, all caught together upon a fabric of hissing. First pack was returning from their ride. I quickened my pace. In the chaos I might be able to slip through into the undercroft unseen, and though I wouldn't be able to talk to Shuala without the iishor, I could see that she was all right.

Without iishor filling my blood, the undercroft was somehow larger, and the noises echoing through it were strange to my ears. They were slower and lower in pitch, the air warmer and the smells sharp and acrid. One after another, dragons were flying in through the great openings to land before an army of stable hands and watchers, and amid the chaos, no one seemed to notice or care that I was there, my footsteps part of the general noise as I made my way through the maze of dens toward Shuala's. A sinking sensation assailed me halfway, when no glints shone from within and no movement promised life. Drawing closer, only darkness greeted me. The oily pakka wool looked old and flat, like it hadn't been changed since our last flight, a single scale caught in its tangles all that shone within.

No Shuala. Injured dragons were likely kept elsewhere, so I wasn't surprised, yet neither was I satisfied. I wanted to see her, to be sure she was safe, so while all around me riders staggered from their saddles, I turned, looking about the undercroft as though for the first time. The open arches stood at one end of the grand space, the armoury entrance at the other, but there had to be other entrances for stable hands and keepers, possibly even dragons.

A hasty search of shadowed walls found no dragon-size doorways, but other passages led off into other parts of the citadel, and I strode toward one, my search for Commander Jasque forgotten.

The acrid smell increased as I entered the first shadowy passage, stone lined and dark, where strange sounds called me toward light more luminescence than open flame. Shouts and footsteps grew louder as I walked—the busy sounds of men hurrying about tasks as serious as those in the undercroft.

At the end of the passage, I emerged into a close space all dim golden light and oily pakka wool, where people dashed to and fro calling to one another in the cheerful way of men at work. Of Shuala there was no sign, but between the bustling figures I could see small alcoves cordoned off from the main length of the room, each a wool-filled den in which snuffled hot breath with gleaming eyes. At the far end of the room stood a bank of glass furnaces roaring hot, and a table on which lay something all too monstrous.

"Hey! You shouldn't be in here," someone called, breaking away from the main group to stride my way. "Who gave you permission to be in here?"

"I . . ." No one had ever asked me that before, my name and status having always gained me entrance wherever I wanted to go. Indignation flared. "I am Lord Ashadi Romm, and I want to see Shuala. My dragon."

Even before I finished the man was shaking his head, a flap of frantic hands hustling me back the way I'd come. "No, no one is allowed to be in here. Leave now or I'll call for the masters."

"But—"

"Out!" Others turned our way at the lifting of his voice—a discordant pause in the midst of their activity. Two stretchers were being hurried in, each with a dark shape atop that bulged more than humans ought, monstrous like the creature on the far table. "Out now, or—"

"Romm!"

I spun to find Commander Jasque hurriedly approaching along the passage, his scowl ferocious in the shadows.

"Commander." I managed a small nod of respect before gesturing around me. "I am looking for Shuala."

"Shuala isn't here and nor should you be." He gripped my arm, turning me about like I was a child to be directed. "I'll have to tell the masters about this, so best if you play along now."

"Play along? Commander, what is going on?"

"What is going on is that you saw nothing and Shuala is fine. Now go back to your room, Romm, and make it quick."

He let go of my arm as we regained the familiarity of the undercroft, but I just spun around to glare at him. "What did I see?"

"Nothing, Romm, I think I made that clear. Now go or the masters will be even less pleased."

"Fine, I'll go, but I didn't come just to see Shuala. I came to ask you a question."

"Then make it quick."

"When Shuala was being shot at, she checked in with you." His expression went blank, but he said nothing so I pressed on. "And you gave her orders to take care of the trouble coming from the ground. Yet now I'm told it was a stray bullet from one of my pack that took us out of the air. Why?"

"Because no one lives in The Sands, Romm. Only monsters. Now go."

He shoved my shoulder, but rather than taking the hint and

leaving, I rocked back and kept my ground. "Mana says that's not true. He says there are people who live out there and always have been. Why don't we know about them? Or is that something else I'm not meant to have seen?"

"No one lives in The Sands, whatever stories your Apaian comes up with. Go."

It was no answer, but I could tell from the stern set of his jaw that I would get no other. So with a stare that lingered as long as I dared, I slowly turned on my heel and made my way out of the undercroft, leaving the dying sounds of settling dragons behind me.

With more questions and fewer answers than I'd had before, I spent the night drinking, shooting, worrying, and then worrying some more, itching for the calm of Qammatz and unable to have it. Eventually, I'd slept, only to wake feeling as bad as I did coming down off iishor, just with less vomiting. Slightly. Mana, however, was far less helpful. His expression owned much disapproval of the you-brought-this-on-yourself variety. He brought plain food and water and looked pointedly at them, before returning to his own tasks. I took a sip of water. Felt awful. Grumbled. Tried to find a comfortable position. Failed. Broke off a piece of bread to nibble. Felt worse. And so pulled the blanket over my head. The darkness ought to have been peaceful, but in that silent, lonely space, thoughts emerged like poisonous blooms. I had brought this on myself because I always did. Because I wanted Manalaii to look after me. To care about me. A simulacrum of care mediated through labour. Beneath me, yet a desperation I always stooped to.

"Nope," I said, throwing the blanket off and sitting up, letting the nausea swirl. "Not doing that."

"Doing what?" Mana asked from the adjoining storage room.

"Thinking. Terrible habit."

"More or less terrible than shooting holes in the walls and drinking too much?"

"Oh, much worse than both."

He huffed a little laugh, and while he went on about his work, I stared around my room and wondered what I was going to do for weeks without a dragon. I'd had hobbies and interests before I'd come to the Shield, I'd had friends and family, commitments and responsibilities, but here there was just iishor and callouts and all too much vomiting. Vomiting was hardly worth missing, yet I wasn't sure what I would do without it.

"Do you know how to play Dace?" I called, levering myself off the bed and beginning the search for my own clean clothes.

Sounds of movement stilled in the storage room. "Dace? Do you mean the card game?"

"Yes. I've never been particularly good at it, but I figure I've suddenly got an awful lot of time on my hands."

Mana appeared in the doorway. "You might, but I—"

A knock sounded on the door—the heavy sort that brooks no refusal. It was the sort my father had mastered, and although it wouldn't be him, it sent a chill up my spine all the same.

With a glance all too like a warning to stay put, Mana made his way to the door. There a pause, then he pulled it open, back straight, shoulders squared. And froze. Something was thrust into his hand, and I moved just in time to catch sight of a servant before he disappeared away along the passage.

Slowly, Mana turned, pushing the door closed behind him, eyes not leaving the paper in his hand.

"What's that?" I said, troubled by his stillness.

Without glancing up, he unfolded the paper and started to read, every second he didn't speak tightening my chest.

"Oh," he said at last, the word coming out on a long sigh.

"What?"

"I've...I've been let go." He looked up, lips twisting into a wry smile. "I'm afraid you'll have to find someone else to practice Dace with, my lord."

For a moment all I could do was stare, horror flooding into

me. Let go. That meant a new watcher. Meant no more Mana. "But..." A demand to know what he could have done to lose his job faltered on recollection of the previous night, when I'd told Commander Jasque there had to be people in The Sands because Mana had said so. I'd asked too many questions and now they were punishing me, sending Mana away—Mana who was not only my watcher but now also my only source of truth.

"No," I said, shaking my head. "No. I refuse to accept it. I will not fly without you. I will speak with the masters. They can't do this. They can't—Where are my clothes? I have to—"

"Ash."

"—go before word of this can get out, before—"

"Ash."

"—it can't be taken back because by the grace of the song I will make them take it back even if—"

"Ash!"

My gaze snapped to him, and my breath hitched at the sight of his twisted smile and damp eyes. "I'm sorry," he said, shaking his head. "But there's nothing you can do and you know it. I wish—" Mana shook his head again and looked down at the floor. "I don't know what I did but I wish I had not. I wish I wasn't leaving you, especially at such a time. I never thought when I came here that I would meet someone who—"

A roar tore through the air, shaking the room. Books and glasses and powder horns hit the floor and we were thrown onto our knees as boom after explosive boom rocked the citadel. I threw my hands up over my head as Mana did, sure the roof would fall in on us so viciously did the floor shake, until slowly the sound and the trembling moved away, fading into the distance like a series of gunshots pulling wide.

"What was that?" Mana demanded, finding his voice first as we scrambled to our feet amid the chaos of scattered books and bottles and bedclothes. "It was right on top of us."

Outside someone shouted, and dodging shattered glass, I darted for the door and tore it open. Loose stones peppered the passage and cracks marred the interior walls, but the shouting sounded far away, muffled and tinny. A shuffle of hurried steps and someone grabbed my arm—Luce—his expression a fearful mask.

"It came from the lower levels!" he cried, his lingering grip tugging me in his wake as he ran. No time to think, only to follow, while behind me Mana called to watchers who stood demanding answers at their doors, unable to leave their suffering riders. Second pack had been called out in the night, leaving only us able to chase explosions.

Like a magnetic bullet, Luce gathered other members of our pack as he ran, out to the main hall and along to the stairs, dodging nervous knots of service staff peppering one another with unanswerable questions. A few called out, but no words seemed to reach my ears as Luce turned down the stairs.

The main floor of the citadel contained our rooms, the dining hall, armoury, and undercroft, while the masters lived above and the serving staff below. Farther below again were the baths and training halls, storage rooms and recreation spaces, and the maze of unused rooms with which every old building is riddled—or at least used to be. In the lower hallway, Luce came to an abrupt halt, all but throwing himself back onto the stones at my feet. The stairs down to the main shooting gallery were gone, torn away leaving every adjoining room a mess of charred stone and debris. The entire eastern wall had been blown out, and through it the view of the Shield Mountains was all wrong. A line of blast craters leading away had torn jagged peaks to dust, flattening passes and caving in hollows.

"Go back!" someone shouted behind me as I stood staring. "Half the fucking foundations are gone!"

Some pedantic part of me, desperate for something else

to focus on, wanted to point out that was an exaggeration, but Mana's hand on my arm restrained such folly. "We should move," he said. "In case more of the floor gives way."

Wise words, yet the scene held me captive. A scene of wreckage, gently smoking, dust still settling, stones thrown miles from where they'd come and everywhere shouts and running steps as people found other ways down to the lower floors. The spaces were little used, but there were probably people in the rubble, certainly supplies, and maybe answers. Had it been an accident? An attack? Everyone in the roiling crowd behind me seemed to have an opinion, but only I thought of the man in The Sands speaking his warning.

We will no longer be your waste pile, your garden, your mine, your slaves. No longer will you take from us and throw back what you do not want. Your next ride will be your last.

"Lord Ashadi?" Mana's grip tightened on my arm and I was about to give in, to step back, when movement below caught my attention. No one else stood close enough to the edge to see it, but at a gasp, Luce and Batien were suddenly at my side.

"What is it?" Luce said. "What did you see?"

"There." I pointed as a low, slinking form dragged itself through the clouds of dust. A form all too familiar from its dull colour to the way it moved. "A fucking monster. No, two of the bastards. How did they get inside?"

"What? Where?" Farisque this time, all shock and no drawl.

"I don't see anything," Batien said. "That's just a bunch of shattered barrels and stone."

"No, farther on, where—"

A rumble shook through the floor, sending us scurrying back. My heart slammed every beat into my ribs as the stones I'd just been standing on tumbled into the crater below.

"Fuck, Ashadi, your imagination nearly got us all killed," Farisque snapped, brushing himself down. "Monsters. Next there will be an army of sand men with fine pistols coming up the non-existent stairs. No, I don't want to hear it," he went on when I spun to glare at him. "There're more important things going on than you losing your mind. And get your death cult watcher out of my way. This is probably his fault."

He slammed a shoulder into Mana, sending him stumbling into the wall, an *oof* of air bursting from his lungs. Batien followed Farisque back toward the stairs, Luce only pausing to grimace at me, their departure leaving me with the feeling I too had just had the breath knocked out of me.

"Are you all right?" I asked as Mana righted himself, shoulders hunched as though to keep himself small.

"Fine, my lord." He brushed hands down his tunic and skirts, fingers trembling. "But I'd rather not remain so close to the...the precipice, if you don't mind. I ought to get down there and help, see if—"

The gong echoed through the shattered citadel and I flinched, expecting the roof to drop on us. It didn't, but at the second ring dread trickled through my body, while the third was like being hit with a whole bucket of cold water. My heartbeat sped in panic and habit moved my feet in the direction of the armoury before I halted. "Should I go?" I said, the realisation that everything was wrong washing over me. "Shuala might be strong enough to fly, but you've been..."

Mana grimaced. "She might not be strong enough, but they may risk it anyway given the situation. If there's another callout today, first pack will have to go out again with less than a day's turnaround. But yes, you'll...have to go without me. I'm sorry."

My stomach churned just thinking about flying out, to say nothing of having to prepare alone and having no watcher to care for me on the other side. "Shit," I breathed, not daring to turn back and look at the hole someone or something had blown in the citadel. "They can't do this, not when they need us."

"Need you," he corrected. "Watchers are wholly replaceable. Although perhaps they will let me do my duty one last time, if they do indeed wish you to fly."

It was not so much a hopeful thought as one that held despair at bay a few minutes longer, and together we made our way toward the armoury—this walk we had made dozens of times turned into a solemn march. Around us the citadel was awash with shouts and running steps, and beneath our feet the floor trembled with aftershocks. Another explosion could hit at any moment, yet I walked in a bubble of disbelief, sure I would soon wake from this strange nightmare.

"Do you think it was them?" I said abruptly as we crossed the main hall. "The people in The Sands?"

"I don't know," Mana replied with a shrug. "But it makes about as much sense as anything, given the warning he gave you."

"You know, it's nice to have someone who believes me. Even if there's only one of you."

"Trust me, you wouldn't want more than one of me."

I glanced his way, retort already halfway to my lips when another explosion roared around us, shaking the citadel. A single burst this time, but as we crouched, hands once more over our heads, fear trembled through me. If they could do this much, what was to stop them taking out the whole building?

"Lord Ashadi Romm!"

As the shaking faded away, I spun to find Master Razard approaching from the direction of the armoury. Never one to smile, his gaze seemed harder than ever, pinning me to the floor.

"Master Razard, I was on my way to the armoury to see if I was needed. If Mana—"

"You are not needed in the armoury, Lord Ashadi Romm. You are, however, needed in Emora."

"I— What? Emora?"

"Yes, Emora," he repeated, his musical voice both soothing

and discordant. "It is clear to us with this latest...setback...that we need the assistance of Lord Reacher Sormei. Hence, we are sending you to Emora as an ambassador while you are unable to fly. We are hoping he will listen to you, where he does not listen to us. We need more riders, more dragons, more funding. It is imperative we rebuild as fast as possible and strengthen our defences, or the citadel may fall. And no, this is not a request, it's an order. You go at once. A ship is due to arrive at Orsu port within the hour and you must be on it when it leaves.

"As for you," he added, turning his piercing gaze toward Mana. "When we said that your services were no longer required, we meant it. So you must also pack your things and be on that ship when it leaves. Another ship will be awaiting you at Remorna, where you will change vessels for Bakii and not return." As another rumble shook the floor, Master Razard flashed Mana something that could have been called a smile. "Congratulations are in order, however, as you will be remembered as both the first and the last Apaian watcher in the citadel's long history."

His words seemed to tear the floor from beneath me, yet with a nod he just turned away, leaving Mana and I nothing on which to stand as our world collapsed around us.

9

Tesha

Morning Bulletin

To all criers for announcement throughout Learshapa

Impressive scenes as the upper city sanctuary prepares for the wedding of Lord Kiren Sydelle and Lady Teshalii Romm tomorrow at noon. The sanctuary, where the divine song has been chanted unceasing for over a hundred years, is proud to now host the grandest wedding in Learshapan history.

Shock news from the Shield as a series of explosions take out part of the historic citadel. The cause is yet unknown.

Horrific scenes as border clashes continue. No mercy expected from barbaric Lummazzt forces as Reacher Sormei's soldiers engage east of Therinfrou and Hospace mines, upholding the reacher's promise that a united Learshapa would not be left to fend for itself.

266:3

From the roof of Romm Manor, the whole city spanned before me, from its gleaming upper rim down its sloping sides, where the people of Learshapa moved about like ants. On the western rim, sand ships came and went from the rocky harbour, the broad glass road they sailed shimmering in the sunlight.

I tightened the wrap around my shoulders. It was too cold and blustery an evening for flies to swarm, cold enough that I ought to have been elsewhere, but I'd run out of quiet places where I could be, for even a few moments, just Tesha. The last two days had been full of intense lessons and practice. Over and over again I had curtsied, had repeated the right greetings, uttered the right niceties, and recited names and places and family histories until my mind turned to dross. Now the house was full of bustle and panic.

On a clear day one could watch the sand ships become tiny dots on the horizon, but with the coming brightstorm the air was damp and heavy, leaving them to come and go through a misty barrier. One ship coming into dock was a large public carrier with multicoloured sails; others had sails of deep red or blue, while another approaching at speed had sails as white as the clouds. White sails wouldn't long stay white in the basin winds, making it the choice of someone who could afford new ones each journey and was eccentric enough to want them.

My gaze fixed upon the white-sailed ship as it drew closer to the city. It was caught behind a public vessel, yet as the road broadened, it raised more sails and darted around the large hull, zipping along like a hawk riding air currents only it could see. I was sure then I was looking at the Sydelle ship.

Footsteps scuffed on the steps and someone called my name, but I didn't turn. Having overtaken the public ship, the white-sailed vessel had darted back in front of it, holding the main line toward the harbour. The smaller ships used different docks, but the Sydelles' might have been large enough to require the big one, and my husband-to-be was clearly intent on making sure he got there first and didn't have to wait for ordinary people to disembark.

"Lady Teshalii!" came my name again. "There you are, my lady, I've been looking everywhere for you."

"Oh, Biiella, we seem to be making a habit of this, I'm sorry," I said. "I just wanted to watch the ships come in. I hope you didn't really have to look everywhere for me."

"Well, no, my lady, when you weren't in your room or in the hall, I did think I might find you here watching for Lord Kiren's ship."

Gesturing for her to join me at the railing, I pointed down at the white-sailed vessel now navigating the harbour's nest of smaller roads. "That one," I said. "I'm sure of it. They were in quite the hurry on the road."

For a moment, she gazed down at the sand ships with interest, before giving herself a shake. "And so will we be in quite the hurry if you don't come now. The party starts in an hour and you aren't ready."

With the wedding taking place the following day, I couldn't decide if kindness or cruelty had prompted Reacher Sormei's request that his brother and I meet beforehand, but either way I could only blame Lord Romm for turning a meeting into an evening party.

And so for the second time that week, I sat by my bedroom window while a pommadeur tidied my brows and knitted my hair into a crown of tight braids. The seamstress had brought yet another collection of the finest skirts I'd ever seen, and I had to chide myself for the joy I felt upon pulling them on. Such extravagant wealth came at a cost, and I hadn't agreed to be an insult bride to gain access to money and finery.

"Guests are beginning to arrive," Biiella said, bringing news while the seamstress circled me, putting the finishing touches to her work. "No sign yet of the Sydelles."

I tried to thank her but found my mouth too dry.

When I was ready, it was Uvao who once again met me at my door. No compliment this time, no lingering stare or reassuring smile, just an arm held out for me to tuck mine into—that small touch the only comfort offered on our walk to the main hall. Since his father and Reacher Sormei had come to terms, there had been no time to talk about our passionate slip in the litter, time only to realise that silence was safer.

While outside the sun set on a damp Learshapan evening, we arrived in the main hall to find it full of guests. Everywhere I looked, knots of people stood chatting, glasses in hand, all multilayered skirts and jewels and pasted-on smiles. I must have flinched on the threshold, for Uvao squeezed my arm. "Steady," he said. "They're all just here to stare. Remember that you're better than them, and you'll be fine."

His provocative murmur made my lips twitch just as the nearest group of guests turned to stare. Others followed, some even gesturing in my direction, and my smile became forced. This was going to be my whole evening—smiling for staring strangers.

With still no sign of the Sydelles, Uvao led me on a slow walk around the room, stopping here and there to introduce me to people amid the overloud chatter. Councillor Angue and Councillor Duzeunde, Lord Broune, Lord Nipralme, and Lord Sactasque—who I had to try not to smile at, recalling the reclamation movement's recent abduction of his ritual carvings. The names kept coming and soon began leaving through the other ear the moment they arrived in my head. When Lord Revennai appeared, he was a welcome interruption in the sea of new faces.

"Ah, there you are, cat," he said, eyes sparkling with humour or brandy or both. "Knew you could do it."

"Even when you were lying on the floor bemoaning our inability to get through a single lesson?" I asked.

"Yes, even then. Never doubted you for a moment."

"Liar."

"Cat."

I could happily have remained trading insults with him, but his mercurial streak kicked in and his expression softened. "You're doing all right? Not too stressed at all this?"

"No, it's fine," I lied. "But I won't remember everyone's name."

"That's all right, by the end of tomorrow you'll be more important than every single one of them and it won't matter. It's only the Sydelles who—"

He broke off as he suddenly found himself the loudest speaker in the rapidly quieting hall. Around us all conversation had dropped to murmurs and everyone not staring at me was craning their necks to see the door. My heart sped, Uvao's warning tap on my arm not needed to know it was time. The Sydelles had finally arrived.

Lord Romm had been holding court alone in the centre of the room, but as whispers heralded the new arrivals, we made our way to his side. And while we waited, I fought the urge to be sick. They were here. I was about to meet my husband, and everyone who was anyone in upper Learshapa had come to watch.

Movement shifted beyond the archway. Heads turned at the approaching footsteps, and in perfectly cut cloth edged in gold, the Emoran god stepped into the room. But for his finery, Reacher Sormei looked the same as when I'd first met him, as at ease at the centre of society's attention as he had been at home on his couch patting his cat. A smile lit his beautiful features, and on show now, he held up a hand in greeting that eased the room's breathless tension.

A servant stepped forward. "Lord Sormei Sydelle, Reacher of Greater Emora and the Celes Basin, Lord of the Shield, and Champion of Rorshendalii."

Reacher of Greater Emora and the Celes Basin, I sneered to myself as he stepped forward into the crowd. One and the same thing to him, no doubt, the whole basin just part of his grand Emoran realm.

"Lord Kiren Sydelle, Grand Archivist of Emora."

My gaze snapped to the archway as a second man strode out of the shadows and into my life. One glance at him and I turned back to Reacher Sormei, sure there had to be some mistake. But no, no mistake, from one to the other I looked, hunting some difference, some unique trait that could tell them apart, but there was none. Somehow, in all the lessons in deportment and small talk and carrying books around on my head, no one had thought to tell me that Lord Sormei and Lord Kiren were identical twins. All that told them apart was their attire, Lord Kiren's skirts simpler than his brother's lush trappings and his armbands less numerous. Two gods. And one was to be my husband.

"Lord Reacher," Lord Romm said, drawing my attention back to the man whose gaze had seemed to look right through me at our last meeting. "You honour my home with your presence."

"As you honour me with your invitation," Reacher Sormei agreed in his deep, slow voice and held out his hands.

Lord Romm lifted them to his lips and, holding them together, kissed them and let them go. Barely seeming to have noticed this courtesy, the reacher moved on, already holding his hands out to Uvao.

"And Lord Kiren," Lord Romm was saying, calling my gaze back to my husband-to-be only for my breath to catch once more at the likeness. No doubt there was some way to tell them apart aside from their clothing, but I could not yet see it. "We are most pleased to have you here as our honoured guest. Your wedding is sure to be the finest Learshapa has ever seen."

"Thank you, Lord Romm," Lord Kiren said, his voice as deep as his brother's but quieter and more gentle. Perhaps the difference between them was less in appearance than in manner, for even his smile was softer, almost shy. "I am most honoured, I assure you."

"—and you remember my cousin of course," Uvao was saying beside me.

"Of course, Lady Teshalii," Reacher Sormei said, standing before me now, the way he lingered on my name almost a purr, his eyes bright. "Quite the pleasure to meet you again and to be able to reassure my dear brother that you are not the monster he feared."

"That *I* feared?" Lord Kiren said, appearing beside his twin and making my head spin. "I was sure she would be lovely, and so she has proven."

"Ah, uh, Lady Teshalii, Lord Kiren Sydelle," Uvao said, his carefully practised words thrown off course by the easy way the brothers moved together through the room. "My cousin has been awaiting your arrival with great excitement. Only this evening, we could not pull her away from the upper balcony where she was awaiting sight of your ship."

Uvao's words brought a smile to Lord Kiren's face and heat to mine, and stuttering something about the ships being so glorious to watch, I made my curtsy. *Greeting. Curtsy. Kiss.* Having risen, I gripped Lord Kiren's hands as I had been shown and pressed them gently to my lips before letting them go, so dazed I took in neither scent nor touch.

Sound didn't break out so much as vanish, leaving silence to bloom through the hall. One glance at Reacher Sormei and I knew at once my mistake. "Oh gosh," I said. "I am so sorry, Lord Reacher, you are just so very much alike!" And taking his hands, I kissed them as I ought to have done before Lord Kiren's.

"Something you will have to get used to, Lady Teshalii," Reacher Sormei said, his amusement sending laughter chuckling good-naturedly through the room. "You are not the first to mistake us and will not be the last. I hope you will be ready to travel as soon as the wedding is over? We do not mean to linger."

"The morning after," Lord Kiren corrected him. "Sormei was

keen on an evening departure, but I convinced him it would be most cruel to expect you to go through an exhausting wedding *and* begin a journey on the same day."

Reacher Sormei flicked a glance at his twin, full of lazy affection. "The day after, indeed. As you see, Lady Teshalii, you are certainly marrying the better of us." He stepped back then, glancing around to be sure every eye was on him. "The fulfilment of this treaty contract with so fine a marriage is a historic moment for us all," he said, raising his voice to ring throughout the room. "And with this morning's explosions at the Shield Citadel it has come none too soon. Long has it been since the Celes Basin stood as one, strong against the threats that batter our borders from every direction. Learshapa has been the missing piece to our strength, the missing piece to our unity, and the missing piece to our soul. May we turn the monsters back into The Sands and stand strong and united against the equally monstrous Lummazzt foe."

Applause met this short speech, and though I clapped because it was expected of me in my new role, part of me had truly been swept up in the emotion of his words. He spoke as if he meant it. As if he believed it. As if everything he had done and ever would do was not for him but for us, the people, and it was intoxicating. Reacher Sormei didn't only look like a god, he spoke like one.

With the formalities concluded, the evening soon became a whirlwind of still more faces, endless talking, and far too much brandy. There seemed always to be a new glass in my hand and a new name to remember, but all anyone spoke about was my wedding or the upcoming season in Emora. Far too many people had advice for me, everything from how best to keep Lord Kiren happy to what colour was most lucky to wear, with one woman even suggesting I recite the opening of the divine song before consummation to ensure the swift conception of children. While her advice was easily ignored, the reminder of what was expected of Lord Kiren's wife was not.

With so many people filling Romm Manor's usually empty halls, it felt like hours before I again caught sight of either of the Sydelles, and catching one's eye across the room, I couldn't even be sure which it was. The creeping sensation I was walking into a trap grew upon me, and though the party would likely go late into the night, I took the first opportunity of escaping, pleading a need to sleep well for the next day.

Mind full and world slowly spinning, I made for the safety of my room. No sooner had I opened the door than Uvao called my name.

"Tesh."

I turned, making the world spin faster.

"Tesh, are you all right? I saw you leave and...wanted to be sure."

His gentle question and concerned expression ought to have earned him gratitude. Instead, I punched his arm. "You didn't tell me they were twins!" I hissed. "I thought I was going to expire upon the tiles."

"What?" Uvao's eyes widened. "Oh shit, no! I assumed you knew. It's common knowledge."

"Perhaps to people who rule cities," I said, hitting him again. "It's not the sort of thing normal people talk about. And I kissed Lord Kiren's hands first."

"And then covered for it very well!"

This earned him a harder punch that hurt my knuckles. "Stop being nice about it! I can't believe you didn't tell me."

"I didn't think to. Will you stop hitting me?"

"Only when you stop deserving it." I spun away to stalk into my room all wounded pride, only to turn back and hit him again. "They're identical twins! How am I supposed to tell them apart?"

"You get used to it. They're very different people. Really, Tesha, that's enough." He caught my fist on the next swing, and I was too tired, too weak, or too drunk to pull away. "You'll be fine. You always are."

The words hung between us, his unblinking stare drawing me in though neither of us had moved. There in the doorway we stood, too close and yet not close enough. I could have stepped back, could have wished him good night, but I just stood and stared, caught to him as he seemed caught to me.

"I should go," he said at last, letting my hand go but making no move to step away. Instead, he seemed closer, his skirts brushing mine, his chest leaving barely the space to breathe between us.

"Yes. No." I shook my head and stepped back into the room. "Don't. I...don't want to be alone. Not tonight."

It was a terrible idea, but before I could think better of it, before I could think at all, our lips met in a hard kiss more heat than grace. As it had back in the litter, sense fled leaving our hands to hunt skin and moans, and to trace familiar paths over once-known bodies. Everything about him was both old and new, combining the comfort of memory with the thrill of forbidden lust. If anyone were to see us or hear us or even guess, the charade would be over, and for a wild moment I didn't care. My world had shrunk to the size of him.

Mirroring one another's groans, we each made quick work of the other's buttons, desperate for skin and heat and sweat. I needed to be wanted and to want in turn, needed to drown in his warmth and his scent, needed to be just Tesha one last time. And so caught together naked and needing, we filled the night with breathless gasps and pleas and promises we would have to forget by morning.

When I would marry another man.

Once again, I stood in in the middle of the room while maids milled about me. I was getting used to the little army that prepared me for every important meeting, though today the usual fluttering anxiety had company—an ache deep in my body that couldn't but remind me of Uvao. Uvao, who'd stayed with me long into the night, keeping both our minds off the morning. Uvao, who'd been gone when I woke.

My stomach grumbled. Emoran wedding tradition meant having breakfast with my husband-to-be, so no tray of food had come with the army of maids, only one of Lord Romm's secretaries bearing the day's schedule—breakfast in the gardens of Romm Manor, before travelling together through the streets to be married at the upper city sanctuary. Celebrations back here would follow, after which I would travel with Lord Kiren to Sydelle House.

Despite my hunger, it was anxiety that churned my stomach as I was led out to the gardens, where the mist had burned off leaving the morning bright and warm. There a fountain trickled its music and birds danced about the flowering trees in a world of their own, and sitting at a large, finely set table full of glittering glassware was Lord Kiren Sydelle. At least I hoped it was him and not his twin.

"Lady Teshalii," Lord Kiren said, standing to greet me. "How troubled you look this morning. Nothing amiss, I hope?"

"Nothing at all, my lord." I slid gracefully into a curtsy, determined to hunt for every tiny difference between the brothers.

As I settled on the cushions opposite, my stomach rumbled. I pressed a hand to it, willing it not to embarrass me, and Lord Kiren laughed. "My stomach was making just such protests when I arrived, I assure you. In fact, I may have been inconsiderate and eaten a small plate of fruit already so I wouldn't feel like I was dying."

"It is very late for breakfast," I said, having dismissed four other things I'd thought to say first. "You were wise to fortify yourself."

He gestured at the food. "Please, do not wait on my account. We can try to get to know one another better when you are no longer starving."

By Emoran standards it was indecorous to shovel food into my mouth rather than pick at it while making small talk, but it was either eat or have my stomach interrupt with growls, so I ate, glad to see that as I served myself so did he. Soon both our plates were full of berries and sliced mango, sticky date cakes and bite-size seed buns dusted with what I knew was powdered tea only thanks to my lessons in rich-people food.

"A very fine spread Lord Romm has served us," Lord Kiren said after a while, nodding at the table. "It is good of him to continue to play host though it's holding up his own journey to Emora, which, after yesterday's explosions at the Shield, I imagine he is all the more eager to make."

"Has there been any further news of Lord Ashadi? Everything has been quite the whirlwind here, so I haven't had time to find out."

"Oh, I know only that he was unhurt in both the accident and the explosions and has left the Shield for Emora. It's all been quite the shock, especially to Lord Romm, I should think. He probably never thought his son would be in any real danger, so it makes sense he would recall Ashadi now—*if* that is what happened to make Ashadi leave, of course. I admit I had rather hoped to find out more from you."

"Then I am afraid I must disappoint you," I said, determined to avoid whatever gossip he was fishing for. "All talk here has been of the wedding."

He accepted my lack of knowledge with a smile and served himself some more food. I would have to find out what had happened to Uvao's brother soon or risk accidentally stepping into a mire not of my own making.

"If Lord Ashadi is to return to Emora," Lord Kiren went on after a thoughtful pause, "that will be quite the change for him after three years at the citadel."

I bit back the urge to ask why it interested him so much and said instead, "I'm sure it will be," and popped a grape into my mouth so he wouldn't expect more.

"As strange a change as this is for us, I feel," he went on, seemingly determined to engage me in conversation. Sensible, perhaps, for a man marrying someone he'd never met, but I wished he wouldn't. It took me so long to think of acceptable replies he would soon think me dull-witted.

"Yes, indeed," I agreed rather than hide behind more food. "Though I've always known I would marry one day; such is my duty to my family."

I was proud of that one and of the sweet smile I conjured for him.

"Very true." He poured himself a glass of the fizzy mountain water that was also listed in my mind under "rich-people food," this carafe filled with slices of orange. "Would you like some, my lady?"

I didn't, but I wasn't sure what excuse to give so nodded and thanked him, not at all looking forward to cringing my way through the sharp beverage.

"I, too, have always expected to marry and expected it would be for the furthering of my family or . . . perhaps, if I'm being honest, the furthering of my brother's ambition," he said as he poured me a glass. "But though it has never troubled me, to be so suddenly informed of its immediate occurrence was still . . . difficult. No. Unbalancing, perhaps, is the best way to explain it. Do not, I beg, fear I have any displeasure in meeting you or in giving our vows today; I just do not wish to begin this marriage on a footing of dishonesty."

His smile was gentle, even slightly apologetic, as though he knew he ought to have prevaricated unconcern instead. Had he spoken less seriously I might have laughed this off, but the man seemed to put his heart into every word.

"How well you express yourself," I said after allowing myself a moment's thought. "It was a shock, I admit, to be so suddenly informed, as you say. But I am also not at all displeased with the choice that has been made on my behalf."

The act was getting easier. Smile, agree, say something nice or talk about duty, be subservient. It was the perfect recipe for an acceptable reply. Or, as Uvao might have put it, just say the opposite of whatever first comes to mind.

Despite my feeling of triumph, Lord Kiren's answering smile was perfunctory at best, and he took a sip of his fizzy orange water. For all he looked like his brother, Lord Kiren utterly lacked Reacher Sormei's intensity. Thoughtful and watchful, Lord Revennai had said of him, painting what was turning out to be an accurate picture of a gentle, considerate soul one could almost forget had a face more suited to art than skin.

"Have you been to Learshapa before, my lord?" I asked to fill the growing silence, hoping it wasn't a stupid question.

A flicker of a smile. "I have, but only a few times and those when I was younger. A lovely city, quite different from Emora, but then so are Bakii and Orsu. Our strengths are in our differences after all."

"That's a pretty phrase," I said before I could stop myself, able only to hope he missed the sharp note it held. "I like it very much," I added. "Wisdom to live by."

"I think so."

With nothing else immediately coming to mind, I focused on filling my stomach until it stopped complaining. At least he had thought nothing of my hunger. How shocked he would have been to know I'd been extra ravenous for having expended far too much energy in bed with Uvao the night before.

"You smile," Lord Kiren said, jolting me from my own little world. "Has something amused you?"

The truth would have ended our marriage before it began. "Oh no, I was just thinking that this time tomorrow we will once again be breakfasting together, just not here."

"How true. It's likely to be a far less relaxed affair though, I warn you. Sormei likes to get the first morning winds whenever we sail, so we're not likely to linger long past dawn."

"Do you always travel in your own ship?"

His brows rose. "Usually. Occasionally in other people's when we have been invited, though Sormei doesn't often leave Emora unless it's very important." He gestured vaguely out into the city to indicate the present situation. "I've sailed on Lord Romm's vessel a few times," he added, nodding my way. "A fine ship to take the winds upon. I hope you will not find ours a disappointment in comparison."

"Oh no, I'm sure I could not. I've always been fascinated by sand ships. I used to love watching them come and go from the harbour as a little girl. All the coloured sails, the flap and snap of the wind and the creak of the rigging, the rushing sound of the silver dust sliding beneath the hull. I used to think that captaining a ship must be the best job in the world. That way I could sail the glass roads back and forth forever, blowing wherever the wind took me."

As I finished I knew I had said too much, but thankfully Lord Kiren's smile was indulgent. "A lady captain, how your family would have raged."

"And how little I would have cared! Well, then."

"I don't doubt it. All the fiercest and most determined people I've ever met are little girls."

Grateful that he'd taken my words in the best spirit, I returned his amused smile. Marriage to him might not be terrible after all—something for which I ought to be grateful, though with all I wanted to achieve, hating him might have been easier.

Although I could have sat picking at the food forever, all too soon it was time to prepare, noon fast approaching. Back in my rooms, the seamstress had provided yet another collection of fine skirts, these in deepest blue and pale cream, fitting seamlessly to a deep blue tunic with tiny jewelled buttons and an open collar. The seamstress buttoned me into it, looking grimly satisfied, while two maids had a hissed argument over which of my armbands ought to go on first. I stood silent as the preparations went on around me, the world seeming to speed ahead like a ship with too many sails. No one came to check on me, not Uvao, not even Lord Romm, servants my only company until I once again joined Lord Kiren, this time in the courtyard. There an open litter sat waiting, pale cushions covering its decorative scaleglass frame.

"We meet again, Lady Teshalii," Lord Kiren said, drawing my attention from admiration of the glasswork. He held out a hand to help me step inside. "You look as dazed as I feel, but I'm sure we can get through this together."

Once we were both settled safely inside, the four oiled carriers gripped the litter's poles and hoisted us into the air, managing the heavy task with barely a wobble. "That was impressive," I said, desperate to say something—anything.

"Wasn't it?" he agreed, flicking a smile my way. "Men with far too many muscles are always impressive, though I do not envy them the work required to maintain them."

"Something you've tried?"

"Only briefly, to my shame. Sormei is far keener on such things, but aside from the occasional sporting activity, I'm afraid the only exercise I get is carrying very heavy books and piles of paper around in the archives."

"Do you enjoy being an archivist?"

We'd already started toward the courtyard gates and our inevitable future, yet he seemed to be in no hurry to answer. "Yes," he said at last, the word unsure of itself. "I think so? It intrigues me and frustrates me in equal measure and is always something of a challenge."

"That sounds like the very best form of employment."

"Sormei would not agree. He is forever telling me to give it up and focus on something more important, but his idea of important is even farther from my idea of enjoyable."

He laughed easily, a man with no ill-feeling toward the twin brother who seemed to control his world, or perhaps a man intent on ensuring my comfort. Either way, I was grateful for his company as we turned out into the street. On the front portico of a nearby manor, two young ladies stood watching and waved to us as we passed. Lifting his hand, Lord Kiren waved back, earning a smothered squeal. Farther along the manor-lined road a group of children had the same idea, their nurse hardly able to keep them from jumping up and down with excitement as we neared.

"We seem to be popular with the young ones," I said, waving back and earning such smiles that some of the worry eased from my heart.

"My youngest sisters are the same," Lord Kiren said, waving to the children as I did. "Not old enough to attend parties, they will nevertheless stay up as long as they can to catch a glimpse of guests coming and going. One of them once snuck into the dining hall and pinched a glass of brandy."

"Oh no!" I cried, laughing at his anecdote. "She must have been quite, uh...happy?"

"Very! Not so happy the next day, however, nor when Sormei gave her a lecture on the proper behaviour expected of young ladies. They adore him, but it's never enjoyable to be on the receiving end of his dark looks."

The picture he painted of his family was warm and charming, making it sound like he lived with all the people he most loved. It jarred with my knowledge of how families functioned in Emoran society, and my mixed impressions of Reacher Sormei, but perhaps Lord Kiren was just a better actor than I'd first thought.

Emerging from the upper city and onto the Grand Way, we passed beneath an arch and turned into a wall of noise. Behind us had been only those too young to attend the wedding; ahead was a whole city. Lining the broad way were people of every rank and class and commune, from wealthy merchants to labourers, from highly ranked artisans and craftsmen to shop women and street boys. From every direction came cheers and the flapping of hand-held flags, clapping and drum beats. Dazed, I looked about me at a city I didn't recognise, joy and ill-ease squirming into a knot in my stomach.

"There are so many people," I said, turning to Lord Kiren and all but having to shout. "Such cheer!"

"You weren't expecting so much elation?" He leaned close to be sure I could hear him, his breath warm against my skin. "People like celebrations, especially weddings."

"Learshapans don't have a lot of weddings; it's not the Apaian way."

"No, but I understand that marriage has been catching on. I did, of course, make the effort to buff up on my knowledge of Learshapan customs before we arrived, just in case the need arose."

"You are quite remarkable."

"Am I?"

I might have answered him, but the clink of glass drew my attention to a knot of armed guards falling into formation before us.

"Were the armed soldiers really necessary?" I said. "Are we expecting trouble?"

His grimace possessed a note of apology. "Sormei expects trouble everywhere he goes, and not entirely without cause. He's had more than one attempt on his life and many attempts on his position."

I nodded, keeping a grim smile to myself. Perhaps I would be the one he didn't see coming, but as we were carried on toward the sanctuary amid waving and cheers, doubt gnawed at me upon a dozen tiny questions. Had I made the right choice? What would happen to the unification when I was uncovered? And what might such deception cost Learshapa?

The doubts rode with me all the way to the sanctuary, right up to the moment Lord Kiren once again offered me his hand. "Are you ready, my lady?"

Was I? There was no time left to doubt, only to pity this gentle man with his kind smile—a smile that would die when he discovered what he'd welcomed into his home.

I took his hand. "Ready, my lord."

The day had barely begun before we were back at Romm Manor for the last of the celebrations. After the ceremony had come an enormous dinner with food enough for the whole city, and amid the drinking and talking that followed, entertainers had sung and danced and spun glittering glass balls through the air. It had all felt so decadent while down in the city wounded miners and soldiers filled Orial Square, and the scale shortage threatened people with ruin. With doubts following me everywhere, my cheeks were beginning to ache with the effort of forcing a smile.

Familiar faces flitted through the crowd of guests. Lord Kiren—now my husband—came and went from my side, as did Lord Revennai, intent on introducing me to anyone I might have missed the night before. Occasionally I caught sight of Reacher Sormei or Lord Romm deep in conversation with other serious-looking men, but Uvao was little more than a hint of dark green cloth darting by, there and gone like a scent I could not catch. As the hour grew later and the time for me to leave steadily approached, I began to hunt him in the crush, unwilling to part without saying goodbye. But each time I headed his direction, he moved away, until at last he got caught in conversation with a group of young men and could not escape.

"Are you travelling to Emora tonight too?" one asked him as I approached. "I heard Lord Romm is to be off the moment this party is over."

Glances flitted my way, followed by a flurry of bows and greetings, but Uvao didn't so much as turn. "No, not until the season starts. Someone has to stay behind and make sure everything is shut up properly here."

This unleashed a torrent of questions, each slightly drunk young lord not waiting for an answer before pelting Uvao with another.

"Did Ashadi really desert his post?"

"Was Lord Romm planning to recall him anyway?"

"Guess you're not the presumptive heir anymore, huh?"

Uvao couldn't keep a flicker of annoyance from crossing his face at that last one, though it quickly disappeared beneath his blank mask. "I have never been under any illusion I would succeed my father," he said coolly. "As to what Ashadi is doing or what my father planned, I couldn't tell you. If any decision was made, neither Lady Teshalii nor I were informed."

In finally acknowledging my presence at his side, he managed to halt the flow of speculation just long enough to add, "Now if you'll excuse us, my cousin and I have a few final travel arrangements to organise before she leaves," and steer me away through the crowd. "If there's one thing you should always remember about Emorans," he muttered as we walked, as though he hadn't been avoiding me, "it's that we always shoot to kill, but sometimes we like to watch people squirm first."

He hurried me away, not seeming to expect an answer, not even seeming to heed where he was going so long as it was away from other people, away from noise and cheer and out into dim, distant rooms where the silence left echoes ringing in my ears. A passageway, a library—I recognised the spaces from my first walk through the manor, yet Uvao didn't slow until he'd marched me between the shelves and into a small reading room softly layered in dust.

"What—?"

His kiss swallowed my question, his lips pressed to mine with such force, such need, that it stole every word and thought and care, until a cold trickle of recollection sped down my spine. "Uvao, someone will see us," I gasped, pushing him away, my gaze swinging to the doorway and the main shelves beyond.

His breathy laugh seemed to mock as he closed the space again, hands to my hips. "Trust me, no one will see us here."

From a peck on my chin, the tip of his tongue traced a line down my throat, gathering a shiver through my skin. "It's too risky," I said, trying to push him away again, though my treacherous body wanted to pull him close. "We can't do this. Please, I can't come this far only to be caught now."

"No one will see," he murmured into my neck. "And I can't let you go without giving you something to remember me by."

His hand slid between my legs as he spoke, the warmth and weight of his touch flaring desire even through my skirts. I swallowed a gasp, shaking my head though I gripped his tunic, keeping him near. "Uvao..."

"Shhh." His breath danced along my jaw. "No one will see us."

"Please, Uvao, don't."

Ignoring my plea, he began hoisting the many layers of my skirts, gathering them around my waist in a hasty rustle of fabric. Without their protection, the chill air touched my bare skin all at once, adding to the shiver of delight as he pushed me back onto one of the narrow reading desks. It was little more than a deep shelf for holding books and couldn't take my weight, but it allowed me to lift one leg and brace myself against another shelf. Realising how widely spread this left me, Uvao groaned and pressed close, and although bookshelves dug into my back I didn't care, not while his lips were on mine and his hands were making quick work of my undergarment lacing.

As he abandoned my lips to run kisses along my jaw, I breathed in the scent of his hair and the hint of panawood that always hung about his clothes. And his fingers slid inside me. I had expected more warning, but there was no time, only need, and it was all I could do not to cry out and give us both away. Slowly, he drew his fingers out again before pressing in, deeper, teasing me with a flick of his thumb, and to keep quiet I bit his shoulder, stifling a groan into the embroidered edge of his tunic.

His laugh huffed against my ear, and after a line of caresses along my jaw, he rescued his shoulder, smothering my gasps with a kiss instead. A kiss I soon pulled away from, fear once more spiking through me.

"Someone is going to see us."

"No one is going to see us," he said, and as though goaded to greater risk, he kept hold of my gathered skirts and knelt between my legs. An attempt at his name, at a final plea, vanished into a gasp at the warmth of his tongue. Tilting my head back, I gave in to the sensations, each filling my world, stealing all sense of time and place. Needing only one hand to hold myself steady, I gripped his hair with the other, wanting to touch him, to know he was there, to tighten my hold as he pressed deeper, so tight strands of his ponytail snapped.

"Uvao," I whispered, as much plea to never stop as fear we ought not to have begun, but it seemed only to urge him on, drawing me toward the precipice. For a moment there was no him, no us, no past or future just the ever-rolling now filled with pleasure I never wanted to end. But it had to end, and at the last moment, I pressed my hand over my mouth. I could hold in the sound of my cries, but I could not hold back the ecstasy that rolled through me, shaking the narrow desk on which I perched, so violently did it rack my body. I groaned into my palm at a final passing of his tongue before he stood almost as abruptly as he had knelt.

Through unfocused eyes I stared at him as he stared at me, the moment so short I had no time to find words or even sounds of gratitude before he spun away. Half a dozen steps to the door, barely time enough to adjust himself to hide his arousal, and he was gone.

For a time, I just sat there as the fading pleasure in my body melded with the discomfort of his abrupt departure. My skirts half tumbled down, enough to cover me but not to hide the truth, and it was a while before I could bring myself to move, to lace my undergarments and shake out my skirts, to set a hand to my hair and straighten my tunic, to dare one step and then another, back out into the real world from whence we'd come. Out to where the noise had gone on unceasing, to the joy and the laughter, the food and the brandy and the whirl of new faces, where I was both no one and yet the most important person in the room.

Of Uvao there was no sign.

Hoping to avoid suspicion, I grabbed a fresh glass of brandy and fell into conversation with someone I'd been introduced to only to forget their name. I tried to focus, tried not to look around while they spoke, but I couldn't see Uvao, and soon I was flittering on to another conversation in another part of the room, still unable to find him.

I flinched at a touch to my elbow and spun, sure it would be him, only to be disappointed by my husband's beautiful face all kindness and consideration. "It's getting rather late, my lady," he said, an apologetic twist to his lips. "And since we must travel with the morning sun, I thought I would see if you were ready to depart."

"Oh, uh…" Another quick scan of the room found it still lacking Uvao, though Lord Romm was playing host by the far arch as other guests made their escape. "Yes, as you wish. I must say all the proper farewells to my family first, of course."

"Of course. Thankfully, Lord Romm is already seeing people off, and you need not worry about your belongings, as I have been assured they were sent over to Sydelle House earlier, along with your maid."

"Oh." Everything had been done for me, leaving me to the sense I'd been cut free from my own life and had no choice but to accept my husband's proffered arm and let him lead me toward the door. The moment we were moving, farewells seemed to come from everywhere until we were the centre of a small storm edging slowly closer to Lord Romm.

Eventually, we stood before the head of my fake family, a man forcing out a fake smile. He took Lord Kiren's proffered hands and kissed them in farewell, wishing him a safe journey—a sentiment Lord Kiren returned before Lord Romm's gaze snapped to me. With a shock, I realised he had to kiss my hands now, and the power of holding them out to him tasted all too sweet. A quick kiss to the back of each and he let them go like it was nothing to him, but when we made to walk on, he took my arm. "Allow me to walk you out to your litter, my dear."

While Lord Kiren went ahead to be sure the right litter was waiting, Lord Romm tightened his grip on my arm, drawing me close, hip to hip. "Don't fuck this up," he hissed under his breath. "If Sormei comes out of this unscathed, you'll wish you'd never agreed to this charade."

And with that, he stepped back. Wishing me a safe journey with the very same lips, he pushed me from the nest to fly or fall alone.

10

Naili

Evening Bulletin

To all criers for announcement throughout Bakii

An explosion at the Shield Citadel fuels fears of a full-scale attack on the northern border, coming after a dragon was shot down over The Sands earlier in the week.

The seasonal guild alliance dinner is to be held tonight at the Bastion. Citizens are recommended to stay clear of Bastion Square and the surrounding streets due to increased security.

Expert scale alchemist Master Occuello says only luck could see a shot penetrate a dragon's scales, as calls to have Shield dragons brought in to patrol the southern border grow with every Lummazzt raid.

Master Occuello—Mistress Occu—*the alchemist* glanced at the scaleglass blade dangerously close to her throat and emanated disdain. "Are you going to cut me with that, little girl?"

"If I have to," I said, standing my ground. "Are you really Master Occuello, the alchemist?"

She tilted her head. "You were expecting someone else?"

"I was expecting a man."

Her laugh held a bitter edge. "Which you are sure I am not? Yet perhaps you also think women aren't clever enough to be masters, so which is it?"

"No, women just aren't *allowed* to be masters."

"Ah, well what people don't know won't hurt them." She shrugged. "But what you think you know will hurt you. No *maid* is going to destroy everything I've built."

She made another move toward the door, but I stepped in her way again, my blade hand shaking as fury lanced through me. "I'm not here to steal your secrets. I'm here because of what you've done to me. To my friends. To all of us."

"Is this about money?" She rolled her eyes. "Threatening me isn't going to get you a raise, little girl."

"This isn't about money!" The blade in my hand shook and I couldn't stop it, couldn't steady myself, anger lifting me from my body. "It's the flowers. The mould. The...the growth. The healing. What have you done to me that I can cut myself and not bleed?"

For the first time, the alchemist's expression was neither disdainful nor amused. Her brows rose, outer edges arching while the inner angled down in irritable confusion. "What are you talking about?" she said, propping her hands upon her hips. The movement exposed the chest she'd been hiding behind folded arms, leaving the gentle curve of small breasts just visible through her thin shift. "What flowers?"

"The flowers growing on my hairs." I thrust out my left arm, a narrow, speckled field of tiny white blooms bared to the light.

The alchemist gripped my wrist, nothing gentle in her touch as she pulled me closer, twisting my arm to the light. She bent her head, breath ghosting over my skin. "Fascinating," she said, turning us both to catch the light at a different angle. "Jasmine, by the scent. Yet with no sepals, and hair has no vascular strength or water. Fascinating," she repeated, and dropped my arm. "But useless to my work."

"Useless to your work?" I levelled the blade at her throat, a hair's breadth from fair skin like the underside of a snake that has seen no sunlight. "How dare you. I don't give a damn about your work; I am here for my *life*. How many laundry maids have you lost recently?"

She laughed, making no effort to step back from the promise of death. "How would I know? And why would I care? Go away, little girl, there is nothing for you here."

"Tell me what you did!" I hissed. "What was on those clothes we soaked?"

"Don't know. Don't care."

We glared at one another, the heat of our mutual anger filling the steamy air more surely than the warmth of her bathwater. My grip on the blade had tightened and tightened until I could no longer feel my fingers. I wanted to jam it in her throat, to slice her skin and pierce her eyes, wanted to throw the blade down and clamp my hands around her neck, squeezing and squeezing until her face reddened and her eyes rolled, mercy begged upon dry lips—she the manifestation of every cruelty Bakii piled upon its poor and its weak, its old and its suffering. Yet she saw my hate and reflected back only bored disdain, her own survival so seemingly meaningless. Her lids slid low over dead grey eyes. "Well, little girl?" she purred, a step closer pressing the point of my blade into her skin but not cutting it. "Are you going to kill me or stand there staring? I've given you all you're going to get from me."

"Why?"

"Because I don't care."

"But you're a woman."

"And a woman should care? Or a woman should care about *you*? Ridiculous. Whatever you think I am, I will say this only one more time, little girl. I. Don't. Care." As each word emerged carefully enunciated and clipped through thin lips, she took another slow step forward. The tip of the blade pierced her skin, bright red blood blooming upon a pale canvas. Another step would cut dangerously deep, yet still she took it, unblinking eyes boring their challenge into mine.

My arm buckled, but though I could not stand there as she impaled herself upon the blade, I wasn't done and didn't retreat. The knife remained between us, little more than its length separating her chin from mine.

"Pity," she said, a thin trail of blood trickling down her neck. "That could have been glorious."

With our bodies close, I was all the more aware of how thin her shift was, how warm her presence, everything about her sharp and dangerous and hateful. And intoxicating. I couldn't look away, couldn't step away, caught to her existence like she'd woven an invisible web into which I'd walked.

"All I want," I said, hating how breathlessly the words came out. "All I want is to know what could have done this to me. And how I can fix it. Flowers are growing out of my skin. Why? What are you working on that could make this happen?"

She shrugged. "The orchis in my new bullets perhaps. Or the vervain. Some effect of the salpo and crystalli in the new scale. It could be anything, but what will knowledge avail you? The damage is done." She took another step closer, her body touching mine, her thin shift like a breath against my rough tunic. I stepped back, heart thumping to a panic though it was I who held the knife. She smiled. "It doesn't matter how desperately you beg my help, little girl, you'll still be growing flowers."

Another step brought her closer still, eyes half-lidded in sleepy threat. I ought to have held my ground as I ought to have let her pierce her own throat upon the scaleglass blade, but I stepped back, hitting the wall. With nowhere else to go, her next step pinned me to the stones. The knife stayed at her throat, but for all I thought of using it now, it might have been an extension of my hand just seeking the touch of her skin.

"If you know what happened, then you can change it," I said, straining to focus on what had brought me here. "You can cure me."

"You want me to save you?" The rumble of her lowered voice shivered through me, and I swallowed the urge to beg such salvation. "You want me to fix you, little girl?"

"It's Naili, not *little girl*."

"Naili," she repeated, rolling my name around her tongue. "Naili what?"

I pressed my lips closed. Foolish to have told her even my first name; it was surely a death wish to give her my last. This woman was not my friend. Working for her had made me one of the lucky ones, that a privilege she could tear away at a word.

"No?" she said, sliding her knee between my legs. "Just Naili? Naili the laundry maid? Naili of jasmine?" Leaning in, her breasts pressed to mine and her lips drew close. "Naili, giver of life? Or how about"—her lips brushed mine, her breath owning a hint of stale wine—"Naili the witch."

Witch. A word so often spat at my mother as she prepared her herbal remedies and sought to help, to heal. *Witch. Monster. Snake.*

"Mmm, hit a nerve, have I?" the alchemist crooned, sliding a hand along my arm. "Shall I kiss it better?" she added, and as her hand reached mine, she gripped the knife, twisting it from my fingers.

"Guards!" The shout jolted through me as she stepped back,

snatching up her formal robes. "Nothing personal, little girl," the alchemist added, fitting the master alchemist's hat upon her dark hair before yanking open the door. "Guards!"

The thunder of approaching footsteps and clinking glass shocked me from my stupor. Had I still held the blade I might truly have stuck it in her then, but she'd played me well, leaving me no weapon and nowhere to run. She blocked the only door, knife held deceptively loose in her hand as she watched me through those sleepy, half-closed eyes. I spun, hunting an exit. Bath. Towels. Hooks upon the walls. Two potted zebarias either side of a decorative window. A pair of light orbs on a narrow side table. Nothing more. The delicately frosted window would break easily enough, but from the second floor it might not matter whether I jumped or the guards caught me, the outcome the same.

"In here," the alchemist called into the passage. "An intruder has interrupted my bath, and I want to know how. I pay you a fortune so this doesn't happen."

Window.

Dodging around the still steaming bath, I sped toward the window, no longer able to hear the guards for the scuff of my feet and the thundering of my heart. And my own shocked gasp as I slid on a pool of water and slammed into a zebaria pot, knocking it sideways. Soil spilled out and flowers dropped, throwing me a wild idea in a flash of desperation.

"Hands where I can see them!"

The shout might have come from far away for all the heed I paid, closing my hand around the zebaria stem instead. Under my touch, it swelled and stretched, narrow branches rushing for the ceiling. A buzz of energy became a roar as I implored it to grow faster, to hurry, to save me. A jolt of growth smashed one leafy branch through the window like a flailing arm. Other limbs and shoots and enormous leaves swung about me as they grew, seeking space in the increasingly cramped room. Roots broke through the sides of the pot to twist along the floor in search of water, filling the space with cries of horror. The alchemist's guards had spilled into the room only to find themselves hacking their way through a jungle—a jungle that kept growing back, kept moving, every leaf bristling with *life*.

Having kicked out the last shards of glass, I climbed onto the window frame, gripping zebaria stems for balance. Night had fallen over Bakii, the city a tangled nest of deep shadows and bright lights dropping away into the funnel. A light breeze rippled my skirt and cooled my burning skin as, like a rearing monster, the zebaria rose on and on like a ladder to the stars. I didn't trust it to hold me all the way to the city's rim, so I gripped one of the smaller branches and spun back to face the room. Guards were stomping on writhing roots and slashing at branches. One man had somehow ended up in the bathwater, while another tried to aim at me through the waving foliage. And still standing in the doorway, the alchemist watched. She hadn't moved. She still held the scaleglass knife loosely in her hand, but she didn't look sleepy anymore, didn't look bored. The stare that met mine was tense and full of confusion.

Glad to finally have rattled her, I took one hand from the zebaria stem and blew her a kiss. She scowled, and with the thrill of it all rushing through my veins, I gripped hold of the zebaria again and stepped back off the ledge.

Air rushed past as I dropped only to be jerked to a halt as the slack stem pulled taut, swinging me into the wall. Hurriedly lifting a knee was all that kept my face from meeting stone, but for all the elation of freedom, fear needled me—they could cut the stem supporting me at any moment. It wasn't far to the dark alley below, but it was far enough that a fall would really test how well I could heal.

Shouts tore through the manor overhead, the muffled thunder of running steps all the more reason to hurry. Loosening my grip, I tried to slide down the stem only to catch on the leaves and nodules and even a yellow flower as long as my leg. Climbing down was awkward, but hand after hand, feet clamped around the stem, I lowered myself into the night—until a jolt shivered down the stem and I was jerked upward. Once. Twice. A foot at a time they were hauling me up, zebaria stem scraping over the windowsill.

Down was farther than I wanted to fall, but with my choices slimming from bad to worse, I let go. No time to even hope for a soft landing before I hit the ground, feet meeting the alley stones, knees buckling, sending me forward onto my hands with a pained gasp. Strain sparked through my joints, but I pulled myself up and made for the end of the alley, hobbling lightly on one aching leg. I had to get away, had to escape, but to where? I'd taken the risk because I was alone in the city, but now I really was alone.

"Hurry!" came a shout behind me, and the alley door bolt scraped. "Spread out. She can't have gone far."

"Shit!" I sped out into the main street, heedless of the pain throbbing in every joint. The street was packed with people, grouped together to point up and wonder, necks cricked at painful angles. Like a fool I looked up, wondering what could be of such interest—what but a giant zebaria, its stems waving in the wind and its leaves fluttering like a loosened shop awning. "Oh, would you look at that," I murmured, and hurried on, winding on quick steps through the gathered crowd in the direction of the nearest shadows. More streets branched off on either side as the main road headed down its spiral path, but most were dead ends, leading to the sheer cliff of the blasting funnel or out onto the overhang. I didn't know where I was going, but taking the path that would allow me to keep running seemed wisest, even if said path would take me down into the damp world of the long forgotten without a pass.

"Out of the way!" A shocked squeal punctuated the shout, and a glance back revealed a trio of guards shoving their way through the curious onlookers, heads snapping about as they hunted me.

I fought the urge to run. Better to walk, ignoring the sting-ing pain still jolting up and down my leg, away through the murmuring and marvelling crowd, away from Master Occuello's and everything I had made of my life.

"Naili!"

I spun at the hiss of my name, catching only shadows and moonlight and the close press of bodies and night veils.

"Naili!"

There, waving frantically from beneath the overhang of a nearby building, stood Alii. She had lifted her veil so I could see her face, but let it drop back as I turned her way. A flicker of doubt battered against the back of my mind like a moth against glass—a moth I ignored in hope of safety.

"Quick!" Alii whispered as I drew close, her hands beckoning me toward an alley. "They're coming!"

I dared not look back, just hurried on through the thinning crowd and into the shadows, brushing past Alii in the narrow laneway. No light drew me on, and the smell of dry, dusty stone heralded the approach of the funnel wall. "Where—?"

Strong arms grabbed me from behind amid a scuffle and a hiss of whispers, and though I tried to cry out for help that wouldn't come, a hand clamped over my mouth. The cloth held to my face owned the sharp bite of alcohol, and something heavy and unctuous swelled inside my mouth. I gagged. Kicked. Screamed. Tried to breathe anything but the pungent oil filling my nose and mouth and mind, but time began to stretch, voices stretching with it. The soft repeat of my name became a drawn-out song, before the dark swallowed it all.

I slept. It felt impossible to do anything else. Half-formed plans swirled into nightmares, each full of fluttering leaves and long, dark hallways clogged with the smell of snuffed candles and clinging bog water.

Whenever some sound or movement broke through my haze and I opened my eyes, I couldn't keep them open, couldn't speak, couldn't move. Could only close them again and sink back into the darkness of my twisting dreams. Trapped to my body's demands, time meant nothing, an eternity yet no time at all passing before the repetition of my name dragged me from the depths.

"Naili? Naili?"

I blinked, my eyes so gritty and sore it was an effort to open them.

"Finally."

The voice came from a hazy figure taking shape beside me—a familiar figure all thorns through frosted glass. "Miiz?"

"Who else would give enough of a shit about you to sit here for half an hour poking you until you woke up?" She sat upon the floor, arms folded, brow knit in annoyance. "Alii says you've been asleep all day."

"All day?" I said, moving an arm just to be sure I still could, so heavy did I feel.

"As in you slept all night and all day."

"She finally awake?" called a voice from outside, disembodied in the way I felt. "Thank the rains, I was so worried you were going to die on me, Naili."

Alii. A glimpse of her face was like a key, unlocking a rush of memories. Chaintho. The flowers. The taste of mould. The alchemist. Being hunted by her guards. The zebaria. Hurrying toward Alii in the crowd only to have a cloth covered in moorgrass oil pressed over my face. "You! You—"

Finger pressed to her lips, Alii hissed for silence, while Miizhei set her hands upon my shoulders to keep me from rising. "I told you to stay outside, traitor," she growled at Alii. "My help comes on my terms."

Alii sniffed disdainfully from the doorway. "Fine, but remember you don't want to make enemies here, Miizhei. Five minutes."

She opened the door upon a distant babble of conversation, only to close it behind her, leaving me alone with Miizhei. I blinked, trying to dispel both my confusion and the exhaustion that kept trying to drag me back into sleep. "Where are we?"

"Some Hood safe house, I believe," Miizhei said. "You appear to have...caught their interest last night. Told you I didn't trust Alii, the traitorous spy."

I switched from blinking to rubbing my eyes, but it didn't help me understand any better. "She's a Hood? But...why do they want me? We're fully paid up!"

"Perhaps because you can make plants grow really fast? What she was doing at Occuello's in the first place is a different question she won't answer."

"I don't understand. If this is a Hood safe house, why are you here?"

Her sharp-edged smile became smug. "Because when you didn't wake all day, Alii was worried she'd killed you, and wanted help from someone who knows you." Her smile faded. "I'm here on sufferance though; she will kick me out soon lest anyone find me here and realise she fucked up. So, tell me what happened. I'm guessing he was home earlier than expected."

He. Master Occuello. Except he wasn't. She wasn't. It ought to have been an easy disclosure to make, yet as though once more pinned by her dull eyes, I couldn't speak.

You want me to save you? You want me to fix you, little girl?

"Naili." Miizhei's voice drew my attention back like a hook pierced through my lip. She had always been a prickly woman, sharp and biting and clever and sure to outlast us all, yet for a moment her expression was all concern. "What happened to you? It's like you're drunk."

"It must be the moor-grass oil," I said. "I can't focus at all. I just want to sleep."

"Well, you're going to have to focus or the Hoods will eat you alive." Her words coiled around me until I could no longer draw breath. "You have to be careful, Naili. You can't trust Alii or any of them. You have to..." She looked down at hands clamped tight in her lap. "You have to be smart. You have to find out what they want and not let them have it all. You have to give them a reason to need you alive. Do you...do you..." She stuttered into silence. Swallowed. Discomfort bulged down her throat. "Do you understand, Naili?" Her voice rasped, edged in fear she once more sought to swallow. "This isn't a game."

The door opened, spilling pale orblight into the room. "Time's up," Alii said as she closed the door, bringing the light closer to sear Miizhei's cheek pale. "It seems you've cured her, so that's our deal done. And no, don't argue. You don't want to be here when the others arrive."

"Just as you don't want me to be here."

Alii's brows creased in irritation, but she didn't bite back. Like two snakes facing off, they stared at one another unblinking, until Miizhei huffed out a humourless laugh. "Don't underestimate us, traitor," she said, getting to her feet and brushing dust from her clothes. "You'll regret it. All of you."

"Thank you for the warning, Miiz. Bye-bye."

Back straight, head tall, Miizhei walked to the door without another glance and was gone. In her absence, Alii folded her arms. "I hope you can walk."

"I hope you're going to explain what the fuck is going on here."

"What is going on is that I saved you from getting caught for growing a freakishly large plant."

"Saved me? Is that what knocking me out with moor-grass oil means? No wonder I feel so safe right now."

Alii clicked her tongue. "You don't need to be so dramatic about it, Naili. Can you walk?"

"I don't know."

"I suppose it doesn't matter. The boys can just carry you if you can't."

"Carry me where?"

A tap sounded on the hollow door, and while Alii turned to open it again I ought to have searched for a way out, have planned an escape, but even moving required too much energy. The lassitude haunting my limbs surely couldn't still be from the moor grass, yet I had never felt so tired in my life.

Footsteps stomped into the room—their owners vanishing from sight as Alii dropped a heavy veil over my head.

"What—?"

"No, keep it on." She slapped my hands away. "For your safety and ours. She may need help walking," Alii added to the others now in the room. "So maybe one of us either side, one ahead and one behind to be sure we aren't followed."

Agreement rumbled and a strong hand gripped my arm, hoisting me up. "Come on," a man growled. "Boss is waiting."

With barely enough time to register how much every part of me ached, I was hauled toward the door, following Alii's retreating voice. Other voices swirled, glass tiles squeaked, and I was part carried, part dragged down some stairs. The last shreds of warm, dry air brushed through the veil as we jostled through a doorway and out into the street.

"Alii, what is—?"

"Not now, Naili. Just walk."

Through the dishevelled, heavy veil, I knew Bakii only by its sounds and the ghosts that moved across my shielded eyes. They called to one another, they laughed and talked, shouted and grumbled, all to the ever-present beat of footfalls and the endless buzz of insects. The air outside was cooler than it had been inside, possessing a myriad of smells I caught filtered through must. The smell of nuts roasting made my mouth water and my stomach rumble, but the hands gripping my arms only tightened and dragged me on.

"Are we in the upper city?" I asked, almost tripping as they dodged me around something on the road.

"No questions," snapped the man on my right.

"Does that mean yes?"

"It means no questions."

The pressure of their grips pulled me left around a corner into a street where the orange evening light was brighter. West-facing then, but I didn't know the city well enough to guess what that meant. After a few more steps, shade flew overhead, something blocking the light there and gone. One of my captors kept swatting at bugs, shaking my arm with every swipe, but with great self-control I supressed the urge to offer him my veil.

When at last we came to a halt, the evening light had gone and every sound came from a great distance, quiet and muffled and tinny. The delicious smells of food had gone too, leaving me with nothing but the musty scent of the veil and something new I couldn't place, something sharp and indescribable.

"What?" came a gruff voice from ahead. "Oh, you."

A chain rattled. A lock clicked. A squeal of hinges and I was yanked forward again, from the cool of the evening street to the damp chill of a stone room, like the laundry before the boilers were lit of a morning.

"I'll take her from here," Alii said, sliding her arm through mine as my other captors halted. "It's not far, you just have to keep yourself upright a bit longer."

My legs wanted to give way beneath the exhaustion, but I refused to show weakness and stumbled on, through a narrower space—another doorway perhaps—toward a growing smell of dust and heat and wax and home. My heart ached. Master Occuello's house had only ever used light orbs and lanterns, like most of Bakii, but here hung the scent of guttering candles. And the quiet murmur of deep voices.

"You're late," a man drawled as Alii slowed our steps.

"I sent a message," she said.

"You're late on top of your lateness. No, don't waste the precious minutes of my life boring me with an explanation. Take off the veil and you can go."

She slid her arm from mine. "Sit," she hissed, hand heavy on my shoulder until my knees bent and I landed on a chair. "And be nice."

"Nice?" I said, my incredulous query lost in the rush of musty netting as she pulled the veil from my head, catching hairs all the way.

I blinked as the static puff of my hair settled around my face. The room had the appearance of a small indoor tavern. A collection of stone tables on one side possessed a collection of silent men, while across the table from me another man filled my future. Sitting half in shadow, his features were mere suggestions, gestures at a face more interesting than handsome and skin paler than most, but it was the way he took up space that struck me—filling the entirety of the long wooden seat by spreading his knees wide and laying his arms along the bench back.

In silence, Alii disappeared through a far door, moth-eaten veil bundled in her arms, and as much as I didn't trust her, it was all I could do not to call her back. All the while, the man sat watching me like I was an interesting specimen.

"What?" I said, determined not to be afraid. "Never seen a woman before?"

"Oh no, I've seen plenty of women," he said with a huffed laugh. "Even Apaian women," he added, tapping his cheekbone to indicate my tattoo. "They just aren't usually brought in with a warning that they're potentially dangerous. You made quite the scene last night, I hear."

"What do you want?"

His lips curved. "You're not afraid of me."

I was very afraid of him, but I would not show it and so lifted a brow. "Should I be?"

"Most people are." As he spoke, he propped his elbows on his knees and leaned forward, bringing his face more fully into the candlelight. The play of light and shadow on his skin exacerbated the sharpness of his features, lit to gold the short stubble on his chin, and made evident the colour of his eyes. Or rather, the lack thereof. My breath hitched.

Black-eyed monsters.

"Ah," the man said. "There's the response I usually get. Before you ask, yes, I'm from Lummazza. My name is Iiberi; what's yours?"

"I'm... I'm Naili."

"Naili." He seemed to swirl my name around his mouth as he sat back, one arm returned to the back of the chair while the other hand rested on his upper thigh against the dark fabric of his split skirt. "Well, Naili. We have a lot to talk about, I think. Feel free to help yourself if you're hungry."

He nodded at the narrow table between us, fruit and nuts and fried sweetbreads gathered in glass bowls around the candles. A jug of dark liquid reflected golden stars of candlelight.

"And risk being drugged again?" I said, trying to shunt my growing fear aside in search of anger. "We sure do have a lot to talk about. Such as why I'm here. We are fully paid up this week, yet for some reason I'm a prisoner?"

His eyelids dropped into lazy disdain. "Are you chained up?"

"I am not such a fool that I think you have to be chained up to be a prisoner."

"One point to Naili," he drawled. "You're here because Alii thinks you might be more useful alive than dead, but it's also my job to clean up the mess and make sure nothing in Bakii is more dangerous than us. So tell me, Naili, why shouldn't I just kill you now and save myself some time?"

The eyes of the watching Hoods were like the pricks of half a dozen sharp blades, a hunger seeming to heat the air. These men would tear me apart at a single wrong move. Miizhei had warned me to be careful, to give them half of what they wanted so they would keep me alive, but if there was nothing they wanted, what was half of that?

The fear I'd been keeping at bay flooded through me. I was sitting in a strange room somewhere in upper Bakii, facing a terrifying leader of the Hoods who was not only Lummazzt but seemed more than happy to kill me for merely being in his way. I'd set out the day before to demand answers, refusing to let my friends suffer at the hands of the rich and powerful, and now here I was because it was always the poor and the weak who lost. And if I died here, no one would even know.

I swallowed hard. "You think I'm dangerous? I'm just a laundress."

Iiberi's unblinking gaze didn't shift from mine, those deep black eyes increasingly hard to meet. "Why lie?" he said at last, his voice more purr than words, a purr that shivered down my spine. "Are you a witch, Naili?"

"Witch," I whispered, the word cutting into wounds both old and new, into a hurt my people had carried for generations of Emoran rule. "That's a rich slur from a black-eyed monster."

His brows twitched, but he made no move, no sound. He didn't blink, didn't scowl or glare or snarl, yet his very stillness, his silence, was more promise of violence than any rage. Here a man who knew exactly where to stick a blade for maximum suffering, who would lick his lips as blood oozed from my wounds, but to retreat, to apologise, would only make it worse. Instead, I raised my brows, trying for faint hauteur even as my heart sped until I could no longer discern individual heartbeats. The hand sitting on his upper thigh twitched, edging nearer his groin. "For the last time, Naili," he said softly. "Why shouldn't I just kill you?"

If I didn't give him something I was dead. If I didn't prove my usefulness, I was dead. If I didn't try to join the fucking Hoods,

I was dead. So with every line of his expression promising pain should I fail, I said, "Get me a plant."

One of Iiberi's brows arched up. "A plant?"

"A plant."

His other brow rose, the slits cut into them lining up neatly. And without breaking our stare, he called to the men at the other end of the room. "Get a plant."

"A plant?"

"A plant!" he snapped. "Pinch something from someone's garden if you have to."

Steps headed for the door amid murmured conversation, but if Iiberi wouldn't turn to watch them then neither would I. In the wake of their departure, a strained silence fell around us. From somewhere else in the building, the faint tick of a clock was all that delineated time.

"Naili what?" he said, not blinking.

"Naili Billette. Is Iiberi your real name?" I returned, determined not to let him taste my fear.

His lips twitched. "Rachetziiber, good strong Lummazzt name. Why a laundress?"

"Why a Hood?" I pointed at one of my eyebrows. "Are you really a lord?"

"Whenever I want to be. No alarm goes off if you cut notches into your brows, you know."

"You're really Lummazzt?"

"What? Haven't seen a Lummazzt before?" he mocked, sending my own words back at me.

I tilted my head, realising how strange my answer sounded even to me. "Only occasionally, from a distance. You're the first I've ever spoken to."

"And would you look at that," he said, feigning incredulity. "I haven't even eaten your face off yet."

Footsteps returned before I could reply, a distant shuffle at first, growing louder. A scuff behind me was the only warning before a plant was dumped on the table between us, a clod of earth stuck around its roots—dirt that scattered onto the small plates of food and trailed across the floor. Iiberi didn't seem to care. His entire presence thrummed with confidence, with power, lodging envy in my gut. He feared *nothing*. Perhaps if I feared nothing, I would get out of this alive.

"Passiflor," I said, finally breaking Iiberi's gaze to look at the stolen plant. "Tell your men to leave."

Iiberi tilted his head as though seeing me from a different angle would allow him to see through me. "And why should I do that?"

"Because I told you to. You can't be afraid of being alone in a room with me and a poor ripped-up passiflor, can you?"

"You know I'm not."

"But do they, Rachetziiber?"

Annoyance and humour fought for his expression. Annoyance won, but he jerked a thumb over his shoulder and snapped, "Out. Five minutes."

More muttering and grumbling, but they went, proof beyond all doubt that this man had more power in his little finger than I'd ever tasted in my life. Yet the last Hood to leave slammed the door harder than was necessary, digging notches of annoyance between Iiberi's brows. "This had better be worth it, Naili Billette, or the city guard are getting a surprise gift of your corpse tonight."

He folded his arms, knees still spread wide as he sat back and waited, watching me with an intensity that burned.

I drew a deep breath, tasting of candle wax and passiflor pollen and a metallic tang I couldn't place. Slowly I let it go again, focusing on the plant rather than Iiberi's deepening scowl. With one pointed finger, I reached for the stolen plant. Its stem was velvety and its green the brightest colour in the room—something simple to focus on as the familiar buzz of energy hummed through me. The passiflor stretched, leaves rustling on the tabletop as they grew, and I let go the fear that *this* time nothing would happen, that somehow I'd been imagining it all along, and let it thrive.

The passiflor stems curled as they grew, circling toward Iiberi on the opposite seat like reaching hands. Flowers burst open. Leaves unfurled. Roots lengthened, snaking across the table and down onto the floor. Growing and growing and—

"Enough!" Iiberi gripped my wrist, snatching my hand from the plant. "Enough."

I looked up, expecting awe or horror and finding neither on his face. Somehow his blank expression was far worse.

The door creaked open. "You called?" someone asked from beyond. Had he? Had I blinked and missed some time?

"Yes. Get this thing out of here," he said, letting me go and sitting back in a rustle of leaves. "Cut it into small pieces and dispose of it."

"No! It can just be replanted, and—"

"Shut up," Iiberi snapped. "Get rid of it."

Without question, a Hood gripped the large plant, its stems still curled around Iiberi's chest, and hauled it off the table. It scraped like he dragged a tree and slammed onto the floor with as much weight, stems snapping. Leaves dropped around Iiberi and stems caught on the plates and candlesticks, but with many grunts and much cursing, the summoned Hood dragged the plant to the far side of the room. One plate had hit the floor and shattered, while both candles lay on their sides, curls of smoke the last memory of their flames.

"Perhaps I should be ordering you cut into tiny pieces," Iiberi said, brushing a knot of hair back from his brow. "I thought Alii was being...overdramatic, but no, you are dangerous."

"But usefully dangerous."

Iiberi folded his arms again as the other man finally departed, trailing cursing and dirt. I'd come with no desire to join their group or even earn their favour, yet as Iiberi considered me I found myself dreading a refusal. The Hoods were brutal and I ought to want only to run, yet to my shame I did not. I was tired of being grateful for the nothing I had, tired of being afraid. I wanted to sit where he sat and know myself powerful.

"We don't tend to take women into our main ranks," he said at last. "Most women here earn their keep by cooking and cleaning and lying on their backs because they don't pass their test."

"Test?"

His smile turned smug. "You don't think we let just anyone join, do you? Even witches who can grow plants with their hands have to prove themselves useful to the cause."

"By doing what?"

Iiberi shrugged, seeming to lose interest. "Each test is specific to the individual, depending on what they can provide. And they aren't decided by me."

"Then who?"

With something of an annoyed sigh, he got to his feet, unfolding as a spider might, stretching from its corner to its full size. Sitting down, Iiberi was an imposing man; standing, he seemed to fill the room, using up its air. "Don't go anywhere, will you?" he said, and before I could think of a reply or even manage to breathe, he was gone, the room far smaller in his wake. I dared a glance around. The Hoods who had been sitting at the stone tables hadn't returned after taking the giant passiflor out, yet there was something watchful about the space, something itchy and strange and wrong, like dozens of eyes upon me.

Barely had a minute passed before the door opened abruptly and Iiberi returned, soft, long-legged steps bringing him across the room to the mess of a once neatly set table. With a waft of salty rose somehow clean and dirty at the same time, he sat, assuming the same knees-splayed position of confidence and ease. "You are to get into Occuello's workroom and steal notebooks and samples for us."

Occuello's workroom. But I'd just escaped from his—*her* house; the most dangerous thing I could do was go back, and they knew it.

"That's impossible," I said, hating the slight tremble in my voice. "He already had heavily armed guards; he'll only have more now."

"Impossible is how we take on the very best, not just fodder."

Fodder. The way he spoke made it sound delicious. As though like the spider he appeared, he would wrap me in silk and devour me if I failed.

I swallowed hard. "But...you already have someone capable of getting inside the alchemist's house."

"Do we?"

His brows lifted in bored disinterest as though he would rather be anywhere else, and it was all I could do not to wither under his gaze. "You do. Alii."

"Ah, but her position is too important to be risked on mere thievery. You, on the other hand, are entirely expendable. Take the test or don't, Naili Billette. Either way, I'll be here to clean up the mess that is your continued existence."

Ashadi

Afternoon Bulletin

To all criers for announcement throughout Orsu and the Shield

Another callout at the citadel sees the dragons saddled up three times in the last day, inciting calls for more riders and greater protection for our northern settlements.

Negotiations conclude on Learshapan treaty as the marriage of Lord Kiren Sydelle, brother of Reacher Sormei Sydelle, to Lady Teshalii Romm has spurred hopes of a renewed, united Basin.

Doubt cast over the safety of all local Apaian artifacts as the reclamation movement strikes Orsu. A burial statue has been stolen from Lord Brosque's estate, and he is offering a large reward for information that might lead to reclamation movement leaders.

90:58

I glared at the approaching ship, hating everything about it from the fulsome billowing of its multicoloured sails to the ornate carvings of its hull. Beautiful only in the faux-grand way we Emoran nobility decorated our houses, competing in the endless game of who could appear most imposing. It reminded me of home.

I withdrew the korsh roll from between my lips and exhaled, smoke tangling into the cloudless sky. Beside me, Manalaii stood watching the ship grow larger, his expression one of reluctant awe.

"Not been on a sand ship before?" I said.

"No." Some of his excitement faded, tucked safely away behind a mask of nonchalance. "But my sister and I used to climb Bakii's ramparts when the guards weren't looking to watch the ships come and go. Before they shut all the walkways off of course. Probably get hung for such a thing now."

"That seems rather extreme."

Mana shrugged. "Not my place to say, but it does mean it's been a few years since I've seen one dock. I'm glad for the opportunity."

"Well then I'm glad we got kicked out too, if only because it pleases you," I said, setting the korsh back to my lips and drawing its smoke in deep to spread calm over ragged nerves. After the lies and the explosions and Mana's sudden dismissal, it said much that it was my destination that hung heaviest over my head. I hadn't seen Emora for three years and hadn't thought to for many more still.

Exhaling the last breath of smoke, I stubbed the korsh roll on the stone railing and flung the end into a nearby barrel. "I hope it won't take them long to unload and turn about," I said. "I'm about done with standing around already."

"It's a few days to Emora though, is it not?"

He seemed determined to be cheerful and who was I to ruin his plans? "Yes, but once I'm on board the ship, I don't have to do anything but drink."

Mana nodded, a slow, solemn gesture that seemed to understand more about me than I did. I took out my korsh pack to roll another. At this rate I wouldn't have enough for the journey, but rationing had never been my forte.

Down upon the rocky desert that made up most of the Celes Basin, a wide glass road glimmered in the sunlight, criss-crossed with the shadows of whipping flags and thick mule posts. In the bright afternoon light, it possessed a pale blue hue shot through with gold, but from certain angles it could look silver or green or even black, like one sailed upon inky nothingness.

I drew a fresh lungful of korsh smoke, its tendrils failing to ease my ragged nerves as well as before.

"You don't want to go to Emora, do you?" Mana said, adding after a pause, "My lord."

I turned my head enough to catch the shape of him at the edge of my vision, yet not enough to subject myself to his expression. "Not especially," I said, blowing free a billow of smoke. "I have never been one for diplomacy when backstabby politics is more fun, and the last time I saw Reacher Sormei he wasn't reacher yet, but he was an irritating ass. I'm allowed to say that," I added, turning enough to see Mana's brows rise. "Because he once sucked my cock. Poorly."

Mana's choke of shock was worth the moment of truth I rarely dared.

"Not sure if that makes it more or less likely that he will listen to what I have to say, or more or less likely he will act to fix"—I gestured in the direction of the distant citadel—"all this."

"I...do...do you all just...know each other?" Mana said at last, though I hoped it wasn't the first question that had come to his mind.

"More or less. By name and reputation if nothing more, but it's fashionable to travel to Emora for the dry season. Lots of parties with little rooms you can sneak off into for such...moments.

Places to make memories you wish you could scoop out of your mind and throw upon the stones with the wet splatter they deserve."

I drew another lungful from the korsh roll, triumphant at having stolen Mana's power of speech however briefly. I would regret it later when he asked more questions or filed the information away with his growing collection of terrible things about me, though it hardly mattered when he wouldn't be with me much longer—a truth that killed off the shoots of joy his horrified expression had sprouted.

We watched in silence as the ship hit the chocks at the end of the broad glass strip, and the last of the coloured sails were hastily furled to keep it from overbalancing in a strong gust of wind. Sand anchors hit the rock and were hammered in by men shrunk by distance who nevertheless had the sort of muscles most could only dream of. Only one wore a veil, the others trusting to the wind to keep most of the bugs off their faces and arms as they sweated at their task.

Once the ship was secure, its sides broke open, great hinged panels dropping down to allow passengers and cargo to pour onto the dock like water from a shattered bottle. Glass barrels and husk-wrapped goods exited upon a trail of equally muscular men following one another like a colony of ants, while the few passengers carried only their belongings. Most wore the dull colours of the lower classes—the only attraction Orsu possessed for the nobility was as somewhere to throw away the sons they no longer wanted.

Once the ship had been cleared, we watched men and mules fight to turn the ship about, struggling against both wind and the temperamental nature of highly polished glass. On board, the rest of the sailors braved the rocking deck to turn the sails and check the wind.

"I suppose we ought to head down there before the ship leaves without us," I said, finally pushing back from the parapet I'd long been warming. "Wouldn't that be an excellent start to my ambassadordom?"

"I'm not sure that's what it's called," Mana hazarded, looping his bag over his shoulder.

"Then what is it called? Ambassadorhood? Ambassadorness?"

"I think just...term as an ambassador? Time as an ambassador? Stint, perhaps."

"How boring. I will insist on being called *your ambassadorness* from now on, none of this dull *my lord* business." Not that he would long have to call me anything. I turned abruptly, snatching up my pair of bags before Mana could reach them. "Let's go, I'm sick of standing here."

"I can carry those for you, my lord," he said, hurrying in my wake. "Since I'm here for the first part of—"

"No *my lords*, didn't I just say?"

"But, my lo—your ambassadorness, please. I would be failing in my duties to let you carry your own bags."

"Lucky for us both that you've already been dismissed then, isn't it?" I threw over my shoulder. "How else am I going to get muscles like those men who hammer the sand anchors into solid rock?"

"I...You...What?"

I turned to grin at him, walking backward a few steps along the stone walkway. "Don't tell me you missed them; they were glistening with sweat and everything."

Mana's brow creased and his lips twitched, reluctant amusement slowly crinkling the corners of his eyes. "It's impossible to know what you're going to say and do next, did you know that, your ambassadorness?"

"No, but thank the song for that, I wouldn't want to be predictable. That way dullness lies." I spun back around on the words and none too soon, the steps having approached far faster than I had envisioned.

Despite the ever-present wind, the air thickened as we descended to the dock, its stones crammed with sweaty bodies and aggressive shouting that hit my skull like the pressure of Shuala's sudden dives. Somehow the noise was worse than the smell, which was a concoction of spices and perfumes and body odours that seemed to cancel one another out, leaving nothing for my nose to latch on to.

"Where do we go?" Mana shouted behind me. "Are we meant to be getting on board yet?"

"Looks like they're only stowing cargo at the moment," I called back. "But if we can find the captain, I can be all important at him until he gives us a good cabin."

In the middle of the main dock, a crier stood upon a pedestal calling the news of the day to the fresh arrivals. His voice sounded hoarse in the hot, dry air, and I didn't envy him the hours he would spend up there shouting the same words over and over to an uncaring crowd.

"—inciting calls for more riders and greater protection for our northern settlements," the man called out as we neared, my gaze sweeping back and forth in search of someone whose entire bearing shouted, *This here is my ship.*

"Negotiations conclude on Learshapan treaty as the marriage of Lord Kiren Sydelle, brother of Reacher Sormei Sydelle, to Lady Teshalii Romm has spurred hopes of a renewed, united Basin."

I stopped abruptly and Mana walked into me.

"Doubt cast over the safety of all local Apaian artifacts as—"

"Did that crier just say what I thought he said?" I asked, turning in the press of bodies to find myself standing all too close to my watcher.

"About Apaian artifacts?" Mana said, adjusting the bag on his shoulder, his forearm muscle taut and sweat beading his brow.

"No, the wedding."

"Of the reacher's brother? Why? Did he suck your cock too?"

"What? Kiren? No! The poor thing has never had a single dirty thought in his life."

Mana lifted a disdainful eyebrow. "And you're so sure about that? Just because he didn't suck *your* cock?"

"Can we stop talking about my cock for a moment? Not something I ever thought I would say, but..." I turned, searching for the pile of crier sheets that were normally nearby before I realised the man was already repeating himself.

"—and greater protection for our northern settlements," the crier shouted. A moment to breathe and then he went on, "Negotiations conclude on Learshapan treaty as the marriage of Lord Kiren Sydelle, brother of Reacher Sormei Sydelle, to Lady Teshalii Romm has spurred—"

"He *did* say *Romm*!" I spun back to Mana. "That's my name."

Manalaii hadn't moved, just stared at me like I'd lost my mind. "Yes, it is," he said eventually. "Relative of yours?"

"No! But she must be!" I turned back toward the crier as though I could ask him for more information, before giving myself a shake. The only person on this dock equipped with knowledge about the Romm family was me.

"Perhaps you would remember her if she'd sucked your cock."

Mana's cutting words tore through my fragile concentration, but despite a brief flare of annoyance, all I could say was "How highly you think of me," and know it was entirely my own fault.

Hoisting my bags with now aching arms, I pushed on through the dense soup of humanity in search of the captain. We found him standing on the steps near the ship's bow, watching cargo being loaded and occasionally removing the korsh roll from his lips to shout.

"Careful with that, you shovelhead!" he called, flinging hand and korsh ash in the direction of a young man who hadn't yet developed the muscles needed for a hauler's job. "Any cracked barrels you pay for with your own tack!"

"Ah, Captain Helliode, I presume?" I said, having to halt on the step below and look up at him. "I'm Lord Ashadi Romm, ambassador of the Shield Citadel."

"Course you are," he said, drawing smoke into his lungs. "And of course you're going to be a pain in my neck like every other fancy ass that steps aboard my ship. Keep to your cabin and I'm sure we'll get along just dandy."

"Give me a comfortable cabin and I'm more likely to keep to it."

The man barked a laugh. "Like I could do else without your dragon masters having my balls for breakfast." He jabbed a finger in the direction of the ship. "Get on board, Lord Ambassador Man, and let the rest of us little people do our jobs."

A deep part of me bristled, but a snappy retort only half-formed before exhaustion buried it. I didn't want a fight, especially not with a man who looked like he would enjoy nothing more than breaking my nose. He was also right. I could have bought his whole ship out from under him, and even as its captain he would have no recourse to take it back—knowledge that ought to have shamed me more than it did.

Belatedly, I realised Mana had taken hold of my arm, his long fingers tightening in warning. "Excellent," I said, smiling glassily at the captain. "We shall get aboard and stay out of your way. And find out what bottles of entertainment are on offer."

The captain let out a little snort behind me but said no more, returning instead to shouting between drags upon his korsh roll.

His ship, unimaginatively called the *Evening Star*, was both more and less grand up close. More because it was far larger than it appeared from the terrace, its hull twice as tall as Shuala and its thick masts reaching far into the sky; less because its side panels were scratched and sun-faded, and its hinges rusting. Only the thin shimmer of scaleglass painted upon its underside had been kept flawless.

"I didn't realise it was so tall," Mana said as we started up the stairs. "Are all sand ships this big?"

"Many of them," I said, grateful for a return to dull, normal conversation. "They need to be big to carry enough cargo to make a profit; also big ships are strong enough for big sails. They might not be fast with so much weight, but big sails mean they move at a more or less constant pace. Smaller ships have to be either very well built for large sails, or have to rely on mules during lulls. My father has a private vessel, and he pays to send mules ahead on any journey he's undertaking because if there's one thing he hates it's being kept waiting."

Mana murmured a reply, lost to the wind, and it was all I could do not to turn around and demand to know if he had just likened me to my father.

Our cabin turned out to be the nicest aboard the *Evening Star*, although it also turned out that wasn't saying much. It was a long, narrow space, at least half the width of the ship but only two arm-spans wide, like someone had taken a slice out of a more spacious room. One end had racks for baggage, a narrow bookshelf with a worn array of uninteresting titles, and an equally narrow table surrounded by cushions. The other end of the room contained a large bed.

Seeming not to have noticed the sleeping arrangements, Mana peered closely at the contents of the bookshelf as though looking for something specific.

"I hope you're not the kind of person who likes the kind of books that get discarded on guest-house shelves," I said, glad my careless drawl was back.

"No," Mana said. "But likely that's because I'm not a great reader rather than because there is something wrong with guest-house books."

"Oh, let me assure you there is indeed something wrong with guest-house books." He shot me a look over his shoulder, and before he could say anything, I added, "Unless one is a Romm family history and can explain how I have acquired a new relative."

"You really don't know her?"

I shook my head. "Not at all. Emoran family trees can get very messy, but likely it won't surprise you to learn that I had to study ours until I knew every branch by heart. And I can assure you, even in the farthest reaches of obscurity, where the cousins of cousins live, there is no Lady Teshalii Romm."

The expression that crossed Mana's features was little more than a facial shrug as he turned to find a rack for his bag. "Seems odd," his only comment on what, to me, felt like a small explosive in the distance that would soon grow too large to ignore.

Having stowed his own bag, Manalaii came back for mine, and I cleared my throat, throwing a glance at the bed. "How much would you be willing to bet the captain deliberately gave us only one bed to annoy the uppity lord?"

Amusement sparkled in his eyes. "Should I go ask for another room and see what he says?"

"Oh no, I wouldn't risk it. That man will eat you alive if you ask him for anything, and I will not have your death by cannibalism on my conscience. Let him think he got one up on the fancy lord, not realising that we already sleep in the same bed almost every night. Unless I snore, and you've just never said anything, then you may go and ask for a separate room."

"No, you don't," he said. "At least not unless you're sick. You do snuffle sometimes though, usually when you're about to wake up from the first deep sleep of iishor withdrawal. It's very cute."

"Oh. Well, you will find it difficult to convince me to go through all the vomiting and exhaustion just for a snuffle."

"Pity."

Perhaps the realisation that he would never again hear me make such a sound occurred to him as suddenly as it occurred to me, for he turned abruptly away to untie his bag, seemingly as intent on sorting through his things as he was on not looking my way.

I squeezed my eyes closed. "Why don't you come with me? To Emora, I mean, instead of changing ships at Remorna. Unless... unless you want to go home to Bakii. Which would be fine too, of course."

Still with his back to me, Mana seemed to slump, stiff shoulders relaxing as though he'd let out a held breath. "You say that like I have a home that isn't with you," he said when at last he turned. "Three years is a lot of habit to suddenly upend, so, yes. Thank you. Yes, I would like to be your watcher for a little longer. Just to Emora and back."

Like I have a home that isn't with you.

My throat constricted. "Oh good. I know it was selfish of me to ask, but— Yes. Good." I forced out a weak laugh. "Song be damned but three years is a long time, isn't it? You must know me better than I do by now."

"Well, I know Lord Ashadi, rider of pack three. But I'm not sure how well I know his ambassadorness. Or even just... Ash."

The sound of my name on his tongue rolled through me with an all-too-delighted shiver. "There," I said, sinking onto the bed with a smile. "You *can* do it."

"Since I don't have to worry about losing my job anymore."

"Perhaps I ought to have called you Watcher Billette, to keep it fair. A good name, *Billette*. Rolls off the tongue much better than *Romm*."

Mana smiled, seemingly as glad as I was to leave the all too emotional waters behind. "That's why my mother liked it. She said it was musical. We grew up on a commune and didn't have a last name like city folk, so when we moved to Bakii she gave us one, Nai and I."

"Is Nai your sister?"

"Yes. Naili. She works as a laundress for some big-shot alchemist in Bakii."

A note of challenge crept into his words, so light he might not have meant it, but a lifetime of edging around my father's moods had made me sensitive to little changes of tone.

"I imagine the smells must be quite interesting," I said, watching his response from the corner of my eye. "Though it seems doubtful anyone gets paid enough to put up with them."

If it had been a test, it was impossible to be sure whether I'd passed, but he deigned to sit on the edge of the bed beside me. "If her letters are anything to go by, then you're right. Although she thinks I'm the one who doesn't—*didn't* get paid enough."

"I would have to agree with her. But then no amount of money is worth so much vomit and ill-temper."

He flicked an impenetrable gaze my way. "She says you're dangerous."

"Me?" I ought to have laughed or agreed or grinned, something—anything but stare at him wide-eyed like the wind had been knocked from my lungs, because what I hoped the unknown Naili Billette meant was that I was dangerous...to Mana. Yet sitting there caught in the heat of his gaze, I couldn't shake the feeling I was the one in danger. "Only to sand monsters, you can assure her," I said.

Mana grinned and I grinned back, but all too aware of a growing constriction around my chest and in my throat, my grin soon faded to a weak smile. To a slightly breathless stare as my heart yearned toward him, like it would leave my chest to live in his if it could. Three years was a long time, perhaps, but it had been filled with callouts and recoveries, with training and work and the endless snipe and gossip and tussle of rich young men set adrift to build their own hierarchy. Rare had been the true conversations. The quiet moments. The silence in which I could hear the hammering of my own heart.

Even when he had lain beside me in my bed, he had done so in the guise of a carer, never a companion. Now we were free of the citadel's constraints, of the need to follow orders and maintain formality, free of the illness and strain of iishor, he seemed like a different person. Manalaii had been my watcher, but perhaps *Mana* was someone else entirely. Someone who drew closer. Whose lashes caressed the air with every blink. Whose lips were suddenly all that existed in my narrowing world. Lips that pressed to mine, slightly dry and wholly breathless. Tasting of old korsh and fresh spiced dates, his tongue slid along the inside of my lip, encouraging my mouth to open, to draw him in, his heat and his closeness everything for the split seconds I allowed myself such joy.

Fear crept in. Fear that this new Mana existed only in my head, that his every move was just Manalaii the watcher taking care of me because he knew what I wanted and how to provide it. Because he pitied me.

I pulled away as certainty solidified, turning everything sour, and in a flurry of dusty linen, I was on my feet. "I'm sorry, I shouldn't—" I cleared my throat. "Not why I asked you to come with me, I assure you."

Still seated on the bed, a troubled notch cut between his brows. "Are you all right?"

"Always. But I think I'd better take myself up on deck for some fresh air."

I didn't await a reply, just hurried out, heart thumping hard. It had just been a moment of weakness, I told myself, and it meant nothing. How could it mean anything when he had always been obliged to fulfil my every request? When his affection had been bought with years of care and forced proximity? No, I'd just let him see too much of my desire and he had done his job, nothing more. A wise man would forget it had ever happened.

I stared at the page before me, gaze sliding out of focus. Outside the narrow windows, the bare rock of the basin slid by, while overhead the ship's crew thumped about shouting. For two days I'd tried to write a damned petition to Reacher Sormei, but every time I put pen to paper, sure of what I wanted to say, of just how to get Sormei to see how serious the situation was, the words faltered. At first, I put it down to my own disinterest, but the longer I stared at my collection of notes, the stronger grew a suspicion that they just didn't make any sense.

For about the dozenth time, I took myself up on deck in the hope that walking would shake loose whatever thoughts had gotten tangled, only to regret the decision at the first blast of wind. It was incessant, hot and dust-laden, every swirl sending the crew darting to adjust the sails. Mana didn't seem to mind. Despite there being nothing to look at but endless rocky wastes, he hardly moved from the ship's railing. At first, I'd wondered if he was avoiding me, but the wind had only to lull for him to pelt the sailors with questions, pointing from rope to wheel to windvane to the complicated chart they used to measure distances and angles. If the deep bass drumbeat of another ship called in the distance, Mana was the first to the prow and there he stayed, watching the other ship pass. It didn't seem to matter whether they were small private vessels or grand cruisers carrying passengers and cargo— he was enamoured of them all.

"You're like an excited puppy darting from one thrill to another and dripping wee all the way," I said, glad to focus on something other than the petition.

"I think possibly that's not a compliment," Mana replied, pausing as he joined me at the railing.

"What gave it away?"

"The wee."

"Ah yes, wee gives everything away. Oh, don't mind me, I'm a jaded grouch you don't deserve."

He leaned at the railing beside me and stared at the dull horizon as though it had answers to all life's questions, his brow creased. I wanted to smooth it, to say something that would bring back his bright smile, but I was just smart enough to know Mana's sister had been wrong. I wasn't dangerous. He was. To what remained of my sanity.

"I understand we should be in Remorna by tomorrow if the winds keep up," I said, because I had to say something. "An hour or two to exchange cargo and turn the ship. You'll love that too, more's the pity."

"Has it ever occurred to you that not everyone has your experience of the world?" he snapped, turning a scowl my way. "Your ambassadorness. I apologise for being so...so gauche as to find something I've never seen before more interesting than your complaints. Not all of us grew up making yearly trips to Emora on a private ship drawn by mules and likely eating fresh fruit and... and chocolate all the way."

His jaw snapped closed as fast as he had let fly his rage, and Mana scowled at the horizon, hands shaking upon the railing. "I'm sorry, I shouldn't have said any of that. It wasn't my place to—"

"Don't apologise," I said. "I might hate your honesty, but if you don't give it to me, I may become an even more insufferable ass."

"Something that is somehow also my duty," he said bitterly.

"Duty? I didn't say that."

"Do you ever owe anyone anything? Or is that just something poor people do?"

I closed my eyes a moment, starting to feel like I'd wandered into a conversation someone else had started. "What? You think I can just do whatever I like whenever I like? Would I be risking my life every callout and drinking iishor if that was true?"

Mana gave a little snort that seemed to mock and disbelieve all in one sound.

"What the fuck is wrong with you?" I said. "Would you like

me to apologise for having been born to a wealthy family? For having a noble name? For experiencing the world in a way you have not? Ought I flay myself upon the pedestal of duty? Or sacrifice myself to the monsters so there's one less rich arsehole for you to share your world with?"

"No! It's just—" Mana's lips snapped shut, pressed to a thin line. "Forget I said anything; it wasn't my place. I have been foolish and taken far too much of your kindness already, Lord Ashadi."

"That's not what you were going to say."

He stepped back from the railing, unfolding to his full height in a way that seemed to leave so much of him tucked in, protected. Hidden. "No, but what I was going to say would only make this worse, so if you'll excuse me, Lord Ashadi, I'll—"

I gripped his arm only to let it go as quickly, my abrupt, desperate gesture staying his escape. "Don't. I'm an ass and I'm sorry." I gestured at the gathering sunset, where the lengthening tendrils of sunlight were growing pink behind a dusty haze. "If anyone should go below and miss the sunset it's me. I've that stupid petition to work on anyway."

Mana glanced at the horizon, hesitant. "It isn't going well?"

"Terribly. It makes no sense at all, in fact, but that's my problem, not yours."

I made to walk back to the stairs, but this time Mana gripped my arm. "Don't," he said, the word an echo of mine that caught my breath. He didn't let go as I had, didn't look away. "Why don't I get us some dinner, and then you can tell me why it doesn't make sense."

I must have agreed, because we were soon settled on the cushions in our narrow cabin, each with a plate of food and the awkward feeling we needed to atone for losing our tempers. Food on board public ships was nothing exciting, but the plain stew-like slop and bread on my plate smelled much better than expected and promised a full belly.

"All right," Mana said, digging into his. "I cleared a lot of pages covered in your writing from this table just now, so what's the problem? It looks like it's going well to me."

"Each individual section *is* going well. I wrote what was frankly a very moving piece about the plight of riders being forced to drink iishor every day, and another one about the efficacy of dragon fire being diminished without enough rest, and my description of the explosion would make a corpse cry. I just don't understand why he needs to hear it."

Mana's brows knit. "I'm not following."

"Well, Master Razard said we needed more funding, but apart from for repairs, why?" I said. "Riders come from elite Emoran families and are sponsored entirely on noble wealth, and more dragons, well, they come from other dragons, don't they?"

"I...assume so?"

"Right, so unless they have to pay dragons to make more dragons, why do they need more money? And yes, I know there are plenty of other people who work at the citadel, but would an increase in riders really cause such a huge increase in required cooks and stable hands to warrant pleading funds directly from the reacher?"

"Not given how little most get paid," Mana muttered.

"Exactly. So, why send me as an ambassador to petition the reacher? I can tell my moving tales of tragedy, but unless he brings in rider conscription—which would be extremely unpopular—he can provide neither more riders nor more dragons. And while he can provide more money, what good will that do? Throwing money at attacking monsters isn't going to deter them."

Mana stared at me, cogwheels turning in his mind as they turned in our ship, seeking the right wind to lead it on. Slowly, he shook his head. "I don't know."

"Neither do I. There seems to be more and more that I don't know, and it's making me twitchy. Why the money? Why send you away? Why were there monsters in that room off the undercroft? How did that man shoot a bullet through one of Shuala's scales? And why? And who the fuck was he? Everyone thought I was mad, that I imagined him in a fit of iishor mania, but I didn't. I know I didn't. As surely as I know that wasn't a stray bullet from my own pack."

I'd barely touched my food but still set down my fork, running my hands down my face to stem the rising panic. "For all I know, Shuala is dead and they're lying to me about that too. Everything made sense a few days ago; now...now nothing does. He took off his glove, Mana. Took it off and set his hand to her scales and apologised, not for shooting her down, but for everything that had been done to her—what does that even mean?"

"I don't know."

"He even had something like a monster that came when he called, tame as a fucking mule, yet for every question I ask I get the same answers. No one lives in The Sands. No one comes back alive. No one can shoot through a dragon's scale. Emora is full of libraries and scholars, and my new relative just married the head archivist, but I'm not going to find any answers there, am I?"

"Probably not, no. The books will all be Emoran books with Emoran lies."

"Then where do I go to find out the truth? Where do I find... other histories? Your histories. Is there an Apaian library?"

Mana shook his head. "I told you, we don't write things down, that's not the way our knowledge has been kept and passed. That's why it's easy to ignore."

"And hard to find. But they exist, don't they? These stories? So where do I find them?"

I had expected his eyes to brighten, for him to smile at being able to share his culture, but Mana's brows sank into the fiercest frown I'd seen him produce for a long time. "Our history and our knowledges aren't just for anyone. They aren't there to...tickle your curiosity."

"It's not curiosity, Mana. I need to know because there's a truth here somewhere, buried beneath the piles of lies; I just can't find it without something to point the way."

"Wanting to know is not the same as needing to know."

"No, but if the lies are this deep, it must be for a reason, and you can't tell me you think it's a good reason."

He eyed me warily over our forgotten meals. "People ask about our history and culture all the time, but it never ends well. No doubt you read *Apaian Culture* as part of your grand education?"

"I think so?"

"Ugly brown cover, depicts Apaians hunting the basin with spears and short skirts."

"Yes, that was prescribed reading. Not sure I read it though."

"You'd know more if you hadn't. The man who wrote it, Elwin Sandarnaque, called himself a scholar and came into our communes, wanting to write about us so everyone might learn. Well, we learned not to trust what Emoran scholars say."

I had the feeling the floor was cracking dangerously beneath me. "That book is quite old, isn't it?"

"It is, yet it has never been replaced or updated because the story of Elwin Sandarnaque is one all our children learn. No one but an Apaian with a right to the knowledge is allowed to write anything down."

"Mana, you know me; I'm the last person alive who would sit down to write a book. I'm not a scholar. I *am* Emoran, yes, but it's not all I am. I'm also a drinking, smoking, sarcastic arsehole who wants to know what is going on before he gets stabbed in the back. Before the Shield falls because we preferred our lies to the truth."

A small smile edged out his wariness. "You forgot keen on shooting things."

"So I did. Whatever will I do without you."

His smile slipped away. "Even if I took you to . . . people who know what you want to know, they might not talk to you. And if they refuse, there's nothing I can do. It's not my place to decide what our elders do with the knowledge entrusted to them."

Remarking that I hadn't known Apaians had official elders seemed unwise, so I just nodded. "I understand, but I want to try."

Mana sighed and made something of a defeated gesture. "Then I will ask around when we reach Emora, see if I can find out which commune we'd have to visit."

"Thank you, Mana. Truly."

"You're welcome. Ash."

His shy smile was like a crooked finger, my name on his lips a hook that tugged me close—a pull I could neither resist nor submit to, leaving myself capable only of eating my meal, bite by bite, without daring to look up from the plate.

Tired as I was, I lay awake long into the night. Sleeping had never been my forte, but the closer we got to Emora the harder it became, dread seeping into my bones. Add the petition and thoughts about Mana, and it was next to impossible. He seemed to have no such difficulties. The bright desert moonlight poured in through narrow windows, laying stripes across his sleeping face. A pale ray cut across his nose and one closed eye, before reaching up into his hair like a lover's fingers. He wasn't exactly beautiful in the traditional sense, with his thick straight brows and untameable hair, but what he lacked in perfect, sculpted lines he more than made up for in flashes of character. In those expressive eyes, that creased brow, and the way his mouth could form smiles that were more frown than smile, and frowns more smile than frown. He was somehow both stoic and mercurial, as dependable as the rising sun yet tumultuous beneath the surface. No doubt he had lain awake watching me sleep any number of times as part of his job. Unwise to wonder if he'd ever had other thoughts in the silent hours he'd lain watching me, yet I wondered all the same. Proximity was proving far more dangerous away from the citadel.

For all I'd told myself I had to stop thinking about that kiss, I couldn't stop thinking about that kiss. But every time I managed to convince myself he'd kissed me because he'd wanted to—really, truly wanted to—doubt returned. Even without the requirement to care for me, I was nothing. In Emoran terms, I'd been taught my worth since childhood, had been sought after for numerous marriage contracts, and had enjoyed the licentiousness of every Emoran season, but the more I saw myself through Mana's eyes the less reason I saw for him to want anything to do with me. And yet I yearned for his touch, for the taste of his lips and the warmth of his body, and I had to roll hastily off the bed to keep my fingers from betraying me against his skin.

Exhausted yet hot with sudden need, I staggered the short distance from our door to the pot room at the end of the passage, to be met with the safety of privacy and the faint smell of old urine. There, perched on the box, I untied the front lacing of my skirts and pulled my cock free, already stone hard as I wrapped my fingers around it. Wrong of me to imagine it was his hand upon it but I did. Wrong of me to imagine his lips upon it but I did. Wrong of me to imagine him pushing me up against the wall, holding me down, needing me so much he cared nothing for my permission and yet I did. There in the safety of darkness I thought of him wanting me until heat spilled onto my hand and shame reddened my cheeks.

It had been stifling at the citadel, caught in our usual routines where we were always being watched and Mana had only ever called me Lord Ashadi, but it had also been so much safer.

After what felt like a lifetime stuck in close quarters with the man I wanted to both fuck and avoid in equal measure, Emora appeared from the dusts of the basin like a bad memory, its outline one I could have traced with my eyes closed. Mana had spent much of the last few days on deck, watching the basin pass in flashes of brown and brown and a brown that had a hint of grey if you squinted, and stood now staring at the grand city approaching far faster than was comfortable. Ships always sped into the underground harbour, but it gave me the feeling I was rushing toward a cliff and couldn't stop myself falling.

"I didn't realise Emora's harbour was beneath the city," Mana said without turning. "Don't the ships need wind?"

"It's not very far inside, but yes, that's why the captain hasn't furled any sails. He wants to have maximum momentum for when the wind drops."

I tried to sound nonchalant, more at ease than I felt, yet as the city sped closer and closer, panic tightened its grip about my chest. I stubbed a spent korsh roll only to immediately roll another and take a drag, desperate for even the mild relief it granted.

Mana glanced my way. "Are you all right, Lord Ashadi?"

Lord Ashadi. Ambassadorness had at least held humour and the sense we were both in on the joke. *Lord Ashadi* just lifted the wall between us and kept it there—a wall I hated as much as I needed.

"Fine," I said as the ship sped into the dark cavern beneath the city. "But I'll be better once we reach our inn and I can start drinking."

With the sudden dropping of the wind, the ship slowed like a cart left to roll, and we joined the rest of the passengers packing the ship's walkways waiting to disembark. Yet despite the jostling impatience, the docking of the ship did not immediately send people spilling down the walkway. Muttering rose. People craned their necks to see the hold up. And as heavy footsteps made their way up the disembarkation ramp, whispers hissed around us.

"City guard?"

"Who do you think they're looking for?"

"Rude to keep us all waiting here for some criminal."

My gut hollowed, ill-ease falling upon me as surely as the man's shadow, the frontmost guard seeming to block the whole doorway. "Apologies for the delay, we'll make this quick," he said. "We're looking for Lord Ashadi Romm."

The urge to shed every part of my Emoran heritage and shrink away was strong, but glances were already flicking toward me. "I am Lord Ashadi Romm," I said, my forced pride coming out haughty. "In what way can I be of assistance?"

With a jerk of his thumb, the city guard let the other passengers leave, and in the slowly emptying passage he approached, something of grim apology about his features. "I'm afraid you are under arrest, my lord. For deserting your post at the Shield. We must—"

"Deserting?" Mana and I voiced our shock as one. "I have not deserted," I added. "The masters sent me as an ambassador to meet with Reacher Sormei."

The man grimaced—the look of one who would rather be anywhere else. "Orders are orders. I'm just here to bring you in, you can explain yourself to them who know more about this than me." He gestured in the direction of the ramp, where the other passengers were slowly making their way down onto the dock. "If you don't mind, my lord. I'd rather not make any more of a scene."

Stunned, all I could do was nod. I went to pick up my bags only to find Mana had beat me to it, his expression grim. Perhaps if he was carrying my bags, they would let him come with me— that the small hope to which I clung as I stepped out onto the disembarkation ramp.

In the cavernous shadows, the dock was full of people finding time to stare at me even as they went about their business. The scene felt surreal, like I might at any moment step from an iishor-fuelled dream—a feeling heightened by the sight of a man standing at the bottom of the ramp, he and his entourage forcing others to bend their paths around them.

"Ah! My son has returned!" he said, lifting his arms as our eyes met. "Song praise this day!"

My father's booming voice seemed to fill the harbour. At any other time it would have frozen me into immobility, but the press of passengers and the guard's guiding hand forced me on. Amid whispers and curious stares, I was borne to the bottom of the ramp, to where my father stood in his fine clothes looking down his nose at the world. From every direction, stares stuck to me and I could not move or talk or even think, could only stand and fear the coming rage.

"Ashadi Romm," he said, clapping his hands on my shoulders. "We welcome you home with great joy." His arms closed around me, and within his embrace the rest of the world vanished to nothing. Tears pricked my eyes, relief mixing with confusion as I couldn't but think of better days when I had been his golden child. Before the first time his fist hit my face, before he'd kicked me in the ribs over and over, screaming that I was no son of his.

Now when he let me go, a warm smile softened his critical gaze. "My Ashadi is back," he said, all gruff and quiet as people milled about us. "I'm glad you are here." And turning to the guards still hovering at my side, his expression hardened. "Now let go of my son."

12

Naili

Evening Bulletin

To all criers for announcement throughout Bakii

*Citizens of Bakii administered justice outside the Bastion today
with a Lummazzt trader guilty of stealing Bakiian citizens
strung up as a warning to others.*

*After being shot down over The Sands, Lord Ashadi Romm has
deserted his post at the Shield, sparking debate over who bears
responsibility for the protection of our northern border.*

*People confirmed missing in recent raids include Lor Mylii,
Pinni Eskaveli, Aber Ronea . . .*

6:49

I crouched in the shadows, staring down into the alley that ran
alongside Master Occuello's house—its side door a dark portal

into an unknown future. Miizhei and Yeloria and the others would be in there, perhaps even in the still-room working on curatives for those in need, yet my thoughts kept slipping to the alchemist. I'd asked only for help. For information. For her to undo the damage she had done. And her refusal had forced me to face down the Hoods and all but beg for my life. Had brought me back here.

I ought to have jammed a knife into her neck while I could.

Beside me on the veranda, Iiberi and his two companions sat in silence as we waited—they the arbiters of my test. Like a stray come to their door, they'd fed me and given me a change of clothes before bringing me back to the scene of my prior crime. One of the Hoods—the one with a long scar down his cheek—had complained about how late it would be by the time we were done, only to swallow his words at the merest glance from Iiberi. The other Hood, who had a bad moustache, dared only a wordless grumble.

Climbing to the veranda of the linen merchant's shop next door to Occuello's had warmed my limbs, only for our silent vigil to stiffen them once more. From our vantage point I could see little of the city, could only hear its hushed life settle with the advancing hour and breathe in its dry, dusty air tinged always with a hint of cooking oil, pepperweed, and korsh, like the city itself smoked to relax. Perhaps a korsh roll would have made so long a wait more bearable.

I glanced sidelong at Iiberi, little more than a heavy cloak in the shadows. Beyond him, his two Hoods kept watch on the alley below. He'd said we needed to wait until all activity in the area ceased so they could keep an eye on me from outside, but hadn't said how long that was likely to take.

"I'm surprised Alii isn't here," I said, giving voice to a question that had been gnawing at my thoughts, along with the larger one of who she was and why she was important that I couldn't yet express.

"It is not your place to ask," Iiberi rumbled back, the words emerging from the deep shadows of his cloak. He seemed determined to remain hidden, unlike the others, who hid by looking exceptionally average.

His reply had discouraged further speech, yet my nerves needed an outlet. "What's with the big hood? Should I have one of those for the whole thieving thing?"

Iiberi turned slowly my way, a hint of his features appearing as dark lines on dark shadows. "Don't listen to the criers much, huh?"

"Criers? Why?"

For a few long seconds he just went on staring at me in silence.

"Maybe you should head back, boss," Scar-Cheek said from Iiberi's other side. "We can keep an eye on the pla—"

"No," Iiberi snapped. "The fastest way to become a slave is to be afraid of them. You know that."

Ragged-Moustache wriggled uncomfortably in his shadow. "They tore him to pieces though, boss."

"I know what they do," came the hissed reply. "I'll be torn to pieces rather than cower. Now shut up about it."

Silence fell, heavy and uncomfortable, my mind full of everything I'd ever heard said about Lummazzt. It was not a pretty list, rather one full of atrocities committed against people all over the basin. Those black-eyed monsters. I shivered as a breeze rippled by, and I brushed my arms, trying to regain warmth only to release the scent of jasmine upon the air. The smell tickled fears now as well as memories, as much mould and putrescence as the safety of my mother's arms. The effects of Occuello's experiments were stealing even my comforts from me.

"Did you hear about that dragon rider who deserted?" Scar-Cheek said, breaking the awkward silence. "People are saying his watcher was a bad influence, but it's not like Emorans are naturally self-sacrificing."

"His dragon did get shot down though," Ragged-Moustache replied. "That'd scare the shit out of me right enough."

Though they both glanced at Iiberi, he seemed to have no opinion on the matter, and maintained his silent stare into the alleyway. "Who was the rider?" I said, trying to make the question sound disinterested. "Did they say his name?"

Ragged-Moustache's equally ragged eyebrows rose. "The lord? Oh, uh, it was…uh…"

"Romm," Scar-Cheek said. "Lord Ashadi Romm. Big fancy estate and everything, I heard, one of those families who own everything you're standing on."

While they grumbled about Emoran wealth, I held a hastily indrawn breath. That was Mana's rider. Of course they were blaming the Apaian watcher for the Emoran's faults, I could only hope it just meant Mana was coming home, nothing worse.

"Something amiss, Laundry Girl?" Iiberi purred at my side. "You seem troubled."

"Oh? Not at all, I—"

"Don't lie. It's boring. You have some interest in the fate of Lord Ashadi Romm?"

I deflated, shoulders sagging. "My brother is his watcher. Or was, I suppose. I'm…concerned he may be in trouble."

"Unlike you, who are not in any trouble at all." He chuckled to himself and jerked his head toward Master Occuello's. "Off you go then, Laundry Girl."

Thieves were surely supposed to have equipment, lock picks and timing mechanisms, ropes and blades, yet what Scar-Cheek thrust into my hand was nothing but a scratchy old sack.

"Don't take too long," he said by way of encouragement. "I'm already sick of fuckin' sitting here."

For a moment I just stared at him as though he'd spoken another language, as though I had a sensible reason to dither, as though I was being careful, not frozen with sudden dread. Only

Ragged-Moustache's snigger broke my fearful trance, reddening my cheeks. I pushed to my feet, all stiff joints and sinking stomach. I had no choice. My future had shrunk to the size of the old sack in my hand.

Climbing down from the veranda was easier than climbing up had been, and I was soon standing in the alley, the city beyond entering the hush only the small hours allowed. I dared not look back up to where Iiberi and the others sat waiting, sure that to risk giving them away would count against me in this strange new game I'd found myself playing.

At this hour, the side door would be locked and most of the house asleep, but I had a plan. Just one plan, and if that failed, then I would panic. Knowing, and hating, that I was entirely visible to the three Hoods on the balcony, I leaned against the still-room's outer wall beneath the high grilles and set a finger to the madrigal we kept there in a hanging pot. A hum of energy vibrated from my skin and into the air around me, as new shoots sped from the dry soil toward the roof's overhang. It was a terrible time to test a theory, yet the suspicion that I could exert some control on the growth had begun with the zebaria in the alchemist's bathroom and been strengthened when the passiflor had wrapped its stems and leaves around Iiberi. Like it possessed my desire to both touch and hurt him in equal measure. Now, I thought only that I needed the madrigal to grow in through the vents, between the metal bars and into the still-room. Shouting for the others to help would earn unwanted attention, but a madrigal made no sound.

Like a slippery shadow, fresh, lithe shoots snaked their way in through the still-room vents. If anyone was still up and working, they were sure to notice. Now I just had to wait. And hope it was too dark in the alley for the Hoods to see what I was doing.

After a few long minutes, a faint click snatched my attention, the sound of an unlocking latch amplified by my knowledge of what it meant. With a tiny squeak, the side door to the servants' quarters edged ajar, a sliver of pale light outlining its black surface. No sign of anyone beyond, no peering eyes or even whispers, yet the door's bright halo called me on. Step one had been accomplished.

Reaching out, I gingerly set a hand to the door as though it might bite.

"Nai?"

"Yes," I whispered back, heart soaring at the sound of familiar voices and new concern. "Please let me in."

I stepped back as the door swung open just enough to let me slip through the narrow gap and into the dimly lit hallway. There, clustered around the door, stood Miizhei, Yeloria, and Kit.

"I told you it would be her," Yeloria hissed as Miizhei dragged me by the sleeve.

"You say that like I argued," Miiz snapped back, pulling me inside the musty still-room. "Shut that door. If anyone finds her here, they'll hand her over to the city guard."

With heavy thuds and clicks, doors were closed behind me, but Miiz didn't let me go. Gripping my arm tight, she said, "What happened? Alii was back after dinner but wouldn't tell me a damn thing."

To think it had been only that evening when I'd woken to find Miizhei sitting at my side.

It had been her question, but the others stared as intently, awaiting an answer. An answer I could give only by recounting everything that had happened since Alii had sat me down in front of Iiberi and pulled the heavy veil off my head. Apart from the occasional snort of disbelief or irritation from Miiz, they listened in silence until the end when Miizhei folded her arms. "And what exactly do they want you to steal?"

"I . . ." I handed over the sack I had clutched tight through the whole story, and Miizhei yanked it open.

"A list," she said, and pulled out a piece of paper with a roll of her eyes. "How useful for you."

"Shit," I hissed. "Of course it's a list. I should have thought of that."

"I can read it," Kit said, holding out her hand.

"So can I!" Miizhei turned to keep the piece of paper out of the secretary's reach, earning a scowl shot at her back. While I shrank, feeling small and foolish for not realising it would be a list I couldn't read, Miiz's eyes darted down the page. "Some of these are books. That will at least be simple enough to match up letter for letter. These ones," she added, making a divot in the paper with a fingernail.

Yeloria let out a small cry. "So we're just going to let her go upstairs and risk getting caught. Again? That's what we're doing?"

"Unfortunately, she doesn't have a choice," Miiz said, continuing down the list with her fingernail. "But Alii has made real enemies here. If the Hoods fail you, they won't see her alive again."

It was the sort of empty threat people made in anger, yet Miizhei spoke with cold promise that shivered pleasant fingers down my spine.

"It's just such a risk," Yeloria worried, rubbing at the flowers on the back of her neck. "There were armed guards hunting through the laundry today. If one of them catches you..."

Her fear for my safety was as welcome as Miizhei's threats, but didn't taste as sweet.

"Don't worry, Yel, I won't let them catch me," I said, glad it sounded more confident than I felt. "I'm going to figure out a way to fix this. To fix us."

Miiz snorted. "Still a dreamer, huh. You cannot fix this, Nai, just like you cannot fix this city or this world. This is the world we live in, and this is the world we'll die in. You just have to pick how you want to live. Or die."

"Not as a plant," I said.

"Very funny."

"I'm serious. I have nowhere to go, so I will fix this whatever it takes. I refuse to die just because powerful people don't need me anymore, and I refuse to sit and wait for this...this magic, or whatever it is, to consume me as it consumed Chaintho. I will fix this. Fix all of us."

Miizhei stared, unblinking at my declaration. Tension vibrated through my skin standing hairs on end, but though some waved their tiny flowers like white flags of surrender, I stared right back. The power in having a goal, however foolish she might think it, was something I never wanted to let go.

"You really think that's what happened?" Miizhei said at last.

"I saw her room."

For a moment we all breathed the sorrow hanging between us, replete with fears of an uncertain future, but the loss of Chaintho was eclipsed by the sudden tangibility of our own mortality. The taste of mould crept back to my tongue, a memory that had imprinted itself so deeply it couldn't be forgotten.

"Maybe one of us should come with you," Yeloria said at last, gripping her hands tight. "We're in this together, and that should mean being in *this* together."

"No," I said, the word emerging without thought, my determination to protect these women the world had forgotten settling like iron in my gut. "No. One of us in trouble is enough. This risk is mine to take; you have done enough just helping me get in here."

"That's nothing," Kit said.

Miizhei shook the list, the snap of paper catching our attention. "Yes, it's nothing, but for now it's our part to play, so let it go. Naili doesn't need to deal with your guilt as well as this." She held the list out to me. "Here, I've marked the ones that are books. The rest are ingredients. Listen carefully." One at a time she pointed to a name on the list and read it out, getting me to repeat it before moving on, until we'd read through them all save one.

"What's that one?" I asked.

"Excre. I'm not sure about that one. Master Occuello isn't a registered gunpowder producer and so shouldn't have any. It's a controlled substance," she added in the face of my confusion. "Legally attainable only if your name is on the list that comes all the way from the reacher's office in Emora. So if the Hoods hold your success on getting that one, we'd better hope he's gotten some illegally. It does seem... unlikely they would ask for something you couldn't get. By the look of the list, they *want* these things, and someone else will come for them if you fail."

"That's the pep talk she needs, Miiz, yeah," Kit snapped. "I'll find out what I can from Mistress Paiwe tomorrow, just in case. She has ledgers of all the materials that come in on order."

Miiz gave a petulant shrug. "Realism is better than optimism, Kit."

I took the list back from her hand. "Thank you. All of you," I added, looking around at the others. "I promise we'll make them all sorry they ever messed with us."

Yeloria gave me a tight hug and Kit a tight smile, before Miiz opened the still-room door for me to leave. Despite my determination and bravado, it took all my courage to step out into the passage.

"Nai, wait a moment."

Rather than closing the door, Miiz had slipped out in my wake and stood, hands gripped tight, watching me.

A breath hitched in my chest. "What is it?"

"I have to tell you something. Just you," she added, glancing back at the door she'd closed behind us. "Because I should be coming with you but I'm not, and... you deserve to know why."

"You don't need to come—"

"Shut it, Nai, you can't read and I can so we both know that's a lie, but—" She huffed out a breath, arms wrapping around herself as though for protection. "I'm not... I'm not actually as unconnected and safe as I've led you all to believe. I don't send money home like the others, but I do send information, and if our alchemist was to find out, if she had any reason to think I was more than a laundress, the trouble would be a lot bigger than just me. I can't risk that and can't risk getting you mixed up in it either. I probably shouldn't have even told you, should have just let you think I was selfish and didn't care. But I do, so here we are."

Her torrent of words ended with her arms crossed and a defensive little pout I wanted to kiss away, yet some of her words picked at my attention. "More than a laundress?"

"I can't explain, at least not now. You have to go, and so do I"—she gestured back toward the still-room—"before there are even more questions. Now go," she added, and with a swift kiss on my cheek that smelled of soft amber, vivid and yet pale like candles beneath a moonlit sky, she was gone. And I was alone.

Despite the nagging questions and the hook Miizhei had slid into my chest with her kiss, I took a step along the passage, followed by another, gaining momentum pulled from some determined depths. Faint light lapped at my feet all the way, thrown by old light orbs, the first bright lights not risking my exposure until I reached the stairs. But the house was silent, just my feet making the softest scuffs as I climbed step by step, one hand on the wall, its solidity reassuring.

The previous night, I'd paused outside the housekeeper's room, knowing that to trespass farther was against the rules of the house. Yet I'd stepped over the crack that marked the transition and walked on like it was the very same floor on the other side, the line not only invisible but insubstantial—nothing but an idea. This time I didn't even pause, just kept walking like stopping would rob me of my momentum and my courage. Past the archways leading to the atrium and on into the winding dark passages filled with storerooms, the whole a maze out of which I hadn't been sure I would ever emerge. I still didn't know the way, but I knew *a* way, and followed my own footsteps, each one a ghostly reminder of someone I used to be.

I found the stairs to the top floor still standing in their shadowed hall. The same dim light from above called me on now as it had then, and without the threatening chink of glass armour approaching, I started up. At the top, guards still failed to materialise, and I hurried on toward the workrooms and libraries, hoping to soon find everything I needed.

The Hoods' list rustled as I drew it from my skirt pocket, the crumpled paper rejecting every attempt to flatten its creases and remove its shadows. Every item hurriedly scrawled across it was neat enough to read, yet all I had was memory of Miizhei's repeated words. By putting their demands in writing, the Hoods had removed at least half of Bakii from their list of possible recruits, including me.

At the doorway to the first workroom, I surveyed its contents. Shelves of labelled jars, dozens of tiny drawers in delicately carved blackwood racks, books and equipment and boxes shoved into corners to gather dust. Miiz had said there was no equipment on the list, only books and ingredients, though whether they would be on shelves or in one of the many secretive little drawers was a different question.

I stared back down at the list, turning it toward the faint orblight emanating from a nearby bench. "Someone needs to make glasses that help one read," I muttered, giving my head a shake and trying to recall Miizhei's words. "Ev . . . eve . . . eveny? Everny? Even—"

"Evernery leaf, perhaps," came a bored voice from the corner, sending my heart leaping into my throat. "Odd stuff, not particularly useful but not easy to get."

In a shifting of shadows, the alchemist unfolded from the dark recesses of an armchair, all sharp cheekbones and disdain. For a moment, I couldn't breathe, couldn't move, couldn't speak. For all some deep part of me had yearned to see her again, her sudden appearance crushed me to the floor. She folded her bare arms, gold bands cutting into her flesh, as much a flashy show of her social status as the notches cut through her brows. They suited her, irritatingly, as the long fall of dark hair at her back suited her. As disdain suited her.

"Lost your tongue, Naili the witch?" she purred, not moving from beside the chair. "You were so full of words and fury last night. Perhaps you need another blade to hand."

I flicked a glance over my shoulder at the workbench, and she laughed low and long. "I'm not that foolish, little girl."

"Just foolish enough to step into the blade like you wanted to impale yourself on it." My voice came out thin and reedy, and I cleared my throat, wishing my heart would stop racing. She hadn't moved, hadn't shouted for guards, yet any attempt to convince myself she wasn't dangerous sounded laughably naive. I'd never met anyone less safe in my life, from the cruelty in her words to the contempt in her gaze and the power of her position. Whatever she wanted the city guard to do to me would be done without question.

With a single slow step, she began her approach, dark skirt stirring about her ankles, as loose as her sleeveless tunic was tight. "Some things are worth risking even one's life for," she said upon another step, her gaze fixed to mine like she sought to hold me with it.

"Death is worth risking your life for?" I said with a breathless laugh, stepping back as she stepped forward. "That makes no sense."

"It does to me."

Half a dozen steps remained between us when I backed into

the workbench, list crushed in my closed fist. She'd still not called for any guards, but she'd lulled me before and could do so again.

"How did you know I was coming?" I said, sliding a step along the bench, hand creeping unseeing in search of something, anything, I could use as a weapon.

"Let's call it intuition. My turn. What do you want the ever-nery leaf for? It's not exactly...medicinal. It won't help you with your little problem."

I didn't glance at the hand that held the crunched list, yet the very act of deliberately not doing so seemed to draw attention to it. Not caring that my other hand was creeping its way along the bench in search of a knife, the alchemist's gaze slid down to my balled fist. "Interesting," she said, her voice dropping into that vibrant purr at odds with the dead pallor of her eyes. "What else is on your list, little girl?"

"Anything that might help me cure myself, since you care nothing for your mistakes."

Still a few steps away, she halted her stalking advance and tilted her head, a hint of curiosity in the way she stared. "On the contrary, mistakes are fascinating. One learns the most from one's mistakes."

"Then study me. Help me. Help us."

"Oh, I don't need to study you to find out what happened, and I certainly don't need to help you." On those hateful words, she held out her hand, long fingers uncurling in a graceful gesture full of assurance her demand would be fulfilled. "The list."

I tightened my grip on the crumpled page. Was there a way out of this situation that didn't involve running from her guards or letting her have the list? Would it even matter if she saw its contents? What would Iiberi say if I came back without it?

"Come now, my little witch, you make plants grow into monsters, yet you fear me reading a few words? I'll just take it from you if you make me."

I met her stare with as much defiance as I could dredge from my rapidly diminishing confidence. "If you want it, you'll have to prise it from my dead hand."

"Oh no, I won't do that. Corpses are so boring."

Like a striking snake, her hand sprang for my throat and I flinched, jerking up a protective arm—only for her other hand to grip my wrist, twisting, bones clenched tight and screaming. A gasp was all I managed before she dug a thumb between my knuckles like it was a sharp-edged blade, shocking my hand open. The crumpled paper dropped free. The alchemist scooped it up and spun away, striding back across the floor before I could even breathe.

"Evernery leaf," she said, reading aloud like an actor on a stage while my hand throbbed and tingled and stung. "Three bottles of black soil. Excre. Fornic acid—interesting, I wonder what they want that for."

Even as she spoke, she sped her pace across the room and pulled open a cupboard with her free hand. "Fornic acid, two jars. Someone who knows how small the jars are then." Having scooped up two jars, she bumped the door closed with her hip and walked on. "Gholiosia...gholiosia..."

A demand to know what she was doing sat heavy on my tongue, but I held on to it, trapped by the fragility of the moment—a moment in which she was reading the list for me and collecting its contents, seemingly intent on helping me steal from her.

Through the warm pool of light and back, the alchemist crisscrossed her workroom, opening cupboards and reaching for high shelves, running a finger down the list again and again as though afraid she would miss something. While she worked, she spoke, listing the items and wondering at them, not once glancing my way. I might have ceased existing entirely for all the heed she paid me—a statue frozen in the shadows of her world. I dared not move. Dared not breathe. With the edge of the workbench digging into the small of my back, I felt pinned, surrounded by cutting boards and twisty glass, bottles and herbs left to dry in neat lines. I touched one. No buzz of life hummed through my fingers for these cut herbs, only a muted, sticky feeling that weighed heavy on my hand. Slowly, the stem began to shrivel, leaves curling as they dried.

"How fascinating." Her voice was a warm whisper by my ear, her armbands hard lines against my bare skin. "I wondered if you could both grow and extinguish when I saw how quickly the zebaria sagged and died. You must enjoy the power it gives you. To create life and dross."

"Enjoy it?" I spun, words spitting from my lips. "This thing you have done to us has already killed one of my friends. It's like carrying an explosive not knowing when it will go off."

She didn't step back, didn't flinch, just stared at my lips with a faint smile as though I'd not spoken at all. "What experiments I would do if it were me, testing every limit and possibility."

"Oh, so you do want to study me?" I sneered.

The brief, bright flare in her eyes died. "Hardly. I am neither jailer nor babysitter. Such tasks ill suit me. I work alone, not even with lab rats." A staccato snap of her heel ended the words, and she was off across the room again, leaving my heart thumping so fast I could not feel my body.

"That they want Hazar's *Encyclopedia of Scale* is perhaps the most interesting of all," she said, skirt fluttering about her ankles as she strode toward a tall bookshelf against one shadow-hung wall. "Voyle knows well how to make the things he doesn't like go *boom*; he hardly needs old theory."

"Voyle?"

She glanced back over her shoulder as she reached the shelf. "The man who sent you, little girl. Don't waste your breath denying it. I've navigated Bakii's troubled waters long enough to know where the currents run."

The sense I had no choice and no power grew, my existence a dry leaf caught in a brightstorm. From the moment I'd first walked up those stairs, daring to seek answers and aid, I'd been at the mercy of powerful people intent on getting all they could from me. Without power, was there such a thing as freedom in a city like this?

Not having waited for an answer, the alchemist had opened a book only to snap it shut in a puff of air that made the soft hairs around her ears dance.

"It'll do," she said, tucking it under her arm. "The excre won't though. That'll have to be changed." Her gaze snapped my way though I was sure I'd not spoken, not moved, not breathed. "Did you bring something to haul all your spoils away in, little girl?"

"I am not a little girl."

"No, but it's surely more polite than calling you a foolish woman. A bag? A sack? Or were you going to balance it all in your arms and stagger down the street looking highly suspicious?"

I wanted to snap at her jibes, to snarl at her contempt, but that would just amuse her all the more, so I gritted my teeth and drew the balled-up sack from the band of my skirt.

Hardly had I pulled it out than the alchemist snatched it, dropping the book in before I could protest. "The book will be fine," she said, seeming to be talking to herself now. "But the vials and bottles will need to be wrapped in something, or you'll be giving Voyle an unpleasant surprise."

"Why are you doing this?" It was foolish to ask, foolish to break the spell that saw her helping me, yet more foolish still to be an unwitting pawn in a game I didn't understand. "If you know I'm here stealing from you for the Hoods, why help me? These are your things they want me to take!"

"And if you don't succeed, they'll send someone else, someone with more skill and equipment. Someone who can read."

She dumped the sack on the workbench behind me. "Yes,"

she mused, needing no reply. "Allic sands look exactly like excre."
Half a dozen quick steps and she was back at the cupboard, glass
clinking as she hunted for something, able to look away from me
because I was no danger. Had I been able to find a blade, she
would still have been right. I had no choice but to do what she
wished, the Hoods waiting outside all too happy to kill me or
hand me over to the city guard if I failed.

"How did you do it?"

She turned at my question, holding two jars taken from the
cupboard. "Do what?"

"Become . . . this."

Her head tilted. "An alchemist?"

"No. Powerful."

A predatory smile spread her lips like she'd come across something tasty. "I knew I was right about you. Your eyes are full of
hunger. Who would seek me out demanding answers but someone who, when the world pushes them, pushes back?"

While she spoke, she carefully peeled the labels off both jars,
not caring that I could see what she was doing. With quick precision, she swapped them over, smoothing the labels back into place
before dropping one into my sack.

"Let me tell you a secret, little witch," she purred upon
approach, all languorous movement and heady, carnivorous
threat. "Power is gained through pushing. But don't just push
back when the world pushes you, push first and never stop." Her
last words warmed my skin, her silky breath like the brush of her
fingers down my throat. I swallowed hard, unsure if I most hated
her, wanted her, or wanted to be her, only that she had disrupted
all sensible thought.

Before it could resume, the alchemist moved away, leaving the
space around me empty yet full of memories. Everything about
her possessed that slipperiness, every attempt to understand her
like trying to catch something unseen in smoky water.

Push first and never stop.

Her words echoed through my head as she crossed and recrossed the floor, list in hand, the ambience almost companionable. "Hmm, not that one either," she murmured, her cape of dark curls trailing in her wake. "How big is your next explosion going to be, Voyle?" she mused to herself. "One day you might take out the whole city."

Returning to my side, the alchemist dropped the last item into my sack with a theatrical flick of her wrist—a small scaleglass canister so dark it was impossible to make out the contents.

"There," she said, leaning her hip against the workbench beside me, arms folded. "All done. Everything he asked for."

She knew that I knew that wasn't true, that I'd seen her swapping labels, but there was something in her knowing smile that was like a gift. Could it mean something for me to know that two items had been switched without the Hoods being any the wiser? As though able to follow my thoughts, the corners of the alchemist's lips turned slowly upward in what for anyone else would have been called a grin. "Good girl. Now, shouldn't you be leaving? Unless there was something else you needed to steal from me."

"No. Yes. A cure."

"I'm not a physician, and I'm not an apothecary, and you don't have the money to buy my services."

"Because you pay me so little to wash your rags," I bit back, pulse thrumming.

"*Paid* you," she corrected. "Now you have no job at all. Just—" She tapped the sack. "Petty theft for criminals who think they're heroes."

"You say that like I have any choice but this or death. All I wanted was information, all I wanted was help, and you refused. But one way or another I will get what I want."

Despite my heated words, she stepped closer, all exquisite threat. "Is that a promise?"

"A promise you will regret forcing me to make."

"Delicious," she whispered, her proximity holding me pinned to the edge of the bench. "I look forward to it. But for now, your new friends are probably waiting."

"Then let me go," I said.

"I'm not stopping you."

"I know what you're trying to do, and it won't work again."

"Oh? What am I trying to do?" Her lips were close now, as they'd been the first time we'd met. "Or perhaps the better question," she added, brushing her nose against mine, "is what am I succeeding at doing? You see, when such hungry eyes wander into my domain, it would be cruel of me not to play along."

Slowly, she slid her hand between my legs, and my treacherous body flared hot as though there had been no fabric at all.

"Please don't," I said, though it was an effort not to beg for more. "I didn't come here for..."

She cupped my heat, the pressure of her palm momentarily suspending all power of speech. "For what? You seem unable to put it into words yet your eyes speak volumes."

"Please let me go," I gasped.

"You're free to walk away whenever you like, Naili the witch. I'm not strong enough to detain you."

Likely it was true, but her hand went on moving and she bit her lip, making me squeeze my eyes shut or risk moaning in delight. "You're very bad at keeping your face from showing everything you're thinking," she said then, lips touching my ear. "Get on the bench."

"What?"

"Get. On. The bench. Or leave. Your choice but make it. Fast."

Before I'd realised what she was asking me to do, she'd stepped away and, in one sweep, pushed the herb-covered cutting board across the bench, clearing space in a crash and clatter of breaking glass.

Whether it was due to such wanton, careless destruction or the lingering heat from her hand, I hoisted myself onto the bench and put myself at her mercy, both shame and desire burning my cheeks.

With hasty gathers of cloth, she hoisted my skirt up around my hips and stepped in close, pushing my knees apart and spreading me open. I gasped, desire fighting with a deep anger that shouted this was not why I had come, that I hated her and everything she stood for—a voice that faltered when she lowered her head between my legs.

Where the night air had been cool, her lips were warm, her tongue hot as it slid slowly along my slit. I wanted that tongue inside me, wanted to know everything she could do with it, wanted to beg and moan and beg some more for her to do whatever she liked with me—the power of her presence more intoxicating than any drug.

From between my legs, she lifted her head just enough to speak. "Say *please.*"

I ought to have been horrified, to have wanted to say nothing so shameful to this woman who could crush me with a thought, but I also wanted her to lick me, to kiss me, to close her hand around my throat and make me hers. "Please."

"Please what?"

"Please do whatever you want with me."

A little huff of warm breath brushed my skin as she laughed. And, satisfied, she slid her tongue inside me. It was all I could do not to buck off the bench so intense did it feel, just because it was *her*. Her knowing exactly what she was doing, exactly how to play me, bringing me right to the edge of ecstasy only to draw back and let it fade. She seemed to enjoy my thwarted moans, and that little puff of air when she laughed teased me as surely as her tongue. Then the warmth was gone and in a blink she was on top of me, dark curls hanging around us. "Do you want to come now?" she said, brushing her lips against mine.

I nodded, pathetic, unsure I could speak.

She slid her hand up over my breasts to grip my throat. "Do you want to come now?" she repeated, by my ear this time. "Say *please*."

"Please," I said, shocked how much I loved the restriction as I spoke.

"So long as you scream. Silence is ever so dull."

Hand still closed around my throat, she slid fingers inside me. Deep. Deeper. Fingertips playing upon every sensitive place she could find. This the moment when so many people sped, harder, faster, slamming hands or bodies into me in a pounding of flesh, but *she* slowed. The pressure around my throat tightened. Another finger spread me wider, stealing the last of my senses. Slower still. Drawing out every sensation with the skill of one trained to notice and remember tiny details, to react intuitively— one allowed to play with her food. In a last movement, she pressed deeper still, knuckles testing the edges of both my body and my sanity.

I could not have kept the scream in had I tried, so completely had she flayed me free from the world. It tore up my throat as my body bucked and spasmed, relieved and yet mourning the loss of fullness when she pulled away. For a moment the euphoria was untainted, heedless of shame or fear. Until a shout echoed in the distance, followed by more.

Sitting up, I found the alchemist watching me through half-lidded eyes, her lips quirked to an amused smile. "Oops," she said as the shouts grew closer amid hurrying steps. "What a loud scream that was. I guess I must be in danger."

Body still tingling, I snatched up the sack so fast the contents clanked. Footsteps approached like a tide of thunder, amplified by the roaring of my pulse, and behind me, the alchemist laughed. "Remember, little Naili, fight even against peace if it's power you want."

Her words followed as I sped for the nearest window, desperation keeping my legs pumping toward freedom as though the glass did not exist—glass that shattered around me, slicing skin as I dropped into the chill night air. And clutched tight in my hand, my permission to live another day in Bakii's strongest gang dropped with me.

13

Tesha

Morning Bulletin

*To all criers for announcement throughout
Learshapa*

*Increased numbers of wounded are expected to arrive in
Learshapa over the coming days as border skirmishes continue.
No end in sight for the scale shortage.*

*The Lummazzt ambassador has ordered the removal of all
Celessi merchants from the southern border city of Elqua, raising
fears that a full war is imminent.*

*A successful end to the treaty negotiations as yesterday's
greatest wedding in Learshapan history went to plan. It is
expected the couple will depart for Emora today along with
Lord Reacher Sormei.*

66:96

I t was barely light when Biiella woke me, and for a moment I was disoriented, emerging from a strange dream already slipping away. Outside of my head, everything was a bustle of hurrying feet and hushed conversation, the smell of cooking on the air.

"You must dress, my lady," Biiella said, skirts and tunic in hand. "The Lord Reacher wishes to be down at the harbour within the hour."

At her words, understanding of where I was filtered back through a deluge of memories. The breakfast. The wedding. All those people cheering as we passed. Uvao's lips. Lord Romm's threats. And when we'd made it to Sydelle House, nothing. I'd been warned that consummation would be expected of me, but Lord Kiren had wished me a good night and left me alone.

As though summoned by my thoughts, a knock upon the door heralded Lord Kiren's arrival, relief chasing concern across his face. "Ah, you're awake. Excellent. We have to move."

He didn't linger, leaving me grateful that hurried preparations gave me something to do other than think. I got up and dressed, letting Biiella ready my hair, pluck stray hairs from my brows, and line up my armbands. I was getting used to their pressure against my skin, and the way they always felt cool on even the warmest day. Not that it looked warm outside today. The mist had dropped again in the night and had yet to dissipate.

Neither Lord Kiren nor Reacher Sormei was at breakfast when I reached the dining room, saving me from the possibility of having to guess which was my husband. With little time to eat, I hardly tasted the breads and cakes and delicately thin slices of fruit that lay before me. A warm cup of chocolate heated my insides but did nothing to lift my mood, and a deep ache formed in the pit of my stomach as I thought of simpler breakfasts with my care group or with Master Hoye while the furnaces warmed, the company far more important than any finely presented food.

When it was time to go, I was hustled out, Biiella meeting me at the door with a wrap in hand. "Here, it is still chilly out this morning, my lady. Unfortunately, it seems the Lord Reacher and Lord Kiren have already left for the harbour."

"They left without me?"

Biiella grimaced. "The staff here say it's quite normal, my lady. It seems they are used to doing everything in their own time and travelling everywhere together. Come. Your cases are already aboard the Sydelle ship, but we don't want to hold them up."

A stubborn part of me wanted to dawdle in revenge; instead I lifted my chin. "Everything is already gone?"

"Yes, my lady. I double-checked."

I wished I could ask specifically about the case containing Master Hoye's box, but until I could find out exactly where Biiella's loyalties lay I couldn't trust her, could only nod. "Very well, let us go then, shall we?"

She managed a smile and fell into step behind the litter called to carry my poor legs the short distance to the harbour. Uncharitably, I hoped people would see me travelling alone and whisper about how poorly my new husband was treating me. It was beneath me, yet I couldn't shake the sense of rejection that had started to fret me the previous night. I hadn't been looking forward to consummating the marriage, but I'd slept with plenty of men I did not care for, and this would be just another such occasion, hopefully enjoyable if ultimately meaningless.

Keeping my wrap tight against the chill, I sat and watched my last view of Learshapa pass by, blanketed deep in mist. It was all I could do not to look back, not to wonder whether Uvao knew I was leaving so early, whether Master Hoye was already at work in the forge, stoking the furnaces, whether anyone had looked at me the day before and seen a woman they recognised, or whether I'd lost that Tesha entirely beneath slit brows and fine hair, layered skirts and a slow, proper voice.

When we reached the harbour, I was somewhat mollified to find Lord Kiren waiting. Of Reacher Sormei there was no sign, but Councillor Angue and Lord Revennai had come to see us off, both wrapped in woollens against the chill.

"Ah, there you are, my lady," Lord Kiren said, stepping forward with a brittle smile. "Apologies for leaving you to travel alone; I needed to be sure everything was ready."

"Lady Teshalii," Councillor Angue said, his bow giving me a moment of panic. Did I outrank him now? Ought I hold out my hands?

Thankfully, Reacher Sormei called out along the dock, summoning both Kiren and Councillor Angue to see something aboard ship, leaving me alone with Lord Revennai. At whom I shot a desperate plea for help. "Who kisses?" I hissed.

"I do. The only people who outrank you now are Kiren and Sormei, and their mother, as matriarch of the family."

A little spark of panic hit at the reminder of what awaited me in Emora, but before I could say so, Lord Revennai said, "You slipped away last night before I could say goodbye. Thus, I have dragged myself out of my warm bed to brave the cold with my father."

"I'm honoured."

"No you're not, cat."

My lips twitched, unable to suppress the smile that nickname brought.

"Be sure to knock over many vases in Emora," he added when I could not find my voice. "Just pick good times. And remember that if you have questions, you can always seek the aid of Lord Romm. No one will think it odd if you visit the head of your birth family on occasion."

I parted my lips to tell him I would rather fail than ask Lord Romm for assistance after the previous night, but the approach of hurried footsteps stayed my tongue. We both turned, but only I caught my breath, joy and dread flaring in equal measure as Uvao slowed to an easy stride. With tousled hair, he looked more like the Uvao I'd known before, back when he'd just been a man I'd met at the commune, when politics hadn't mattered. But for the fine clothes, I could have believed it.

"Tesh..." For an age my name hung suspended on his lips and he stared at me, a man who saw nothing else in the whole noisy harbour. "I was afraid you had left already."

"No. No, not yet." My words were breathless, meaningless noise, but they were all I could utter as his stare hooked me in, reminding me of the previous night pressed up against the shelves while—

"Careful," Lord Revennai rumbled, flicking a glance along the dock.

Uvao didn't seem to hear him. "I'm sorry about last night, Tesh, I just...I couldn't..." He ran a hand through his hair, further tousling the mess, but his dark eyes never once left my face. "Just...just tell me something, please. I have to know. Do you love me?"

"Uvao!" Revennai hissed. "Snap out of it or you're going to get us all shot. Tesha, you—"

"Yes." It was both the easiest and the hardest word I'd ever spoken, but also the most true. "Yes, I do. I love you. I tried to stop and I thought I had succeeded, but...being around you again, I..."

At the edge of my vision, Lord Revennai hissed expletives that seemed to bounce off the glass bubble in which we stood. Every fibre of my body yearned forward, but I retained just enough sanity not to move. Uvao stood his ground as I did, but our eyes locked and our hearts entangled.

"I love you," he said, the words a hoarse whisper. "I need you to know that. To know I never stopped and I never will."

Revennai gripped his shoulder. "Enough of this. We should go now. Shit, Kiren is—"

"Ah, Lord Uvao, how good of you to see us off at such an early hour," came Lord Kiren's voice, preceding his return along the dock. For a moment Uvao's gaze went on holding mine, before he dragged it away like a man fighting gravity. In its absence my heart hammered sickeningly fast and my knees were sure to give at any moment.

"Lord Kiren," Uvao said, somehow managing to sound bored. "One must do one's duty, even in the cold."

"Shall we be seeing you in Emora this season? It's been a few years, has it not, but with Ashadi possibly returning it ought to be...interesting."

"Yes," Uvao said almost as quickly as I had. "Yes, I'll be there. There is little in Learshapa to keep me here now."

His meaning thrummed through me, and I stared at the side of his face, his every effort not to glance my way like fuel thrown on flames.

"And you, Reve?" Kiren said, turning the question on Lord Revennai. "Shall we see you again this coming season?"

"Yes, of course." Revennai managed a bland smile, somehow adding tension to an already tense moment. "It is the highlight of my year."

In the wake of his words, taut silence stretched, seeming to tear at my whole body with sharp, desperate claws, until at last Lord Kiren cleared his throat. "Well," he said. "It will be good to see you again. In Emora. When—if you come."

"And you."

"My lady?" Kiren's hand touched my arm. "We ought to embark. Sormei fears that if we don't catch the wind soon we won't outrun the brightstorm, and there's nothing he hates more than having to anchor in the middle of nowhere."

"Of course," I said, the calm words seeming to belong to someone else. "I'm ready whenever you are, my lord."

With a nod to Lord Revennai and Uvao, Kiren turned away,

and I had no choice but to turn with him, arm in his. But while he spun quickly on his heel, I lingered just a breath, taking in a last lungful of the city and of Uvao's scent. No time for more words though they banked up on my tongue, time only for a lingering stare and the shattering of my heart as I turned away, regrets pooling with my grief.

Vision blurring, I let Lord Kiren lead me along the dock to the embarkation stairs, where Councillor Angue stood admiring the ship. Reacher Sormei was already climbing aboard, shouting something to the crew hidden in the mists while the councillor bid us farewell, kissing my hands one after the other. When it was our turn to embark, my stomach flip-flopped all the way up the stairs, Lord Kiren behind me. It was the first time I had been on a sand ship. The first time I'd left home. The first time I'd ever truly felt alone. And by the time I'd reached the top and looked back, the dock was empty. Uvao had gone.

Determined not to collapse, I pulled myself together and looked around. Everywhere were masts and rigging and sails, folded and furled amid coils of rope. Bare-chested men strode about, paying no heed to us as they carried things and pulled things and did any number of important-looking tasks. Reacher Sormei had disappeared into the thick mist, nothing but a voice still calling his orders like he was the ship's captain. Perhaps he was. It was his ship and he didn't seem the type to lie idly by while there were things he could be doing—be controlling.

"Come, I'll show you to your cabin," Kiren said, arm touching mine as he passed. "Best not to get in their way when they're preparing to catch the wind. Likely to get stepped on."

Not daring to look down at the dock again, I let him lead me a safe path through the chaos to a short flight of stairs and a lit interior. It was like walking into a manor house shaped like a ship, and I had to turn a gasp of surprise into a cough. Furniture, windows, curtains, door, even an atrium open to the sky through a grating above—everything but a fountain and the birds that usually colonised any open space with water and shadows.

"We're only using the upper floor this journey, so don't worry about the other stairs." Kiren walked on, heedless of the splendour around him like this palace that rode the desert wastes was nothing out of the ordinary. "We'll eat here, and there are a few sitting rooms along there where you can relax during the day if you'd rather stay below deck. There are books in this one, if you enjoy reading, else there are stitchery supplies and paint and other such things in the next." A few more hasty steps along the passage and he halted outside doors almost as grand as the ones in Romm Manor. "This will be your cabin. Your maid will be in the adjoining room should you need anything during the journey."

We'd stopped at my door, but the corridor continued on a way, more doors leading off to more places. "And where is your cabin, my lord?"

"I am—" He counted quickly beneath his breath, pointing a finger at each door in turn. "Three doors along, my lady, should you have need of me. Sormei's room is at the end, and he keeps the rooms either side as working space should he need to write letters or take meetings."

"Or hide away from his guests."

I said it with a laugh, but Kiren grimaced. "He is not the most…warm of men," he said, glancing over my shoulder as though to be sure his brother wasn't near. "But he is loyal and determined, and no one works harder. I hope there will be more time soon for us to all get to know each other a little better, but until then I assure you that, for him, he is showing you great regard."

I kept to myself a wish to know what poor regard would look like, and as eager to escape the awkward moment as he was, excused myself to get settled. My cabin was smaller than my room at either Romm Manor or Sydelle House had been, yet still larger than anything I'd ever slept in as just Tesha. It had an enormous bed draped in fine linen, a collection of carved wooden furniture, and even some broad-based vases full of fresh flowers. Yet for all its grandness, its smaller size gave it a cosy feel, a closeness and warmth that promised safety.

While Biiella bustled about, unpacking cases and stowing others, I sat on the edge of the bed and looked out the window. One half of the view contained Learshapa Harbour, a scene in which people bustled about in the mist, silenced by distance. There, other ships sat in other docks, some packing or unpacking, others entirely still and lifeless. The other half of the view was all basin—the dry, rocky ground that connected our cities and estates like they were islands in a grand sea. One couldn't build and live just anywhere in the Celes Basin, which left whole swathes of it untouched by any but the Apaians who chose to remain living out on communes.

A shout sounded above, followed by another a little farther away, and the ship jolted. "What was that?" I said, gripping the bedpost.

"Likely we're about to catch the wind, my lady. That was probably the sail test to be sure they have the direction correct. Are you all right? You don't get sail sick, do you?"

"I don't think so. I mean, I never have before." I gave myself a little shake and got to my feet. "I've never really paid much attention to the workings of a ship though, so I might head back up."

"As you wish, my lady. I'll get your cabin sorted so it's comfortable when you return."

"Thank you, Biiella."

The shouting continued as I made my way back through the living quarters, no sign of either Kiren or Sormei below deck. From the base of the stairs the shouts became more intelligible, most calls of direction and numbers that sounded important.

Partway up the stairs I recognised one as Sormei's voice, and at the top I found Kiren perched on a reel rope, watching.

"My lady." He stood at my arrival, but I gave him a tight smile and waved such formality away.

"Do call me Tesha, my lord. I think it will be more pleasant for both of us."

"Then you had best call me Kiren. Tesha."

It felt like something of a truce, here at the beginning of my journey into the unknown.

"Did you come to watch the sails?" he asked when I perched on the reel at his side. "It doesn't seem to matter how many times I've watched them unfurl, I always get a thrill, like I'm a small boy again, riding the glass for the first time in my father's sloop. Sometimes," he added in a lowered voice, "Sormei orders them to unfurl two or three sails at once. It's not the smoothest ride, but the sudden burst of speed is like learning to fly."

It was the first time I'd seen his face truly animated, his eyes bright.

"Perhaps he will do that on this journey too," I said. "It sounds exciting."

"You think so? Not a very comfortable way for a lady to travel, jolted about at the wind's whim."

"No, but I think sometimes it's nice . . . not to be a lady?"

His lips twitched into a smile. "I do sometimes find it's very nice not to have to be a lord too. We'll have to try it together sometime perhaps."

Before I could answer, the great flap of a sail unfurling whipped overhead, and the ship slid forward. It was no jolt of speed, rather a careful navigation out of the tangle of docks at Learshapa's edge, but it blustered the mist into my face and sent my hair tumbling.

"The first sail is always the most difficult," Kiren said. "They have to be sure the direction is right or the ship will crash into something. Or veer off the road. Once we're moving it gets easier, and they can unfurl more sails. Unless the wind gets really swirly, then only the sailors who don't value their lives dare keep at full sail." He glanced my way. "That's why Sormei wanted to get away before the front of the brightstorm comes through. Secretly I think he's always wanted to sail through one, but his ambition is stronger than his love of risk."

"A love that you share, I'm beginning to think?"

"It would be thrilling, navigating a storm as it swept over, but I'm not sure I'm quite prepared for that kind of excitement yet. Certainly not on this journey. Ah, they're letting down a second sail."

Thankfully his excitement and desire to share his knowledge meant I didn't have to ask questions, only wait for him to explain each step as we wound our way through the main docking ports toward the open road ahead. A road I'd seen many times from the harbour, but never from above as it stretched away, its perfect glass surface gleaming and glittering with silver dust. A magical path, leading us out onto the basin's wastes.

In a flurry of unfurling canvas, the central sail tumbled from its ropes to billow as it caught the wind. A shout followed, and the masts turned with a rattle of gears beneath our feet. With nothing ahead but the road, another sail soon followed, along with a course correction that made barely a wobble.

My attention had been all ahead upon the glimmering road, but as the ship hit its stride I stood to look back. Back at Learshapa, the only home I'd ever known. Despite knowing most of the city would not be visible from the outside, I was shocked by how small it looked. How flat. From within, it was deep and wide and full of life, but from the basin wastes, there was just the outer rim—the harbour complex, the palatial estates, the glass waterlines slipping from view—nothing of the rich culture and life of its people. And no sign of Uvao.

Kiren's hand touched my arm, and with a jolt I looked down at him still perched on the reel. He didn't say anything, his expression all the understanding I needed for tears to prick my eyes.

"I think I might rest now," I said, needing to escape.

"Of course. I'll be here if you need me."

Brushing tears from my eyes, I went below, wishing I could breathe the scents of Learshapa one last time and wondering whether I could ever trust the man I now called husband.

The magic of sailing along glass soon wore off, leaving hour upon hour of barren landscapes and rushing winds. Every now and then a change of wind would animate the crew to rapid motion, furling and unfurling different sails and turning masts to compensate. Of the other ships we passed upon the road, only the large public vessels caused any grief. They lumbered, slow and heavy and capable of crashing every other ship off the glass with a single turn of the mast, and so had to be watched carefully.

With the Sydelles often busy, worry was my constant companion. Worry about Learshapa, about Uvao, about what awaited me in Emora, about Lord Romm's warning and what would happen when the Sydelle twins found out I wasn't who they thought me. I'd set out on this journey with a plan—a plan that felt shakier by the hour.

At the end of the second day we reached Remorna, the basin's central hub where ships could be turned and traffic directed—a great crossroads of sorts where large pools of glass allowed for free movement. Part of me expected Sormei to order his crew to weave with the wind, making the road his own, but despite his hurry, we slowed in preparation to dock. For all the effort of furling sails, the ship stood still for mere minutes—long enough for a sheaf of papers to be brought aboard and nothing more. The papers disappeared below deck, and as quickly as we had stopped, we were off again, all other traffic halted to ensure our swift passage. And swift it was, our sails soon catching full wind and leaving Remorna behind.

I soon discovered it was news for which Sormei had halted, two days without reports from the rest of the basin enough to make him foul tempered. My opinion of him lifted a notch to know he took such personal care rather than leaving the work to others, even going so far as to run through some pages with Kiren over dinner. Much of it meant nothing to me—all names of people I'd never met and places I'd never been, but when they moved through the Learshapan dispatches it was an effort to continue eating while concentrating on their words.

"The scale situation in Therinfrou is worse than expected," Sormei said, ignoring his meal as he shuffled papers. "Nothing from the other mines yet. Six blasts so far. Minimal casualties, but the Lummazzt are closing in."

From the other end of the table, Kiren swallowed a mouthful. "That war is starting to feel inevitable. Faster than I'd expected."

"Much faster," Sormei agreed. "I hate to think what would have happened if we had waited for that vote before being able to help. Better this way." He glanced at me as he spoke, proof he hadn't forgotten I was present, as I had hoped. "Especially since it meant welcoming a new member to our little family. You are the linchpin holding us all together, Lady Teshalii; what a heavy responsibility."

Lord Kiren laughed the laugh of a man softening a blow and patted my arm. "Not that it's a responsibility she has to work to maintain now that we're married."

"Oh no. Of course not."

Sormei's gaze lingered on mine, dark and heavy, with a twitch of amusement flickering at the corner of his lips—a man laughing at a joke we both shared. A chill trickled through me, and for the second time I had the unshakable sense that he knew. And as his attention returned to the papers in front of him and the news coming out of Learshapa, the weight of his words settled in my gut. *What a heavy responsibility.* Because the only thing that could harm the unification now was an insult bride being found out, forcing a renegotiation.

While the Sydelle brothers ate and talked, I stared at nothing and yet saw the healers performing hasty triage in Orial Square and the crowds gathered to cheer our wedding, hope in so many faces. I'd been so sure about fighting against unification in fear of losing Learshapan power and Learshapan culture, but if it fell through now, if I was discovered, Learshapa might lose so much more. To protect my home, I could not let myself be exposed. Not until Learshapa was safe.

Sormei straightened his dispatches with a small sigh. "It will be good to get back and have a steadier stream of news."

"While *I* am looking forward to a bed that isn't moving all the time," Kiren said, a laughing glance thrown my way.

I smiled, taking a bite of rolled beef but tasting nothing. I could maintain the fiction as long as necessary, I was sure, but Lord Romm's parting threat sat like a stone in the middle of a glass road. He wanted Sormei disgraced. Wanted Sormei out of the way, and would expose me to see that done, Learshapa be damned.

In front of me, Reacher Sormei pinched a bit of spiced flatbread free between thumb and forefinger and placed it delicately in his mouth. There were no food tasters here, I had noticed, no heavily armed guards in clinking glass armour. Kiren had said his brother's wariness wasn't without cause, that people had made attempts on his life and his position, but perhaps he took other precautions here. No sooner had I begun wondering what they could be than I realised I could get Sormei out of Lord Romm's way without having to be exposed, and without risking Learshapa's safety. All

I had to do was poison the reacher. And be sure no suspicion fell upon me. Not here, but...

"Are you feeling all right, my lady?" Kiren said, sending my concentration smashing to the floor in so many pieces of shattered glass. "Something amiss with the food?"

"Oh, oh no, my mind was just wandering. I've never been very good at sleeping aboard ship, and it's catching up with me."

Sormei shot me one of his half-lidded, sleepy smiles across the table as he wiped his fingers and went back for another piece of flatbread. "As well for you that we won't be stuck on board much longer then, Lady Teshalii. The winds are steady and we're on course to beat the brightstorm to Emora. May you find such news relaxing enough to sleep tonight."

I didn't, too caught in thoughts of my new plan, and as though I'd brought sleeplessness upon myself with my lies, the following day saw me wake tired and heavy. With the dawn came lightning strikes, beginning to etch the horizon we'd left in our wake. Throughout the afternoon they brightened, creeping ever closer, while bruise colours bloomed across the sky. With pink clouds swirling upon a blue-black canvas, I stood at the back of the ship and watched the storm chase us across the plain. It would already have rolled over Learshapa, and even if we outran it, it would hit Emora within hours of our arrival—a dramatic welcome to my new home.

"Beautiful, isn't it?"

I flinched, not having heard anyone approach. For a moment I thought it was Kiren who joined me at the railing, but something in the slowness of his voice and the faint almost mocking smile gave him away.

"Lord Reacher," I said, and curtsied.

"No need for that; we're family now, are we not?" He set his hands on the railing beside me, staring out at the approaching storm. "You seem to have gotten better at telling us apart, I see."

"It takes only one embarrassment to inspire speedy study."

His laugh was more abrupt and brusque than Kiren's but seemed to come more easily. "A wise saying."

When he said no more, the silence took on a tense quality as though imbued with the tightly coiled energy of the storm. The suspicion he knew the truth returned, and on its heels gratitude that poisoning him would rid me of that fear too.

"Do you think we will outrun it?" I said, gesturing at the brightstorm to break the silence.

"I should think so. But I am wary of absolutes. The winds have a mind of their own and can sometimes drop at a moment's notice as though suddenly called away. Sailing the basin is a good reminder of just how little of life is truly in our hands."

I glanced at him, expecting something of a knowing smile but finding serious contemplation instead. "I should think as reacher you have rather more power in your hands than most."

"Perhaps. And yet the wind could abandon me, or the rains fail to come, and the tiniest speck of poison in my food could be my end. We are all of us, even the reacher, at the mercy of other people, and nature is our true master."

I wanted to argue, to point out that while what he said was true of everyone, he had the money, the resources, and the power to minimise the effects such things had upon him. He had food tasters. He had more sails upon his ship. He would not be the one to die of thirst if the rains failed. But as Lady Teshalii Sydelle, I could say none of it without giving myself away.

"Do you know that you take a sharp little breath whenever you think of something you should not say?"

"What?"

Sormei's lazy smile held a quiver of genuine amusement. "Something you ought to work on perhaps."

With those words he patted the railing, took a last look at the gathering brightstorm, and turned away, leaving me to the speechless agony of realising I hadn't been as clever as I'd thought. And a doubled determination to begin the destruction of Emora with his life.

The brightstorm chased us all the way to Emora, nipping at our heels like an excitable puppy. Unlike how Learshapa had seemed to disappear the moment one stepped outside of it, the city of Emora was visible for miles in every direction. It rose like a mountain, or rather a small range of them, all hills and valleys and caverns hewn into stone. The story went that it had been built from the rubble of the great city of Tehewin hundreds of years ago, but I'd not expected it to look true. Nor for the grand waterfall to be so...grand. For water to spill so through warm, dry air seemed a dangerous waste, yet it poured from a high ridge to splash in endless thunder into the pool below—a giant fountain of sorts, a beautiful artifice built from wealth.

"There is always something nice about coming home," Kiren said as the buildings emerged from the lingering mist. It hung about Emora like clouds dropped too low, blanketing and caressing the pale buildings, all turrets and domes and round coloured windows of fractured glass. "Even dense mist can't ruin it," Kiren added. "Though I wish the city had put on a nicer face for your arrival."

"Does anywhere in the basin have a nice face when staring down a brightstorm?"

"Likely not!"

For all I'd read about the city, the closer we sailed the more questions I had. What was the tall building on the high spire that looked like it was trying to spear the clouds? Where were the workings of the waterfall hidden? Where was the water harvested? Had the glimmering white stone come from the mountains into which Emora had been built? But none of my questions felt safe, so instead I watched the city approach in silence.

Unlike Learshapa's external harbour, the harbour at Emora was a cave system, its towering ceiling high above us as we sped from daylight to sudden darkness. Like every sail had been furled at once, the ship slowed, momentum all that pushed us on toward the myriad pinpoints of light within. As my eyes adjusted, I realised it was hundreds of light orbs, each hooked upon the belt of someone working to bring the ships in, guide them to berth, and unload the goods. Some were even attached to the reins of mules, groups of which lined up ready to pull ships in the still air.

"Welcome to Emora," Sormei said, a bitter note in his voice despite the undeniable natural beauty of their harbour. At first it had seemed just dark, but the longer I looked about the more I saw. Flowering vines grew from somewhere above to dangle overhead, and water seemed to seep from the very stones themselves, dampening the ground to a slick as shiny as the glass upon which we sailed.

From the main cavern, we slid slowly toward a smaller cave, empty of all but a few private ships moored and quiet. In the distance the echo of shouts and bustle promised another cave where merchant vessels and public ships pulled in—a noise I was grateful not to have to bear upon already strained nerves. Beautiful Emora might be, but everything about it was strange, from its harbour to the very way it had been built. Nothing looked right, nothing sounded right or smelled right, and that wasn't going to change.

The feeling grew heavier as we left the ship behind and found no stairs up into the city. Instead there was a door that led into a small metal room like a box with lattice sides, and I gasped as it seemed to unfurl all its sails at once and rise upward. It took me a moment of thudding heart and panicked senses to recall they used counterweights in Emora to scale the great heights and to feel like a fool. A fool horrifically out of her depth in water that tasted all wrong.

I wished the day might return to dullness so I could breathe and rest and acclimatise to my new surroundings, but it was not to be. Not when there was a palace to be shown around and a home to see and a whole army of servants to be introduced to as my staff. Not when there were dozens of names and rooms to memorise, not when every step took me more out of my depth like I was striding into an ocean and couldn't turn back.

The Emoran reacher's palace was enormous, taking up the entirety of its own plateau on the north side of the city, its six wings forming something of a star around the central halls. Only three were in use—one was Sormei's private residence, another was where the rest of the Sydelle family lived, and the third was Kiren's. Mine. Ours. I wasn't yet sure how I felt about that. I was a false bride, a deliberate insult, yet I had married Lord Kiren and was a lady now for better or worse—one of the very Emoran nobles I'd railed against all my life.

However fraught our relationship was destined to be, Kiren was both kind and observant enough to soon realise I was in need of peace. "Foolish of me to get carried away trying to show you everything in one go," he said. "Here, let me show you to your rooms."

From the large central room of our wing, I followed him along a passage, around the edge of an atrium, and toward a pair of wide double doors.

"Your rooms, my lady," he said, bowing as though he had been a servant and I the lord. "I do hope you will find everything satisfactory."

He pushed the doors open on the words, revealing a large, ornately decorated sitting room full of light. It held a short central table with elegant chairs, shelves of books, and more cushions and trinkets and curving glass vases full of flowers than I had ever seen in one place.

"You like it?" Kiren said, something of hope gleaming in his eyes.

"Like it? It's beautiful."

"Good. The servants have been busy since our marriage was announced. I hope you like flowers." He crossed the sitting room as he spoke, showing me into a slightly smaller room that was still larger than any bedroom I'd ever seen. A wide bed sat in the centre, covered in embroidered wool covers and pale linens, while in an adjoining dressing room a washstand tinkled with running water like my own personal fountain. "Your maid's room is through that door," he added, gesturing to a door set into the tiling and almost invisible. "It looks like your things have already been brought up from the ship, though I imagine it will take a few days before you're comfortable. If you want anything changed, just say so. This is your home now, and these are your rooms to do with as you please." He smiled, a soft wry smile tinged with something like pity. "I'll let you get settled. Mama wishes to meet you, but I think you'd best rest and change and fortify yourself beforehand. She can be...a little tiring if you're not used to her."

On that troubling note, he let himself out, leaving me to the peace of my beautiful new rooms. They had everything, even a balcony, half latticed in for privacy, and the large window that looked out onto one of the many gardens was clear glass at the bottom rising to a rainbow of varying colours, no two pieces the same. It was art, and I loved it as I loved the rooms and wished I didn't. The need to remain aloof and not get sucked into their world nagged at me. I had not come to be comfortable. Had not given up my life and my home for luxury.

Although my chests were half-unpacked, there was no sign of Biiella, so I dug through the remaining chests until my fingers found the comfort of Master Hoye's wooden box. Pulling it free, I carried it into the bedroom and closed the door. There, sitting on the floor, I cracked open the lid. The same array of small glass bottles peered back, each symbol-etched stopper gleaming with promise.

I ran my hand over the little army of vials and tried to remember the names marked on the underside of the box. Arscotor—poison. Turum powder—slower poison. Shele—desiccant. Ulgele—regurgitative. Siline—abortive. Melchidor—somniferent. The ways they could be used felt infinite, the possibilities for disruption unparalleled. All I needed now was glass. And a way to get some into Reacher Sormei's hands.

With a plan beginning to coalesce, I felt far more in control when I ventured from my rooms. Only an hour had passed, yet the looming brightstorm brought darkness to everything it touched. Out in the main living area, all chaises and thick carpets, bookshelves and paintings and vases, the full-length windows that spread along one wall seemed to bring the billowing storm clouds inside. Yet for all their ominous roiling, cheerful laughter lit the space, pausing only as I entered. Two young girls sat on the floor, hands frozen in the middle of a clapping game, while on chaises to either side sat Kiren and an older woman I knew immediately for his mother. She had something of her sons' look, though her heavy brows sat lower and no smile lit her face. This was the woman I needed to charm, needed somehow to befriend if I was to end her son's life.

Knowing my plan, I had a sudden urge to run, to hide beneath a blanket rather than face her. No part of training to work with glass had involved learning how to extract information from Emoran matriarchs.

Kiren rose as my breath threatened to abandon me. "Tesha, allow me to introduce you to my mama, Lady Sydelle. Mama—"

"Oh pish, Lady Sydelle indeed," she said, her voice far from the intimidating tone I'd expected from her appearance. "You may call me Mama, dear. Or Mama Juri if you prefer, a shortening of Jurique. Generally I like shortening names, but I must say I cannot abide Tesha as a shortening of your lovely name, so excuse me if I don't use it. Teshalii, so pretty. Don't you think, girls?"

The two girls on the floor had shifted to their knees, watching me eagerly. The elder one, ten or eleven years old and possibly the one from Kiren's tale of stolen brandy, looked to her brother. "I think *she's* pretty. Do you think so, Kiren?"

"I should think only someone without eyes could claim otherwise," he said easily. "My sisters," he added to me. "Desa and Luave. They have been waiting very patiently to meet you."

Their mother barked a laugh at that. "Patience is not a virtue that runs in this family. But there, girls, you have seen her and must be satisfied. Now, run along so we can chat."

"Come with me, girls," Kiren said. "I'll show you the pretty things I picked up in Learshapa."

They both leapt up, thrilled to hang upon their older brother's arms as he fielded their torrent of questions all the way out of the room. Step by step, their talk faded into the gathering thunder. And with them gone, Lady Sydelle lifted one of her heavy brows at me, each slit through half a dozen times. "Come sit with me, Teshalii; let me look at you properly."

I walked over, keeping my gaze demurely lowered even as I hardened myself to meet her every challenge. Hardened myself to find her every weakness and exploit it for information.

"You know I was most upset not to be at your wedding, my dear, and I do apologise, but Sormei, you know, must have everything exactly as he wishes with no thought as to what anyone else wants, and it didn't matter how often I begged him to have the wedding here so I could be present; he wouldn't hear of it!"

I settled on the chaise beside her, and she peered closely at me. "Yes, you have a very determined look, I like that. None of this namby-pamby nonsense will do for my boys. Both too clever by half and would be bored within a day to share their home life with someone lacking a brain and her own ideas. I assume you *do* have your own ideas?"

"Many, Lady—"

"Uh-uh," she tutted. "Mama Juri. Please."

"Oh yes, of course, Mama Juri." The words felt strange upon my tongue, yet they were warm and pleasant too, a taste I'd never tried and had only heard described. "I shall do my best to remember."

"Of course you will. And you'll have plenty of occasions to practise now we are family. This palace is quite ridiculously large, but in general terms, I am always just next door. Unless I'm out. Which I frequently am, when my health allows, of course, because one must be seen in society. It is quite exhausting though, my dear, being the reacher's family. Take whatever you thought you knew about the exigencies of social life and multiply it. It is far worse for Sormei, of course, dear boy, and he does work so very hard. No wonder he struggles to sleep more than a few hours even with the help of a nightly glass of strong carvales." She gave a theatrical little shudder. "Horrible stuff, but one does what one must in this world, and I shall not poke at him for that."

A demure nod hid the thrill that shivered through me at such detailed information easily given. "No, of course not, Mama Juri. He does work very hard."

"Yes, and he was always the sicklier of the two," she went on. "You'd not think so to look at him now, but it's still true. He has to take great care with his food, and if there is an illness going around he is sure to catch it. The only time Kiren has ever been sick is when they both had that dreadful southern fever. Although even then, Kiren was fine while for a few days there we thought we would lose Sormei." She sighed and patted my hand. "But enough of such morose stuff. Truthfully, my dear, I'm very glad to have another woman in the house. It's been rather lonely here since my Alliqua married—my eldest daughter, you know, although"—she flicked a glance around the room as though to be sure we were alone—"I suppose of everyone my son might have married you know she's not my eldest. How very…amusing… it was to learn that our families were to be united after all, but no matter, the past is the past, as they say, and we do not speak of it, of course and— No. Where was I? Oh yes, I am so very glad to have you here, dearest, and I do hope we shall be good friends."

Swallowing both the questions that came to my tongue and guilt at how easily she was confiding in me, I set my hand on hers in turn. "Oh, I'm sure we will, Mama Juri. I'm very sure we will."

I let her talk on as she wished, drinking in every detail until Kiren returned with the first close rumble of thunder, his sisters in tow. Having let the girls pepper me with a few questions, the three Sydelle women then took their leave, and I managed to carry my guilt back to my room before my knees gave way beneath the weight. There, in safety, I laughed. I laughed at how easily such information had come to me, laughed at how trusting she had been—they had all been. Laughed until tears spilled down my cheeks and it was grief that poured through my fingers.

Outside, the thunder grew louder and light flared. All crackles and flashes in pink and green and blue, the brightstorm rolled over us as realisation of what poisoning Sormei would really mean rolled over me. He wasn't just the reacher, wasn't just the man Lord Romm wanted out of the way, he was also a son and a brother in a family that had welcomed me without question. He worked hard, cared about his empire, and had done more to protect Learshapa from the Lummazzt threat than I had ever expected. But I could not let such knowledge stay my hand, for if Lord Romm exposed me as an insult bride, the unification would be renegotiated and Learshapa would be left without aid as war stormed ever closer. It had to be done, and as tears streamed down my cheeks, determination hardened to a solid core in my chest. If it meant saving Learshapa, I would kill him. To save Learshapa, I would kill them all.

Naili

Evening Bulletin

To all criers for announcement throughout Bakii

Lummazzt ambassador calls off talks with the Bastion, claiming a lack of confidence in his own safety while the remains of a Lummazzt trader still hang as a warning outside the city.

Increased attacks at the Shield have seen dragon riders called out without rest, while an investigation suggests deserting rider, Lord Ashadi Romm, was unduly influenced by his Apaian watcher.

Seven more citizens have been confirmed missing. Val Corinthe, Chaintho Hamash, Glori Diin, Barash Hadamarkii, Lee Verique . . .

10:26

He lounged, everything from his posture to his golden mop of hair like that of a lion. Even his sleepy smile that didn't reach his eyes held more threat than welcome, like he was tolerating my presence only until he decided whether I was food.

"Voyle." Iiberi spoke the name like a cough, seeking the lounging lion's attention.

"Mmm?" the man said, not taking his heavy-lidded eyes off me.

"This is Naili, the one who successfully completed her challenge to steal from Occuello."

Voyle blinked slowly, seeming to be in no hurry for anything. "Ah yes, the witch," he said at last, and with a groan of effort, straightened himself somewhat in his chair. "The one who tried to kill you with leaves."

"I didn't—"

"I never said—"

Iiberi and I spoke at the same time and equally in unison snapped our mouths closed. My cheeks began to heat as though my words sharing the same space and time with his had been too intimate, and I was glad he didn't look my way.

"An Apaian woman who can steal from our favourite alchemist and grows plants by touching them. I'm not sure what else I ought to call her but a witch." Though he still sat at his ease, eyes half-closed, Voyle possessed the same intensity of stare with which Iiberi had pierced me upon first meeting, both men the sort to snap one in half at a thought. "And it was you who used an overgrown plant to escape Occuello's house. Caused quite the stir, you know."

He paused, but I had the feeling it wasn't so I could speak, so I didn't. He tapped a rhythm upon the arm of his chair, seeming to be thinking. A glance risked at Iiberi, still standing near his boss's chair, didn't help.

"What else can you do?"

I ought to have expected that question. Anyone who wanted

to take me on for my strange new skill would want to milk it for all it could give.

"I don't know," I said. "I've...I've only been able to do this—the plant thing—for a few days." Determined to keep my rapid healing to myself as long as possible, I shrugged. "I tried to ask the alchemist what he'd done to me and...and what would happen now, but he refused to answer."

"So you leapt out his window."

"Rather than be caught by his guards, yes."

Voyle turned his head, glancing at Iiberi. "Thinks fast on her feet, it seems." He held out his hand. "Give me the sack."

Instinctively my grip tightened, but if Voyle noticed he ignored it and waited patiently. I'd intended not to hand the sack to anyone before I was given assurances, before I was accepted, but once again my belief in my own power had been grossly naive. I gritted my teeth to hold in grief. I had no power here.

The sack made the muted sound of shaking items as I handed it over, the move to grasp it the first Voyle had made since I'd entered his room. No lazy movement this; his hand shifted so fast he could have caught the sack before it hit the floor had I let it go.

With the sack settled on his lap, the Hoods' leader untied the neck and tugged it open, his brief wrestle with the stiff rope the first sign he was just a man.

"Well, would you look at that," Voyle said, a lion now languidly examining the spoils brought to him by others. "Even the excre. Count me impressed, Billette, I didn't think anyone would be able to get all these. Turns out all I needed was someone who used to work for the dread alchemist."

Dread alchemist. I'd not heard Occuello called so before, yet somehow it fit. All that disdain and contempt and manipulation, all that shuddering pleasure and overwhelming guilt. I'd loved every moment.

"Well, Iiberi," Voyle said, tugging the sack closed and tucking it beside him on the chair. "It looks like we have a new, and rather unexpected recruit. You'd better find her a room and some better-fitting clothing and all that nonsense. A blade too, if she knows how to use one."

I'd once held my ground with a scaleglass blade as the alchemist let it pierce her skin, only to buckle at the last moment.

"She'll pick it up quickly, I'm sure," Iiberi said.

"And if not she can murder us all with plants, eh?"

"Indeed." Iiberi's tone had chilled, but his nod was respectful as he turned to leave. Voyle had barely moved since I'd arrived, yet the urge to beg Iiberi to stay almost betrayed me. The boss wasn't frightening in the way of sharp teeth and pain, but his very existence was a threat, inevitable like the coming night. And he knew it. Enjoyed it. Wanted me to be afraid.

Unable to hear my silent plea, Iiberi departed, closing the door behind him with all too definite a snap. Voyle seemed hardly to notice.

"Tell me," he said, leaning forward. "Could you get back into Occuello's place?"

"Probably." It would be simple, really, but better he didn't know that. Better he didn't know about the other laundresses and the alchemist who had waited in the shadows to fill my sack with her own stolen goods. "Though it might take some work a second time."

"Mmm," he said, watching me from his wide chair, draped with furs despite the city's warmth. He looked dark enough to be pure Emoran, yet he wore his skirt skewed to the side, revealing a length of leg covered in wiry hairs—something no Emoran would ever bare to the world. He seemed to be built of such inconsistencies, his golden hair as out of place as the furs, and his posture lazy despite bulges of muscle. Even his room, small and windowless, had been packed with decorative riches of the sort an Emoran lord might own—paintings, chests, glass sculptures, heavy candelabras, and oil burners. It all carried the scent of mouldering wealth.

"But if you got in," he went on after one of his long silences, "you could get anywhere in the house? Is that how you got me these?"

"Yes, but there are guards. Likely more now."

He blinked slowly. "You seem like someone who gets things done, whatever it takes."

I hadn't been. I had worked for Master Occuello for years without complaint as though the labour had owned me, had worked through me, rather than the other way around. Growing small flowers on my arms had pushed me from my comfortable, hated rut, and now here I was, standing before the man who had grown the Hoods from an organisation of petty thieves to Bakii's most chaotic power brokers. I was blowing dust off forgotten ambitions, each unfurling with a thrill of fear.

Voyle leaned back, stretching out his legs and crossing his ankles. "Tell me, Naili, what do you want? And don't give me a trite answer. What do you really want?"

What did I want? I'd been just surviving, head barely above water for so long that I'd ceased to dream, only to live. But I'd had dreams once. I'd wanted to fight, to fix everything that was wrong, and some of that fury was slowly trickling back.

"I want to change the world," I said. "Break it if I must. Before it breaks me."

A smile slowly spread his lips, and he began to nod. "Yes. Yes, I thought I might like you. You do what you're told and none of us will have any regrets. Welcome to the Hoods."

Iiberi stood waiting for me outside Voyle's room, leaning against the passage wall with his arms folded. At sight of me, some tension eased from his features and he straightened, pulling himself to his full height. "Finally. I was getting very bored of waiting. Come," he added, already striding away along the passage. "I'll show you where your room is."

A murmur was all I had to thank him as I shook off the lingering discomfort from being in Voyle's presence. He'd said nothing to worry me, done nothing to trouble me, yet the feeling I didn't want to be anywhere near him remained.

"This place is quite the maze," Iiberi said, not glancing back as I followed. "You'll get used to it eventually. This is the part where we live, mostly; each of the doors along here is someone's private room. They aren't all the same, some bigger some smaller, but it's nothing personal. People get the room that's free when they join, nothing more. This is yours," he added, halting outside one with a curly symbol painted on the door—a way to differentiate them from one another, at least for those who could read. "Leaf"—he pointed at the word—"fate or irony that this was the room free upon your arrival, we may never know."

The latch clicked and he pushed the door open, freeing a scent like high-pitched hissing, roses and sun-warmed wood. The room lacked both wood and roses, but I'd been me long enough for that not to bother me, long enough too that I was grateful for a place to call my own. A small room, it nevertheless had space for a neat bed and some shelving, even a tiny metal table and a chair so battered it shone. It was all I could do not to thank Iiberi tearfully.

"I should have stolen my own clothes while I was at Occuello's," I said instead, eyeing the empty space while owning empty hands.

"That is one thing you never need to worry about around here; we have quite extensive collections of clothing for all occasions." Iiberi leaned against the door-frame. "Looking like you belong is more than half the battle, you know."

I didn't, but I nodded all the same.

His soft laugh mocked. "Come on, I'll show you where you can find what you need."

Closing the door behind us, we returned to the passage. Other passages with other doors led to other places and more private quarters than I could count, but with only the occasional faint murmur to break the silence, the place was quieter than I'd expected, and I said so.

"Because it's the middle of the day," Iiberi said, leading me on again with his long stride. "We don't keep our place as Bakii's gang of gangs by sitting around chatting. Anyone here is working or sleeping in preparation for a night shift."

"And you're stuck showing me around." I said it merely to say something, but when he didn't answer, questions began worming their way into my thoughts until I had to voice one. "Why are you showing me around? Aren't you a boss around here? Surely some lowly recruit should get this job."

"Your acuity is a mixed blessing, Naili Billette. Noticing things is good. Pointing them out not so much."

"But why would—?"

Iiberi stopped in the middle of the passage, and I almost ran into him. "And continuing to point them out when you've been warned is something akin to a death wish." He glanced back over his shoulder, his eyes like dark shadows. "The way to succeed as a new Hood is to do what you're told and not ask questions more momentous than 'Where is the pot chamber?' The answer to which is through there." With a gesture to a narrow arch into something like a small roofed atrium, he walked on, leaving me to hurry after him with the feeling I'd stepped on a snake.

Succeeding as a new Hood had never been my plan, a resentful part of me wanted to rage. I was only there because they'd given me the option of joining or death, a straightforward decision for which I was now being punished. But I kept my annoyance to myself, held tight the rage that had grown hour by hour since finding Chaintho's room, and followed Iiberi on. Better to pretend, to do as I was told and say what they wanted to hear, to gain their trust and then find ways to make use of them in silence.

The extensive collection of clothing Iiberi mentioned turned out to be no exaggeration. The room he led me to was twice as large as my private quarters and lined floor to ceiling in shelving and racks on which hung every colour and fabric of skirts and split skirts I'd ever seen, more tunics than a whole army would have needed, and boxes and boxes of wraps, scarves, veils, and armbands. "This is where you'll find everyday clothing," he said, striding in to light a second lantern halfway along the wall. "Nothing fancy or specific, and no armour or weapons, but everything you could need to look like a normal person going about normal business in Bakii. It might take you a while to find something in the right size, but keep it all tidy. Hoods who make a mess in storage rooms get all the worst jobs, and that's a promise."

I stared around the room, unsure where to even start. "You mean there's more than this?"

"Oh, much more, but we keep the fancy things for specific occasions, not for fun."

He'd taken up a spot near the second lantern and leaned against the wall—a habit of his, I was beginning to notice, that made him look smaller and less imposing. "But what do the Hoods need all these clothes for?" I asked. "And fancy ones?"

Iiberi smirked. "There's a lot you don't know about us, Naili Billette. But around here answers are earned not given."

"I'm not even allowed to know what the Hoods *do*?"

"We do a lot of things, some of which you already know, some of which you'll have to find out."

"What about why you had me steal from Master Occuello? Am I allowed to know that?"

"That is hardly a secret. Why steal things if not because you want them?"

"Including the excre?"

Iiberi's smile froze in place, becoming toothier.

"You can hardly blame me for reading the list you gave me," I said, unable to ignore the sense I was edging around something important. One wrong move and he wouldn't tell me anything, but with the right words I might get something I could use to leverage Occuello's help. "Surely it was too small an amount to make gunpowder," I went on, hoping I was right about that. "But just enough, perhaps, to prove someone who shouldn't have had any did actually possess some."

Iiberi's frozen grin took on a sneer. "And so your acuity earns you an answer, Naili Billette, but next time you may not be so lucky. Yes, the supplies you stole from Master Occuello were not things we need, rather things we wish to prove he is making use of. We believe he may have a . . . politically interesting client."

A politically interesting client. The words conjured my memory of Miizhei standing in the dim still-room passage, all sharp edges and worry. *I don't send money home like the others, but I do send information,* she'd said. Whatever Master Occuello was doing, she'd gathered many watchful eyes.

Perhaps thinking he'd said too much, Iiberi scowled. "And that, Billette, is all you're going to get. Here, this looks your size," he added, pulling a grey skirt from one of the many racks.

He was right, but I didn't thank him. I refused to be grateful when I'd become a Hood against my wishes, just as I refused to be grateful for the cursed magic living in my skin. I was here at the whim of more powerful people, but if I played along, I could find a way of turning it all to my advantage. My friends needed a cure, and I needed leverage against the dread alchemist, the seeds of which Iiberi had just given me.

Getting no reply, Iiberi pushed himself off the wall. "Well, take your time, Billette. Find yourself some clothes and get yourself settled. Dinner is served downstairs."

"That's it?" I said as he made to leave. "Nothing else I need to know or see?"

"You're sharp, you'll figure it out. And if you have any questions, you know where to find me."

He walked out on the words, leaving me to the mountains of clothing and the slowly dawning realisation that he was laughing at me as he strode away down the passage, because I didn't know where to find him at all.

Despite my determination to make use of the Hoods, fear clung to me as I made my way down to the dining room for my first evening meal. I'd lingered longer in my allotted room than I'd planned, meaning many Hoods had already gathered by the time I arrived. Voyle rose at sight of me, his broad smile oozing pride neither of us had earned.

"This here's Naili Billette, and you don't cross her or you answer to me. She's a Hood now, like any other of you bastards." He slapped me on the back, broad hand all but sending me staggering. "Get yourself some food and join us, Billette."

Some two dozen men filled the long dining table, so like the one back at Master Occuello's that I wouldn't have blinked had Miizhei appeared. But there was no Miizhei and no other women, not even Alii, just the curious gazes of all too many men. Only Iiberi seemed disinterested in my arrival. With one elbow propped on the table, he was spearing the contents of his hvarda with a knife and lifting each, almost daintily, to his mouth.

A long arch took up the entirety of the far wall, from beyond which came the familiar sounds of a kitchen at work. The scrape of thin metal dishes mingled with the clink of scaleglass, the crackle of coals, the hiss of hot water, and the low hum of chatter—the distinctive chatter of a room full of women working in concert.

The sound tugged at my heart, its strings both yearnful and yet repellent, reminiscent of so much suffering I hadn't realised was suffering. It had just been life lived one day at a time until the future faded from view.

On the counter under the arch, a half-empty pot of hvarda sat between a stack of flatbread and a deep dish of stewed and dried fruit, scented with vanilla and cinnamon. A stack of thin metal bowls sat haphazardly at one end, and a pile of spoons and knives at the other. Shamefully glad I didn't have to speak to the women in the kitchen, I served myself the largest amount I could fit in the bowl and hoped I could come back for seconds. My stomach hadn't stopped growling all day.

Back at the table, some of the men were already finishing up and departing, while others took their time or seemed happy to linger, talking while they wiped up the last of the hvarda sauce with their fingers. Voyle sat at the head of the table like a king of old watching over his people, commanding their attention whenever he spoke.

I took an empty place next to a Hood intent on his meal, though my appearance made him pause, hvarda-dipped flatbread halfway to his mouth.

"Hello," I said, reminding myself I was allowed to be there, however strange it felt. "I'm Naili."

The man bit a chunk off the flatbread and, while chewing, said, "Vedu."

Too hungry to make small talk, I dug into my meal, letting the low rumble of chatter wash around me. Farther along the table someone was talking about a city guard they'd gotten information from, while another was bemoaning the disinterest of a young woman who seemed to work at a nearby tavern. I ate and listened, while beside me, Vedu ate as fast as possible and made good his escape. I'd not expected a warm welcome, but I'd expected something, even if it was jibes about the markings on my cheek or what I kept between my legs. Instead the dining space had taken on a wary tenor, conversations seeming to falter whenever I looked up from my meal. I reminded myself that Master Occuello's servants had been cold and unwelcoming to newcomers too. And at least for now, being ignored was safe.

By the time my hunger was finally sated, I was one of the few Hoods remaining at the table, the others left nursing glasses of date wine over an absorbing argument about which glassroad had been built first. Despite being quite sure it was the Shield road, I just listened until movement in the doorway heralded the late arrival of Alii. Unlike me, she earned respectful nods and murmurs from the remaining men as she complained about how late she always was for meals now.

"The bastard doesn't feed you?" one of the men asked.

"Oh, he does, just not very well. Isn't that right, Naili?"

The sudden question was like having a searing light shone in my face, and I flinched. "What?"

"Occuello. Food isn't good," she said like someone breaking down an obvious statement to explain it to a child, before she moved away to serve herself from what was left. When she joined the table, she evinced not the smallest surprise or curiosity about my presence, nor offered any apology for having attacked me. Everyone accepted my existence like a dull fact, as though I hadn't had to fight for it, as though I wouldn't have been dead had I failed. I ought to have been grateful for safety on whatever terms, but the alchemist's words had spun in my head all day.

Power is gained through pushing. But don't just push back when the world pushes you, push first and never stop.

I glanced up at Alii, sitting a few seats away while the small group of lingering men went on with their argument. "So," I said. "Who are you?"

"Alii," she said without looking up from her meal. "You?"

"That's not what I meant."

"Then ask what you meant."

What had I meant? As I thought about it, the question fractured into dozens. How and why was she a member of the Hoods? Why did they seem to respect her? What was she doing pretending to be a laundress at Occuello's? Did she know about the source of my apparent plant magic and the danger of sticking her hands in the laundry tubs? But in the end the question that nagged most was "Who are you to these men? Who do they see when they look at you?"

A wry smile flickered on her lips, swallowed with her next mouthful of food. "The daughter of someone they respected very much," she said. "Does that make you feel a bit better? I'm not so much a Hood as I'm just Alii."

"Who is your father?"

"My father *was* Voyle."

She must have caught my confusion for she huffed a soft laugh. "Oh, not Linden. Yes, you're right in thinking he isn't old enough to be my father, don't worry. But he's also not old enough to have been the original founder of the Hoods. The real Voyle. Think of the name as something like a title, and that might make it easier."

"So you're here because you have nowhere else to go or because they can't get rid of you without spitting on your father's memory?"

Her laugh became bitter. "You're sharp and nasty, Naili, I hope you know that. But let's say it's a bit of both, shall we? And no, I am not telling you what I'm doing laundressing at Occuello's, so don't ask."

"Does he know? Occuello?"

"No."

"And if I threatened to tell him?"

"Then I would threaten to tell Linden about your magical friends. It's a good thing we're not actually threatening one another here, isn't it?"

I envied the ease with which she spoke, and said, "You should give me something, you know, if only so I don't accidentally fuck up your plans when Voyle has me go stealing again."

She shook her head. "That isn't how we work. And besides, you won't last here because women never do. Neither do decent people. Or people who dream. And you, Naili, are all three." She started clearing away her meal to depart, but paused to add, "Let me give you a piece of advice. A warning, if you will." With a glance at the few remaining men at the other end of the table, she lowered her voice. "Linden takes whatever he wants, whenever he wants. I'm protected by my father's ghost, but I've seen women come and go from these ranks in silence because of that man. As this is your first night, you can be sure he will come knocking, and there's nothing you can do to keep him out. One woman even married another Hood, sure that would end it." Alii clicked her tongue and, carrying her bowl, moved away from the table leaving me to imagine the horrors she had planted in my mind.

When she made for the door without returning, I sped after her, accosting her in the dim hallway. "Nothing?" I said, unable to hide the note of fear that tightened my voice. "What about you? You can protect me?"

"I can barely protect myself. I'm sorry, Nai, I really am. Iiberi is the only one who can face him down."

With a grimace, she walked on, wishing me a good night as I stood trying to keep my knees from collapsing beneath me. Everything about Voyle repelled. All lazy, cruel power for the sake of lazy, cruel power.

I ran after Alii's retreating back. "Alii," I hissed. "Can you do something for me?"

"If it's protecting—"

"No. Just...can you take Iiberi a message? I don't know where his room is, but I...He said that if I had more questions I ought to just ask, and I have more questions. And I would appreciate him enlightening me. At once."

Alii sighed. "Other people have tried this too," she said. "He's notoriously disinterested in being a protector. But all right," she added when I made to insist. "I'll give him your message. And now, Naili, I'm sorry, but good night."

On that dismissal I had nothing to do but return to my room and pace, dreading the coming hours and once more hating my own naivety. But even as I considered my options, determination settled like scaleglass in my bones. They had forced me to become a member or die, and I would turn it to my advantage whatever it took. When Linden had asked what I wanted, I'd said I wanted to change the world, to break it before it broke me, and with every step around the small room I now had to call my own, I meant it all the more.

Eventually, heavy footfalls heralded the arrival of someone outside my door, and trying to will Iiberi into existence, I opened it. The man who'd filled the world when Alii had first brought me in stood on the threshold, arms folded, his loose tunic shouting his Lummazzt identity even more than his face.

"Well?" he said. "You wished to see me?"

"I did, yes. I have a lot of questions. Come in."

"I don't do that."

"Why not?"

"Call it a cultural memory. Many are the Lummazzt men chased from women's bedrooms with sticks around here. Better never to fall into the trap in the first place."

"Who is going to chase you? I'm the only one here."

He tightened his folded arms and waited expectantly for the questions. I could ask them, but standing in the doorway wouldn't be enough, I was sure. "Will you come in if I tell you something I kept secret? About...my magic."

"Information in return for my presence? That seems a high

price to—ah. I see. Alii has warned you about Linden." He sighed. "This secret of yours had better be worth it, Naili Billette, or you can be sure this is the first and last time I will even consider being your shield." At last, with the hesitance with which I'd once crossed the line of light emanating from Mistress Paiwe's office, he stepped inside and closed the door. "What is it?"

Just inside the door, he stood with his arms folded, a sign his continued presence was entirely dependent upon my reply and I could not fuck this up. To give up my secrets felt weak, but at least in doing so I was choosing which evil to saddle myself to.

"My...*magic*," I said, the word *magic* feeling wrong and strange on my tongue; yet to call it anything else would be ridiculous. "It doesn't just let me grow plants at speed and...control them, somewhat."

"Ah, so you *were* trying to strangle me with that damned passiflor. Good to know. Do go on. What else can you do?"

I parted my lips to exclaim I had not been trying to do anything, but thought better of it. "I can...I can heal. Really fast."

Iiberi didn't look impressed.

"I first realised when I cut myself on a piece of scaleglass," I went on. "It was a deep cut, but by the time I got a bandage, it was gone. I'm also quite sure I broke something when I dropped into the road escaping Master Occuello's house the first time, but by the time Alii attacked me, it had healed. Here," I said, holding out my arm. "Test it."

Not something I'd ever thought to offer, but I held firm despite my doubts, despite even Iiberi's doubts as he stared hard at me like a man waiting for me to recant. When I didn't, he gave a lopsided shrug. "All right."

He drew a small knife from his belt and, without hesitation, set the tip of its blade to my skin. To heal didn't mean to feel no pain, yet I set my teeth as he sliced slowly through my flesh, determined to give away nothing but the blood that poured freely.

Having sliced a long, straight cut, he ended it with a curve, like a painter adding a final flourish to his work. And then he watched. Watched as the blood slowed its spill, as the skin at the beginning of his cut began to close, as his handiwork was undone by flesh determined to knit back together and keep itself whole. And though it was my skin, I shivered at fully seeing it for the first time.

Iiberi's grip on my arm tightened. He seemed closer, his breathing heavier, his gaze unshifting from the wound that was almost a wound no longer, the healing tracing his cut as it spread.

"God have mercy," he murmured, proving to anyone who might have missed his eyes that he was Lummazzt. "That's not something I ever thought to see." Seeming to realise how intently he stared and how tightly he held me, he looked up. "You weren't kidding."

"Seems a strange thing to joke about," I said, my voice more breathless than I'd expected. Some deep, primeval part of me wanted him to do it again. Wanted him to lick the skin he had cut. Wanted him to hold me down and do what he wanted with me like the alchemist had. But I hadn't parted with my secret just to invite a different vicious man into my bed, so I reined in my unruly lust as best I could, the act like trying to stuff an enormous blanket into a tiny purse.

Iiberi let my arm go, and I stepped back. "So you'll stay and answer my questions?" I said.

"I rather feel it is I who should be asking the questions."

"I wouldn't have answers if you did. But perhaps you can tell me why you don't like Voyle. You don't have the same reason Alii and the other women have, and yet you seem to share their dislike."

Iiberi scowled. "You ask very personal questions for someone I've only just met. Does it occur to you that perhaps you have to prove yourself trustworthy to earn the answers?"

"All right, then tell me something I'm allowed to know. What power do the Hoods really have?" I said. "When it is Emorans who rule the basin."

"We have power; it just might not be the sort of power you want." Iiberi shrugged. "Bakii is a web of people all striving for their own ends; with the right knowledge and a bit of pressure, any string of a web can break."

His eyes brightened as he spoke, his lips twitching into a half-smile as though catching sight of his next meal—truly the spider I'd thought him, stalking about his web in search of prey. I couldn't supress a shiver despite how much I wanted him to keep talking, to detail everything from the feel of the sticky webs to the taste of each crunchy wing. Perhaps if I could learn how the web had been strung, I too could play the game as he did.

The scrape of a step halting on the floor outside was all that heralded a knock at the door, a sharp, imperious rap of knuckles that seemed to warn the hand could as easily have broken through the soft wood. My next question froze on my lips, and Iiberi turned, his scowl returning as he stared at the door. Rather than immediately open it, he hissed a few swear words, grumbled something unintelligible like he was having a conversation with himself, and scuffed his feet on the floor. Eventually having reached the door, he waved fiercely for me to get out of sight, and tugged it open.

"Oh, Linden," he said, tone as bored as it was surprised, a unique combination I would have to practise. "Something amiss?"

From out in the passage came Voyle's voice, his words as capable of taking up all the available space as his presence. "Nothing amiss at all, Iiberi," he said, a toothy smile present in his tone. One that barely reached his lips let alone his eyes. "I'll bid you good night."

A pause. The movement of shadows upon the wall. Then footsteps retreated, all while Iiberi remained standing at the door, blocking entry as much as inviting question. He nodded a few beats as though counting, then closed the door and spun to lean against it, back flat to the warped wood. There he stood with his eyes closed, every breath faster than the last, until eventually he seemed to regain a sense of his surroundings and glared at me. "He won't be back tonight at least," he said, pushing himself upright. "Hopefully longer. Now if you don't have any more questions, I'll leave you."

"Only one question," I said, a squirm of fear in my gut at how difficult that had seemed for something so simple. "Will you come again tomorrow night?"

"That depends," he said, reaching for the door again. "How many more secrets do you have to share with me?"

He didn't wait for an answer, just pulled open the door. "By the way, you have something in your hair, in case you hadn't noticed." A gesture at the narrow, cloudy brass mirror on the wall and he was gone, closing the door in his wake like a snap of censure.

Barely had the sound faded away than I was standing before the mirror, clawing through my hair in search of what he'd seen. The scent of warm jasmine radiated into the air, and tiny specks of yellow pollen dusted my hands, pale petals soon adding to the horror. They were larger than the ones that had been growing on my arms and legs, but nowhere near the size of a full jasmine flower—a clump together the only reason Iiberi had been able to see them from a distance. At least so I hoped.

A dusty, almost milky scent joined the jasmine as I yanked the flowers out, yet with every broken stem I found yet another flower, the small blooms seeming to have spread from the back of my ear to the back of my head.

"No," I whispered, tearing out hairs with the flowers now, each sting possessing the satisfaction of cleansing horrors. From my hair, I moved to my arms and legs, stripping naked to hunt out every errant flower and rub it from existence. With every one I brushed away, another seemed to appear, the endless sprouting a nightmare from which I needed to wake. But no matter how much I shook myself, or how hard I scratched my skin, I could not wake. The effects were getting worse. How long had Chaintho known about the flowers before—

The taste of mould leapt to my lips as though it had never left me, as though I stood in that room that no longer looked like a room, its every surface covered in rotting growth and creeping putrescence. My room here was no bigger, a space that could so easily become filled with reaching roots and giant leaves unfurling to the ceiling, each possessing a glistening sheen. And like a cocoon my skin would split, a rush of jasmine flowers pouring forth in place of blood, mould in place of guts, my entire body becoming earth as I ceased to be. I saw it all so clearly as though it was no dream but a vision of the future in which I became the same forgotten dross as Chaintho, left to be swept off the floor like so much dust.

Tears were falling before I felt them, hot and angry, and I sank onto the floor, sucking great, shaking gasps of air. I'd told Voyle I would break the world before it broke me, but I was already running out of time.

15

Ashadi

Afternoon Bulletin

To all criers for announcement throughout Upper Emora

*Morning heralded the return of Lord Reacher Sormei Sydelle and
Lord Kiren Sydelle with his new wife, Lady Teshalii Sydelle,
prompting an afternoon full of palace visitations akin to those
when Reacher Sormei first took the reachership.*

*It is believed that sunrise also brought Lord Ashadi Romm
to Emora, who deserted his post at the Shield after three
years spent serving to protect the basin from enemy
attacks.*

*Several items of historical and cultural significance have gone
missing in Emora this week, as the so-called reclamation
movement gains momentum throughout the basin.*

190:13

I stared at the contents of the room—a room I'd lived in almost every day until I'd left for the citadel, yet one I no longer recognised. Everything was new. The curtains. The bed. The plants. Even the tiling on the floor had been replaced with what was, apparently, the latest style in colourwork. And hanging in the dressing room was a whole new wardrobe's worth of clothing in the current style—more clothes than I'd ever had at one time. My father had even ordered a new holster made, and a new make of Hiburque pistol lay on a side table, gleaming.

Being left alone for the first time since stepping off the ship was like slowly rising through dark water in search of air. Everything that had happened in the last half an hour sped by like a blur. My father's demand for proof and his determination to make a scene had saved me from arrest for now, and we'd left the harbour trailed by his retainers, so like a parade that we'd turned heads. I'd had just enough sanity to ensure Mana was with us before being swept away on my father's arm. He'd walked slowly and talked to as many people as he could find on the way, laughing off the charge of desertion as ridiculous since he had himself recalled me. The same story over and over, and all I could do was smile and agree and assure people I had suffered no injury being shot down in The Sands before walking on to do it all again. Eventually we'd arrived at the gates of Romm Manor to a formal greeting, every servant lined up like an honour guard. I was sure I hadn't drawn breath the whole time.

I drew breath now, each coming fast like an excitement I could barely contain. My stomach fizzed, and as I emerged from confusion into daylight, I possessed a restless energy that sent me flitting about the room. I'd been sent to Emora as ambassador to the Shield, was somehow also a deserter, and had been recalled by my father at the same time. Now I was meant to be preparing for dinner, but as I strode from the dressing room to the balcony and back, the next step eluded me.

A gentle tap at the door heralded Mana's arrival, although *arrival* was too strong a term for the wary way he peeked around the edge of the door.

"Lord Ashadi? Do you...do you wish any assistance? I'm...not sure I have any role here, but if—"

"Yes, please," I said, clinging to this one moment of familiarity. "I am meant to be dining with my father, I think, but...I don't know...can't...What do I need to do?"

I hated how pathetic the words sounded, but he seemed to understand. And finding the dressing room, Mana set to work on what had always been the smallest part of his role as a watcher—sorting out my wardrobe.

"Do you have a colour preference?" he said, rifling through the embarrassingly large amount of clothing my father had purchased. "Or any particular style?"

"I...no. I don't know. I want to be...covered. Appropriately."

"I think they will all perform that function, yes."

I shook my head, trying to clear the daze. "I'm sorry, I don't seem to be thinking straight. I feel a bit...drunk. I didn't drink anything, did I?"

Mana emerged from the dressing room carrying a short stack of clean clothes, which he sat on the bed. "No. I think you're in shock. Quite beyond the whole being-thought-a-deserter thing, I assume you weren't expecting any of...this."

"No! I didn't even know he would be in Emora, let alone want to see me, and—I...I don't—"

Mana wrapped his arms around me and held me tight, chest to chest, my rapid heartbeat against his slow, steady rhythm. He didn't speak, didn't move, just held me to him, grounding me in the physical world in which our bodies existed. The twitchy, restless part of me wanted to pull away and pace, but enough of me wanted his touch, wanted to drink in his calm, his warmth, his care, that I stayed where I was, just breathing and being held until little by little the clouds of confusion began to part, sinking me back onto my feet in a real world. A real world in which I could remember the soft touch of his lips, and the slip of his tongue along mine.

I pulled away, ruffling my hair and achieving only a sheepish grin. "Thank you, I needed that."

Mana stayed where he was, watching me. "I thought you might. It's not what most people think of as medicine, but my mother was a great supporter of touch in healing. Hugs help people slow down and remind them where they are."

"A very wise woman."

"She was, yes. Are you ready to dress now?"

"Yes. That was obviously the next step to getting ready for dinner, yet somehow, I couldn't find it."

"Like I said, you're in shock. What do you mean to do?"

I had no answer, but while he helped me dress for the first dinner I'd had with my father in three years, I thought through my plans and found them all in tatters. I'd come to Emora because I'd been ordered to do so as an ambassador, only to realise on the journey that Reacher Sormei could not provide what was really needed. I'd begun to wonder since whether they'd just wanted to get rid of me, wanted to stop me asking questions—a possibility made all the more likely when guards awaited me on the dock.

"Perhaps a message to the masters will sort out the confusion," Mana said, filling the silence his question had left. "And then you can—"

"It's not a confusion." My words emerged with more assurance than I'd expected, but even as I spoke, I knew them to be true. "The citadel masters don't accidentally accuse the heir of one of Emora's wealthiest families of being a deserter. That's a deliberate choice to discredit me. Or perhaps they hoped to get me out of the way entirely, assuming my father wouldn't lift a finger to protect me after having sent me to the Shield in the first place."

Mana seemed to have frozen in horror, my armbands caught in his fingers. "That seems like a great risk," he said at last. "Just for asking questions?"

"I'd say for asking questions and not being satisfied with the answers," I said, holding my arm out for him. "And I saw...monsters...in a room off the undercroft. Just like the ones we fight, but also not quite. Commander Jasque was shaken when he found me there. There's something they don't want us to know, and I'm going to find out what it is."

"Ash, they've already tried to arrest you once. They might do worse when they find out that didn't work."

The quiet worry and care in his tone warmed me like nothing else could, and as he slid an armband up my arm, I laid my hand on his. "They are just old riders sitting in a broken castle at the end of the world. I know the most powerful people in the basin by their first name. Don't worry about me."

He didn't look convinced, but he nodded and slid his hand from beneath mine to add a second band to my arm. "Just...be careful. Not only of them, but also of Lord Romm. This...grandiose display must have a purpose."

"A purpose beyond caring for his son?" A flare of anger nipped at my skin. "Need he have another?"

A light tap on the door stole his reply, and the unsmiling face of Torl, father's steward, insisted its way into my world. "Dinner is ready, Lord Ashadi," he said, and flicking a glance at Mana, added, "Your...*friend*...can dine with the servants."

"Thank you," Mana said before I could retort. "I would be honoured."

"Honoured?" The question was barely past my lips before Mana was out the door, leaving me little to do but follow under Torl's insistent gaze.

I found my father waiting in the dining hall antechamber, casting an eye over what appeared to be the most recent crier sheet.

He looked up as I entered, tucking the sheet away and smiling broadly. "Ashadi." As when I'd stepped off the ship, he crushed me into a stiff hug, but unlike Mana's, it left my body tense.

"Father," I said, and in the standard greeting, took his hands and kissed them. "I apologise I did not greet you properly at the harbour, nor thank you for meeting me. It was undutiful of me."

He waved an indulgent hand at this. "It is nothing. A man who has spent days on a public ship isn't expected to have his full senses about him. I see a brief rest has now returned you to full mind, however, and to fine attire!" He stepped back, the better to look me over. "I knew that colour would suit you. And this season's collar shapes are very much in your favour. As well you were not with us last year when we had to suffer through *rounded lines*."

Before I could answer he gestured toward the dining hall. "Come, let us eat. I hate to think how long it has been since you tasted the sort of good food only our cooks can produce."

Borne in his wake, I let my fingertips drag lightly across the wall and the fine wood of the door, needing something real to calm my leaping thoughts. Thankfully, although my room had changed, the dining hall was the same as it had always been, a grand space open on one side to the central atrium. Heat and flies weren't a problem at the citadel, but here netting hung over the open atrium and water trickled, every shadow a pool of life.

Upon the table sat a spread fit for the grandest party, yet it was set only for two. "Very fine, is it not?" my father said, gesturing for me to join him at the table. "I even had the kitchens make your favourite—gashana with wild honey."

Gashana with wild honey had been my favourite as a child until a bad batch of honey had left me sick for weeks—something I dared not remind him of as I took my place opposite.

"So, do you get news out on those mountains of yours?" he said as though I'd chosen to go to the Shield for the joy of it. "Quite a lot has happened in the last few weeks."

"I heard about Learshapa," I said, waiting for him to serve himself before I could begin—the social customs so baked in that even after three years without them they were still second nature. "And about Kiren's wedding."

I spoke as lightly as I could, hoping to skirt around the edge of what had been a very dangerous drop I didn't want to fall down again. The observation that our families were at last connected would have done me no favours.

As he finally served himself from a dish of salted cuttlefish, my father's low chuckle had a sharp edge. "Yes, my greatest triumph, that. They arrived this morning too. You'll have to be introduced privately to keep up the pretence you know each other already, but your brother did a decent job training her. Pulling his weight around here for once."

Knowing it was always safer to leave Uvao out of the conversation, I said, "I take it that I was correct then, and there never used to be a Lady Teshalii Romm in our family tree."

"Of course not! But she's there now, and what a fine mess she'll make of the Sydelles for us."

I'd had bigger things to worry about than the sudden appearance of a new relative, but his words shook comprehension from the foggy corners of my mind. "An insult bride?"

"Naturally."

He said it with such ease, like we were discussing nothing more significant than the weather. The hollow feeling that bloomed in my gut seemed not to affect him. "That's... quite the risk."

"Nonsense. It's all planned. So long as everyone does what they're told."

"I don't think I understand. Her discovery would trigger a renegotiation of the treaty and likely a vote of the conclave that might oust Sormei, but there will also be an uproar, and that uproar may well be aimed at us. That won't do you any favours if you're planning to stand for the reachership."

"Only if we don't expose her ourselves."

He spoke lightly, more interest taken in selecting a bunch of grapes than in the fate of our new family member. "You're going to expose her yourself? And put the blame on her?" I asked. The wisest course would be to change the subject, to not know, but I was back in Emora at least for now, and that made his plans my problems. "She must be a clever woman to be able to instigate all this herself and somehow force her way into our family unbeknownst to us."

The expected snap of irritation didn't come. He just set the chosen grapes upon his plate and moved on to examining the skewered pakka drenched in herb sauce. "She's an old... *friend* ... of Uvao's."

On anyone else's lips it could have been an idle observation, but in my father's brittle tone it was all threat. A demand to know whether he would really sacrifice his son to give himself the strongest position at a conclave leapt to my tongue only to be swallowed, the answer as clear as his rage had been when I'd last refused to play his game. Uvao and I had never gotten along, but to even think about his destruction in the name of political advancement sickened me to the core.

Though I didn't speak, something of my thoughts must have leaked out across the table, for my father huffed an irritable breath. "It is all done. It has been set in motion and cannot be changed now. And this may yet be the greatest contribution Uvao has made to this family. In the meantime, we must officially return you to society. There's to be an evening party at the palace tomorrow in celebration of Kiren's new wife, and we will be there. Together. Never again will the Romm family fall to being a laughing stock."

I murmured agreement around food that no longer had any taste. Mana's warning that my father's display must have a purpose echoed awfully in my mind.

"I imagine you'll be quite the star once we get past this foolish desertion business," my father went on. "Everyone has been talking about your incident beyond the Shield, and we can play that up instead. Then, between you and Lady Teshalii, we will be the centre of attention."

"There is little to say about my…misadventure," I said, realising he hadn't asked me about it, nor the explosions and the endless callouts for endless monsters. "Except to wonder what a man was doing out in The Sands to begin with."

"No one lives in The Sands. Likely it was a stray bullet—one I have to thank for bringing you back to me at just the right time. I have begun conversation with Lord Mior about your marriage to his daughter, Lady Ibella. I think she wasn't old enough to attend parties last time you were here, but you will meet her tomorrow. The connection will be integral to gaining the support of the southern estates at the conclave."

Each word left me increasingly bewildered. "But…I am a rider of the Shield. It is my duty to return and—"

"No. You are the heir of this family before anything else."

"I was. Until you sent me away to be a rider."

"And now I am recalling you as is my right. I have already written to the citadel masters to rescind your obligation—necessary to quash the talk of desertion even if I didn't need you here. But you *are* needed here. You have the skills to rise, Ashadi, to lift this family back to where it deserves to be. You are sharp and cunning and know everyone's weak spots, but you are also charming and handsome. And you are my heir. This city used to be your plaything; you can make it dance for you again."

Not once in three years had I been able to say I enjoyed life at the Shield. Like most riders, I had been there not because I'd dreamed of protecting the basin, but because I had no choice. The feeling I had no choice remained, yet even with the knowledge that the citadel masters had decided I was dangerous, some part of me clung to that terrible life, to Mana and Shuala. "But the Celes Basin is in grave danger, Father, and it's my duty—"

"Your duty is to me!"

His growl silenced even the fountains, the whole house seeming to hold its breath at his fury. Even when he breathed out, forcing a smile, his frustration remained, stuffing the room like a swollen bruise. "Given your desertion, it is surprising that you feel your duty to the citadel so strongly. But what happens at the Shield is of no great importance after all. This is where futures are made. Where families rise and fall. And this is where you need to be now. I will not have my son and heir in danger of being shot out of the sky again."

My heart swelled. This was the care my father had used to show me. Why was I fighting it? Why would I want to go back and drink iishor amid secrets when I could return to my real life and find truths? It didn't even matter what I thought. As he'd had the power to send me to the citadel, he had the power to recall me. And the power to send me back again if I didn't do as he wished.

"I...I didn't desert, Father," I said. "I was sent by the citadel masters to meet with Reacher Sormei about the trouble at the Shield. As an ambassador. I think...I think they did not appreciate the questions I asked about the man who shot me down and are punishing me with this lie, but I will fulfil the mission they sent me on all the same."

My father shrugged, taking another skewer and pouring himself more wine. A man who cared nothing for my explanation, resentfully putting up with small disruptions to his plans.

"I can send a petition to Reacher Sormei tomorrow and—"

He waved this away, slipping back into his earlier ease. "Never mind petitions. That is for commoners. You are Lord Ashadi Romm and you are my son; I will organise for you to meet with the reacher the day after tomorrow if that will satisfy you."

The reminder of how easily my name and wealth allowed me

to move through the world was more alluring than I wanted to admit, but it was with misgiving that I agreed, because it was his power, not mine, and I would have to do what I was told if I wanted to use it.

Once dinner was over, my father dismissed me in his usual high-handed manner. He had somewhere to be and I needed rest—words he would have used even had they not been true.

Unsure I had even eaten, I returned to my rooms as dazed as when I had left them, only to find an argument filling the space with spittle and rage. On one side of the room stood Mana, staring down a pair of men who only stopped shouting at my arrival, and bowed.

"Uhh...what is going on here?"

"My Lord Ashadi," one of the men said with an obsequious smile. "We have orders from Lord Romm to have this...*person*... escorted from the house. As he is responsible for your desertion, we have threatened to call the city guard, but he has still refused to budge. Apologies for not having this sorted before you returned from dinner, my lord, we will send for the—"

"No, you won't." I glanced at Mana, whose expression could have been hewn from stone. He made no attempt to defend himself or request my assistance, just stood his ground with a determination that would have impressed even Shuala. "This man is here because I wish him to be here, and he has no crime to answer for. Anyone who sends for the city guard will struggle to find work in this city ever again and that is a promise. Now out, both of you."

The men shared a glance, before the second one bowed. "As you wish, my lord, but I am to wait on you. On Lord Romm's orders."

"No, I need only Mana." Stepping aside, I gestured to the still open door. "Leave. Now. Both of you."

Shocked stares turned from me to Mana and back again, before the nameless servants gave little sniffs of irritation and stalked out.

"I'm sorry," I said to the still motionless Mana. "It is very like my father to not mention this to my face, just give orders behind my back."

"It seems I am now to blame for your desertion. I suppose it was only a matter of time before they pointed at the Apaian."

The words held more reproach than I had expected. "I tried to explain to my father that I didn't desert at all," I said. "But he seems not to believe me, or not to care. He's too busy smoothing it over and turning it to his advantage. He says my duty is here anyway, and that my family is more important than what is happening at the Shield."

Mana stared at me, gaze seeming to rake my face. "More important than there being more attacks than they can fight back? Than explosions levelling one of the passes and taking out a wing of the citadel? How?"

I threw up my hands in defeat. "I don't know! It's all a fucking mess. That new relative of mine? Insult bride. He is going to expose her and sacrifice my brother to the horrified masses to force a meeting of the conclave. Lord Reacher Romm, at last." My laugh had a hysterical edge that only sharpened at sight of Mana's stare. "Yes, that's exactly what I thought too, but to ensure he'll have enough votes, I'm to marry some daughter of a southern lord though I can't for the life of me remember which one now, only that she was too young to be at parties a few years ago so I may as well be marrying a child!"

"Whose name you don't know."

"Exactly! But I shall take heart. This plan is so risky it'll surely blow up in our faces, and once we've been stripped of our estate, I can become a beggar. I think I would make a pretty good beggar once I let my hair get dirty, don't you?"

Mana stilled, something wary in his stance. "Ash? If your father smooths over the claim of desertion, the citadel masters will have to find another way to discredit you."

"What else can they do? My father is too powerful."

"Yes, but mine is not. If they plan to get to you by attacking me, then I'm not safe here. I should go before—"

"No. Don't. Please." The words were out before I could think better of them. The same selfish words with which I had begged him to come with me in the first place. "No, I'm sorry. You are free to leave. You're free to leave anytime, but since I got you into this mess, I would rather get you out of it first. Rather you left as a free man than one wanted for a crime you didn't commit. I'm to meet with the Reacher the day after tomorrow and can plead your case. I'll make sure you're safe here until then."

As I spoke, Mana's brows drew together in confusion. His lips parted as though to shape a question, only for him to tuck it away unspoken. "All right," he said instead. "Until the day after tomorrow."

"The day after tomorrow," I agreed, tension easing.

"Right, well. I guess, in the meantime... does this house of yours have one of those fancy big Emoran baths you sit in? If I'm going to risk my life sticking around, I may as well enjoy the only good thing Emorans have ever made."

"Of course it does," I said, hiding the jolt of fear his blithe words sent through me. "This is a manor in upper Emora. Here we build the baths before the rest of the house, because we know what's important. I shall let your insult slide, however. I accept being second best, but only to baths."

With the comfort of a destination and something I could control, I gathered up what we would need and led Mana out into the passage. It was strange being back home, but at least in my father's absence, the house possessed the silence of a released breath, and we slipped through it unheeded.

Emoran baths came in a variety of shapes and sizes, but they were all deep pools in which one could be fully submerged, and all were hot enough to sear away aches and sometimes even skin. Usually private baths were large enough to fit half a dozen people at once while public baths could fit dozens, but whichever Romm had built our city manor had preferred the smaller variety. Our bathhouse had four, each a glory of translucent dark scaleglass with gold needle inclusions, poured in place as a single curving piece of glass. Between each bath, crackle-glass partitions provided a modicum of privacy, though the heat all came from the same floor and the steam rose to a collective ceiling. Steam into which Mana's low whistle carried.

"Not bad," he said. "I've seen finer, but this is very impressive."

"You've seen finer?" I said, glancing back as I made my way toward the farthest bath. "*Where?*"

"That is for me to know and for you never to find out."

"You are a tease, you know."

I dropped our towels on the bench against the wall and, dodging the reaching tendrils of an overgrown plant, took two dressing robes from the shelf and added them to the pile.

"Towel. Robe," I said, stripping out of the fine clothes Mana had so recently helped me into. "Feel free to take them to the more impressive baths."

I was fully undressed and ready to step into the water before I realised Mana hadn't gotten further than his tunic. He'd slept in my bed, cared for me, cleaned me, dressed me, and seen me naked more times than I could count, but all that had only ever gone one way. The realisation hit me like a punch. I tried not to show it, not to appear conscious of his existence as I stepped into the water, but the effort of not turning to stare at him as he revealed more and more of his skin was almost too much.

I focused on the extremely important task of scooping a few fallen leaves from the water and returning them to the pot of the offending plant, until a small splash told me it was safe to turn without embarrassing him.

"I forgot how hot the water is," he said as he settled into it. "You'd think that in a desert we would want cool baths, not hot ones, yet here we are." Reaching up a hand, he pulled the tie from his hair, sending dark strands tumbling about his shoulders, tips reaching for the water.

"Perhaps it was cooler in Old Emora, and we are just bad at letting go of traditions. Although, I think there's something to the idea of being hot by choice."

Mana sat on the bath's underwater ledge and leaned back with a sigh, tension leaking out of him. I wished it were so easy. Instead, I dried my hands on a towel and reached for the korsh pack I'd brought with me, rolling more than usual into a paper. Having lit it, I threw the striker back onto my towel and turned to find Mana watching me, something intent in his gaze that seemed to preclude either of us breathing.

"No need to look at me like that," I said as lightly as I could. "It's not like you haven't seen me smoke in every possible situation. Being here only makes me worse."

"Emora is more stressful than riding dragons?"

I laughed, blowing out a cloud of smoke. "Yes, the dragons here walk around on two legs and breathe out worse than fire."

"But at least there are nice baths."

"That is definitely an upside, yes."

He rose to dry his hands on the same towel, before holding out a hand for my korsh. "May I?"

The unexpected request reminded me of our brief kiss back on the sand ship and the taste of korsh on his breath, and I swallowed a demand to know since when had he smoked. Instead, I handed him the roll and watched as he set it to his lips and drew deeply, every movement owning the fluid grace of a man well-practised in the art.

"You know," he said, exhaling. "If it worries you at all, I just want you to know that I'll be all right. Leaving, I mean. I'll go back to Bakii and see what trouble I need to get my sister out of. Never was wise to leave her alone for so long."

"If it worries me? *If?* What kind of monster do you think I am that it wouldn't worry me?" I held out an imperative hand for the korsh. "I am human, you know."

"Oh, I know." Mana set the korsh to his lips and drew a deep breath into his lungs, showing no sign of giving the roll back. I twitched my hand, but he just smiled, the look he threw me all challenge.

"You're going to make me roll another?" I grumbled.

He blew smoke in my direction. "You don't have to. Just come and take it."

The challenge quivered heat through me and filled my head with steam, and yearning more than thinking, I started toward him through the water. He watched me beneath half-lidded eyes, but rather than offer the roll, he just turned it around. Lit end inside his mouth, he held the roll pinched between his teeth and leaned forward. My heart thudded into a sea of fog and I froze. Holding the end steady, he said, "Don't lords know how to share?" in husky challenge, before once more offering me the roll caught between his teeth. I could no more refuse the offer than sprout wings, and wanted to even less. So leaning close, I parted my lips and took a drag, inhaling as he exhaled, all smoke and heat as both korsh smoke and Mana's breath coursed through my body.

Whether it was the hardest hit of korsh I'd ever taken or just the existence of Mana, I stopped thinking. He drew from the roll again, our lips close. A breath, a gasp; for a moment it seemed he was inhaling me until we were kissing—a kiss that picked up where our last had ended, not tentative but hot and desperate. So close were we that the smallest movement brought us skin to skin beneath the water, my hard cock yearning to press against his body as much as I yearned to melt into his kiss.

Beneath the water, his hand closed around me, sending a pleasurable shudder up my spine. I gasped against his lips, and with a small chuckle he tightened his grip, his other arm snaking about my waist to hold me close. Chest to chest, I sat astride him on the bath's underwater ledge, my body nothing but an internal scream of desperation as my cock pressed up against his. Until he shifted his hand around us both and I let out something more whimper than cry. He didn't seem to notice. All was heat and pleasure and need and the lingering buzz of korsh as his long fingers worked, stroking us against one another in the warm water. Our kiss stilled, lips touching but letting out only moans and gasps in the airless steam, his every little shudder of pleasure pushing me further and further until I couldn't have stayed silent had I tried, so completely did the sensation tear through me.

For a moment I seemed to be both all too connected to my body and yet to have transcended it entirely, and a series of awestruck expletives hissed past my lips. There in the hot bath, I remained pressed against him, unwilling to move lest the scene fracture into a thousand tiny pieces, impossible to recreate. I wanted our chests pressed close, wanted our bodies entwined, wanted to press my lips to his neck, to his jaw, to his lips. Wanted never to let him go. And maybe, just maybe, I could build a future where I didn't have to.

"Feeling a little better now?" he said, the words rough and warm against my cheek.

And the relaxation that had melted me against him began to recede in the face of an increasingly familiar fear. That Mana only cared for me because it was his job, or perhaps more accurately because the proximity and intensity required of the job had induced such care. And even if that wasn't true, I was heir to one of the most powerful families in the basin. People had always given me what I wanted, even when it wasn't what they wanted to give.

I pulled back, a chill spreading through me despite the heat of the bath. "Thank you, yes." The words sounded ridiculous, but in that moment even ridiculous was better than honest. "Something tells me that's not the first time that's been done in here, though would you believe it's a first for me? You are very good at your job."

Mana's brow furrowed, an unspoken question once more hovering upon his lips. I should have let him leave Emora, should have freed myself from the pain of his presence, freed us both, but I'd been too weak. And now I could not even run without giving myself away.

"Looks like I need a fresh korsh roll after all," I said, trying for drawling ease as I dried my hands on the towel. "Do you want one?"

"No, thank you, my lord." Water streamed off him as he pulled himself out of the bath and snatched up a towel. "I am finished and so shall bid you good night."

Before I could think of anything to say, he'd wrapped the towel around his waist and started in the direction of the door, and the farther away he walked the harder it became to call him back—and the more it would mean if I did. And so I let him go, as I ought to have let him go when we'd left the citadel, swallowing every foolish hope that we could ever have a future.

Grateful for strong brandy and exhaustion, I somehow managed sleep, but morning brought recollections of the previous night that hit me like a runaway sand ship careening off its road. My father's cold plans. Being recalled from the citadel. The marriage he was setting up for me. The life he was once again tearing from beneath my feet—all leading up to Mana's decision to loosen some of my tension with a moment of utter bliss I wanted to both relive endlessly and completely forget so nearly had I thrown all caution to the wind. There ought to have been words that could sort out such tangles, that would remake the road along which I sailed at breakneck speed, but when Mana arrived to help me prepare for the day, I had nothing.

For a time, he just worked in silence, fetching my clothes and readying my shaving water, until he said abruptly, "You know that I don't work for you anymore, don't you?"

"Oh, of course you don't, I just hadn't thought..." I trailed off, flustered at the spikes he'd just laid upon my road. "I should get someone else to wait on me. I'm sorry."

"I don't want someone else to do it, I just...just wanted to know that you know. That you know I'm no longer being paid to take care of you."

"Shit, I should be paying you, shouldn't I?"

"No! I mean yes, I suppose, but—" He shook his head and turned away to find my shoes. "Don't trouble yourself over it, Lord Ashadi. I have been well compensated with your hospitality. I just..." Mana sighed. "When you asked me to come with you back on the ship, I thought it was because, well, because you didn't want to be without me. Was I wrong?"

His words hooked into my heart, asking for a truth I dared not give. "Of course I want you with me," I said, with all the ease I could muster. "But I will still make sure you get paid. Although right now I had better get to breakfast before my father starts shouting."

And so I escaped.

My first full day back in Emora would culminate in that evening's party at the palace, but my father insisted on much before then, on doing everything possible to be sure I was *seen*. That meant stopping in at Master Pirellei's to sit eating fine cakes while questions gathered around me like flies, taking my new pistol to the shooting gallery to rub shoulders with the young firecrackers, and strolling around the garden square to smile and kiss the hands of every matriarch who marvelled at my return. And paying a call on Lord Mior to be introduced to the newest woman unlucky enough to be picked out as my bride.

All in all, it was a day in Emora much like any other day in

Emora, full of familiar people and forced smiles, and dull conversation that papered over what everyone was really thinking, over the city's heartbeat and the ever-simmering mire that was Emoran social life. I'd never had any illusions about it, but neither had I expected to have missed it.

That night the palace was full of people, familiar and new, all talking, laughing, kissing one another's hands, nibbling on bite-size cakes, and drinking from ever-renewed glasses of wine. Every room had giant coloured-glass windows, mosaics and fountains, greenery and glinting light, yet the presence of Sormei's personal guards gave the place an oppressive quality with their scaleglass armour, heavy scowls, and repeating pistols.

Although we had arrived together, I soon left my father behind and started a lap of the main rooms, searching for the one person in all Emora who might have answers. While I walked, people accosted me, some with greetings, others with questions about my choice to desert my post, and I parried them all with the ease of long practice and walked on, eyes darting. Until a familiar voice called, "Ashadi!" and I turned to find Lord Kiren crossing the floor toward me. "I was hoping to see you this evening. It's been an age since you were last in Emora."

"Ah, Lord Kiren, I too was hoping for a chance to speak with you," I said, taking his proffered hands and lifting them to my lips. "You look well," I added. "And I understand congratulations are in order."

"Thank you," he said with the sweet smile that had captivated so many. "Tesha is around here somewhere, but it is quite the crush, is it not? Lord Pasque tells me we haven't had this many people at a palace party for at least forty years."

"Trust Lord Pasque to be in possession of such a fact. What's really impressive is that he's still breathing. How is the old boy?"

Kiren chuckled. "Old. Cranky. He still comes to the palace daily to wait upon Mama, and what can I say? She enjoys the attention. Although since she has taken a liking to Lady Teshalii, perhaps she no longer needs his dull attentions quite as much."

"Likes her, does she?"

"Yes, I really should find her for you." He craned his neck and looked around, somehow managing to still look dignified as he did so. "It must be some time since you last saw each other."

I realised then that I'd been hoping he knew the lie for what it was, that perhaps he was just testing my loyalty, but Kiren wasn't that good an actor.

"Prior to my arrival yesterday, it had been quite some time since I saw any members of my family," I said, choosing my words carefully just in case. "But I'm sure I will find her in the course of the evening, despite Lord Pasque's insistence the palace is at present more crowded than ever."

"No, not ever. Just the last forty years." A smile danced about Kiren's lips, reminding me that while he was often considered dull by those who didn't know him, there was a reason he was well loved all the same. "He mentioned something about a trial having been held here back then that brought the whole city. I can't recall learning anything about it, can you?"

"No, but then history books, I've discovered, are quite unreliable."

His expression took on an arrested look, brows slightly raised. "That's an interesting observation. Something particular that makes you say so? Wait, first let's walk." He took my arm as he spoke, leading me off through the crowd. "This way we're less likely to be interrupted."

The urge to claim it had been merely an off-handed comment flared, but however foolish my concerns might appear to him, he was the head archivist and I had to try.

"I don't know which tale of my misadventures is being told here," I said as we strolled slowly across the room. "But I was shot down by a man with a very fine firearm who, from his warning to me, appeared to live in and know about The Sands, and who apologised to my dragon for what was done to them. Tell me how this is possible when everyone says, and every book claims, that only monsters live in The Sands, and that no one has ever come back from an expedition to find out where said monsters come from."

It was more than I'd meant to say, but once I'd begun my story it had all come out, the scintillating party around us fading to a muted nothing. Through it all, Kiren kept us to a sedate walk, a vague smile plastered to his face for anyone who might look our way.

"I...admit I have heard both versions of your story," he said after a long pause. "The first hastily adjusted by the second, you might say. As I have also heard you were both recalled and deserted your post, and yet are to visit us tomorrow to petition Sormei for assistance because you are also an ambassador."

"I did not desert my post," I said, words low and vibrant. "I just asked questions no one wanted to answer. Are you going to treat me to the same assurances that no one lives in The Sands too? Or set your brother's guards on me perhaps."

He huffed a laugh. "It may surprise you to know I have neither the power to do so nor the inclination. As to your question, there is nothing in the archive about The Sands, which, yes"—he nodded when I scoffed—"likely doesn't surprise you, but there are... let us say *gaps* in some of the correspondence between reacher and citadel going back decades that feel...unnatural. One of those problems I've been picking at for some time now, though I'm told it's nothing. I was, in fact, hoping to ask you a few questions about it while you were here."

"You think someone is hiding reports, or orders?"

"Both."

"But why? What is there to hide, and who actually looks in the archive except—"

"Me." He halted, turning to face me as we reached the end of one grand room. "I look in the archive. I don't think it is safe to be seen talking any longer right now, but I wanted the chance to warn you before you see Sormei tomorrow. There is something going on, and I can't find out what it is, so tread carefully. He is not your friend."

It was all I could do to keep my expression neutral with so many people watching. "You don't trust him?"

Kiren shook his head yet smiled all the while. "No. I haven't trusted him since he sent Mitzy away." A fleeting grimace. And a squeeze of my arm as that name punched me in the gut. "He named his cat after her, did you know?" He gave a breathless little laugh. "And now you're the only one I've dared tell and I'm terrified that I did, so here we are. But you deserved to be warned. You could be on dangerous ground asking these questions around him."

"Thank you." He'd given me no answers, but the sense of solidarity was new and strange, and though I ought to have thanked him and moved away, I lingered a moment longer. "Do you...do you know if she's...all right? Or..."

"No, we have no communication with her at all, and I don't know where she is," he said, yet as the official statement left his lips, he quirked something of a wry, ironic smile and once again squeezed my arm. And I knew she was all right.

And of all the men in all Emora, this was the one my father would break to get what he wanted. The urge to tell Kiren about his insult bride was almost too strong, and if he hadn't held out his hands at that moment to part, the admission might well have spilled from my lips heedless of the consequences. But he did hold out his hands, and I kissed them and was walking away in search of air before I could even wonder whether silence or honesty was wisest.

I found a small courtyard before anyone else could accost me, a thankfully empty space all netting and twinkling golden lights. Leaning against one of the warm stone walls, I lit a korsh roll and drew deeply, tilting my head back to release smoke into the sky.

"Just pretend I'm not here."

I flinched, the voice all the more familiar because I'd just left its twin inside. Lord Reacher Sormei Sydelle sat in the shadows on a corner bench, a pair of his guards even shadowier figures behind him. Though the sight of him dropped my stomach through the floor, I conjured a smile.

"That's difficult to do when you're the reacher these days," I said, and feigned the kissing of hands. "Lord Reacher."

"You've still got it, huh?" he said with a wry laugh. "Even two years at the end of the world haven't blunted you."

"Three."

He raised a brow. "Three? Really? No wonder I'm starting to feel old." He waved a vague hand. "Do ignore me. Since you're coming to see me tomorrow morning and I'm not allowed to wriggle out of it."

"We could save time and talk now."

He laughed a harsh bark. "Oh no, that would be a waste of time. I already know everything you're going to tell me. I know about the explosions. I know about the callouts. I know about the man out in The Sands who shot you down. I know that bullet went right through the middle of a scale. I've even seen it."

After Kiren's warning, it wasn't surprise but a wariness bordering on fear that settled over me. I blew more smoke out into the dry night air. "Then you're going to do something about it all?"

"Oh, I'm always doing something. You should know that."

Sormei rose and strode over, all loose, easy strides and lazy, half-lidded eyes that made his beautiful face a threat. He held out his hand, and after breathing in another lungful, I handed over the korsh.

He dragged in a breath and slowly let it trickle out between his lips. "Run along, Ashadi. Everything is going perfectly well, and you wouldn't want to step in it now, would you?"

With Kiren's warning fresh in my mind, I swallowed every demand, every observation, every snarky retort, and just said, "I assume, since you know everything, you know I didn't desert my post. And that my watcher had nothing to do with it."

"Oh yes, I know, but I also know you're a determined arsehole who doesn't know when to stop. So take this as your final warning, Ashadi. Don't come to see me tomorrow and don't ask any more questions. Be grateful your father has forgiven you and get on with your life. If you don't, you won't be the only one who suffers, and surely you have enough blood on your hands after last time." He blew korsh smoke into my face and waved a dismissive hand. "Walk away."

Under the watchful eyes of his guards, there was nothing else to do, and so I spun on my heel and walked away. And once I'd started walking, I kept walking, out of the palace and back home, pleading exhaustion but carrying the feeling that I was standing on a precipice. I had starting asking questions to understand what had happened to me out in The Sands, and the more answers I failed to get the more important they felt, but if I didn't stop there would be no going back.

I arrived home to find Mana sitting in the corner of my room—a very different shadowy figure to the one I'd left in the garden. "I hope you haven't just been sitting there all—"

"Vimi," he said, without moving.

"Uh, Vimi?"

"Yes, you asked me to find out which commune you would have to visit to learn about dragons and the people in The Sands."

Walk away, Sormei had said, and walk away was what I ought to do. Yet I had only to contemplate such a course to know I could not. And so I stepped over the precipice, taking lives in my hands and trusting to the unknown on the other side. "How many days?"

"That depends on how we travel," Mana said, rising from the chair like for once I'd said the right thing. "It's overland, so anything from ten days or more on foot to somewhat less if we can ride."

Riding that far sounded hideous, but walking sounded worse. "Riding it is. How long will it take you to grab your bag?"

His brows rose. "A few minutes. Why?"

"Because we're leaving. Now."

16

Tesha

Morning Bulletin

To all criers for announcement throughout Upper Emora

*Onlookers say last night's party to welcome Lady
Teshalii Sydelle, new wife of Lord Kiren Sydelle, was
one of the finest gatherings ever held on the palace grounds,
with hundreds of guests also making it one of the
most crowded.*

*Upper market tragedy with two shops burned down overnight.
The fire broke out in the back of Mistress Kayra's famed
establishment, destroying hundreds of rolls of fabric and
numerous fine skirts.*

*Rejoice! No time wasted as Lord Peteus Euchard and Lady
Elbetta Souilsin announce betrothal ahead of the new season.*

349:15

I learned a lot from Mama Juri, and even more from the grand party thrown the following evening to celebrate my marriage and the unification of the Celes Basin. Every member of the Emoran upper class in the city had been present, at least so it seemed for how crowded the rooms had felt. I'd done my best to set still more names to still more faces, but it had been Reacher Sormei's movements throughout the evening I'd found most interesting. Or rather, his lack thereof.

While everyone else was using the opportunity of such a gathering to swirl about negotiating their status and discussing marriages, using everything from the look of their clothes to the time of their arrival to claim a place in the hierarchy, Sormei hardly moved. Having laid claim to a collection of heavily cushioned settees at the narrow end of what Mama Juri had called the conservatory, he had remained there most of the night. People came to him, he didn't go to them, and I couldn't decide if it made him look powerful or childish.

Two days in Emora had done nothing to ease the sense of being wholly out of place, but I was beginning to feel more comfortable in the grand rooms that were mine to call home. I was finally getting used to having a maid to wait on me too, and to caring about such things as my appearance and the maintenance of my slit brows. Waking up and donning the persona of Lady Teshalii was slowly getting easier, though the mere thought of home made my heart ache in a way that threatened to steal it all away.

"Do you have plans this morning, my lady?" Biiella asked as she searched my wardrobe for appropriate attire. "If you are staying in or going shopping—"

"A quiet morning, Biiella, but I'm to visit Lord Romm before lunch."

Though my heart thumped at the admission, she just nodded and set about finding skirts most suited to my plans. I'd hoped to avoid another meeting with Lord Romm for as long as possible, but he'd requested I visit to be formally introduced to Lord Ashadi, Uvao's older brother, a man both heir and outcast. The prospect held as much apprehension as curiosity, though I had the doubtful confidence that, no matter what he had done, he couldn't be as bad as Lord Romm himself.

Once Biiella had finished getting me ready for the day, she left me alone for the hour left until we had to depart. Likely she thought I would sit on the balcony and enjoy the morning sun or entertain myself with one of the many books provided on my shelves, not that I would immediately kneel beside one of the large square vases and slide a box from its dusty shadow. Its base slid out easily with a flick of increasingly practised fingers, sending a trio of pages fluttering loose with it. Two I caught, the other escaping to glide onto the floor as though it wasn't heavy with plans to poison Emora's reacher.

Having laid the three pages flat and turned over the box base, I sat and stared at them—these my only friends in this strange new life, my only advisors. Here I asked my questions like a supplicant at a sanctuary of the world song, seeking answers from a sea of words. Though there was only one question. Could I poison Reacher Sormei without anyone finding out it was me?

From one page, notes about his schedule and possible opportunities stared back. From another, ideas on how to swap in tainted glassware, from where I could steal glasses to copy or alter, and notes on which glasses seemed to be the same in every wing of the palace. The third page was the most important, containing my scribbles as I tried to understand which poisons would work, but it contained more questions than answers. The box base held a lot of information on each poison's persistence once in the glass, its comparative strength as a factor of time, and even the occasional note on unexpected side effects added in tiny handwriting, but it couldn't solve my biggest problem. That I had no forge and no hot glass.

Without being able to make the glasses myself and add the

poisons at the appropriate time in the cooling process, any substance labelled with a small *H* was out of the question. Those labelled *D* seemed to need an even more complicated process of being part of the glass from the beginning, leaving only those labelled *A* available for easy use. *A* was for *acid*, it seemed, for these substances could be added to already formed glass by softening some part of it with acid—a small, crusted dropper of which sat tucked into one corner of the box.

For the dozenth time, I ran my finger down the list of substances the box contained, looking for the *A*s. Ettrikot—euphoric. Doma—laxative. Ulgele—emetic. Po—desire. Tammittotra—sleep. And that was it. I kept hoping something more deadly would appear with an *A* beside its name, but hope had yet to manifest anything more useful than giving the reacher an upset stomach. Had Master Hoye been present, I could have asked him whether the poisons would still work on their own, or when pressed into the glass cold, but in Master Hoye's absence I could only doubt. I could try, and hope for the best, but half murdering the man would be the worst of all outcomes.

I added a few notes to the page about Sormei's schedule, more to feel like I was making progress than because the added details were useful, then stared at all the information as it failed, yet again, to provide me with a workable idea. And as time ticked on, drawing my meeting with Lord Romm closer, I got up to check the two glasses I'd left to set on a high shelf in my dressing room. Using a scarf so as not to get fingerprints all over them, I took one down and gingerly prodded the spot in the base where I'd dripped in acid the day before. The glass had set, though felt softer than it ought. Perhaps that was just how it worked. There was no time to change it now, only to wish, once again, for Master Hoye and slide the glasses back into their box.

Once the papers were safely stowed and the poison box hidden, I rang for Biiella, and set off on my morning call with what I was coming to think of as my entourage. Wherever I went, whether to walk around the markets or pay a social call, Biiella always came with me. Having one's maid alongside was quite normal for Emoran women, I'd discovered, though no other women also had to suffer the endless scrutiny and company of Reacher Sormei's personal guards. From the moment I left the palace grounds, two fully attired in glass-scaled armour followed a step behind me everywhere I went. For my safety, the Sydelles had said, that they could keep an eye on me only an incidental bonus.

The two guards remained outside when I arrived at the Romm family manor—a grand building much like their manor in Learshapa, yet distinct in ways I was beginning to recognise were particular to this city. Here, external walls made each manor into a closed-in compound, and where most buildings had corners in Learshapa, so much of Emoran architecture was sinuous, flowing, alive. And there were dragons everywhere. Dragon statues, dragons made of glass, dragons painted on frescos, dragons battling in large mosaics—the dragon seemed to be the most important symbol of Emoran life, though the citadel that housed the beasts was far away.

Having been let in through the outer wall, a servant welcomed me into a grand entry hall, before taking my veil and gesturing where to leave my shoes. "His lordship is in his retreat, if you would follow me, my lady. Your maid may wait in the hall."

This seemed quite ordinary to Biiella, who handed me the gift box she had been carrying and left me to face Lord Romm and his threats alone. My heart thudded hard against my breastbone as I followed the servant through a pair of large doors at the far side of the entryway and out into a long passage. It ran alongside an atrium full of greenery, so much like the manors of Learshapa that my heart ached.

The servant didn't once turn to be sure I followed, just walked on with the plodding step of someone who had made this journey many, many times before. When at last he turned through an arch, it was into a well-lit room filled with refractive crystals, each one spilling rainbows of light across the floor and over a wall of shelves filled with artifacts. More Apaian artifacts, just like Lord Romm's collection in Learshapa only bigger, though thankfully lacking another skull.

"Ah, you have noticed my collection."

I jumped and spun, not having heard the servant announce me nor noticed Lord Romm sitting cross-legged on a long cushioned bench beneath one of the windows. Coloured light danced across him as it danced across everything, though it did nothing to lighten his hard stare, at odds with the curl of a false smile upon his lips.

"Y-yes, my apologies, my lord," I stammered. "I was just so immediately struck. It is even more grand than your collection back in Learshapa."

"Yes, I thought you were interested in that. It's important to maintain a connection to history, you see." He nodded at the box gripped in my hands. "You have brought something for me?"

"Oh yes, I have brought you a gift." I passed it over with a curtsy. "A small token of gratitude to the head of my family. For everything you have done for me."

His lips twitched into a lifeless smile. "And so the tool thanks her maker," he murmured, opening the box with a flick of his thumb. Dipping one hand into the nest of soft fabric, he withdrew one of the wineglasses and held it up to the light. "Quite a nice piece of work. It has a reflective quality to the shape that not all glasses have."

Rather than thank me, he grunted a sort of acceptance as he pulled out the matching glass, and called to the servant still waiting by the archway. "Bring wine."

"Yes, my lord."

The man walked out, leaving us alone. As though he'd been feigning some friendliness for the servant, Lord Romm's expression immediately soured. "It turns out I have invited you here for no purpose this morning," he said, each word bitten out. "And I am left to make Ashadi's excuses. He has disappeared without a word. Likely on some important mission for the citadel we mere mortals are not to know about. Ashadi is...unpredictable, I'm afraid. It is part of his charm, I'm told. Once he makes decisions it is very difficult to shift him from them."

Unsure whether speaking well of his heir or poorly would be most likely to gain Lord Romm's approval, I settled for "I am disappointed not to have the opportunity to meet—to renew my acquaintance with him."

Lord Romm's lips smiled without the rest of his face. "You may speak freely here, girl. The only people listening here are my people. I note you have Sormei's glass tigers following you around— take care there; they are both spies and guards, but rumour has it they also possess many other skills and play many other roles. Not the most popular part of his reachership, the reinstating of personal guards for the reacher's family, though it seems the idea has caught on. I've already noted some half a dozen families who have some form of personal guard with them this season."

He harrumphed at this, and for a brief moment he was just a grumpy old man—a grumpy old man who realised with a sniff that he'd said more than he meant to the upstart sitting across from him.

Thankfully the servant returned then with a refreshment tray. Noting the wine glasses already on the table, the man left behind the ones he had brought, instead pouring what looked like a light morning wine into the glass closest to Lord Romm. When he turned to me, I sat a hand over my own glass. "Just water at this hour, if you please."

Lord Romm snorted. "That's a habit you'll soon lose spending time here, my dear. Wine is the only way to make it through a day. You see, being a nobleman means having too much time in which to get bored, a problem much compounded for our wives and daughters who have nothing to do at all. Except drink."

At that he lifted his glass in something of a salute and drank deeply. While the servant poured water for me, I watched the liquid slide into Lord Romm's mouth, unsure it had sat long enough in the glass to have an effect. It had taken a full day to prepare, to check and recheck the dosage before adding it to the soft spot at the bottom of both glasses, and now these few moments would prove whether it had all been worth it.

I dragged my gaze from his glass lest I give myself away, and stared at the artifacts instead. I'd left occasionally helping the reclamation movement behind in Learshapa, though if I could find a contact in Emora, perhaps I could do more than just loosen Emoran power while I had such free access to their homes.

"There's a piece missing at the moment," Lord Romm said, recalling me from my thoughts with a jolt. "From the collection. A string of charms. Very fine. Thought to have been carried by an Apaian leader into battle for good luck. The house is being searched as we speak, but I don't think it will suddenly turn up. More likely that damn reclamation movement or whatever they call themselves have gotten a thief into my staff. If I were reacher, I wouldn't let them run free through our cities making a nuisance of themselves like Sormei does."

The flicker of an ugly scowl looked out of place in the light-filled space, all slowly shifting colours in the gentle breeze. He sat back and drank the last of his wine, pouring it down his throat in a way that seemed to emphasize his lingering, festering anger. "The day I can oust him from his precious reachership will be a good day for us all," he added, gesturing at me with the empty glass before setting it on the table.

He reached for the wine decanter and poured himself another glass—much fuller than the one his servant had poured. I watched the liquid swirl in, wondering how new wine would affect the softened glass in the bottom. For the hundredth time, I wished Master Hoye had been present to ask, since in his absence I could only try and fail. And hope that with only water in my own glass, I would not soon feel unwell.

"In the absence of Ashadi, there is little for us to say to one another," he said, sipping from the fresh liquid. "Sormei's gaining popularity in Learshapa faster than I thought possible with these border skirmishes, so we may have to bring everything forward. I'd expose you to trigger a renegotiation and conclave now if I had everything in place, but I don't, so keep your head down a bit longer. You have consummated?"

He asked as though it was nothing, an off-handed comment as he ran through the steps he needed to take, but when I didn't immediately answer, his gaze came to rest on me heavy and dark. "Have you?"

"No, my lord, we have not." The shame at having to admit so to this of all men heated my cheeks to a searing glow. "Lord Kiren seems... entirely uninterested."

"Then make him interested! It's your one song-be-damned job, and if you can't get it done then all of this is for nothing. I told you back in Learshapa you'd regret failing me, and I meant it." More wine was poured down his throat. He seemed untroubled by the taste, and the only change so far was the slight sparkling of sweat at his hairline. "I will not have my plan thwarted because you couldn't get Kiren Sydelle hard."

I flinched, hating his harsh snap and his scowl, his demands and his threats. I'd never met anyone I disliked more, and for a wild moment I hoped the ulgele I'd put in the wineglasses would somehow kill him. Poisoning him instead of Sormei would have had the same effect, saving me from exposure that could end in Learshapa's ruin, but there was no saying what Lord Ashadi would do as head of the family in his place. Without a chance to meet him, it was too risky.

"If you're going to drag this out," he went on, swallowing the rest of his wine, "you had better start bringing me good information I can work with. Find out who Sormei is meeting with and what he's planning so I can get ahead of him, especially as regards the fighting at Therinfrou Mine. You need to find a way to disrupt his popularity there, to make him look like he's doing a bad job, because the more he helps the harder he will be to oust, and I refuse to lose to him in another conclave because the people around me couldn't do their fucking jobs."

His rant ended with a cough and he hit the flat of his hand against his chest as though to clear something offensive. It didn't work and he coughed again. More sweat sparkled on his brow, and he rang the bell at his side, summoning his servant.

"My lord?"

"Pour water." His voice was a little strained, but he waited while his servant poured water into one of the original, untainted glasses.

Lord Romm gulped the water down, and I knew immediately he ought to have been more careful. Nausea demands sips over gulps, and Lord Romm's face paled. "See Lady Teshalii out," he said, growing almost green. "I'm feeling a little unwell."

"The doctor did warn you to take care with wine at an early hour, my lord," the servant said, clearly a man who had been with the family long enough to dare opinions.

"Yes, yes." Lord Romm waved this information away, and gestured almost frantically at me. "Just show the girl out, Torl. And you just do your damned job," he added to me, lips tight. "I want better news next time we talk."

That he was daring speech and clinging to his dignity was, I had to admit, impressive. Rising from my chair, I thanked him for the hospitality and said all that was proper, before letting Torl usher me from the room. I didn't hurry. There was all too much joy in lingering a little longer to make him suffer.

Although the ulgele didn't seem to have dissolved into my water, my stomach churned all the way back to the palace. I might have been able to swallow Lord Romm's hateful words, but his complaints about Reacher Sormei's popularity being built on helping Learshapa gnawed at me. Helping Learshapa was all I'd set out to do, and I couldn't but wonder if I was as wrong about Sormei as I had been about the unification vote.

I carried my worries back to our wing of the palace, only to walk into the most delightful collection of smells. It was all charred meat and sticky sweetness, possessing even something of the dust of Learshapa's streets.

"What is that?" I breathed, looking around the main living space.

"Tesha?" Kiren appeared from the dining room, a smile playing about his lips and his eyes bright. "Ah, you're back just in time. Come, have lunch with me."

A little thrill trickled down my spine at finding him so happy to see me, a feeling that grew immensely upon stepping into the dining room. There I found the most impressive spread of Learshapan food I'd ever seen, everything from street skewers to date cakes, dried and salted slivers of fish to spicy mango on shredded greens, and my mouth watered.

"What is this?" I said, looking about to find still more hidden treats. Even spiced orange brandy and wafer-thin cinnamon crisps dusted with sugar and vanilla bean.

"I know you've been feeling homesick," Kiren said, glancing rather shyly at me as he gestured at the table. "So I asked the kitchens to cook a spread of eastern cuisine. I understand the fish is more of a city dish than a reaches one, but I'm sure you've spent enough time in Learshapa to know it well. On the other hand I'm told this wobbly thing is a dish particular to the northern reaches, and I hope the cooks were right about that because otherwise this speech is a little embarrassing."

"I cannot say I have travelled enough to know the precise regionality of our food, so all I can say is it looks delicious. Thank you."

"You are most welcome." He beamed, an expression I could not imagine ever seeing on his twin's face. "It's nice to have a change from the usual fare too, so if the cooks have done it justice, we could add more Learshapan dishes to our everyday spread."

Such words did more than waking up in a palace to remind me I was no longer just Tesha. I was Lord Kiren's wife now, and together we settled at our very long dining table loaded with far more food than the two of us could ever manage to eat. It was an unnecessary waste, yet in that moment, breathing in the scents of home, I didn't care.

"Did you enjoy your visit to Lord Romm?" he asked, poking the wobbly thing as though deciding if he wanted to try it.

"It was very pleasant, yes," I said, unable to trust him with even the vaguest sense of why I'd gone. "Although when I left, he didn't seem to be feeling very well."

"That's concerning. Not an illness in the house, do you think? Ashadi didn't show up for his meeting with Sormei this morning. Was Ashadi there?" he added, having decided against the wobbly thing in favour of a skewer. "I hope he's not unwell too."

I shook my head, choosing a date cake from the platter. "I'm afraid I don't know. Lord Romm said Ashadi wasn't at home, but wasn't sure where he'd gone. Something to do with his duties to the citadel, he thought."

"Duties to the citadel? That was exactly what he was coming to see Sormei about."

While Kiren frowned, I bit a corner of sticky date cake and closed my eyes, easily able to imagine I was sitting back in my favourite public house being serenaded by the trickle of water and a symphony of swear words.

Kiren brought me back with a sigh. "I hope it turns out things aren't as bad at the Shield as we fear, but I said the same about the situation with the border mines, and look how that turned out. Sormei is far better at predicting what is going to break next. Truly an excellent trait in a reacher, though I doubt people know just how much work he puts in."

"A lot more than past reachers?" I asked, thinking of Lord Romm's complaints of Sormei's rising popularity in Learshapa.

"Oh, far more. Even the archival record shows that reachers well before our time wrote far fewer letters, held fewer meetings, and gave fewer instructions. Either that or they were all terrible at maintaining their personal archives to the proper standard while in office. The majority of Lord Reacher Olbor Eurche's archive from some hundred and twenty years ago is gossip sheets interspersed with letters demanding new ships. I can't be sure, but he seemed to have a habit of crashing them."

Listening to Kiren talk about his twin made Sormei sound like the god he appeared, as perfect as the face they both carried but only Sormei truly owned. Where Kiren glowed like a candle, Sormei blazed like the noontime sun.

"Any other news while you were out?" Kiren asked when I didn't answer. "Has Lord Romm got his full household in residence yet?"

"Oh, I couldn't say I noticed," I replied, unsure what he even meant. "But Uvao isn't with him yet."

I'd hoped I could say his name without my heart fluttering in my throat, but I was wrong. Thankfully, Lord Kiren didn't seem to notice. "Oh, that doesn't surprise me. They've never gotten along, and likely Uvao will stay in Learshapa as long as his father will let him, as he has every other season. Ashadi was always the golden child. Oh, but what am I saying, you know all this, of course. I forget who I'm talking to in a childish desire to gossip."

"Perhaps because of who I am, I don't hear the same things you do. No one says a word against Lord Romm to me."

It sounded true, and though he had been trying to glean gossip from me, it was gossip I wanted from him. I had spent every free moment of the last two days trying to figure out how to poison Sormei, with the answer increasingly clear that without access to a glass forge I could not. But there was a way to ensure Learshapa remained protected that didn't require poison—telling Sormei everything. It would destroy Lord Romm, but perhaps that wasn't such a bad thing.

"Oh, there's nothing bad to say about Lord Romm!" Kiren said, all easy cheer. "We just like to gossip because what else is there to do?"

It was a diplomatic answer, and for a moment I considered reaching across the table and gripping his arm to share a desperate moment of honesty, but fear held me still and silent, and the moment passed, leaving me carrying my burdens alone. And so I swallowed his lie along with a sliver of dried fish and forced out a smile. "Of course."

Silence reigned for a time, until Kiren rose from the table with a sigh. "I have to get to a meeting, I'm afraid, but you linger over the cakes as long as you like. I'll be back for family dinner later of course."

"Of course," I said again, and though the words were dead on my lips, I thanked him again for the lunch.

"You're most welcome, Tesha," he said, stopping beside my chair to kiss my cheek. Not a quick, obligatory peck, but a lingering press of his lips that held some affection had I wished to read it so. But while I ought to have been pleased, have seen it as a step toward the consummation our marriage needed and Lord Romm demanded, all that remained in his absence was worry.

With no one to talk to and no one I could trust, I took that worry back to my rooms and paced. Up and down, back and forth through the bolts of sunshine, hearing birds chirp on my balcony but not really listening to anything but the dull thud of my heart. I had to make a choice. I could stretch it out, knowing

Lord Romm couldn't expose me until I had consummated with Kiren, but that might get me only a few weeks if I was lucky, and they were dangerous weeks in which our marriage could collapse without the proper legality. Poisoning Lord Romm was a risk, not only because his heir was an unknown quantity but because suspicion could blow back on Uvao. Poisoning Reacher Sormei would be harder, but with so many people sure to profit from his death it would be impossible to pin on anyone, and it would lead to a more predictable outcome—a conclave and new reacher. Yet it would leave Learshapa—leave the whole of the Celes Basin—in Lord Romm's hands, and that, I feared, was the very worst thing I could do. The only other option was telling Reacher Sormei the truth, exchanging my own safety and the safety of the basin for political leverage against Lord Romm. It sounded sensible, yet I had only to think of Sormei's intent stare and his cat-like smile, his ambition and his armed guards, to lose all confidence. The Sormei that Kiren knew was not the same Sormei to whom I would have to spill my secrets. Not for the first time, I wished there was someone I could ask for advice, wished Master Hoye had come with me or even Sorscha, someone who would tell me not what I wanted to hear but the truth I needed to know.

When my thoughts became too tangled for pacing in front of my windows, I took them to the gardens. Fresh air did not help, and striding around amid the greenery achieved only sore muscles and the endless crawl of time toward a point where I would have to make a decision. Even lying on the grass and staring up at the sky brought no insight beyond a growing wish I'd never come to Emora at all. I told myself that such a thought was unworthy of me, yet I thought it all the same.

By the time I had to dress for dinner, my world had shrunk to nothing but the cycling of my own thoughts. Without perspective, I had only panic, without advice, only gut reactions, and no amount of time would bring me either—I could only keep running and hope I chose the right path.

In preparation for dinner, I washed and changed and let Biiella redo my hair, something relaxing about falling back into the rhythm of this strange Emoran life. Teshalii was becoming like a piece of my wardrobe I could don and remove with greater and greater ease, a game of pretend I could never stop playing.

Kiren was waiting for me, thoughts seemingly as far away as mine as he offered me his arm with only a brief smile. We made the journey from our private wing of the palace to Mama Juri's in silence, under the eye of servants and guards alike. It was my first family dinner, as Kiren called it—Mama Juri's insistence that on the first day of every week the Sydelles ate together—and as we arrived in the matriarch's sitting room, I was forcefully reminded that I was an intruder here. Not only an impostor forcing my way into the Emoran palace, but into a family.

Mama Juri sat on one of the long couches, while her daughters, Desa and Luave, sat on the floor at her feet. They had a spread of coloured cards and seemed to be playing a game I didn't recognise, along with Reacher Sormei. Except here he wasn't reacher, he was just a big brother laughing with his sisters, under a mother's fond gaze. Learshapans didn't live in families, yet at the sight, the strength of their bond nagged at my heart all the same.

"Ah, Kiren, love," Mama Juri said, rising to greet her son. "So glad you're here. And you, my dear, welcome," she added to me, embracing me with a soft, rose-scented hug rather than a formal kiss of the hands. "I meant to ask you to join me for afternoon tea, but I admit I had a nap instead. It's this weather! I'm always so unsettled after a brightstorm. A difficulty poor Sormei shares, of course, having taken all too much after me, poor dear."

The Emoran reacher showed no sign of embarrassment at this pronouncement, but shared a glance with his twin, full of the same fondness she possessed when looking at them. "Taking after you is a boon and you know it, Mama," Sormei said, rising to his feet with loose, easy grace. "If we are unsettled by brightstorms it is merely because brightstorms are, one must admit, very unsettling things."

One of the young girls, Desa, I thought, hoping I'd remembered which was which, jumped up to whisper something in her mother's ear.

"Come now, Des, you know it's not seemly to whisper in company," her mother chided. "But yes, I'm quite sure that if you ask nicely, Teshalii will indeed sit and play a round of Dace. Though you might be asking too much for her to have dear Sormei's skill."

"No one is as good as Meimei," Luave said as both girls turned their beseeching gazes my way. "But would you play with us, Lady Teshalii?"

"Oh, you don't...you don't need to call me that," I said. "I mean, I would really rather if you didn't, since we're...family now."

"Well said," Sormei said, and when I met his gaze, it was full of lazy mockery that reddened my cheeks. "We are all family here."

Giving in to the insistence of a pair of hands tugging me toward the floor, I knelt beside Desa as she gathered the cards in preparation for another game. "It has been such a long time since I played," I said, breathless with sudden dread. "I'm not sure I remember all the rules."

"You'll soon be an expert again with these two around," Reacher Sormei said, and though he'd moved away to a seat near his mother, he abandoned it, adding, "Here, we can play a hand together and see if that helps jog your memory."

"Oh no, that's all right, I don't—"

His arm brushed mine as he sat down, the warmth of skin against skin more shock than it ought to have been. Touch had been so common in my old life, but here it was all formality, all Kiren holding out his arm and Biiella fixing my hair, nothing hot and vital and real. Accident though it was, I became suddenly aware of Sormei's presence at my side like it had weight, like he depressed the floor at my side to draw me in.

"I don't...?" he prompted my unfinished sentence, his shoulder bumping mine as he settled into a comfortable position.

"Oh. Um, you don't need to trouble yourself."

"Not at all. There is likely still at least ten minutes until dinner, and if I teach you to play well, perhaps these two brats won't ask me to play quite as often!"

One of the girls threw a cushion at him, and as air whooshed past me she laughed, saying, "You have to play extra now because of that!"

"Ah, but maybe that's exactly the outcome I was hoping for," he retorted, throwing the cushion back and tapping the side of his head. "I'm clever like that, you know."

He winked at me as he spoke, and for a moment everything about him was warm and approachable, his manner with his family utterly unlike the Sormei of legend. And because thinking hadn't gotten me anywhere, I ran with instinct. "Sormei," I said, a thrill tingling through me at being able to call the most powerful man in Emora by his first name. "If you have a moment after dinner, might I speak to you about something?"

Before I could doubt the wisdom of such words, they were out of my lips and unable to be recalled, prompting only a slight lifting of Sormei's brows. "If you wish, dear sister. I am, of course, at your disposal. We could speak now, if it suits you."

"Oh." My heart thrummed fit to make me sick, and though I wanted the declaration done and over as soon as possible, I also wanted to run and run and never look back. The desire not to embarrass myself trying to play a card game I'd never seen before won out. "Yes. That would be good. If you don't mind."

"I don't mind at all. Sorry, brats, you'll have to make Kiren play this time."

As he got to his feet, every eye in the room seemed to be upon us. Our exit from the game caused groans from the two girls, which in turn earned remonstrations from their mother, and though Kiren took our place, it was with a lingering look my way, full of questions I could not answer. Stupid to have said anything here, to have made this familial space into my confession, but it was too late to escape as Sormei stalked to the far side of the room and offered me one of the chairs by the window. And so I found myself sitting in beautiful sunshine, facing the man whose ambition had upended Learshapa.

"Well, my dear, what is it you wished to speak to me about?" he said, something of his lazy threat returning upon half-lidded eyes and an amused smile. Sudden fear froze my lips. What madness had made me think that this man, of all Emorans, was the one I could most trust?

When I didn't answer, Sormei sighed, and nothing had ever sounded as deeply disappointed as that sound. "And here I was hoping you were about to surprise me with your bravery and tell me the truth. I ought, perhaps, to have brought our little game to an end sooner, but I admit I wanted to enjoy some more cat and mouse."

I could not speak, could only sit and stare, a scream trapped in my lungs. His smile broadened. Just like the cat his words claimed him to be. "You ought to take more care over your facial expression, my dear, unless you want your far-too-kind husband to ask what I said to trouble you."

As though summoned by the warning, Kiren glanced up from the card game, and for a moment I held his questioning gaze. Before his sisters recalled it to the action, leaving me to stand alone. I swallowed hard, at last finding my voice. "You know?"

"Yes," Sormei said, a sneer flitting across his features. "But let us be very clear about what it is that I know. I know you were not a member of the Romm family. I know that you are an insult bride. I've known since the moment we first met, and yes, I let the marriage go ahead because your existence suits my purpose, and so here we are. *Mouse.*"

The name was the twist of a blade, chilling my blood all the more for how fondly Lord Revennai had called me *cat*. Surely he couldn't know about that too, yet looking into his beautiful, cruel face, I knew in my sinking gut that he was capable of anything.

Across the room, the two young girls laughed at Kiren's card choice, and Mama Juri watched on fondly—the whole a world away from the icy cage constricting around me.

"Don't worry," Sormei said, the words almost a croon. "I don't intend to tell them. It will be our little secret, you and I. You and I against those who seek to keep the basin divided when we need to be strong. The Lummazzt came for Emora once, and we weren't ready. We were almost entirely destroyed. Now it's happening again, and I am the only one prepared to fight them. So no, there will be no secondary negotiations, no conclave, no new reacher. I assume you agree, or you wouldn't have brought me Lord Romm's head. That was your plan, wasn't it? To trade your safety for that of your charming benefactor? Almost I feel sorry for you that I already knew."

Nothing about his expression looked sorry. Eyes bright, lips formed into a cruel curve, he was enjoying himself all too much. And a flare of anger melted the fear that kept me frozen.

"I believed you more likely to fight for the basin, yes," I hissed. "But any idea I might have had that Lord Romm was a fouler human than you has proven incorrect."

A flicker of genuine humour softened his sneer. "I thought you had fire in you. Too hot for Kiren to handle, that's for sure, but then that's why he needs me."

"What do you want? Why not just out me before the marriage went ahead?"

"Because then they would have found another way to attack me. This way, Lord Romm is tied up believing he's got me, and in the meantime you work for me. You tell me all Lord Romm's plans—including the mess Ashadi is making. And you find out what Kiren is up to."

Questions multiplied on my tongue, but at his last words I could only say, "Kiren?"

Across the room, sitting on the floor with his sisters, my husband appeared to be good-naturedly losing. Luave prodded his shoulder, gloating, before turning to us. "Meimei! We beat him!"

"Well done, brats," Sormei called back. "If only we could all be so skilled."

Desa and Luave giggled, applying to their mother for further praise, but Sormei's words seemed to suck the last of the air out of the room. From his place on the floor, Kiren stared at us unsmiling, and Sormei stared right back.

"Yes, Kiren," he said, finally answering my question while staring right at his twin. "He is a lot more than the sweet face he shows you, but he's also very good at hiding his tracks. He has been very busy in those archives of his, looking into my past orders, and I want to know why. He has a secret correspondence with someone in Bakii and I want to know who. So when he asks you why you wanted to speak to me, tell him you'd had some troubling news from Learshapa—that attacks on people there were becoming like those in Bakii—and see what he says. And don't bother refusing," he added, smiling not at me but across the room at his twin. "You hold nothing over me and nor does Lord Romm, because until your marriage is consummated, it's just words."

I flinched, but I could not let my expression give me away, not with Kiren watching us.

Sormei seemed to lack such worries, his grin broadening. "Oh, don't bother denying it. I know my brother better than anyone else ever will, and if there's one thing most people fail to understand about him it's that he has no physical interest in anyone he doesn't love. Of course, he would attempt to overcome that should he have reason to try, but that would require admitting all of this and begging his forgiveness. And hoping, somehow, that despite such a pitiful tale of betrayal, he could still get hard."

"You. Are foul," I said with a forced smile.

"No, I am honest. A rarity around here, you'll find. Now we had better part before Kiren burns a hole through us with his stare."

Before I could answer, he got gracefully to his feet and held down a hand to me. "Well, Lady Teshalii? I hope you agree to my terms."

17

Ashadi

We left Emora in the cool of the early morning, alongside a handful of other travellers—a merchant with a train of mules, another with a cart, a pair of young men who kept to themselves, and an old woman with the bored look of one who had ridden the basin far too many times to care what might lie ahead. At first the heat had been bearable, but by noon we were caught between the competing forces of searing sun and baking rock. And the wind, intent on buffeting us off the track. Only the desert mules seemed not to mind, plodding on at a constant, loping pace, each long leg like bony string. Their city-based cousins were stockier, made for short distances and steep hills, but out here fat and muscle weren't needed, just water.

Thankfully there was plenty at the first campsite, its deep pool having been topped up by the recent brightstorm. There were stone huts too, for those of us who hadn't brought our own tents. It was the most uncomfortable sleep I'd ever had.

The second night was little better. Sitting on the loping desert mule all day was taking its toll, the ache in my backside continuing to throb even once we'd dismounted. Fewer travellers shared our camp this time, yet I still felt eyes on me wherever I went. Despite Mana's best efforts to disguise me, it seemed I still carried too much Emoran lord with me to easily hide.

"Hopefully no one actually recognises me," I said as we sat gnawing on the jerky and dense bread Mana insisted made the best travel fare. It was certainly made to last, which also made it impossible to eat.

"It's the way you carry yourself, I think." Mana tore off a chunk of bread with his teeth and sat chewing rather than elaborate. Overhead the last of the light was draining away, leaving behind a blanket of stars.

"How I carry myself?" I prompted.

"You stand upright."

"As opposed to what? Crawling around?"

"No, as opposed to standing like normal people."

I glanced around at the others sharing our campsite. Most were sitting, but one recent arrival was still untying saddlebags from his mule. "Normal people like that man?"

"Sure."

"I'm not seeing your point."

"Perhaps it's your hair then."

"My hair?"

"Mmm," he said, once again chewing a mouthful of bread.

If one could call it bread. I would rather have called it vaguely bread-flavoured stone. Swallowing hard, he added, "It's clean. You can tell because it does the fluffy, floofy, waving-in-the-wind thing whenever you take your hat off."

"So does yours."

"Only because I had a bath the other night."

The words were quiet, seemingly innocuous yet reverberating meaning. The other night when we'd bathed together. When we'd pressed against one another, breathless with need, and for a foolish moment I'd dared to think we might have something more than we ever could.

It was my turn to swallow hard and try to turn my thoughts. "Well, but they're not staring at you."

"Because I stand like a normal person."

Unable to shake the feeling I was being punished, I thrust the remains of my meal—for a given value of the word *meal*—back into our supply bag and withdrew a white scaleglass flask. Water flasks weren't uncommon, but unlike the thick, heavy ones most travellers carried, mine had glass so thin it weighed little more than the liquid it held. I just had to hope no one could tell from a distance.

"You'd better not drink the day we expect to reach the commune," Mana said, eyeing the flask as he rolled himself some korsh to wash down the meal.

"Why? Is alcohol not allowed?"

"Not...culturally, but most communes have banned it."

"Is that why you don't drink?"

"Partly. Why let merchants sell you misery when they'll just use your money to create more misery?"

"It's not all misery, drinking, I mean."

Mana shrugged, and exhaled a cloud of smoke from the korsh roll pinched between long fingers. "You always look miserable when you drink. Besides, it tastes like piss."

"Never having tasted piss, I will have to bow to your better judgement."

The look he threw me spoke volumes—volumes I would rather have thrown in the fire than read—and I got to my feet. "I'm going to walk about a bit, see if I can loosen my legs."

Awaiting no answer, I brushed dust from my simple skirt and started off in no particular direction, needing space to breathe away from people's interested stares. And away from Mana. Two weeks ago, I'd been sure I understood him and understood...us. Because there hadn't been an us, could never be an us, my all-too-frequent yearning stemming only from gratitude over his gentleness and care. Now it felt complicated. As complicated as the tangle of lies into which I'd fallen when that sharpshooter had shot Shuala out of the sky. What ought to have been simple questions had led me farther and farther from the citadel, leaving my world to collapse piece by piece in my wake. Sormei knew a truth he wanted to hide, and I would find it.

Mana leaned forward on his mule, dropping his face into his free hand with a stifled laugh. "That's not how you greet an elder. That kissing the hands thing is something only Emorans do. Or people who work for Emorans. Or want to be liked by Emorans."

"Ah, that must have been what my tutors meant when they said Apaians would do anything to get away with not showing proper respect."

"Most likely," came his grim reply as he straightened, having to unstick his veil from his sweaty brow. "Although in your case, whenever I am appropriately respectful you tell me off for calling you *my lord*."

"Of course I do. Because I don't think I'm better than you, what-ever the citadel masters say about it. Now," I added, determined to escape any deeper conversation. "Before all this talking dries out my throat, tell me how I *should* greet an Apaian elder."

For a moment it seemed like Mana would say something else, but shook his head like a man clearing unwelcome thoughts. "You approach them, respectfully, and place your offering on the ground—still some feet away—then you step back, respectfully, and bow your head. You then don't move—"

"Respectfully," I interjected, earning a glare.

"You don't move until they've examined the offering and decided if you are worthy to meet with them and make a request."

"So even with a gift—"

"Offering," he corrected.

"Even with an offering, they could still refuse to speak to me."

"Yes."

"Seems a bit rude."

"As is the assumption that everyone is always ready and willing to talk to you. Politeness, as you see it, is almost completely devoid of consent."

I looked sidelong at him, his features made hazy by the thick veil upon which a few flies were hitching a ride. "You have a lot of thoughts about this, don't you?"

"I suppose so. You could call it one of the risks of growing up on the outskirts of a city, with all the other people who had been cast out. Not me," he added in response to my sudden stare. "My mother."

"Your mother was an outcast? Why?"

He huffed a humourless laugh. "Because she thought about these things too much. And because she made healing poultices and suchlike. People called her a witch."

"Of course they did. Is that why you're such a good watcher?"

"Because my mother was a witch?"

"No, because you learned a thing or two from her about taking care of people."

"Oh, I suppose so. I'm...I'm glad you think I was good at my job."

"And I'm glad you were good at your job, you know, since that involved looking after me and all."

Another of his humourless little laughs and we slipped into an awkward silence, made all the more uncomfortable by a whip of dirt as the wind changed direction. It was impossible to know what was going through his mind, but mine had leapt right back to that evening in the bath and how he had asked if I felt better now, like it had been nothing but a service rendered. I had asked myself whether it mattered how or why I got what I wanted so long as I got what I wanted—got him—but unfortunately it mattered all too much. At the citadel, he'd had to obey my every order, and while we weren't at the citadel anymore, such habits ran deep.

Mana cleared his throat, and the weight of his gaze fell upon my cheek. "I guess the thing about growing up around outcasts is that they're outcasts for a reason. They don't look at the world the same way most people do. *I* don't look at the world the same way most people do."

"Given how terrible the world is, that's probably for the best," I said with forced lightness, not meeting his gaze. "Right, so, these elders. I give my offering, then bow my head until they answer, and if they refuse?"

"Then we leave."

"And if they accept?"

"Then you're invited into their home and have to behave accordingly."

"Respectfully, you mean."

A flash of humour escaped upon a laugh. "Respectfully. Yes."

That night we stopped at our first campsite attached to a noble estate, its distant presence making me feel all the more exposed. Mana had said I looked Emoran by how I stood, so I tried hunching my shoulders to see if that would help—a task made easier by the exhaustion beginning to weigh on my bones. There were many travellers making use of the campsite, but there was less water, and the collection funnel looked like it hadn't been cleaned for some time. Despite having no owners as such, the other sites had been well looked after by those passing through, and I had to wonder if this one had been ignored because it ought to have been the responsibility of its Emoran owner—Lord Vief, if my geography hadn't failed me.

"Another day, I think, and we'll be close," Mana said, untying a bag from his dull-eyed mule. "Although we may have to sleep two nights to be safe."

"We couldn't push on and sleep at the commune?"

"Without having been invited to talk, let alone stay? Not a wise start if you want to talk to the elders."

I grimaced, but held back the disparaging comment about poor hospitality that leapt to my tongue. Likely Mana would tell me a better word for it was *presumption*.

The strangeness of setting up camp outside Lord Vief's estate grew as the sun sank. I'd never thought much about the campsite on the edge of the Romm estate. We always passed it in our shuttered carts whenever we travelled, never troubling to look out at who else might be travelling in less comfort. It would be better tended than this one, I was sure, if only because so much of our wealth had come from building the trade trail to the eastern sea, which passed by our estate.

Our. It had always been a painful word to hold, so completely did we lack any true sense of family, but it was even harder to let the word go.

"Are you all right?"

I turned to find Mana unpacking more of the same non-perishable and hardly edible food, a slight frown caught between his brows. "Yes?" I said. "Is there a reason I shouldn't be? It is possible for me to go a few days without someone peeling grapes for me, you know."

"No, I mean, you're bending over like you've hurt your back."

"Practising not standing like a nobleman."

"Oh."

He stared at me and I stared back, slowly straightening. "Not doing it right?"

"No, not really. It's more...relaxed."

"Relaxed. Is this better?"

"No, but don't worry about it. At least your hair is starting to look more basin dust than..." He waved a hand, looking for the right word.

"Floof," I said. "And that's a direct quote."

Mana grinned as I dropped down beside him, taking the food he held out. "Floof," he agreed. "Though I must admit I like the floof."

"Well, I can assure you that I'll be washing it at the first opportunity, even if that does out me as a..." I looked conspiratorially around before lowering my voice. "...*lord*."

His smile grew a wan edge, and he dropped his hand into his lap, food untouched. "I'm going to miss you and your stupid humour. There is no way your father will let me remain in Emora for even a second after stealing you away on this escapade. I can't say I'm looking forward to going back to Bakii, but I'm done at the citadel even if I wanted to be someone else's watcher."

"I imagine that's for the best since there's only so much vomit one should have to deal with in a lifetime," I said, trying not to sound like his words were hollowing out not only my stomach but my soul.

He fixed me with one of his long, unblinking stares I could never decipher. "You say that like cleaning up your sick was the worst part of the job."

For a moment there was just the shiver of the wind, all attempt at reply lumping into a mass of unspoken words in my throat.

"I'm...I'm sorry about the other night," he went on when I didn't. "I should have asked your permission rather than just..."

Just closing a hand around both our cocks and proceeding to destroy all ability to even think for a good few minutes. Permission. Perhaps it was a cultural difference, like the expectation of hospitality, but I didn't want him to have asked for permission. I wanted him to have wanted me so badly, for himself, that he didn't care about asking. The knowledge had a shameful edge, built on a lifetime of possessing all the power, of living at the centre of society, of being Lord Ashadi Romm. I ought to want from him only what I could take or pay for, not something I couldn't even express aloud.

"Nothing to apologise for," I said, waving his words away. "I did feel better afterward."

I bit into my small bread boulder and chewed the requisite four dozen times before it was soft enough to swallow. Mana took a bite too, but made it look far easier despite how much it hurt my jaw.

"I don't know what's going to happen when we get back to Emora," I said, the words forcing their way out. "But it'll be safest for you not to be there after this as I'm going to be Reacher Sormei's least favourite person. It's enough to make me wish I was back at the citadel, because I'm going to miss you too. And Shuala. I won't miss this though," I added, disliking the way serious conversation tore at my skin like a sandstorm. "Out here the heat is unbearable, the wind is atrocious, and there are too many flies. Also I think my mule is broken. His bumpy gait has forever injured my arse, and brandy is the only thing that gets the dusty stink of his fur out of my nose."

I reached for my flask as I spoke.

With a wry, tight smile, Mana nodded at it. "Last night," he said. "In case we make good time tomorrow. Sorry."

"Likely I will survive. No, don't look at me like that; water is horribly dull, but maybe I can spice it up with some dirt."

"Most of the water out here comes...uh...pre-spiced. Hard

to keep it clean with the winds blowing everywhere." He picked at the bread with his fingernails, not looking up. "How worried are you really? About going back to Emora after this?"

"Honestly?" I said, abandoning the rock bread to light a korsh roll. "*Worried* doesn't even begin to cover it. If Sormei is so deep into this that his own twin is scared, what chance do I stand if I get in his way?"

Mana's brows rose. "Your name doesn't protect you from him?"

"The man threw his own sister out of the family for refusing to marry me, for which he blames me, I might add. So I'm already his least favourite person even before my father ruins his Learshapan contract with an insult bride."

"That's why you ended up at the citadel."

"Oh no, I ended up at the citadel because *I* refused to marry *her* despite my father's insistence, though likely I would have done if she had not been intent on marrying someone else. Let's just say Miizhei and I were not meant to be."

"Oh."

While Mana frowned at me like a man trying to understand a book in a foreign language, I rolled more korsh and tried not to think about what the future might hold. Better to stay in the moment, listening to the other travellers' low chatter, the night music of insects and wind, and the slurp of mules enjoying Lord Vief's dirty water. It was nothing like the entertainments that would have been on offer inside the estate's manor, a manor I would have been welcomed to with true Emoran hospitality had I strode to the door. Yet even the prospect of another night sleeping on the stones didn't make me want to move.

Two days later, the low mounds of the Vimi commune came into view, and I was very much sober enough to appreciate it. Not that there was a lot to appreciate. Built from the stone of the basin, the mounds blended in, and I might have ridden right past had Mana not been with me. There were no markers and no campsite, and the last well was half a day's ride behind us—a fact I would have questioned had I thought my belief in communal trails could survive more of Mana's well-reasoned arguments.

"Well hidden," I said instead, blowing a fly from the front of my veil. "One would think they don't want visitors."

Mana shrugged. "And one would be right. Besides, people who can't be found can't be blamed for the world's troubles."

By the previous night we'd left every traveller we'd crossed paths with behind, each having a different destination to the one we faced. Likely a more welcoming one, but I reminded myself I hadn't come to be treated to fine hospitality. I'd come in search of the truth, to end the feeling my world was unravelling and there was nothing I could do to change it.

"Remember everything I told you?" Mana asked, glancing my way as we approached the nondescript mounds.

"Respectfully something something respectfully."

He rolled his eyes, trying to hide his smile. "Really?"

"I remember," I said. "I might have a bad sense of humour, but I have a good memory."

Mana nodded. "It's important. Mistakes are fine, so long as you show you're trying to meet them on their ground rather than yours."

He articulated it well, like always, and I couldn't but watch him out of the corner of my eye as we traversed the last of the distance. He'd been quiet at the Shield, a watcher intent on doing his duties as best he could no matter how difficult I made it. He'd always practised loading every one of my pistols until he could do it faster than I could, always ensured I had clean clothes and fresh water, and was there to catch me when I collapsed beneath the draining strength of iishor. But now he rode across the basin with his head held high, taking the lead on everything from our rations and supplies to the direction we travelled. I'd been swept along in his wake yet had nothing to complain about. There was no way he could have said the same of me as his dragon rider.

A short way before the closest mound, Mana brought his mule to a halt and dismounted. The commune's only nod to the notion of hospitality was a metal pole upon which we could hitch our mounts, and a water trough for them to drink. Its cover was surprisingly heavy, until I realised it was made of old scaleglass, semi-opaque and the colour of heavy cloud. It wasn't the sort of thing one could transport or reshape, which meant the commune had been here for a long time.

With the trough cover open, Mana looked my way, his expression impossible to read. "Are you ready?"

"As ready as I'll ever be."

"You have the offering?"

I patted my skirt pocket. "Has been safely tucked away since I repurposed it."

"Right. Well. I guess we'd better not dawdle out here in the hot wind then."

"Probably not, no. Is this... are you sure this is going to be all right?"

Mana heaved a sigh and nodded. "It'll be fine, it's just... always a bit nerve-wracking seeking time with the elders. Even for me."

"That doesn't make me feel any better."

He patted my shoulder. "Good thing that you're the bravest person I know then. Let's go."

On that strange utterance, he gestured toward the wide hatchway. Unlike the trough cover, it was made from light, battered wood and lifted easily, revealing a steep stairway leading down into the ground.

"Wouldn't want to have to carry supplies down here," I said, eyeing the narrow, shadowed steps.

"Oh, there's a ramp on the other side for carts and the like, but it spirals and always makes me feel unwell. Shall I go first, or would you like to?"

"After you; I don't want to get lost trying to figure out where I am, thank you very much."

"It's just a stairway, but sure. Close the hatch cover behind you."

Mana started down the stairs, one hand lightly touching the wall for support or balance or because even before I closed the hatch it was difficult to see. After I let it down, the shadows only deepened.

"Should have brought some fresh light orbs," Mana said, his voice muffled by the closeness. "There's more light ahead at least."

Ahead, or farther down depending on how you looked at it, a trio of light orbs hung from hooks on the low ceiling, though they too had seen more energetic days. Thankfully the stairs didn't take us as deep as I'd feared, and we soon reached the bottom, where a room had been carved into rock. Broad grooves in one wall made a series of shelves, each owning a variety of simple shoes, some fully closed in for work, others strappy sandals.

"Shoes off," Mana said, bending easily to untie his travelling boots. I did the same, able now to hear a distant murmur of muffled voices. At least voices meant life and we hadn't come for nothing. At least not yet.

With our shoes nestled together on one shelf and our hats hung opposite, Mana made for the door—another old scaleglass relic that would have been impossible to open had its hinges not been well lubricated. As it was, Mana pushed it open with ease and stepped into a space filled with natural light and the sweet smell of pressed dates. It was enormous, with rough sandstone walls curving to create something of a bright cavern. Water trickled from somewhere and large palms stretched toward the ceiling, beneath which sat clusters of Apaians in skirts of ochre and russet.

At the slight creak of the old scaleglass hinge, every voice broke off and every head turned, leaving some two dozen pairs of eyes staring at us as we entered. Some looked bored, others curious, a few like they hoped a glare would burn our skin and send us running.

"Don't talk to anyone remember?" Mana whispered as he turned to close the door gently behind us. "Acceptance by the elders comes before everything."

I nodded, not wanting to break the silence, not when, in Mana's words, I talked like a rich Emoran even more than I walked like one.

One by one the Apaians went on about their tasks in the vast space—a space that only grew more vast as I took it all in. The high point of the roof seemed to sit beneath one of the domed mounds we'd seen outside, leaving light to spill in through what looked like round holes but were likely balls of glass.

"This way," Mana said, and unlike in the stairway even his whisper seemed to echo. From the entry door he led the way directly across the space, changing course only to avoid small groups of people sitting in the light to weave or talk or peel vegetables—people who paid us no heed, like we had ceased to exist the moment they decided we weren't an immediate threat. Off the large, round hall with its swept stone floor, passages led away into other parts of the commune, likely to kitchens and bedchambers and whatever else one needed out here. The one Mana led me toward looked the same as all the others, lacking any extra decoration or grandiosity that might have allowed someone without Mana's knowledge to find their way to the elders.

This new passage led slightly upward, growing dark and cool, the scent of crushed dates giving way to old vellum and dust. Not a long passage, however—the commune seeming both larger and smaller than it had first appeared—which brought us face-to-face with the elders before I'd had time to wonder if I was going to fuck this up. No closed door separated the elders from the rest of the commune, but their room possessed some of the domed hall's vastness, lacking only the height. Low-ceilinged and rectangular, the space had a coal pit in the centre and images painted on every wall. To one side, a low table and a rack of rolled and ragged vellum; to the other, three people seated together on cushions. They wore deep blue skirts and heavy veils—the sort they could see through, poorly, but through which we could not see them.

At a nudge from Mana's elbow, I swallowed hard and started toward them. Silence seemed to roar in my ears, though it was probably just the thundering of my heartbeat as, after a whole journey, it came down only to this. Approach, but not too close, Mana had said, and so I did, trying to keep my breathing even and my hands steady. At what seemed like a respectful distance, I knelt and, pulling free the string of charms I'd liberated from my father, set it carefully on the sandstone floor.

The moment it emerged from my skirt pocket all the air seemed to leave the room and I was glad I couldn't see their faces, glad I could not look at them, that all there was left to do was stand up and step back, head bowed. And wait. I did so, swallowing the urge to glance at Mana to be sure I'd done my part right. I couldn't have offended them too much at least, since the scuff of bare feet on the slightly dusty floor heralded them rising from their cushions. Silence returned all too soon, until at last a tinkle as the charms were lifted. More silence. Then in low voices they spoke, not to me but to one another in the Apaian dialect that could at times be hard to understand though it shared most of our words. And then once again came the silence. A silence that dragged, owning nothing but my breathing and the panic of my inner thoughts.

"Where did you get these?" spoke a crackly voice, finally breaking the silence. It spoke in the same dialect, but louder and clearer, as one might if unsure of being understood. It made me feel foolish, yet at the same time I was grateful not to have to ask Mana for a translation.

"My father's collection," I said, having been coached to speak honestly whatever truths it might reveal.

"Stolen?"

"No, being brought back to its rightful owners."

The silence came again, heavy now with the fear I had said the wrong thing, my heartbeat so loud it seemed to fill the space.

"Welcome, Emoran," another voice said, this one easier to understand. "We grant you the position of guest within our commune, but you must leave by sundown."

"Thank you." It was much better than the swift kick I'd been expecting, but when I looked up it was no sense of true welcome I received. The elders remained veiled, standing now but still in their little knot as though for safety. Of the charms there was no sign.

One of them gestured behind me. "And you, Dragon, may stay as long as you wish with the blessing of us all."

"Vesenemae," Mana said, appearing beside me. "I am most honoured."

"As are we to have your presence. Now, do tell us what has brought you here."

Mana looked my way, and I had to swallow the urge to ask why they'd called him Dragon and remember instead why I'd come. For my own dragon. For the truth.

I cleared my throat. On the journey I'd practised what I might say when I reached this moment, but all my fine words of explanation disappeared leaving me with "Dragons."

"Dragons?" one of the elders repeated, one flicking their gaze to Mana.

"Yes. And the people beyond the Shield. In The Sands. I...I wish to understand how they are connected, and connected to us, if you—" I dredged up recollection of how Mana had worded it. "If you would honour me with the sharing of a story."

I'd hoped we'd had enough of silence, but once again it hung over us as the elders looked at one another. For a moment I wondered whether they could communicate without speaking, so little did they seem to need their voices, but with the passing of a minute or more a murmured exchange ended with a brief nod from one.

"The story you seek is one we possess and one we are able to share. In part. No story," the elder added abruptly, "can be shared in full to outsiders, this you must understand."

"I understand."

"Very well. Erebei will tell you the story as you are allowed to know it, as it has been entrusted to her. The knowledge you take from here is never to be shared; that is the understanding you accept in hearing it. Yes?"

"Yes, I understand," I said, having to clear my throat to raise my voice above a whisper. The importance of their stories and their histories, of this very moment in being allowed to hear one, was beginning to weigh heavily on my shoulders.

Beside me, Mana turned as though to leave, only for one of the elders to shake their head. "No, Dragonborn, stay. The flames tell us you must also hear this story and carry this knowledge. You have come to us at the right time."

Something in the way they spoke to him was deferential, like he was the elder, but there was no time to do more than wonder why before another elder beckoned. "Come," the one called Erebei said, gesturing toward the coal pit. "Sit. Both of you. This will take some time."

A long time passed, yet it seemed no time at all before Mana and I walked out of that room in silence. There was something almost offensive about the chatter back in the domed hall, like it was wrong to act as though the world had not changed. It had. It had rocked beneath my feet, yet it rocked still more when all the people who had ignored us earlier began to gather around. All at once they were on their feet, charging forward, sending a shock of fear jolting through me. But none of them so much as glanced my way. It was Mana they sought.

"Child of Dragons."

"Honourable One."

"Dragonborn."

"Please, take this."

"Dreamer, honour us with your presence awhile."

They pressed in around us like a whispering tide, and I had to clench my fists, fighting the urge to push them back, to shout or shake them until they understood the weight of all I now knew of the world. The realisation that they all knew the truth already struck me harder than it ought, as hard as the stares that began turning my way.

While the people pressed ever closer, murmurs of thanks dropped from Mana's lips along with excuses that he could not stay. One young man reached out to touch him like he carried divinity within his skin, and an older woman begged he grant her a breath of his strength. All the while, he edged toward escape, the way increasingly blocked.

"Please, Honoured Dragon, stay with us awhile."

"May the time come soon, Dreamer. May the world change."

Mana tried to keep walking, but there was no space to move. He stepped back, and the voices around us grew more insistent. Desperate. Pleas rose on wavering tones like a keening song, and beside me, Mana tensed. A small sob convulsed in his throat, and when I looked his way, I hardly recognised the wide-eyed young man at my side. Pale, with his jaw set, Mana seemed to see nothing, only to shrink like he wished to manifest a shell to hide in. I knew the feeling all too well, and stepped forward.

"Excuse me," I said. "If you could step aside and make space, it would be greatly appreciated."

Simple words, but possessing all the command of my rank and the biting drawl that had shamed dozens of presumptuous hangers-on over the years, they might as well have been shouted orders. Attention drawn to my existence, gazes swept me up and down—that too something I was well used to.

"Thank you," I said, using the confusion to step toward the exit, giving the gathered Apaians little choice but to step back. Before they could renew their protestations, I grabbed Mana's hand and pulled him along in my wake. Embodying my father's stately march, I carried us both through the chaos toward the door. It was working, but perhaps they would follow us up the stairs and out onto the searing rocks of the basin, at which point I would be out of ideas beyond an ignominious retreat on mule.

Thankfully, they didn't follow. Once we stepped through the door, they seemed to accept that Mana wasn't staying and fell back, eventually abandoning us so completely that we donned our shoes and hats in silence. We made the walk back up the stairs in silence too, my thoughts caught between the Apaians' behaviour toward Mana and their elder's story.

Back out in the basin's heat, both seemed fanciful.

"Thank you," Mana said, the words little more than a whisper above the buffeting wind as we made for our waiting mules. "I . . . didn't think it would be that bad."

His hand trembled as he reached for his reins, and I took hold of it, as though my tight grip could contain his shaking. "Are you all right?"

His gaze snapped to meet mine, all surprise, before he looked away. "Yes, I'm fine. But we should go, or we won't make it back to a campsite before dark."

It was no answer, but it was the best I was going to get.

"Wise as ever," I said, trying for a light tone. "Perhaps we can race our mules and see who survives longest without falling off."

"I think I'll pass," he said, managing a chuckle. "Let's just not dawdle."

We didn't talk on the way back to the nearest campsite, just rode side by side through the oppressive heat, caught in our own thoughts. The longer I kept mine trapped inside my head the more they started to circle, catching on the same idea over and over.

I needed to talk to Shuala.

They were the first words out of my mouth when we reached the campsite, just as the setting sun turned the rocky wastes golden.

"I know," Mana said.

I'd expected to defend my reasoning, to have to explain, and his agreement left me deflated. "It's a long way back to the citadel though, and that's if they'll even let me in."

"Maybe you don't have to go that far."

He spoke so quietly I almost didn't catch his words. His attention seemed to be elsewhere, dark eyes staring into nothing. "What do you mean?"

"Dragons can talk over any distance," he said. "You just need iishor."

Iishor. I'd always thought of it as a foul brew cooked up by some Emoran alchemist. The truth had been harder to hear. At least for me. "Did you already know? About the iishor?"

"Some. I knew we made it first. And yes, before you ask, I do know how. It's been a while since my last brewing stint at the citadel, but so long as we can get the ingredients, it's not as hard as you would think."

"At least not for the Honourable Child of Dragons," I said as we sought out a free spot in the camp to sit and eat, though I'd never felt less like sitting and eating in all my life. "They don't call you that because you worked at the citadel, do they."

It wasn't a question, but he answered all the same—a slow, solemn shake of his head before he murmured an excuse and walked away. Perhaps in search of water or in need of stretching his legs, it didn't matter, mattered only that the man who walked away bore no resemblance to the watcher whose gentle hands and sweet smile had long troubled my dreams.

18

Naili

Morning Bulletin

To all criers for announcement throughout Bakii

*The watcher wanted for questioning in regards to Lord
Ashadi Romm's desertion from the Shield has gone missing.
Originally from Bakii, the Bastion is requesting
information on the possible whereabouts of one
Manalaii Billette.*

*Rationing required! Gun owners expected to ration
gunpowder over the next weeks as a valuable shipment from
Emora fails to arrive. The reason is yet unknown.*

*Unconfirmed numbers of missing people are pouring in. Those
confirmed by family so far include Leosha Tii, Hem Iilorono,
Naili Billette, Torrah Kine . . .*

Breakfast in the Hoods' hideaway was a far more subdued affair than dinner the night before. While dinner had been a communal gathering, breakfast appeared to be the kind of meal where everyone came to it as they needed, men passing through the shadowy dining room and out again in small groups, sharing whispers. Thankfully they didn't seem to be whispers about me, the Hoods present all focused on other, far more important things. They did glance my way though, and I was glad I'd checked in the mirror before leaving my room, sure at least for now that no obvious flowers sat on my skin and hair. And that the tearful red rings around my eyes had subsided during a fitful night.

Iiberi sat halfway along the table, a large ledger open in front of him covered in brown ink. Half a dozen Hoods sat around him, nodding and eating as he spoke, gesturing as though giving orders.

"Noon, at the tower," he was saying as I passed, eavesdropping on my way to the kitchen arch where plates and baskets of food sat waiting. Again the only sign of the women who worked in the kitchen were the fruits of their labour and their distant chatter amid the clatter of washing up. "And if he's more than five minutes late, you're out of there."

Iiberi spoke like a commander, and the Hoods around him made murmurs of agreement, sharing low-voiced stories, no doubt of what had happened on other occasions when the man they were meeting had been late. Loading up their plates from the spread of food, two other Hoods were having an intent discussion about the safest route to somewhere on the far side of Bakii, and as I slipped past them I had the feeling I was skirting around secret knowledge. Perhaps one day I would be as knowledgeable about the city and its power brokers, rather than a very hungry ex-laundress covered in flowers.

But first, I had to find a way to force the alchemist's hand lest I crumble to dross, which meant getting a message to Miizhei. She wouldn't be able to meet me until after—

"Billette."

I spun at the sound of my name, almost losing a round of flatbread off my plate. Iiberi beckoned imperiously, the men around him having dispersed about their given tasks leaving plates and bowls and cups full of thick dregs. More Hoods looked my way than had at my arrival, perhaps to see whether I would do as I was told.

"Iiberi," I said in greeting, carrying my bread over to the table, stomach rumbling. "Or should I call you something more formal when you're being my boss?"

Annoyance flickered across his face, there and gone and leaving me triumphant. The ability to unsettle him, to have power over even something as small as his frown, felt good.

"I am always your boss, and Iiberi will do; we don't do formalities like that *yes, master, no, master* stuff you're used to with Occuello. Sit."

I could have enlightened him that until a few days earlier I'd had no interaction with the alchemist for whom I'd worked, but truths were currency now, and I kept that one to myself.

Setting down my plate, pitifully lacking in sustenance, I slipped onto the long bench and stared expectantly at him. It didn't fluster him, Iiberi folding back within the protective carapace he seemed to carry everywhere.

"We need to find out what you know and what you have to learn. Let's start with the basics—knife-work. Any good?"

"Only with the sort of knife-work it takes to chop herbs." And threaten purring, disdainful alchemists who kept stepping closer, daring me to slice their throats.

Iiberi made a note, and I leaned one reddening cheek on my palm to hide my embarrassment.

"The streets of Bakii?" he went on without any comment. "How well do you know them?"

"Depends on which part of the city. I know the streets around Occuello's pretty well, and out into the middle market."

"The deep?"

"Only as far as the deep market."

"And the upper city?"

I shook my head. "I've never even walked through it. Poor Apaian women in serving clothes don't get to do that."

"Poor Apaian women in serving clothes can go almost anywhere," he said with a twitch of his lips I could have called a smile, before going on. "Politics?"

"If you mean do I know who rules here, then yes."

"Then no." He made another mark in the ledger, and I had the distinct feeling I was failing a test. "Contacts?"

I blinked at him, trying to get my head around his meaning before I failed even more. Fortunately, or unfortunately, Iiberi took pity on me. "I mean do you have any close and trustworthy family and friends, or acquaintances in . . . high or interesting places."

I'd lain upon the alchemist's workbench and moaned. "No," I said. "The only people I know are the laundresses I worked with and some of the other servants. No family here anymore."

"You didn't get out much, I take it."

"The matron wasn't keen on letting us have free time, so I only got a weekly pass."

Iiberi grimaced, but at least he didn't make a mark in his ledger this time. Around us the rest of the Hoods were getting on with their meal or their preparations for the day, paying us little heed beyond a few glances, and I could only hope none of them had acute enough hearing to know what I was saying.

"And you can read and write?"

A simple question with no simple answer. If I admitted I couldn't, he would ask how I'd read the list of items to steal and who had helped me, but if I said I could I would be setting myself up for more trouble. Embarrassed as much by the situation as by the truth of my poor education, I pressed my hands to my hot cheeks. "I...I can't write," I said, the admission as heavy as the coming lie. "Reading is all right."

Another note in the ledger.

"And do you have any particular skills beyond killer plants that we should know about?"

I wasn't sure if I ought to thank him for keeping my other secret skill to himself, so just said, "I know how to scrub blood out of almost any fabric."

"That's less useful around here than you'd think," he said, shutting the ledger with a thump of heavy paper. "Most people who end up with blood on them are too dead to care about the state of their clothes. You start knife training with Scoria tomorrow. His real name is Envolii, but no one has dared call him that since he cut Shalla's earlobe off."

On those words, Iiberi rose from the table.

"And today?" I said, trying not to sound hopeful, not to sound like I needed desperately to meet with Miizhei rather than run errands for a gang. "Can I do whatever I wish, or is that not allowed?"

"You're not a prisoner here, if that's what you mean, but you have to put the Hoods first and not do anything that could bring us disrepute."

"A fancy way of saying I should keep to myself and not tell people I'm a Hood."

His weak smile came with a humourless laugh. "This time I choose to be grateful for your dreadful acuity, because otherwise I would find the list of things we need to teach you daunting. As for this morning, you and I are going for a walk. After we find you something...better...to wear."

I nodded, though my stomach sank. Getting a message to Miiz would have to wait.

The something better to wear was the finest-looking something I'd ever seen. Faintly scented with vanilla and cinnamon and a hint of sand rose, the full-length linen skirt was embroidered and dyed, gathered and pinched and jewelled—the sort of skirt the very richest noblewoman in Bakii might have worn. A plain cream tunic accompanied it, no less fine in stitching for its demure colour.

"I can't wear that," I said as the Hood acting as my wardrobe set down a wispy, light veil and a trio of armbands. "I…"

The man watched me, unmoved, as I trailed off. "Unless I've underestimated your size requirements or you're allergic to linen and silver, yes you can."

He walked out on the words, leaving me to dress. It wasn't something that I usually took a lot of time over, but by the time I'd pulled the clothes on, adjusted them, patted them, adjusted them again, run my hands down the smooth panes of the skirt and spent all too much time rubbing flowers off my arms, Iiberi had knocked four times to see if I was yet ready to go. Peering into the cloudy brass mirror, I finally tied my hair into a neat knot and was as happy with the outcome as I was ever likely to be.

He was leaning against the wall outside my door, arms folded, but he straightened as I stepped out. "Finally. I hope you don't mean to take that long every time, or you'll be getting very few tasks in the upper city."

Without comment or compliment, he looked me critically up and down before adjusting one of my armbands, his hands warm as they slid the band a touch higher. "Put that veil on; there are always swarms of flies by the north door and we need to hide your face."

With that he strode off, leaving me to tie the veil around my waist as I hurried in his wake. In his cream-and-gold embroidered skirt and tunic he looked out of place striding the rough, dim passages of the Hoods' hideaway, yet I had to admit he wore it well. The light fabric saved his paler skin from standing out, but I found myself staring at his arms all the same, at the lines of his lithe muscles cinched by fine armbands and covered in a faint gleam of sweat.

The route Iiberi led me through the Hoods' enormous old house carried us away from the living areas to a flight of stairs, and up into a light-filled space with high ceilings and smooth clay walls. Several rooms fanned off what looked to be a central atrium, a slice of each visible through broad archways, all deep, vibrant green fabrics, gold-edged murals, and dark hardwood furnishings.

"What is this place?" I whispered, staring about.

"Our frontage," Iiberi said, not bothering to slow, familiarity stealing all awe from him. "It's important to have the right kind of space in which to do certain kinds of business."

"What kinds of business?"

"Questions here are earn—"

"Earned not given," I finished. "All right, but if this is part of your ... *our* ... property, why doesn't anyone live in this bit?"

"Because the places people live shape who they are, and we don't want to be like them."

Them. Just as we'd always referred to Master Occuello as *him* or *the man upstairs*, *them* had only one meaning in Bakii—the lords, the elite, the rich, Reacher Sormei and his ilk, and for the first time since setting foot in the door, I felt like perhaps I was in the right place after all. The Hoods had the money, and the space, yet lived like they didn't, keeping their fine halls empty in silent protest.

Without slowing, Iiberi led the way to the main door—a great arched entry surrounded by rows of coloured glass. A smattering of fine dirt had blown in to pepper the white tile, providing the first sign the world outside still existed. Warm, dusty air seeped in too, taking over from the empty, lifeless smell that had pervaded the rooms, a smell so faint it teetered upon the knife-blade of existence. Beyond the coloured windows, the hum of flies grew louder, each a black speck upon the glass.

"Unfortunately it's time to fight our way through the flies for the pleasure of breathing upper Bakii's baked air," Iiberi said, halting before the door.

"I'll take baked air over damp any day. And both over the faceless smell of these rooms."

Iiberi lifted one of his notched brows. "Faceless? I didn't think lack of visage had a smell."

"Everything does. Can't you smell it?"

He looked around, breathing deep, his brow notched in concentration.

"It's like...a smell that is no smell," I said. "Not the absence of smell so much as one that consumes other smells, desiccating them to nothing."

"That has to be the creepiest description of a smell I've ever heard. And no, thankfully, I can't smell that. Here." He drew a small blade from the pocket of his skirt and held it up to my face. "Stand still."

I leapt back. "What? Why?"

"Eyebrows," he said, tone long-suffering. "Although I can cut your nose off instead if you'd prefer. It might help with the phantom smells. So long as it wouldn't just grow back."

"I'll pass on testing it, thank you."

"As long as you'll also stand still, that's fine. Don't want to botch your brows or you'll look ridiculous."

I clenched my fists and lifted my chin, unsure how I felt about having the notches of a noble cut into my brows. It felt wrong, yet deliciously so, my many misgivings balanced by the thrill of transgression. As he brought the blade slowly closer to my face, I closed my eyes instinctively, only to flinch at the first touch of cool metal. I'd never done more than pluck the occasional errant hair and didn't like the scrape and sting of the blade, but thankfully he made quick work of the task and had soon switched to the other brow.

"There," he said, stepping back. "And I didn't cut your nose off after all. Veil up."

The fine, wispy veil had seemed too delicate to possess any functionality, but the fabric was surprisingly strong and the clip well made, leaving me floating in a soft, protective bubble as Iiberi opened the door. I squinted, momentarily stunned by the bright light as the second door opened, and amid a symphony of insect humming, Iiberi tugged me out into the hot street. Let go as suddenly, I stood blinking, trying to adjust to the brightness, while he closed the door behind us.

"Lesson number one," he said, rejoining me. "Upper-class women don't stand foolishly in the middle of the doorway trying to rub their eyes through their veil. The way you act is even more important than the clothes you're wearing. Thankfully, this is just a practice. Now, walk."

He soon settled into an easy stroll, leaving me to keep pace at his side, so disoriented from the bright light and the strange location that I couldn't tell which direction we were walking. "Where are we?"

"This is Upper East Crescent."

"Upper East—"

"You are staying at number five Upper East Crescent, also known as Haber House."

Rather than attempt to further articulate my shock, I stared at him, hoping the information would soon make sense. It didn't. Iiberi just stared back, faintly smiling through the diaphanous material of his veil—a veil, I realised, that hid the colour of his eyes as surely as mine hid the dots tattooed beneath my eye.

"Are you...are you safe out here?" I asked, recalling his discomfort sitting on the balcony across from Occuello's. "Am I?

And please don't damn my acuity again; I'm not trying to prise information out of you."

"Are you not? That I don't believe, but yes. We are safe so long as we look like we belong, but I have blades should that go awry. In truth we are both safer here than anywhere else in the city—a strange feeling I find I quite enjoy."

"Is that why we're out here?"

"In part, but you said you had never been to upper Bakii—a must for understanding this city." As he spoke, he gestured to the street around us, bustling with familiar sounds of life yet unfamiliar faces and forms, smells and signs and details. Everywhere were fine skirts of every colour, each a pleated, gathered, and embroidered masterpiece of clothcraft, clean and unique. Even on the main street where the alchemist lived I had never seen so much colour. The number of wealthy citizens was usually outweighed by the poor with our plain clothes and moth-eaten veils, while the smell of damp was always present like a promise in every breath. Here the deep was so far below that no hint of damp escaped to trouble us.

"It's like a whole different world," I said, gazing around at a streetscape so unlike the rest of the city that its very existence left a sour taste in my mouth. "How can they—?"

"They don't care," Iiberi said. "And on the rare occasions one of them does feel bad, nothing changes; they just make sure the suffering of others is kept farther and farther out of sight. I would take you to see the Bastion, home of uncaring, but I don't think you're ready for that."

As he spoke, we entered a large market square full of people, and never in my life had I seen so many beautiful, useless things for sale. Glass figurines in every colour, embroidered veils, cloth dolls with real hair, painted plates, scented cushions, and artistic scenes picked out in miniature mosaic. There was even a stall selling what Celessi people thought of as Apaian treasures. I turned away, knowing to look would only enrage me.

In the middle of the square, a crier stood shouting that morning's news to the uncaring crowd, and as we drew nearer his words washed over us. "...valuable shipment from Emora fails to arrive. The reason is yet unknown." He drew a deep breath. "Unconfirmed numbers of missing people are pouring in. Those confirmed by family so far include Leosha Tii, Hem Iilorono, Naili Billette—"

"Did he just say my name?" I said, turning on Iiberi.

"He certainly did," he returned, sounding wholly disinterested. "But do keep walking or you'll draw attention to yourself."

"But why—?"

"This is why it's good to read the crier sheets every day so you don't get surprised by the news."

After a brief break to wet his lips with water, the crier returned to the top of his call. "The watcher wanted for questioning in regards to Lord Ashadi Romm's desertion—" My stomach dropped through the stones, and with my hand on Iiberi's arm, I stopped walking entirely. "Originally from Bakii, the Bastion is requesting information on the possible whereabouts of one Manalaii Billette."

Iiberi tugged me on with a warning I didn't hear, not speaking again until we were well clear of the market. "You need to be more careful. We cannot have members who draw attention to themselves in any fashion, even when their brother's wanted notice is the first item of news for the day."

Given how completely I had failed, the knowledge it had been a test ought to have troubled me, but fear for Mana was all that sped my heart and sank my stomach. Wanted by the Bastion. I'd always said it was only a matter of time before his beautiful lord got him in trouble, but I'd imagined the trouble of being fired for fraternisation, not this.

"I take it you don't know where he is?" Iiberi said, turning us away from the main thoroughfares and into a narrow tributary road.

"No."

"The no of someone who wouldn't admit it even if they did. A pity, given the value of information in this city."

"A pity?" I halted my steps, safer here away from so many watching eyes. "Why was my name in the list of missing people? I have no family here to confirm anything!"

Despite his veil, Iiberi's expression of mock pity came through clearly. "What? You think the crier news is all true? Someone will have noted your removal from Master Occuello's payroll and decided to make use of your name to stir up panic and anti-Lummazzt sentiment. There is only one place in this city where you can trade truths. Come on, it's time you met the most powerful man in Bakii."

While his words swirled around my head, questions mounted, but Iiberi just sped his pace. At a small fountain, another turn took us into an even narrower street, where houses butted up against the small workshops of craftsmen with expensive wares. Another turn and Iiberi was leading the way down a flight of stairs, from light into shadow. It wasn't the shadow of depths though, where darkness bred mould and mildew, rather the cool sort gentle on the skin. A faint breeze rippled the hems of our skirts.

"Where are we?" I asked, looking about at the dark brickwork and the old lantern sconces. "This doesn't even look like Bakii."

"These are some of the few remaining streets from old Bakii. Most of them got lost, pulled down, or built over, but there are a few here and there. They're special in a way, I suppose, but I always feel like ghosts live in their bricks. They have a sad, eerie quality. Here, at the red door. Careful not to say a word while we're inside. Everything you say will be remembered, recorded, and used. Takes some getting used to."

Before I could ask what he meant, he'd pushed the door open without even pausing to knock. Air filled with the scent of dust and paper and ink, old books and flickering stars wafted out to greet us, but the room beyond owned nothing but a table—red like the door—and a man sitting with his hands folded before him.

"Good afternoon, Murmur," Iiberi said, having closed the door behind us.

"Is it?" Murmur sounded bored and looked like a man who rarely left the dim light of his room.

"It is actually. Fine weather."

Murmur stared back, blinking slowly. "And?"

"I'm here for an exchange."

"Very well. Go."

Without glancing my way, Iiberi said, "The Hoods have a new member, a woman who goes by the name of Naili. She used to work at Master Occuello's as a laundress."

Had he not already taken the choice out of my hands, I would have snapped at him that my identity and history were mine to give away. Instead, all I could do was try to keep the scowl off my face, sure the watchful Murmur would notice it and write it down with all the rest. Not that he seemed to be writing anything down, at least not yet.

"I see," Murmur said. "Well, I do have something I think will interest you greatly today. Only half the usual gunpowder shipment is expected to arrive, not just today but all week." Murmur's lips spread in a smile of someone who had completed a good business deal. "Goodbye, Iiberi."

"Farewell, Murmur."

And with that, we were done. Iiberi made for the door, his brow stormy, but not as stormy as I felt. "Why did you tell him that?" I hissed the moment we were back in the narrow brick-lined alley. "I don't want everyone to know about me."

"Information is currency, and the Hoods will spend you whatever way they see fit," he said, walking on. "Be grateful I didn't tell him other things."

"Wait." I hurried after him. "That was the most powerful man in Bakii?"

"You doubt it? Murmur is a whisper monger, like... that person in every workplace who knows everyone's secrets and gossips about them all, only it's for the whole city."

"But how does he know what is true if he just listens to everything people say? Couldn't people use that to spread falsehoods?"

"They could, but he's never been wrong. Don't know how he does it, but he's never wrong."

A man who was never wrong, who knew the secrets of a whole city and only parted with them for other secrets—no wonder Iiberi had called him the most powerful man in Bakii. Murmur hadn't asked what Iiberi wanted to know, had just traded one secret for another according to his own whim or, perhaps, his own plans.

"Who does Murmur work for?" I asked, following Iiberi out of the remnants of old Bakii.

"Everyone and no one. He doesn't refuse to do business with anyone, but is beholden nowhere that we've ever been able to discover."

Doesn't refuse to do business with anyone. I tucked this new information away for further consideration. A dangerous plan to force the alchemist's hand had slowly been forming in my mind, and as I followed Iiberi back to the Hoods' hideaway, another piece twisted into place.

Perhaps knowledge really could be power after all. Now I just needed Miizhei.

I sat picking at a sticky patch on the table, trying not to think through all the ways my message could have gone astray. The messenger could have pocketed my coin and not taken the message at all, could have given it to the wrong person, could have been intercepted by Alii. Foolish to leave anything to chance, but I didn't yet have any choice but to hope.

Upon our return from upper Bakii, Iiberi had insisted I change out of my fine clothes before passing me off to a Hood named Caldec, whose job seemed to be something like a quartermaster and mail clerk rolled into one. He'd rolled his eyes at the instruction to make use of me, but by the end of the afternoon I'd learned enough that he'd stopped grumbling, and I'd discovered how the Hoods sent messages. Kids in need of food or coin came and went from a small nook in the corner of Caldec's domain, carrying messages and bringing back news. The one I'd sent to the servants' door of Master Occuello's had eyed me like I'd spoken nonsense, but had taken the coin all the same and scurried out before Caldec was any the wiser.

By the time the old Hood sent me off at the end of the day, there had been barely enough time to scrub my skin clean of flowers before daring my first solo trip outside the Hoods' headquarters. I still wasn't entirely sure I was allowed to leave, but could not risk asking permission. I had to see Miizhei.

Yet though I sat waiting in a dingy little tavern near Occuello's, the jug of sweetened orange water I'd ordered remained untouched. She was late.

Eventually, when I was beginning to wonder how long I ought to wait before giving up in search of another way to contact her, the doorway darkened and there stood Miizhei, a wrap caught about her shoulders and the delivery sack in her hand. Shame jolted through me at the sight of it, at the realisation that in the last few days I'd not once thought about the people who needed my help with draughts and tonics and salves.

Having hesitated a moment in the doorway, Miizhei entered, yet the steps that brought her across the small, crowded room toward me were slow and unsure. "Naili," she said when she drew close, not immediately taking the place opposite. Instead, she gestured to her thick, dark eyebrows. "New look."

I'd forgotten about the slits Iiberi had cut in my brows and lifted a hand to them, enough shock in the movement that she deigned to sit, folding her sharp edges onto the floor across from me. It had been a long time since I'd sat to drink with anyone, and I found myself glad it was her.

"I almost didn't get your message," she said, settling her plain skirts neatly about her. "Quite the risk you took."

"Worth it, if you know what I think you know."

She paused in the act of pouring herself a glass from the jug on the table. "Straight to business then, huh?" She seemed to be trying not to look around, trying not to appear conscious of our surroundings. "I should never have let my guilt get the better of me. More fool me."

Her words were quiet and she didn't meet my gaze, and belatedly I realised Miizhei was afraid of me. Or if not of me, of what I might say, of why I'd asked her to come.

I reached across the table, a quick squeeze of her hand all I dared. "I can't stay long, but I promise I'm not here to harm you, or expose you. I think I've found a way to save us. Or rather, to make the alchemist save us."

Miizhei huffed a mocking laugh. "Even if I believed that possible, she doesn't help people."

She. A deliberate admission, and not, I realised, the first time she'd spoken it. "You know."

"Of course I know. There is only one way for a lower house servant to get information from their employer. It took a while, but I found ways to catch her attention—his attention, I thought at the time. I was hoping for a fool who thought little of his servants, only to get a spider who likes to play with her food." She laughed softly, more at herself it seemed, yet I couldn't but wonder if she knew just how much I knew. "And now you want my hard-won information. For yourself? Or for your new friends?"

"Neither. You don't need to tell me what you know, just... who you are. More than a laundress."

She drank from her glass, shaking her head even as she swallowed. "No one is allowed to know that, not even you."

"All right, then tell me who you spy for."

For a long time Miizhei stared at me, seeming to ask whether I knew that the two questions were one and the same. I did, but tried not to show it. "I want to trust you, Naili, but I've been wrong about people before. What good will my answer be?"

"It could give us a future," I said, looking down at my hand rather than at her. "I know you don't think we can save ourselves. But I refuse to give in. Refuse not to try. At least for the others if not for myself, for the women the world forgot. If you tell me why you're here, I should have everything I need to force the alchemist's hand, and maybe then all of this will mean something, not have been suffering in vain."

"Suffering in vain," Miiz whispered, her gaze seeming to look through me and beyond, this Miizhei troubled, her edges softened as though by the laundry's steam. "Why I'm here is a very long story I will tell no one, but... when I write letters, they go to an old friend, a maid who works in a very prestigious household. I assume you've heard of the Sydelle family?"

I had expected a high-born Emoran name, one politically fraught enough that she feared blackmail, but not that of the lord reacher.

"I see you have," she said, her smile pressed flat. "But she does not work in the household of Reacher Sormei, rather his brother, Lord Kiren Sydelle." Again she seemed to resist the urge to look around, to be sure of safety in a way that would have risked attention. Instead, she shifted onto her knees and leaned across the table, beckoning me close. The choice to whisper in my ear would appear suspicious to anyone watching, but I did as she bade and leaned my elbows on the table. Met not with a whisper but a kiss, I forgot for a moment why I had come and what I had asked, thinking only of the desire she sent shivering through my skin. Until she pulled back just enough to part our lips and no further. "Lord Kiren believes the reacher has secret contracts with Occuello," she whispered, lips brushing mine as she spoke. "Contracts neither would want anyone to know about. For bullets that can pierce scaleglass, among other things."

Bullets that could pierce scaleglass. Like those that had brought down Lord Ashadi Romm's dragon, before Mana became a wanted man for his rider's desertion. The thought whirled through my head, pulling at fears. "But be careful," Miizhei added, her lips barely a breath from mine. "Reacher Sormei is a dangerous man." On that warning, she kissed me again, her lips soft and welcoming and perfect, drawing me in like a deep breath before pulling slowly away, touch and taste lingering long into the empty moment that followed. A moment in which sound slowly returned to my ears and I realised Miiz was watching me with an amused smile. "You'd better run along and play saviour now, Naili," she said, patting my cheek. "And don't make me regret that kiss."

Darkness had fallen by the time I found my way back to the red door. Iiberi hadn't knocked, but given the hour, I couldn't summon that level of confidence and tapped upon its solid wood. For a dozen heartbeats I stood in the silent, cool street and waited, before Murmur opened the door and peered out.

"Naili of the Hoods," he said, pulling the door wide. "Come in."

"Before I do, I have a question."

"One to ask in the street?"

"I...I just want to know whether you do other sorts of exchanges, with information, than just the usual. For instance, could I ask you to hold a secret, as...protection?"

For a moment he looked me up and down, before once again gesturing inside. "Come in, Naili of the Hoods."

Leaning back against the parapet, I stared up at the dark, star-filled sky and kept my fingers on a vine taken root in the gutter. I'd been focusing on where I wanted it to grow and was sure it must soon catch her attention. And I was ninety percent confident she wouldn't send her guards. All right, eighty-five.

No doubt the Hoods would be wondering where I'd gone by now, but there was no saying when I would next be able to steal freedom or how many days I had left while flowers grew out of my body, so I'd risked another hour. Somewhere along the way, wasting time had become a death wish.

With a crack of old wood, the roof hatch finally arced open, all squealing hinges and dust. A scowling face emerged, and it was all I could do not to grin despite the rapid thumping of my heart. I was really going to do this, really going to go toe-to-toe with this woman used to getting her own way.

Fight even against peace if it's power you want, she had said, and here I was.

"Fancy running into you here this fine night," I said with all the ease I could muster, and let go of the vine.

"Isn't it though," the alchemist said, hauling herself up the last steps and into the moonlight. No loose curls today. Every last strand was tied and tucked into her master's hat, yet I could remember her hovering over me, hair falling in curly curtains.

"What do you want?" she snapped. "This is wasting my time, but unfortunately ignoring your little trick was starting to become a problem." A few steps closer across the roof and she halted again, folding her arms as I did. "What is it, o thorn in my side?"

"Bullets."

Her eyes narrowed. "What about bullets?"

"You told me the first night I came seeking help that you were working on new bullets."

"And?"

"And then a dragon got shot down in The Sands, by a bullet that went through scaleglass."

"That's it? That's what you wanted to talk to me about, little girl?"

"No. I wanted to ask if that was a commission for Lord Reacher Sormei Sydelle, since I know you work for him."

For a time she didn't move or speak, just stared at me, expression blank enough that it didn't give anything away. Eventually, she brushed invisible dust from her sleeve. "That is a very odd assumption. Surely if Reacher Sormei wanted an alchemist, he could find one more easily in Emora."

"Oh, likely he has one there too, but you do the things he doesn't want people to know about, don't you?"

The alchemist rolled her eyes. "That is a wild supposition, little girl."

"Is it? You'd be surprised what secrets people leave in their pockets for laundresses to find."

She stared at me, gaze raking my face for a lie I was determined she wouldn't find. Likely she was careful, but could she be sure she was *that* careful, when plenty of notes and lists and half-empty jars found their way to the laundry every week.

"You can't read," she said at last.

"No, but I know people who can. I'm good at listening, you see, and at being in the right place at the right time. And while I don't care who you work for or why, there are plenty of people who would. Voyle, for instance. A man who would steal from you just to prove you have illegal substances in your workshop must have something of a grudge. I assume you know that's why he—"

"Of course I know," she snapped, something fragile in the

way she threw out her hands only to let them fall, awkward, by her sides. "He's wanted to ruin me ever since I cut in on their powder trade. He's a monster, you know, hardly worth betraying me to, I assure you."

Stepping forward, I faced her over the empty darkness, my anger all I needed now. "And you are worth saving? I came to you that night because I needed help, because something in your clothing or your washing liquids had changed me, but I didn't do it just for myself. When you refused to help me, it was my friends you condemned. They are the women the world forgot, but I will not. You want my silence, and I want your help—help I once asked for. Now I demand it."

"Ah, the sweet little bud has grown teeth," she said, all drawling boredom. "How exciting. But you've forgotten the reason I didn't have to listen to such dross the first time was because I have guards and you do not. I can have you killed, and there's nothing you can do to me. And so I bid you farewell, little—"

"I wouldn't do that if I were you."

In the silence, a gentle breeze brushed between us, rustling our skirts and pulling at loose strands of my hair. The alchemist didn't blink. "Why not?" she said at last in the crisp syllables that seemed to emerge from her lips in moments of stress.

"Because if anything happens to me, the whisper monger behind the red door will tell everyone that underneath that hat and binder you're a woman doing a man's job. You know, that secret you were willing to kill me to safeguard."

"Not just teeth you've grown," she sneered. "Perhaps I should be proud of the monster I've created, but I would rather damn you. Very well, little girl, you have a deal. My help for your silence, but if you think it will make a difference you will be disappointed. And if I find the Hoods have caught even the tiniest hint of what I've been up to, our deal is off and it'll be your friends who suffer, since you've protected yourself so nicely."

She must have caught the horror that her words hollowed in my gut, for something of a smile returned, mocking and amused. "Too late to run now, and too late to change your mind. You've put every card on the table, risked everyone you care about, and now we both have to win or we both lose. And to think, most people don't go courting a reacher's fury. How very delicious you are, little witch."

19

Tesha

Morning Bulletin

To all criers for announcement throughout Upper Emora

Every gunpowder seller will be imposing limits of sale on customers with production halved. It is unclear what the cause is or how long the shortage will last.

Emoran meteorologists warn the first day of the social season may be ruined by another brightstorm.

Nine days until the start of the social season, there are already more families in residence than usual. Recent arrivals include Lord Duzeunde, Lord Vuove and his family, Lord Revennai Angue, and Lord Uvao Romm, younger son of Lord Romm.

Crouched on the floor with only a dim lantern for light, I read through the notes on the back of Master Hoye's box for the hundredth time to be sure, really sure, I hadn't missed anything. No new poisons appeared, no new methods of introducing them into glass, yet Sormei had left me with no choice. He had to die, and soon, before his plans ruined all my own. Before he made me dance to his tune, too afraid to even remember why I'd come. But I'd not forgotten yet. I'd come to Emora to dismantle the power structure that kept the world as it was, and I could start with him. Sormei held every string of power, and without him so much could change. And so I sat up late into the night, preparing a poison glass I could sneak into his room for the nightly drink his mother said he couldn't sleep without.

My whole body buzzed with fearful determination as I squeezed the dropper, sending acid to swirl in the bottom of the first glass. It wasn't how any of these poisons ought to be incorporated, but I was out of options and out of time. While the first glass softened, I added acid to the second and the third. Without knowing which of the palace glasses Reacher Sormei used for his nightcap, I had stolen one of each and chosen three different quick-acting poisons in the hope that one, at least, would work when used this way. It was all such a risk, but I had run out of good ideas.

When the glass had softened, I sat in near darkness and added the poisons—double each dose in case that would help them to work when used this way. Again I wished for Master Hoye, again I wished I had never come, again I wished I had punched Sormei's face until it swelled up and bled.

Eventually, when there was nothing to do but wait for the glass to set, I tucked each glass safely onto the top shelf of my wardrobe and tried to sleep, only to lay awake long into the night amid increasingly wild flights of panic. When at last I slept it was fitful, and I woke unrested, feeling as fragile as the glass I'd once worked with every day. Not wishing to face Kiren, I stayed in my room, periodically checking the glasses and trying not to submit to bouts of tears and panic that threatened to overset me.

Having spent the day shut up in my room, I was unlucky to find Kiren in when I emerged that evening. Sitting at a table in the main living area with stacks of paper all around him, he had a pair of spectacles perched upon his nose and was frowning at the page in his hand. His brow lightened when he looked up. "Ah, there you are, Tesh, I feel like I haven't seen you all day."

"I feel like I can hardly see you now," I replied as lightly as I could, forcing myself back into the guise of dutiful wife. "You seem to be hidden behind stacks of paper."

"It's a new archive that's just arrived from Bakii. It's better suited to our library here, but damned if I know how to catalogue it."

He has been very busy in those archives of his and I want to know why. He has a secret correspondence with someone in Bakii and I want to know who, Sormei had said, and hating myself for it, I feigned an interested smile and asked, "Don't you have people who do that sort of work for you?"

"Yes, of course," he said. "And generally I would leave it to them, but it's a collection of letters and sketches and treatises written by Kamadan in the years he lived in Emora. Some are observations of the day, some are deep political theory, some are poetry, and some are love letters, sketches of naked women, and dirty limericks!"

I settled beside him at the table and took a piece of paper off the pile. "This one seems to be a letter to a butcher in Eley Street, thanking him for the...'juiciest haunch I've eaten in many a year.' I see what you mean." I set the page down. "Not sure why that's worth archiving, honestly."

"Because it was written by Kamadan."

"Well, then does it matter how you catalogue it?"

Kiren's expression slid into what I was coming to know as his serious face. "It does, actually, because if someone is looking for something in particular, such as"—he picked up the page he'd been scowling at—"dense papers about political theory, they want to know where to look. If I catalogue this as poetry, people won't look through it for political writings."

"Or dirty limericks."

"Or dirty limericks," he agreed with a laugh. "Truly the most important part of the whole collection. But no matter, I don't mean to bore you with the petty grievances of my work."

"It's not boring," I said, because until I could kill him I was Sormei's spy, yet I was also surprised to find I meant it. "It may mean nothing to me," I added. "But when people talk about things that interest them, it's always interesting."

Kiren tilted his head to the side, a bit of flyaway hair escaping the arms of his spectacles. "That's a nice way of looking at it. What's something you're interested in?"

"Glass."

"Glass? Do you mean like...windows or..."

"I mean just glass. It makes such interesting shapes. Something that can make a plain window, a delicately stemmed wine glass, and a sculpture that looks like fluid would be fascinating enough without the ability of scaleglass to make roads through the basin and veins upon which water condenses at night."

He took his spectacles off, holding them loosely in his hand as he stared at me. "I see what you mean. Something I don't care much about is far more interesting when someone else loves it."

My cheeks heated at the intensity of his stare and the knowledge of my treachery, and I looked away. "Glass also makes your spectacles, of course. Which I admit I didn't know you needed."

"Unfortunately, yes, although just for close reading, nothing else. Sormei says it must be because I have spent too long staring at paper instead of at the horizon, since he doesn't need them for anything."

Faced with Kiren's endless gentleness and the care he put into something as seemingly unimportant as cataloguing the archive of a long-dead, lustful poet, I couldn't but wonder again at Sormei's belief his twin was up to something.

"Why don't you just catalogue it under his name?" I said. "Surely Kamadan is well enough known for having had many interests that his name would get across how broad the archive is."

Kiren looked at me, his thoughts impossible to divine. "That's an interesting idea. We've catalogued by person before, but always using their position rather than their name. Like how the personal papers of each previous reacher is catalogued as 'reacher of Emora.'"

"That makes sense if they have a position, but I feel Kamadan defies such...narrowing of his scope."

"That is certainly true. And thank you, I will put the suggestion to the others tomorrow and see what they think." He pushed aside the stack of papers in front of him. "Enough dusty pages. Shall we dine together tonight? I thought it might be nice, just the two of us, rather than joining the family."

With my plan to poison Sormei, I had no desire to dine with him and Mama Juri and the girls, but being alone with Kiren wouldn't be much easier. When I didn't immediately answer, he took my hand and lifted it to his lips in gentle salute. "Your choice, my dear. I am happy with whatever you decide."

I opened my mouth, unsure what would come out, only for the click of an opening door to interrupt my spiralling thoughts.

"Your lordship," one of the servants said. "My lady. Lord Revennai Angue and Lord Uvao Romm are here to see you; shall I show them in or tell them you're not at home to visitors?"

"Oh."

Kiren's face froze into an expression wholly unreadable, in keeping with the shock that had sent my heart racing. Uvao was here. Since leaving Learshapa I'd thought about him far too often, memories joining me when I lay alone at night yearning for his touch. Just the knowledge he was in the same city, let alone the same building, ought to have set my heart racing, but it was fear not lust that filled me now.

"Yes," Kiren said, unfreezing at last. "Of course. Show them in. How very ungracious it would be of us not to welcome such guests."

"As you wish, my lord." The servant went back out, and a moment later, before I could prepare myself, Uvao walked in, Lord Revennai at his side. Often since reaching Emora I had wished for them both, wished for their counsel and their acceptance, but it was too late now, and they arrived like ghosts into my shattering world. Both exquisitely dressed in the latest fashion, they could have been portraits of themselves for how unreal they seemed. Rather than joy, the sight of them sparked only a repetitious mantra I wished they could hear. *It's not safe here. You can't stay. It's not safe here. You can't stay.*

"Reve." Kiren rose from his chair and strode forward, his gaze upon only Revennai until at the last moment he seemed to register Uvao's presence. "Lord Uvao. What a pleasure it is to see you. You have both arrived for the season then?"

"Lord Kiren," Revennai said, taking Kiren's hands and raising them to his lips. "And Lady Teshalii, how very glad I am to see you both well."

He came toward me as he spoke, and exactly as he had once taught me, I rose and held out my hands to go through the formalities. "Lord Revennai," I said as he took my hands to kiss, though he might have kissed air for all I felt it. "I hardly thought to see you here so soon."

I could come no closer to uttering my warning aloud, but no matter how many times I shouted the mantra in my head, neither of them heard me. Not even when Uvao took my hands and kissed them—a swift kiss all social nicety, though the way he looked up through his lashes asked questions I could not answer. Did I still love him, did I want him, had I missed him? Better that they had come days from now when my deed had been done, when I could feel again.

With the niceties over, a strained silence blossomed, seeming to fill the room with spiky thorns. Kiren glanced at Revennai and then at me, pressing out a thin smile as Lord Revennai made a poor show of interest in the papers Kiren had been looking through.

"Dirty limericks, you know," I said—anything to fill the silence. "Kamadan was an interesting man."

Lord Revennai's laugh shattered the awkward tension. "So I understand. This, however, seems to be a letter to his local butcher. About a—"

"Juicy haunch," I said at the same time he did, causing him to turn a grin my way full of warmth.

"There is rather more to the archive than dirty limericks," Kiren said stiffly. "Such is not the mark of a man."

"Perhaps not," Lord Revennai said, turning his warm smile toward Kiren. "But I recall a time when you were quite good at writing them yourself."

"Oh!" I crowed like I was a wholly different person, like I was watching someone else act my part. "How very much I would like to hear you read such glorious poetry aloud, dear husband."

They both laughed, but Kiren shook his head. "I'm afraid I haven't kept any, and my memory isn't very good."

Revennai scoffed. "No, that at least is true."

True to his mercurial temperament, Lord Revennai had swung from good humour to a bitter glance, and a stiff, poisonous silence grew once again, all thorns and broken glass. Lord Revennai had always spoken oddly of Kiren on the occasions I had managed to badger him into speaking at all, and now their forced smiles and their stiff manners had fractured, unearthing something I began to suspect was both beautiful and dangerous. Something to watch. Perhaps even something I could use.

"We were just discussing dinner," I said, looking from Lord Revennai to Uvao and back to Kiren. "Perhaps you would like to join us?"

"I'm sure Lord Revennai and Lord Uvao have other plans," Kiren said. "Having only just arrived."

"No," Uvao said with quick ease. "We have no plans yet, do we, Reve? And both of us would merely have an empty house to ourselves were we to dine at home."

"That is certainly true," Revennai said, though he had to swallow something all too like reluctance. "We would be honoured, of course. So long as that's acceptable to you, Kiren."

"Of course. Yes. Please do stay."

And so we dined and we drank. We laughed and talked and even sang a Learshapan folk tune, much to Kiren's amusement. And when, much later, it came time for our guests to depart, the lingering of Uvao's lips on my hand was a promise he would soon find a way to see me alone. I wished I could ask his advice, wished I could feel his love for me in the absence of any confidence I'd made the right choices, but though Kiren shyly invited Revennai to remain, I could not do the same.

Yet in the silence that followed their removal to Kiren's rooms—for a final nightcap, no more—I sat and rifled through my husband's papers. For a long time I found nothing that could be of any interest to Reacher Sormei, just file after file of Kamadan's writings, letters from a group of scholars in Bakii, and scrawled notes about cataloguing. I was about to give up when I found a tightly folded missive in a pile near an unlit brazier. Most of what Kiren was preparing to burn looked like tattered filing records, but what unfolded was a short letter. It wasn't addressed to anyone, but at the bottom it had been signed, *A Cat*.

He ordered the bullets, it said. *Though I think the design is stolen.*

More lies in the crier sheets too. He wants these wars. Found nothing about the monsters, but is it really a coincidence they shot down Ashadi's dragon? I have my doubts.

I read the page again, and again, trying to divine sense from all the words and gaining only an unshakable sense the *he* was Sormei. Was this what he had wanted me to find? Was it evidence of my husband's treachery? Or Sormei's? Unsure, I folded the letter back up and tucked it into my skirt, flicking my gaze about the room to be sure I was still alone.

Biiella was waiting to help me into bed, and while she undressed me and brushed out my hair, the words of the letter circled back through my mind. *More lies in the crier sheets too. He wants these wars.*

It seemed I hadn't just been wrong about Sormei, but about Kiren's devotion to him. And as I climbed into bed, more aware while my husband had company that I was wholly alone, I couldn't but wonder if anyone in Emora was who they pretended to be. It wasn't until I was at last drifting off to sleep that I realised I was no better.

I woke in the pale light of the early morning, restless and drained. In the silence of my rooms, the previous night felt like a dream, but I could remember every word of the letter as surely as I could remember the looks Kiren and Lord Revennai had shared as the dinner wore on. It was too early yet for Biiella to be waiting, and though I could have rung for her, I found I wanted no one.

Gingerly, I pulled a wrap on over my bedclothes and stepped out into the main room to see if Kiren had yet emerged, and all but ran into his twin.

"Ah, good morning, sister," Reacher Sormei said from one of the large chairs, successfully shocking wakefulness into every corner of my body.

"Oh, Lord Reacher," I said, the words little more than a ragged breath. "I'm sorry I did not realise you were here."

He waved this off with a lazy hand. "It is of no matter. I have correspondence to read while I wait."

"Would you... shall I let Kiren know you are here?"

"Oh no, that won't be necessary. I like to allow him his privacy after all. I heard that Lord Revennai came to visit last night, so perhaps it was foolish of me to arrive at so early an hour."

I ought to have been grateful he made no mention of Uvao, yet his erasure from the scene was further reminder of how alone I was. Some of that grief must have shown on my face, for Sormei hooked a finger beneath my chin. "Come now, no need to be sad. After all, we are all but supplicants outside Kiren's walls. Those he allows in are not always the most deserving, but they do make your job much more difficult. Cruel of Lord Revennai not to warn you, don't you think?"

It had been, I realised, but I wished I didn't think so, and pulled away. "I must ring for breakfast," I said. "You are, of course, welcome to stay and eat with us."

"How very generous you are, sister," he said, those bright eyes laughing at me. "It would be truly monstrous of me to reject your invitation when you have already been so cruelly abandoned."

Hating his sympathy, I excused myself, gave instructions to the servants, and returned to my rooms to dress. And there in my wardrobe I found the three glasses I had prepared and a startling realisation. Sormei was here. Right now. Without any of his guards to test his food and drink. It was either take the risk, or play his game and give up the letter, outing my husband's treachery in return for my own safety. In the end it was no choice at all.

I didn't ring for Biiella, instead choosing just to change my wrap for something larger and more respectable. Then, using the wrap to keep the glass clean, I took it from its high shelf, before hiding it behind the fall of fabric. Out in the main room, I could hear the servants arriving to set the table and knew I was running out of time, but a quick glance in the mirror reassured me the wrap looked natural and hid the glass in my hand.

Back out in the main room, Kiren had emerged, heavy-eyed. "I didn't realise you were joining us for breakfast," he was saying. "Oh, Tesha, you are looking very well this morning," he added at sight of me, his kind compliment washing over me like the lie it was.

"Thank you," I said as I held tight to the glass and waited for my chance. "Nothing is so good for one's appearance as a long sleep."

A frown flickered across his face as he searched my words for hidden meaning, but with the piles of Kamadan's archive blocking the servants from finishing the table, there was no time for him to say more.

No doubt curious what the archive contained, Sormei got up to help him remove the stacks, and I took my chance. Glass in hand, I made a show of bustling about fixing the servants' work before I set it down in the guest's place, removing the other to the tray on which it had come. With the task done, I drew a deep breath to settle my racing heart, but I could hardly breathe when at last Sormei sat before the altered glass. There was no wine, but according to the notes on the box base, fizzy water ought to exude the poison almost as well as alcohol—assuming it worked this way at all.

"So, did you visit this early for a reason?" Kiren said, serving himself an enormous plateful of breakfast.

"It is not so very early," Sormei murmured, flicking an amused glance my way. "But yes, I did come for a reason. I've had news from the Shield. It isn't yet known beyond these walls, but I wanted to warn you since it will be all anyone is talking about by tonight."

On that alarming remark, he served himself a few pieces of fruit and picked up the glass. At any moment he would drink from it, though that wasn't what held Kiren frozen. "The Shield?" he said, the words constricted. "What news?"

A simple question, yet it seemed to suck all the air from the room. "The Shield has been breached," Sormei said as though it was nothing, before he drank a mouthful from the glass.

"Breached?" Kiren repeated, the sense he was deliberately holding words behind gritted teeth making it even harder to breathe. I needed Sormei to drink more, the efficacy of the dose given this way entirely untested, but having read that letter I also needed him to explain. And fast.

"Yes. The monsters have already reached Orsu."

The table shook as Kiren got to his feet, looming over his forgotten meal. "What have you done?"

Sormei chuckled and downed the last of his drink—the last of his possibly poison-infused water. "I have done what I needed to do, like always, because no one else will. Especially not you. And now"—he too got to his feet, but slowly, meeting Kiren's glare across the table—"because I set it in motion I am the only one who can fix it. The only one who can unite the basin, who can make us strong, who can ensure we never again have to run. This land is ours. What's left of the scale is ours. I will—"

He swayed abruptly, catching himself on the laden table and sending glasses tumbling.

"Sormei!"

Fury banished, Kiren lunged to catch him as he staggered, only for Sormei to fall full weight against him and send them both crashing back onto the table. The soft wood cracked and dishes smashed, food flung far amid the cries of horrified servants. Frozen in place, I could only stare as shattered ceramic gathered in my skirts, as heedless of the cuts on his own face, Kiren shook his twitching twin, shouting for help. Somehow I heard it all yet there was no sound, everything heavy like we were facing down a brightstorm, its static dancing down my spine. Monsters had breached the Shield. The Celes Basin was under attack. And I'd just poisoned the only man who knew what was really going on. The only man who could lead us through the chaos.

20

Ashadi

Morning Bulletin

To all criers for announcement throughout Lower Emora

Enemies closing in as yesterday's breach of the Shield worsens. The citadel's dragon riders fight to contain the threat north of Orsu, but there are reports of destruction as far south as the Grulinasque estate.

More losses reported on the eastern border as Therinfrou Mine falls to Lummazzt forces. Further attacks expected in the coming days.

"You are the difference between our survival and our destruction." Reacher Sormei calls for all Celessi citizens to unite to defeat the current threats. Anyone who wants to fight to defend their homeland and their families should contact [local officer] at [local governing office].

349:63

Our journey back to Emora seemed to take forever and yet be over in a heartbeat, so entirely did I spend those days living in my own head. I had a whole new history to fit into the space lies had filled, and Mana may as well not have existed for all he spoke. We must have appeared utterly unapproachable too, for even other travellers had avoided us, leaving total silence where conversation and connection had once been. By the second evening, we'd already smoked through my stash of korsh, and I had determined to never again travel with less than twice the amount I thought I would need.

The relief I felt when Emora emerged from the dusty horizon owned a breathless quality, built on the knowledge that now there really was no going back, that it was time to do what I'd spent days only thinking of.

Returning to the upper city was too dangerous now, so as we dismounted our hired mules and entered the noise and chaos and stink of lower Emora, we sought the first inn we could find with a vacant room.

"...as the Grulinasque estate," a crier shouted by the lower gate as we hunted an inn sign. "More losses reported on the eastern border as Therinfrou Mine..."

The first inn had no spare rooms. Neither did the second. To find a third we had to cross the bustling square once again, dragging exhausted legs as we brushed past beggars and traders and even more mules, hardly able to hear ourselves think for all the shouting and movement. The crier was struggling, his voice hoarse as he shouted to all who were close enough to catch snippets of his news, "...homeland and their families should contact Governor Heign at the Lower South House."

Unable to follow his words, I snatched up a crier sheet from a pile beside his plinth and hurried on after Mana. It wasn't until the fourth inn that we were in luck. It was a slightly more expensive establishment, yet the landlord was nevertheless a grumpy arsehole who barked a room number at us and left us to find it on our own. Everyone seemed too busy, the whole city on edge, a feeling that was fast seeping into my bones. I swallowed my only tenacious desire—to ask where the closest baths were—and followed Mana up the stairs.

"It shouldn't take too long to buy the ingredients I need," Mana said, the exhaustion in his tone mirroring my own. "You should be able to speak to Shuala within a couple of hours. After that I think you have a lot of decisions to make."

The sense of urgency we'd lost in having to make the return journey sped upon his words, so much suddenly riding on so little. Barely had Mana dropped his dusty saddlebags than he was gone again, pausing only to accept the purse I thrust into his hand.

Alone, I paced. There seemed little else to do, our arrival having sped the world to a pace that scoffed at simple things like washing and finding clean clothes. So much had changed between leaving Emora and returning that I no longer understood what a dragon rider was meant to be or what I ought to do—the intersection at which I stood owning so many paths, some yet invisible to me. Somewhere along the way I'd lost even the comfort of being sure of Mana.

Child of the Dragon.

Honoured One.

The desperation in those gazes and those whispered voices haunted me. Even when I closed my eyes, I could still see the hands reaching out and the bodies closing in. The air vanishing. Despite the Apaian insistence on consent and respect, every one of those people had been so desperate to talk to him, to touch him, to take some part of him for themselves, that they hadn't seen him as a person. But why? Mana still hadn't explained, and it felt wrong to do as they had done and make demands upon him, yet the question gnawed at me as painfully as the fractured crossroads at which I stood.

After pacing, I tried sitting. Tried staring out the small window. Tried finding some clothes in my pack that passed for clean and failed. And eventually, I uncrumpled the crier sheet I had picked up in passing and began to read. And then ceased moving altogether.

It could have been minutes or hours before Mana returned with a waxed-paper parcel tucked under his arm. He looked dead, but I must have looked worse for he froze on the threshold. "What happened?"

His words shook life back into me, enough at least to look again at the page in my hand. To lick dry lips. "'Enemies closing in as yesterday's breach of the Shield worsens,'" I said, voice hoarse. "'The citadel's dragon riders fight to contain the threat north of Orsu, but there are reports of destruction as far south as the Grulinasque estate.'"

My voice faltered before the end, the last words coming out on a half-whisper. Somehow saying it aloud made it worse, made it real, and the tense, bustling city beyond the inn's walls made sense. As did the lack of vacancies at most of the inns.

"Shit," Mana hissed, setting the waxed-paper bundle on the table. "Does it say what happened? How it happened?"

I shook my head. "No details. But it was only a matter of time before we were overwhelmed. Before we couldn't keep up that many callouts." I squeezed my eyes shut. "I should have gone to that meeting with Sormei, should have demanded answers then and there instead of traipsing out into the basin. I might have been able to do something about this, I could—"

Mana gripped my shoulders and shook me harder than he ever had before. "No," he said, the word as fierce as his scowl. "You know there wasn't time for anything you did or didn't do to have an effect. You could have gone to that meeting, and even if the reacher had miraculously had a change of heart and told you everything, what difference would it have made? Even if he'd sent more money, or more riders or dragons or stable hands, they would have gotten there too late. And no, before you blame yourself for not being there, they sent us away! And one rider could never have made a difference, even if Shuala had been strong enough to fly."

"Shuala," I breathed, a new fear creeping upon me. "Do you think...?"

"We'll find out. I have everything; I just need time to prepare it."

The table was soon covered in paper-wrapped ingredients, a small set of measuring scales, a variety of spoons, a scaleglass bowl, and a pair of drinking glasses empty yet ominous. While he started working, I paced. While he scribbled notes for himself, I paced. While he measured everything once, twice, even three times to be sure he got it right, I paced. For three years he'd been my watcher, and yet not until that moment had I seen—truly seen—how much care he put into his work. Into me. And still I paced.

"How is it going?" I asked after a time, unable to hold in the question any longer.

"Fine," he said, not looking up from his task. "It's just a bit finicky. At the citadel one watcher measures, another checks it over, and a third brews, and we can all watch each other to be sure there are no errors."

"I can watch you if it would make you feel better. Although possibly I would feel worse, you know; actually seeing what goes into the damn thing might make it even harder to drink. Did I ever tell you that when we first started at the citadel, I thought the iishor was made from dragon blood?"

"I imagine a lot of people do," he murmured, tipping some silvery powder onto the measuring scales.

"It just tastes so tinny and looks foul," I went on, the need to talk momentarily overtaking the need to pace. "I thought I would be sick the first time I drank it. Actually, I still think that every time I drink it. Remember that time Luce—"

"Ash."

"Yes?"

Mana tilted his head to the side. "Do you want me to make this properly, or accidentally poison you?"

"Right. Yes. Shutting up."

I went back to pacing.

An hour later, as the sun was beginning to set and the main room of the inn below us came to life with chatter, Mana sat back, satisfied.

"Is it ready?" I asked, my stomach already churning at the knowledge of iishor to come.

"Not quite. It has to sit and stew for at least half an hour, or the effect isn't strong enough."

"Half an hour?" It wasn't, objectively, a long time. And yet it was also, actually, an eternity.

Mana pressed a wry smile between his lips. "I'm sorry, but we have to do this right the first time as we may not easily get a second."

"I know, I just…" I heaved a sigh. "Excuse me while I pace for the next half an hour. You may want to find somewhere quieter to sit."

"I have a better idea." He drew a fresh korsh parcel from the remains of his bundle and held it out to me. "Why don't you roll us each a smoke while I tell you a story."

The knot of anguish in my gut loosened a little at the sight of korsh, but I lifted a brow at him. "A story? What kind of story?"

"The Apaian kind. Assuming you want to hear it."

An Apaian story, I now knew, held elements of truth within its tapestry, and was not granted to just anyone. Especially not an Emoran.

I nodded, unsure I possessed the right words to express the breathless cocktail of gratitude and confusion his question provoked. But I could have rolled korsh with my eyes closed, and so sat on the end of the bed and let my fingers work while he cleared away the leftover ingredients like someone packing away one thought before beginning another.

"This story is mine to tell," he said at last, glancing briefly at me only to stare at his hands instead. "Although in a way it has become everyone's to tell. You asked why they called me Dragonborn, or Honoured Dragon. Well, our word *dragon* doesn't mean the same as your word *dragon*. After hearing Elder Erebei's story of where your dragons come from, you probably could have guessed that."

While he spoke, I handed over a lit korsh roll. His first inhale was deep and full, and he held the smoke in as long as he could before letting it go with a rush.

"Long ago, when the basin was all Apaian land," he went on amid the dissipating cloud of faintly blue smoke, "we lived in clusters, like our communes now but more... connected. Like a family, you might say, though larger, and they didn't work the way your families do. But one's cluster was the most important thing, because out there the conditions aren't exactly hospitable. Especially before the drilling and blasting for water, there were only the natural aquifers. So I guess you could say that if your cluster was everything, then anything beyond your cluster was nothing. Was the enemy." He grimaced and breathed in another lungful of korsh. "There was no such thing as *Apaian* then. I suppose you could say there's still no such thing as an Apaian now. We are Vimi or Luunsii or Jaarkeel or Liina"—at this last he gestured to the markings on his own cheek—"which is perhaps why you Emorans found it easy to colonise the basin at first. We weren't exactly united."

Mana waved a hand, seeming to dissipate all he had already said along with the smoke. "That's not important, really; what's important for this story is the part of Elder Erebei's story I already knew. That there used to be big herds of animals that roamed the basin, which we hunted for food, bred for fur, and used for transport. They were called dragons. That's what Erebei meant when she said that some Apaian clusters bred dragons from dragons. Your dragons from our dragons."

"And now yours don't exist anymore?"

He shook his head. "Not that I've ever heard. I've certainly never seen one. They were all killed in the wars, whether by the Emorans or the Apaians, or both; the basin is now empty."

"Seems strange that a space that once maintained life now doesn't," I said as he paused to stub out the end of his korsh roll. "You'd think something else would move in."

"Something did." Mana's raised brows mocked. "Us. We took over. Filled the space."

It was a depressing thought, but not one I could refute.

"That isn't important though," he went on. "What's important is that there were once herds of animals in the basin, and Apaians of all kinds built their lives around hunting, travelling, and fighting one another. You might have noticed," he added, holding out a hand for another korsh roll, "that none of those things happen anymore, do they?"

"No?" I had the uncomfortable feeling that my initial reaction— that the lack of attacking and hunting was a good thing—was wrong.

"No," he agreed. "The Emoran conquest changed everything, and it doesn't matter whether that change was good or bad, only that it all changed. We don't hunt dragons anymore. Wild dragons don't even exist. And Apaians are Apaians now, more often than we are Vimi or Luunsii or Jaarkeel or Liina. Imagine, if suddenly there was no Emoran political game, if the estates no longer mattered and you had no duty and no family, how would you know how to live a good life? If you took away everything that structures Emoran society, what would you do?"

I stared at him, realisation seeping into me upon cold fingers. His words were just words, but his meaning haunted. Every possibility I came upon for what I would do was rooted in the present, in the way Emoran society functioned. Without it, who would I even be?

"Now imagine this problem isn't just your problem," he went on. "Imagine it becomes your children's problem. Then their children's problem. And their children's problem, until you have a collection of people who know who they are but not how to be who they are, and then you'll be ready to hear this story."

Holding his second korsh roll between his lips, Mana took a moment to stir the contents of the scaleglass bowl, its soupy texture beginning to take on the lumpiness I knew from experience. He seemed satisfied and sat back again, staring at me now rather than his hands. "Emorans see the future in stars, but Apaians see the future in dreams and trances, in flickering flames and moments of madness. The mind acting...beyond normal, you might say, is what connects us to the world. You think the world is already written and has to be maintained through chanting; we think the world has already been written but only because every moment exists at the same moment. Right now is also yesterday and last year and five seasons from now; we're just passing through it in a linear fashion."

He waved away my look of confusion. "Don't worry about that. What's important is that dreams and trances allow glimpses of the future, and some years ago there was a boy who had a dream as part of his initiation rites. In that dream, the boy walked. He walked and walked and walked like there was no end to the world, and as he walked the world changed around him from dry gravel to lush grass to shadowy caves and on, until at last he could walk no longer. Broken, his legs gave out beneath him and he collapsed beside a wingless, scaleless dragon that had been licking its skin as though covered in wounds. After that, the beast licked the man's wounds and he found life again, and was able to stand, to live, to continue his journey, riding upon the dragon's back."

"And that boy is you," I said, realising as I asked that it wasn't really a question.

"It was, yes." His nod was slow. Contemplative. "The elders said it meant that I would one day bring back the dragons—not literally, I should think, but that somehow I would one day renew what was lost, would find a way to be truly Apaian again. And so I became a symbol of both everything we had lost and everything we wanted to regain, but I was only ten and didn't really understand what it meant. Didn't understand how big it was. But my mother did, and so we left the commune before the year was out. Naili was only six and hardly remembers the fighting."

"Your mother didn't want you to be a hero to your people? My father probably couldn't think of anything better."

His huffed laugh held no humour. "Perhaps she wouldn't have minded had she believed it possible, but my mother didn't want them to use me, to consume my future, out of a need for them to find their past. A past that is never coming back."

"And what do you think?"

Mana shrugged and, having stubbed out his second korsh roll, poked the iishor again. "I think this is almost ready for you to drink."

"Really? That's your answer?"

"That's my answer, because I don't have a better one. You aren't the only one who has made an art out of running away from their problems."

For a moment his gaze was intent, heavy with meaning, before he took up the bowl and carefully poured half its contents into each glass. "The recipe makes four doses, but I've halved it. Two doses allows us to have another on hand just in case, though I don't think it keeps well. Here," he said, pushing a glass across the table. "I don't know for sure it'll work the same. I've done the best I could, but some of the ingredients might be fresher or staler than what we normally get, so, well..." He trailed off, the pair of us staring at the dark liquid in the glass—a liquid I had never wanted to drink, yet here we were yet again. Mana looked around the poorly furnished room. "Where do you want to do it?"

"I don't know, I guess I'll...sit on the bed?"

"Lying down for this would certainly be an improvement."

My laugh wholly lacked humour. "Already prone rather than you having to catch me as I fall."

"Certainly less likely to hit your head."

"Have you ever let me do that?"

"We're stalling."

"Yes we are."

I picked up the iishor. "I hate what this stuff does to me," I said, and realised it was the first time I'd ever said so aloud. "And what you have to do because of it."

"It's not so bad for me." He pressed out a thin smile. "All I do is look after you, and that's always been more than fine with me."

For a moment we were back on that bed on the *Evening Star*, and I wanted to kiss him again more than I'd wanted anything else for a long time, but the iishor was the least of what stood between us now.

Tightening my grip on the glass, I said, "I refuse to be emotional in slow motion, so maybe say that again when I come down from this trash."

"I'll be right here for you," he said, squeezing my free hand as I lifted the glass to my lips, the iishor scent all deceptive sweetness. Yet the moment it touched my tongue it was bitter, tinny and slightly congealed like old blood. I swallowed it down in one go because to draw it out was torture, and habit kicking in, I let the glass drop from my hand. It hit the floor, cracking into a dozen large pieces. Not the satisfying shatter I was used to on stone, yet it seemed right for this moment in which everything was slightly wrong.

Normally while the iishor took effect I would be shouldering rifles and beginning the walk to the undercroft, but with no rifles and no undercroft, I sat gingerly on the edge of the bed, half expecting it to collapse beneath me. Like water spreading paint, colours slowly started to shift. The noise from downstairs sped into a collection of strange voices and sounds that seemed to warble against my ears like hummingbirds.

"Ash?" Mana bent his head to look me in the eye. "Is everything all right? If you're not feeling good, you have to tell me. I could have messed up the—"

I waved a hand like I could swat away his speeding fears, each word lifting in pitch. "I'm fine," I said, everything taking on the thick slowness like I stood in the centre of a brightstorm. I closed my eyes. "Shuala?"

Something scratched at the edge of my mind, a crackle like all sound was going out of focus.

"Shuala? Shu, can you hear me?" Again the scratch and crackle like if I turned my head the right way I might find her voice. The urge to shout was almost overwhelming. "Shu, please!"

I opened my eyes. Mana had retreated to the table and sat watching me, gaze steady, chin on his hand. He was all the wrong colour, bright red with the heat of life caught in a fading room. On the table sat the second dose of iishor, one step all it took to reach it. Mana's outcry was shrill, blending into the inn's noise, but before he could stop me, I poured the second glass down my throat. I didn't even hear the glass hit the floor.

With eyes closed again, the darkness was full of colour. The noise around me ceased being discrete sounds, instead melting together into a wad of stretchy mud that pulled thin or bunched with every rise and fall. The room disappeared. Or I did. It was hard to tell.

"Shuala?"

Ashadi Romm? came her rasping voice from the void around me. *What are you doing?*

"I need to talk to you, Shu. But first, are you all right?"

Her rasp became a rumble of dry amusement. *Trust you to run far away when there is a fight. Running away for good, I hear.*

"Shu, are you all right?"

Glorious. Better now you aren't here.

"That's my Shuala. I hope you're safe and that you can keep being safe."

No rider, no flying. I admit I'm glad you aren't here, Ashadi Romm; there is no rest here anymore. Callout. Callout. Callout. By the hour they lose more ground.

"How?"

Because there are more of them. There have always been more of them.

"The failures."

Silence. It ate at me, shredding my confidence with the fear she'd gone or would not speak to me, that her disdain had hardened into true dislike and now I'd overstepped a boundary I hadn't even known existed and—

How do you know? she asked at last, voice echoing about me.

"Doesn't matter how I know. It's true, isn't it? That you were...made. You were all made. By the Apaians who fought back. Who needed stronger weapons. The ones now out in The Sands."

It does matter. It matters because you aren't allowed to know. Because the last rider who found out the truth lost his life. Because that cannot happen again. We are caught together, you and I, trapped in a cycle of our ancestors' making that cannot be broken without destroying us all.

Word by word her voice grew louder and the sparkling colours drained from around me, leaving only darkness. Darkness that wobbled like I was peering through water. Muffled sounds. Men stared through cracks in glass, talking, talking, always talking. Gloves on their hands as thick as hide. A nod. A number. They moved on. In a sleepy stupor every part of me was examined. Skin, eyes, jaw, wings, down my throat to the flames that boiled.

Everywhere mewling and roaring, and always the talking, talking, talking. These creatures never shut up, never stayed still, never made any sense. Pain followed. Pain and pressure. Slicing my skin with blades of glass and pushing still more glass into the wounds again and again, over and over with the pain, always pushing, always deeper, each pretty tinkle as the scales tapped together a reminder that they were there, embedded in my flesh. I woke from that sleep with a roar that covered the stones in flame, each and every cut upon my skin oozing as it healed, drawing the glass into my body.

That roar of agony and hate boiled up my throat and I raged into the darkness, alone and yet not, for her mind still felt close. With the last of my breath no longer able to sustain it, my roar faded and died to fierce, sharp breaths. Disembodied, I yet breathed and crushed my hands to fists. "You're...you're all made like that?"

We are. At least, those of us who are not broken. Who do not go mad. Who are not discarded to The Sands. But you cannot know, Ashadi Romm. They will not let you know.

"They? Who are they?"

Your people. Your friends. Your family. Your everything. You cannot know. Forget you know and stay far away, Ashadi Romm; let us fall to our brethren. Let it end and walk away.

No doubt it was wise advice, but I was fast realising that *wise* had never been my forte. My father had been right about that if nothing else. Too reckless. Too emotional. My best skills for manipulating society coming from my worst traits. But perhaps I could use them for something better. What, though, I didn't yet know.

"Let them try to silence me."

Ashadi.

"Shu, I'm not going anywhere. But you could come to me."

And why would I do that?

Because one man's words hadn't stopped haunting me. Because a stranger in The Sands had shot us down, drawn off his glove, and laid his hand upon her. *I'm sorry for everything that has been done to you*, he had said. *May you one day find the grace to forgive us, and we the courage to forgive ourselves.*

"Because this needs to end. It's time we met your makers, Shu. I want to take you home."

The story continues in...

AGAINST THE HUNGER OF TYRANTS

Book TWO of
the Shattered Kingdom

Acknowledgements

I must admit that I made the grave error of starting my acknowledgements in a separate document right back at the beginning of the drafting process, thinking this would make it easier to keep track of people I needed to thank as I went. It might have, had I not lost said document. Thus I start from scratch, here at the turning in of final edits, and must pre-emptively beg the forgiveness of everyone I will inevitably forget.

Many thanks to editor new, Angelica Chong, and editor old, Nivia Evans, for their help in guiding this book toward the best version of itself. Thanks always to Julie Crisp, my ever-patient agent, who has to put up with my most dramatic self whenever things go wrong, and to the whole team at Orbit for bringing my books to life.

In many ways, this book was a very solitary labour of love, but I owe a great debt to my many friends in the bunker (you know who you are) for the endless encouragement to write what I wanted to write, and to keep going when it all felt hopeless. Especially given the year I worked on this book was a cursed year in almost every way, and I'm very glad to be leaving it behind. Immense thanks are also due to my husband, Chris, for putting up with my shit, talking through book problems, and hastily reading the whole thing in a few days when panic that I'd written the most terrible book ever overtook me. Also to Belle and Amanda for their gentle variants of pat-pat there-there and sorrows, sorrows, prayers that were required to keep me sane while editing. And Sara, my endless font of joy, best friend I've never met, for always being there for me even when I'm a sad lump of sadness.

And a final and very great thanks to Anne for answering my weird physics questions on Twitter some years ago now, which led to even cooler ideas and a greater understanding of sound waves, colour, and perception. If you thought it was cool that Ashadi's perception of sound and colour change when he drinks iishor, you too should thank Anne.

extras

orbit

meet the author

Leah Ladson

DEVIN MADSON is an Aurealis Award–winning fantasy author from Australia. After some sucky teenage years, she gave up reality and is now a dual-wielding rogue who works through every tiny side-quest and always ends up too over-powered for the final boss. Anything but Zen, Devin subsists on tea and chocolate and so much fried zucchini she ought to have turned into one by now. Her fantasy novels come in all shades of grey and are populated with characters of questionable morals and a liking for witty banter.

Find out more about Devin Madson and other Orbit authors by registering for the free monthly newsletter at orbitbooks.net.

if you enjoyed
BETWEEN DRAGONS AND THEIR WRATH

look out for

THE SCARLET THRONE
False Goddess Trilogy: Book One

by

Amy Leow

Binsa is a "living goddess," chosen by the gods to dispense both mercy and punishment from her place on the Scarlet Throne. But her reign hides a deadly secret. Rather than channeling the wisdom of an immortal deity, she harbors a demon.

But one cannot remain a living goddess forever. When her temple's priests decide that Binsa's time in power has come to an end, a new girl, Medha, is selected to take over her position as goddess. But

Binsa refuses to be discarded into a life of uncertainty as a young woman, and she strikes a deal with her demon: She will sacrifice her people's lives in order to magnify his power, and in return, he will help her seize control from the priests once and for all.

But how much of her humanity is she willing to trade for the sake of ambition? Deals with demons are rarely so simple.

1

The False Devotee

A woman had been crushed by a goat that fell from the sky.

Her husband, Uruvin Vashmaralim, humble spice merchant, now kneels before me, haggard bags underlining his eyes and tear stains slashing down his cheeks. He laments the loss of his wife and the suspicious circumstances hanging over her death. She was a pious woman, he claims, who always set the mangoes and wine before the family shrine and prayed to them three times a day. One day, however, a terrible illness befell her. She didn't place her offerings before the family shrine. She died the next week, not from illness, but from a goat falling on her while she was drawing water from the well.

Lies, a childlike voice hisses in my head.

The man bursts into sobs at the end of his tale. I observe him with my back straight and hands folded demurely on my lap. My lips are pressed into a thin line, but my brows are soft and relaxed. My brother has told me that this is my best regal pose, assuring everyone that the spirit of the goddess Rashmatun lives in me, with every muscle, every limb perfectly poised.

Even if Rashmatun never possessed me. Even if Rashmatun doesn't exist.

"My goddess!" the man wails. "Please, have mercy. I know not what my wife has done wrong, save for the one day she forgot to placate our ancestors' spirits. Her death has grieved me so. Rashmatun, what can I do to rectify the calamity that has fallen upon me?"

I stay silent, contemplating the situation. A goat dropped on an unsuspecting woman. It would have sounded ridiculous if not for Uruvin's solemnity as he delivered the tale. In fact, I am still in disbelief, even though I allow him to continue wailing.

Meanwhile, Ilam, the demon inside me, trails slow, taunting circles in my mind. His presence is as unnerving as a monster lying beneath still waters.

"Uruvin, how long has it been since your wife's demise?" I say, my reedy voice amplified with deeper, overlapping echoes. The acoustics of the concave niche carved into the wall behind my throne creates an incandescent quality to my tone. My brother did it himself, claiming that the sculpture of Anas, the ten-headed snake god, would protect the living goddess from any harm. What the temple dwellers do not know about is the hollow that lies beyond the niche, large enough for a grown man to squeeze into and eavesdrop on my daily audiences.

"Two weeks already, Your Grace," Uruvin replies. He wipes a tear away from the corner of his eye. "I miss her terribly."

Two weeks. Snivelling Sartas. They'd have cremated the body by now. "Pray tell," I resume smoothly, "was she a good woman?"

"Why, of course, Rashmatun! She was everything a man could ask for." He waves his arms in a vigorous manner, as if it can convince me of his sincerity. "A wonderful cook, a meticulous cleaner, a patient listener. Oh, my dear Dirka!"

He falls into another round of incoherent sobbing, forehead planted onto the fiery red carpet beneath him.

I narrow my eyes at Uruvin, studying him intently. The hems of his suruwal are suspiciously clean, neither a trace of ash nor dust on them. He probably never visited his wife's remains after the funeral. The Holy Mound is where we keep the ashes of our dead, open to the public and frequently flooded with visitors. If he were truly mourning her, he'd have spent plenty of time there.

Or perhaps he is so overwhelmed with grief that he cannot bear to step into the Mound.

Lies, lies, lies, Ilam chants with sadistic glee.

Where is the lie? I ask.

Open your eyes, girl. Open your eyes and see.

I draw in a breath, and Ilam gets to work. He worms his way to the front of my mind, shoving me aside and suffocating my thoughts. After nearly ten years of communing with a demon, you'd think I'd have become accustomed to the constant crawling up my spine.

But I endure it to have this power.

The demon burrows straight into Uruvin's mind; the man himself is unaware of the intrusion. A rush of resounding *truths* pours into me, and a brief flash of pain splits my skull before fading into a dull pulse. My senses sharpen, so sensitive that I can hear Uruvin's erratic heartbeat and catch the faint scent of perfume on his smooth, creaseless clothes. Ilam's magic amplifies the truths such details carry. Each of them pierces through my mind like a fire-tipped arrow streaking across a moonless night.

Throughout this, I maintain my tall, unflappable posture.

Then Ilam is done. He slowly retreats, and the world fades into its usual palette, the saturation of sounds and scents ebbing into the background. I inhale deeply. Using blood magic always leaves me with a discomfort that carves deep into my bones. After all these years, I still cannot tell if it's an inherent side effect of blood magic, or if it's my own revulsion towards the practice.

Meanwhile, Uruvin is still choking on melodramatic sobs.

I wait for him to swallow his tears. Now I see where the lie reveals itself. If not for Ilam, I would not have caught the subtle yet alluring fragrance of frangipanis on him, commonly used as a perfume by Aritsyan women to usher good luck in love and life. I would not have seen the shrewd gleam in his eyes.

The part about the falling goat must be true—as absurd as it is—since Ilam did not say it was a lie. A mystery to be dealt with later. But Uruvin is no honest, grieving husband.

He hopes to earn some sort of compensation for his unprecedented losses. Just like many of the insufferable fools who walk in here. Some devotees are genuine, but plenty are out to take a bite out of the goddess Rashmatun's bursting coffers.

Fortunately, I'm not as gullible as these people would like me to be.

"You live by the banks of the Nurleni, Uruvin?" I ask after the man wrests his sobs under control.

"Yes, my goddess. I'm sure that the chief priest would have told you all you needed to know." He sniffs loudly. Perhaps he's wondering why the great Rashmatun is asking such menial questions.

"Is it Harun who will relieve you of your plight?" I say, allowing an edge of irritation to coat my tone. "No. It is I. So answer my questions without hesitation nor falsehood."

Uruvin's fingers drum against his thigh. "Yes, Your Grace. My humblest apologies, Rashmatun."

"Excellent." I tilt my head. "Is your business doing well, Uruvin?"

"Why, of course! The demand for spices is always there, no matter how poor the economy. And the river always brings good business." His fingers continue to *tap, tap, tap*.

Interesting. It hasn't been raining for the past few months; the waters of the river have receded so much that large boats can barely sail down without their bottoms scraping against rocks. Does the merchant think that I am ignorant to the workings of the world at large because I don't step foot outside temple grounds?

I stay silent for a while, tempering my anger.

"Do you think me a fool, my child?" I finally say, voice dangerously soft.

His eyes spark with alarm. "Your Grace?"

"I have given you a chance to speak the truth, and yet you have lied to me." I lean forward ever so slightly, careful to not let the weight of my headdress topple me forward. My shadow, cast by the braziers above my head and distorted by Anas's ten snake heads, stretches towards Uruvin. "You call yourself a follower of Rashmatun, yet you dare to let falsehoods fall from your tongue in my presence? Why must you use your wife, even in her death, to compensate for your failing business?"

Ilam cackles in delight. He loves it when I truly *become* a goddess, when none can defy me and all must bow to me.

Even I have to admit I enjoy the feeling.

The rhythm the merchant taps out grows even more erratic. "Your Grace. I assure you that I have been speaking nothing but the truth. My wife—"

"Is dead. That much is certain." I pitch my voice low; the echoes induce trembles in the man's limbs. "But for all her wifely qualities, you never did love her, did you?"

Uruvin's lips part dumbly. "I—I—Rashmatun, no," he stammers. "I loved her, with all my heart!"

"You are lying *again*." I slowly adjust my arm so that my elbow is propped atop the armrest encrusted with yellow sapphires, my temple resting against my fingers. "If you did love your wife so, why have you found yourself another lover already?"

I cannot widen in shock and guilt; his expression is stripped see all. It was foolish of me to even think of deceiving to a panicked bow. "Oh, Rashmatun!" he cries. you. Please, my goddess, I beg for your forgiveness! Please grant your servant mercy!"

I close my eyes, exasperated. Sweat trickles down my neck; the back of my jama is uncomfortably soaked. I am eager to peel off the four gold chains weighing down my neck, and my rump is sore from sitting the entire morning. I've given this man more than enough time to redeem himself.

"For your transgressions, you shall be prohibited from entering the temple for the next five years," I declare, opening my eyes languidly. "And you will pay a twenty percent increment of yearly taxes, since according to you, your business is bustling. My priests will ensure that the necessary paperwork is filled out."

His face takes on a sickly pallor. "My Rashmatun has been merciful," he murmurs.

"Get out," I say, quiet.

Uruvin ducks his head and rises to his feet. He scuttles backwards until he is out of the worship hall. Ilam's amused laughter continues ringing somewhere at the back of my mind.

With a tired sigh, I sink into my throne, "Harun." A portly man whose eyes resemble a bulging frog's steps into my direct line of sight. I've grown somewhat accustomed to the chief priest's permanent expression of gross surprise. "Anyone else?"

"No, my goddess," Harun replies. He adjusts the orange sash thrown over his left shoulder. "That was the last worshipper for today."

"The land is in a dire state now, Rashmatun. *Which* the port a sizeable portion of our grain store_ *the armies' sup-* ply centres before the drought hit us." He sta_ *dio* his frog eyes. "Your people are growing despera_, *supies_* flooding your temples, and more still wish to have *be with* with you."

"I see."

Clever, clever goddess, Ilam laughs. *How your people love you* ...

I try not to bristle in reflex. No use getting furious at a demon you cannot control.

Harun clutches onto the length of prayer beads around his neck; his eyes slide towards the priests lining up behind him, their mouths shut in an eerie, complete silence. "My goddess, perhaps if you actually do something about the drought—"

"The Forebears bide their time, Harun," I say, waving a dismissive hand. "Is Hyrlvat thriving? Are the cornfields of Vintya lush and abundant? The gods are staying our hands for reasons that will be clear in a time to come."

Harun presses his lips into a thin line. I've been using that same vague reason for the past two months now. Even as most of our supplies are being given to the Aritsyan army, who have *been battling* the Dennarese Empire for *decades,* leaving precious little in our silos. Even as our crops wither and the prospects of a hungry winter grow exponentially with every passing day.

Do I have a choice? No. The only reason why the people of the city of Bakhtin have not rioted against me is because the rest of the country is suffering as well. Anyway, this is not the first time such a drought has occurred, and certainly not the first time Bakhtin's goddess stayed her hand from bringing food to her people.

The chief priest still doesn't look convinced, though.

"Why do you not use your own magic to enchant the clouds, then?" I suggest scathingly. "If you're so worried about the drought?"

"My goddess, you know that our power has greatly weakened over the years. Besides, we can only cast enchantments—"

"When I'm around. Yes, I am well aware," I cut him off. *Excuses*, I think, but don't say out loud. The priests have no problem coaxing trees to bear fruit and casting needles to mend their elaborate garments when they think I'm out of sight. Minor spells, but ones that speak volumes about the temple's priorities. "Enough," I continue, vexation growing in me the longer this topic drags out. "I will only admit twelve devotees per day. At most. Am I clear?"

He dips his head in deference. "Yes, Your Grace."

"Good. And see to it that the necessary compensations and punishments are dispensed."

"Of course, Your Grace."

I dip my head. "Till tomorrow, Harun."

"Till tomorrow."

I stand up and step off the elevated dais. My bare foot touches the carpeted floor. Immediately my posture is not as straight, my head not held as high. I let my knees buckle, as if they were not accustomed to the weight of the ornaments I wear. Harun reaches forward to steady me, a fatherly smile on his face.

In a split second, I am no longer Rashmatun. I am Binsa, vessel of the goddess of wisdom, an ordinary girl whose life was touched by the extraordinary.

"What did she do today?" I ask Harun. My routine question after I've broken out of my "trance."

"Many things. Many great things." His routine answer.

"Will she bring rain soon?"

"She..." His grip on my shoulders tightens ever so slightly. He shakes his head and presses a hand against my back, guiding me out of the Paruvatar, the worship hall. "Come, child. You should rest."

I follow his lead without another word. We exit into a courtyard shadowed by long, straggling branches and lush emerald leaves. The rhododendron bushes planted all around the space are at full bloom, the vibrant red of the flowers resembling cloaks woven out of fresh blood. The sun overhead blazes bright, yet its full heat is lost on me with the mountain winds cocooning the temple, which lies high atop blustering cliffs. All enchantments by the hands of the priests; while the rest of the city withers, the sanctity of the temple must be maintained, which includes tending to its environment.

Harun claps his hands. Muscular palanquin bearers materialize before us. I step into the litter; the chief priest walks alongside.

The palanquin sways with a rhythmic lull as the bearers walk in perfect synchrony, marching through the various temples in Ghanatukh's complex at a languorous pace. They let me down before a two-tiered building, its red walls basking in the glow of the sun. I enter the Bakhal, the goddess's place of residence. A tall, imposing woman appears from behind one of the pillars, her generous girth clad in white. Jirtash claps her palms together and bows her head. Harun nods, leaving me to her care.

We wind our way through the sprawling maze of the pillars and shrines in the Bakhal's lowest floor, the scent of sandalwood drifting lazily through the air. We cut through another courtyard—a dry fountain in the middle, a luxury the priests didn't bother with—before arriving at my chambers. The furnishings hardly match the grandiosity of Rashmatun's power; while they are not falling into decay, they are as plain as a commoner's taste in fashion. The size of the room makes up for the lackluster decorations, though.

Any room is better than where I used to live, back when I was a child.

Jirtash tugs me towards a full-length mirror. I follow her like the obedient girl I'm supposed to be. She's the chief of the handmaidens and the oldest, having attended to four other vessels of Rashmatun before me. She carefully lifts the headdress away and places it on a finely embroidered cushion; the absence of its weight is liberating.

Meanwhile, Ilam has curled into a comfortable ball at the back of my mind. The demon rarely emerges during my day-to-day activities, only coming to life when something catches his interest or offends him, or when he wants to taunt me. Typical of a demon, only giving attention to matters that involve them, and remaining apathetic towards everything else.

More handmaidens scuttle towards me, peeling away the layers of my uniform with reverent efficiency. The four gold chains, each with a different design, representing the four cardinal directions. The bhota and jama, both fiery red and embroidered with golden flowers, catch the brilliant rays of sunlight streaming in through tall, narrow windows. My earrings and bangles are removed. Jirtash wipes my forehead with a cloth soaked in coconut oil, removing the seven-pronged star painted onto it. She whispers a quick prayer, a plea for forgiveness as she temporarily breaks Rashmatun's connection to her chosen vessel. With the star gone, she moves on to the rest of my face—the thick lines of kohl around my eyes, my bloodred lips.

Soon I am left naked, save for a pendant of yellow sapphire hung from a crude length of woven threads. Its uneven surface rests comfortingly against my chest, where my ribs protrude beneath my skin. My arms and legs are as thin as sticks, and my breasts are pitifully small. Not that it matters, since no one dares to comment much about my appearance.

The handmaidens unwind the thick coils of hair piled atop my head. It falls almost to my knees, thick and luxuriant, a soft sheen running down its trails. The only physical trait I am proud of.

Jirtash takes my hand and leads me toward the bathtub. I sink into its waters, contentedly allowing the handmaidens to lift my arms and legs and scrub them clean. A layer of grime gathers and floats on the water.

When I'm done, Jirtash towels me down and outfits me in a red kurta—I must always wear a hint of red somewhere—and a loose-fitting suruwal. I sit before the vanity table, and she braids my hair as her helpers tidy up the place.

"Oh child, what a woman wouldn't give to have hair as gorgeous as yours." Jirtash sighs in admiration.

Ice seems to gather at the nape of my neck. The ghost of a rough hand yanks the ends of my hair and sets it aflame.

I play with a near-empty bottle of perfume on the table, pushing the memory away. Jirtash has combed my hair almost the past ten years. This is just another day, another routine. She has no ill intentions. She has nothing to do with my past, I remind myself.

A past that she can never learn about.

I hope she doesn't notice the tremor in my fingers as I run them over the perfume bottle. "Thank you," I murmur.

She doesn't say anything else. I know what is on her mind: If only the rest of me were as gorgeous as my hair. I am close to sixteen now. Other girls my age have developed bosoms and swelling hips already. Me? I might as well be a withering tree trunk.

It's unusual for a girl to not have menstruated already, she told me two weeks ago, and what is even more unusual is that I have not shown signs of puberty. She once suspected that I was malnourished, but quickly dismissed the notion when I pointed out that I ate three full meals a day.

I did not tell her that I always dispose of two of those meals.

She finishes braiding my hair and claps her hands over my shoulders. "All done," she says. "There now, don't you look pretty?"

I don't agree with the sentiment. My nose is too large for my pointed chin and thin lips, my cheeks are as hollow as empty bowls of alms, and my eyes are too large, too fierce. But she is trying to be kind, so I muster a smile. "Thank you."

She nods, then releases me from her grip. A platter of food has been served, placed on a table by the window. I polish off the meal thoroughly; it's my only one every day. When no one is watching, I retrieve a vial from under my table and pour a drop of its contents into the clay cup of water, turning it into a murky solution. I drain the cup, trying not to wince at the foul taste. This is forbidden medicine that poisons my ovaries—another one of my methods to delay my bleeding for as long as possible. A small price to remain a goddess for a little while longer.

But my medicine is running dangerously low.

I haven't heard from my supplier in weeks. I grit my teeth, suppressing the anxiety rising up my throat.

When I'm done, I head towards the exit. I sense a hint of grim disapproval from Jirtash. "Off to your lessons, now?" she asks, more out of courtesy than genuine interest. She does not think that I should be paying so much attention to books and education. I should be more concerned about growing into a woman and finding a good husband, like the many girls who came before me. The latter won't be too hard, considering that everyone wants to receive some form of blessing from a former living goddess. Assuming that I choose to marry.

However, that means that I have to give up my status as the vessel of Rashmatun. The thought hollows out my stomach, as if someone carved my skin open and emptied my insides.

Who am I, if I am Rashmatun no longer? A scrawny girl with no inherent title or wealth to her name. A nothing, someone whose face will fade from the memories of all who have seen her.

I shake the notion out of my mind. I am still a living goddess, I remind myself. "Of course, Jirtash!" I chirp innocently. "Lessons won't wait!"

I traipse out of the room.

Follow us:

/orbitbooksUS

/orbitbooks

/orbitbooks

Join our mailing list
to receive alerts on our
latest releases and deals.

orbitbooks.net

Enter our monthly
giveaway for the chance
to win some epic prizes.

orbitloot.com